Praise for *How It Was*

'Janet Ellis writes with tenderness and wisdom about how you can lose a child while they are still under your roof – and how a child long-lost will never leave you. I veered between laughter and a lump in the throat, often on the same page. This book will sneak up behind you and break your heart.'
Erin Kelly

'A wonderful book – so beautifully written, what an incredible piece of storytelling. A brutal tale of the mother-daughter relationship, told elegantly and poetically. The intensity of it! And the misplaced longing of the bored housewife. I am so impressed.'
Emma Kennedy

Praise for *The Butcher's Hook*
Longlisted for the Desmond Elliott Prize

'Ellis excels at the poetics of flesh . . . There's a wit and a richness to the writing, a nice way with pastiche, and a real feel for the macabre. And, in Anne, she has created an engaging and at times daringly amoral heroine.'
Observer (Paperback of the Week)

'Ellis knows how to keep her audience hooked.'
The Times

'A high-finish performance . . . *The Butcher's Hook* will hook you.'
Observer (New Faces of Fiction)

'One to watch . . . a sharp eye and a sharper wit.'
Guardian

'A dark, weird, gloriously feminist story.'
Elle

'A story of dispassionate, bloody brilliance rich in believable period detail.'
Metro

'A surprising blend of psychological thriller and revenge tragedy . . . timeless.'
Daily Mail

'Ellis weaves her tale with deft skill, striking imagery and a boldness rare in a first novel.'
Mail on Sunday

'An absolute page-turner.'
Sunday Express

'Dark, packed with surprises and with a feisty, unforgettable heroine, this is a top-class debut.'
Woman & Home

'A cracking read.'
Prima

'Fun, grimy and romantic, as well as being a properly rollicking adventure.'
The Debrief

'A triumph; dark, shocking and funny. The voice is perfect and the words glitter like little black jewels.'
Erin Kelly, bestselling author of *He Said/She Said*

'Dark and utterly mesmeric. This is historical fiction as I've never encountered it before: full of viscera, snarling humour and obsessive desire. I loved it.'
Hannah Kent, bestselling author of *Burial Rites*

'Beautifully crafted. Janet Ellis is a masterful storyteller.'
Clare Mackintosh, bestselling author of *I Let You Go*

Also by Janet Ellis

The Butcher's Hook

How It Was

How It Was

Janet Ellis

TWO ROADS

First published in Great Britain in 2019 by Two Roads
An Imprint of John Murray Press
An Hachette UK company

1

A CIP catalogue record for this title is available from the British Library

Hardback ISBN 978 1 473 62517 4
Trade Paperback ISBN 978 1 473 62518 1
eBook ISBN 978 1 473 62519 8
Audio Digital Download ISBN 978 1 473 62520 4

Typeset in Hoefler Text by Hewer Text UK Ltd, Edinburgh
Printed and bound in Great Britain by Clays Ltd, Elcograf S.p.A.

John Murray policy is to use papers that are natural, renewable and recyclable products and made from wood grown in sustainable forests. The logging and manufacturing processes are expected to conform to the environmental regulations of the country of origin.

John Murray (Publishers)
Carmelite House
50 Victoria Embankment
London EC4Y 0DZ

www.tworoadsbooks.com

To Mike and Judy, my Ma and Pa.
Good people.

You can see how it was:
Look at the pictures and the cutlery.
The music in the piano stool. That vase.

Philip Larkin, 'Home is So Sad'

Chapter 1

How does it feel, watching Michael die? Slow. Confining. Sitting for hours in a brightly lit room on an uncomfortable chair makes me heavy with inertia. I feel as if I'm swelling beneath my clothes. No one insists, but I feel I need permission to leave his side, even for a moment. Yes, you go and get yourself a cup of tea, they say. We'll fetch you if anything happens. But nothing will happen, yet, for a while. He's stable.

I haven't got this washroom to myself: a young woman moves aside as I come in. She's been drying her hands on reluctant paper towels; a pile of them sits on the wet tiling. She gathers them up. The lid of the rubbish bin opens with a loud clang as she depresses the pedal. I lean over the basin. It's difficult to see myself clearly past all the notices. One sign would do. You can hardly forget about hygiene in a hospital, can you, there's scarcely a wall without a sanitiser unit, or instructions on where to find one. I apply my lipstick. I watch my lips part and enjoy the sliding pout that spreads the colour. I could still pleasure a man with this mouth, if I chose to.

The young woman watches me. She sees what you see: an old woman. She'll note I'm plainly and practically dressed. A little vain, perhaps: my scarf was obviously tied in front of a mirror. A little selfish, certainly: I am not curious about her, after all. She will never hear me called by my name. She doesn't know I have scarcely slept in years. She can't tell how often I have either fled grief or sought love. My scars and wounds and welts are concealed beneath my skin. From time to time, though, they chafe. I catch the young woman's eye and smile. She doesn't smile back, she just makes some sort of adjustment with her eyes to let me know she's seen me. She is probably wondering why I use make-up at all. Some foundation to cover up the cracks, perhaps, but who cares if my lips are bare? Michael would notice if I didn't make an effort any more. Even now, with the mask over his face, forcing air into his lungs, although he's pinned to the bed with a relentless web of tubes and wires, he'd still notice.

'Are you all right?' the girl says. She doesn't move towards me, but I feel her gaze sharpen.

I look at her in the mirror, then at myself. I can see why she spoke. Despite the brave red of my lipstick and the careful set of my hair, I'm crying. 'I'm fine,' I say. 'Might not bother with mascara, though.'

She turns away. If I'm able to joke, then Death isn't sitting by anyone's bed.

Oh, but it is, I think. Death is stroking Michael's face. Death is in the voices of the young doctors who attend to him and the older nurses who examine the clipboard at the end of his bed and shake the plastic veins that seep their fluid into his arms. 'Are you comfortable?' they say to him. They mean, *are you still here?* Death is the ventriloquist who impersonates concern. Michael can only nod, the mask denies him speech.

I am not crying for him. They say when someone has an amputation, they often experience phantom sensations in the lost limb. It troubles them, aching or itching with infuriating accuracy. This is the opposite. Michael is still present. He is visible, but even if I were to stick pins in the part of me that once cared, I cannot feel anything for him any more. I pity him, of course. I am sorry that he has to wait until his cup of tea has cooled to a tepid, unthreatening temperature before he can drink it. He used to like it hot, sweet and strong. He can only take one or two sips of the milky, bland offering now, before shaking his head and refusing more. Afterwards, inside every cup, there's a brown ring half an inch above the level of remaining liquid, like a calibration of disappointment. I regret for him the flowered gown he wears. They promised him a plain one but no one, including me, has taken responsibility for exchanging it yet.

If I could carry them, I'd bring in all the photograph albums he so carefully tended. Look, I'd say to the nurses, this is who he was when he didn't have to endure every breath going into his body as if it were a landed punch. When he wasn't a pile of hospital notes and his name on a wipe-clean board above his bed.

The years inside are picked out in gold lettering on the front of each album. Proper corners on all the photos and a layer of crisp tissue between each page. Michael's neat handwriting records the details of every photograph because, in those days, we knew exactly who those people were. We could recognise every background. We could label which bridge we were crossing then or identify the church that we were admiring. We remembered all those birthday parties and the names of the other careening and gesticulating children. We knew then on which beach we stood, our eyes shielded. Pages of people, many lost now because they're dead, or they might as well be. Last Christmas, I caught myself hovering over some names in the address book because I couldn't remember if they were actually or metaphorically gone.

You know how the victims of a crime struggle to identify their assailant in a line-up, even if they're definitely there? The police get all the suspects to repeat a phrase, something that was said at the time. As instructed, they intone, *'Shut up or I'll kill you,'* or *'Give it to me,'* but without a rush of adrenalin the words are flabby. *'I love you,'* the photos in the albums say, without conviction. *'You're happy, we're safe, all is well.'* There's me, with a swelling belly, and Sarah, half toothless at six, standing by my side outside the cottage. Here's Eddie, squinting at the camera as he holds out a caterpillar for his father's attention, its black body curled on his palm. The four of us, all smartly dressed for someone's wedding. Michael's second cousin's, I think. I'd wear that coat now if I still owned it. It was just like something Doris Day would have worn, its spotted lining matching the trim at the cuffs.

The albums do not continue past a certain time. There were photographs taken afterwards, of course, but they stay in boxes, uncollated. I have carried these heavy books with me, unopened for the most part, for many years. Last night,

I prised several pictures free of their mountings. It didn't take much effort; the glue only whispered a faint protest before it gave up its charge. Several were already detached, floating away from their descriptions. I had a half thought that I'd spend some time putting them back into position, but there will never be an afternoon rainy enough to spare for that task. One was missing entirely, corners and all. Michael's caption, *'Marion, Sarah and Eddie'*, illustrated only the blank space above. Beside and around it, we celebrated Christmas – caught holding half-unwrapped presents and sitting in front of heaped plates. We smile, all of us, easily, in every one. I plan to show the photographs to Michael. I will remind him of our life, in the time before.

I will take him the letters, too. I didn't need to reread them to remember their contents. Like the lyrics of a song you don't like, they stick in my head on a loop, once I've let them in. Whole phrases – *'it gives me no pleasure to tell you this; and from that date, access is denied; the view is amazing, you'd love it, come!'* – swim up and slide away again, as slippery as eels. Last night was the first time in a long while I'd retrieved them all from the box.

I laid them out in date order. As usual, I was irritated by their different shapes and sizes. As they always do, the edges of one envelope caught against its neighbour. One cellophane window showed only blank paper, where I'd returned it the wrong way round. I had no doubt I'd do exactly the same again, affronted once more by its contents and unwilling to accept they should be addressed to me. I will leave a note permitting all the letters' disposal, when someone clears the house after I'm gone. There's no need to contact anyone mentioned here. Whoever finds these missives will dismiss them, anyway. They'll appear an inconsequential collection. *Dear Mrs Deacon, We have great pleasure in confirming that your daughter Sarah has successfully passed her entrance examination to St Thomas's School and we look forward to welcoming her; Dear Mrs Deacon, Thank you for volunteering to visit the residents of Hillview, they will be very grateful; Dear Marion, I was rather upset by the tone of your last letter, but Rosalind has persuaded me to forgive you because . . .*

I held each one in turn, as if I laid my fingers against my wrist, anticipating an acceleration of my pulse. There was no reaction. I was calm. I gathered them together and put them with the photographs. A parcel of time.

The smell of hospitals is the same as it ever was. I cried when they walked Michael on to the ward, flattened on a gurney as if he were already laid out. But it was Eddie I saw, small and narrow in the middle of the bed, his eyes closed as if they would never open again. Michael was staring up at a rushing ceiling, blinking under intermittent spotlights. One of the orderlies put his hand on my sleeve, not quite meeting my eye. They can't get too involved, can they? I should know that, if anyone does. You'd be tangled up in the family's fears and anger if you got to know them, you can't risk anything beyond the immediate, brisk comforting that goes with care. When I worked in a hospital, the relatives were rarely more than an impediment. Their outdoor clothes always looked lumpen beside my neat uniform and the patient's flimsy bedclothes. They'd shrug off their bulky coats as soon as they could, the wards were always kept very warm. There was never anywhere to hang anything, and the bed was off-limits. You were constantly handing scarves and hats that had slipped free from chairs or laps back to their owners.

I go back to Michael's bedside, carrying a polystyrene beaker of coffee I don't want. Someone has changed the date on the whiteboard above his bed to read: *10 October*. Eventually, soon, the last date recorded for him will be wiped away and someone else's countdown will begin. I pick up the carrier bag. He dozes; the skin around his mouth and nose is swollen with the mask's constriction. When they remove it, it leaves a deep indentation on his skin. The rush of returning blood is painful and makes him wince. They've moved him to a room on his own now. That's because they know they'll get it back soon. This is how it ends, I think. This room will be the last one he sees. Through the window, behind a venetian blind that rises unevenly to one side like a lifted hem, there's a petticoat glimpse of rooftops, aerials and chimneys. His hands on the counterpane are yellow and dry. You wouldn't ask him to remove the lid of a jar now, or circle your fingers round his, stroking them, to promise love, later.

I feel suddenly nervous about speaking to him. His closed eyes and inert body exude an authority I don't recognise. The room squeaks and buzzes with the machines that measure and support him. 'Michael,' I say aloud. He opens his eyes with some effort, as though the remaining number of times he'll be able to look at me are now rationed and he's reluctant to use one up if there's no point. 'I brought some things to show you.' I slide my hand into the bag without looking at the contents, choosing at random. It's a picture taken in the garden of the old house. An inflatable pool takes up a great deal of the little lawn. Sarah stands up in it, her ruched swimsuit snug over her pot belly. She is about, what, nine or ten? Legs apart, unselfconscious, her two front teeth slightly too large for her face. Eddie sits beside her, leaning on the inflated rim, his hand making an indentation that isn't large enough to displace any water. I am sitting on the grass beside them, looking at Michael holding the camera. We are all smiling. 'Eddie was only three,' I say. 'He could almost have swum in it, couldn't he?' His name reverberates for a moment.

'It rained, do you remember?' I say. Great, fat drops had begun to fall into the pool out of what had seemed to be a clear sky. Sarah had looked at me nervously. She'd have expected me to react with a brisk change of mood, hurrying them into the house, gathering their clothes and toys. But, that day, the rain itself had some warmth in it and the loud *plink* as it hit the water made Eddie laugh. Sarah had sat down too, sending waves over the side. When I didn't admonish them, they wallowed in the disorder, splashing me and paddling their hands in the spreading, muddy lagoon that surrounded their rubber island. 'We all got soaked,' I say. 'You stood in the doorway with towels, waiting for us to stop our game and we kept saying, *Not yet, not yet*.' The happy people in the picture in my hand hold my gaze. The rain has yet to fall, but when it does, they will not mind.

The venetian blinds let in lines of light, they lie flat and seemingly solid on Michael's blanket. The image catches me sharply, as if I'd run headlong into a hidden spike. It picks open the scar of a memory and prods at the open wound. Where else was there a shaft of sunlight like this, drawn on a bedspread? I'd actually thought it was a solid thing that day, a scrap of fabric, perhaps, but when I'd tried to pick it up, I'd dissolved it with my shadow. I'd laughed, standing alone in Sarah's room. Sarah's bedroom, yes – that was where I was. A weekday. There was still a nursery china nameplate on the door, a picture of a little Peter Rabbit saluting her name although at fourteen she was far too old for it. She'd made her bed before she left for school because, if she didn't, if she'd left the sheets and blankets runkled, she knew it made me cross. I seemed to feel a thousand tiny aggravations then. My anger was constantly simmering, easily brought to a spitting boil by some transgression or other. Her unmade bedclothes carried the warmth of her, long after she'd left the room. I disliked touching them. Recently, and unexpectedly, there was something in her physical presence that made me squeamish.

Does anything really happen by chance? I'd put my hand into a drawer, looking for the other sock. I'd found only one of Eddie's, in the washing basket. The name tape sewn on to it read: *E M Deacon*. I had opened several drawers in Sarah's room without finding its partner. My hand closed around a little book, leather-bound: *Sarah Jane Deacon PRIVATE DIARY. Keep out.* If I hadn't had time that day, I wouldn't have opened it, but the fates cleared the way. I wasn't busy. I had nothing to do but read it. That's how it was.

Chapter 2

20 September

I am definitely going to give all my toys away to Eddie. I've been thinking about it for a while but whenever I open the cupboard to have one last look at them, I feel queasy. I've been trying to play with him for months but every time we start a game, I feel so frustrated I want to hurt myself. I decided to start by giving him the horse. I hid it from him ages ago. I'd kicked it away so he couldn't see it and then pretended I didn't know where it was.

I had to lie flat on my front to slide my hand under the sideboard. Where my bosoms are growing it hurt like bruises. The dining room floor is hard wood blocks laid in diagonals and there is loads of muck trapped in the gaps between them. I swore because my feet hit the wall as I stretched my legs out behind me. Eddie snorted. All I could see of him were his fawn wool socks and his school shoes. He can't tie his laces properly, they're always coming undone. I wiggled the little plastic horse out of its hiding place and brushed away the grey fur of dust that clung to it. It made me sad. I used to think the heat of my hand would be enough to start its heart. I could see a whole world through its hard eyes. It felt like a long time ago.

I gave the horse to Eddie and told him I was too old for it. Eddie said I was only twice him, because he is seven. He adds himself up all the time. He said it wasn't fair if I stopped playing anyway because we'd laid out a whole farm. He pointed at the fields and lanes we'd marked out with knitting needles and at the reels of cotton that stood for hay bales. I told him he could have my whole farm set. He gasped and said, Really? Really? because he'd often begged me for even one small part of it, even a lend of it. He asked me to tell Mum it's all his now. He was scared I'd go back on my private kindness and make him out to be a liar. Fair enough, I usually do. I said I'd tell Daddy too and we should shake on it and I held out my hand and he put his whole little fist into my open palm.

I am lying on my bed writing this, trying to remember what I used to care about. Everything is muffled and stale. All my Beatrix Potter china animals face in different directions because I haven't arranged them properly for weeks. I have an essay for homework I can't be bothered to do. Mrs McCain set it as she lifted her big bum from her chair at the end of the lesson. She paused mid-rise, her palms flat on the desk to support her weight. I could tell she said the title without really thinking. *Describe Your Environment, Inside and Out*. She had to give us some homework, it's in the timetable. She'll be bored to death by my essay, anyway. I'm going to write about how we live in a small semicircle of houses at the edge of the village. I'll describe how you can see the footpath and the fields beyond from Eddie's room at the back of the house. Our window cleaner is so old that he can remember when it was all fields here. He told me our houses were built because of the baby boom. He made it sound like a bad thing. I'll write about how our gardens never seem to be in full sun. I'll say that you can see everyone's lights turning off at night, but you hardly ever catch sight of the other people who live here. Except Sheila from three doors down who patrols all the time, like an old sentry.

I'm not going to say how much I want to look out of my window and see a boy standing there. He'll be coming to see me. I haven't met him yet. I don't know what he'll look like. I can't even give him a name. But I'm going to matter to him. I wish this could be the last Monday *ever* that I don't have a boyfriend. The next time there's a full moon, I'm going to wish like mad on it. Otherwise, I can see all the boring Mondays bobbing across the weeks and months and years for the rest of my life, like boats on a flat sea, with nothing exciting to disturb them. Ever.

There were thick, grey stripes across the bottom of my white school socks. I must have dusted the top of the skirting board with my feet. That shows you how gross and low her standard of housework is, which is ALL she has to do all day.

Chapter 3

Michael sleeps. It gives his body something different to do. You wouldn't say he sleeps like a baby; he looks guarded and wary, even in slumber. Over the years since everything happened, he's had to stay as ready for action as a soldier in the trenches. He can't risk mistaking any silences for a lull in the fighting. I'd like to close my eyes, too, but if someone came in, they might think I was ignoring him. I feel the contents of the bag as if I could identify each letter by shape alone. They don't give themselves away. I pull one out as if I'm drawing a raffle. My prize is a card with a picture of a building on the front. Though it's taken from what must be its best angle, nothing could enhance its squat shape and featureless exterior. It's not where you'd choose to end your days.

18 December

Dear Mrs Deacon,

I write to thank you on behalf of the residents of Hillview Residential Home for your splendid contribution to our Christmas party. The decorations looked wonderful and were much admired. Please accept this invitation to our small staff gathering on Tuesday for a mince pie (or two), to herald the festive season.

The decorations were some old-fashioned paper chains and the balding tinsel saved from last year. I remember Helen, in the same tartan skirt she always wore, holding the coloured links between finger and thumb. 'Careful with these, Marion,' she'd said, passing them to me as I stood on tiptoe on the refectory table. 'I can't entirely vouch for them, there was only so much glue left by the end of the session. But I wasn't allowed to interfere, you know what they're like.' And sure enough, by the end of the afternoon, two or three chains broke free and dangled just above head height, trembling. And the old women (it was mostly old women) warbled carols and brushed cake crumbs from velvet tops, worn specially. I had a reindeer brooch they used to like; its red nose flashed on and off. I can't reminisce with Michael about that time, he didn't share it with me. So much of my life, afterwards, is solitary.

There's a jacquard dressing gown on the chair. I packed it with his things, but it seems unlikely he'll need to wear it. Monogrammed pyjamas, too. That's an upgrade. I had to pack his bag very quickly; I didn't want the doctor to see I didn't really know where everything was and have him watching me open all the wrong drawers. 'Thank you, Mrs Deacon,' he'd said. 'It *is* Mrs Deacon, isn't it?' I close my eyes. I always seemed to be tired when I was young. I used to wake in the morning feeling as if I hadn't slept at all. When I was pregnant with Sarah, I burrowed into bed every afternoon without guilt and drifted in and out of sleep. Make the most of it, the health visitor said. She'd woken me with one of her visits and without apology. After the baby comes, she'd said, you won't be able to take yourself off like that. You will chase sleep like an escaped balloon on a windy day. She'd looked askance at my unkempt hair and watched me stifle a yawn.

Chapter 4

I see myself the day I found Sarah's diary. I'd held it for a few minutes before I'd opened it. It wasn't honour that held me back, I didn't value her secrets. The ebb and flow of her days was well known to me. Her school timetable was pinned to the cork board downstairs and I organised all her other appointments. I thought her diary would reveal – nothing. It would be only an amusing catalogue of forgettable events, childish ambitions and daydreams. I was afraid that her adolescent musings might reveal a certain small-mindedness. She was so lacklustre these days, so seldom moved to any displays of emotion beyond anger or spite. What if her assumed indifference to the world concealed genuine hostility? There was always a possibility that she didn't really like us. That she really didn't like me.

When I was her age, I'd sought out the wilder girls, the ones who were so busy being bohemian they expected nothing from me. They certainly didn't want competition. I was admitted to their ranks only because of a single fact – my mother had recently died. This made me interesting and stopped further conversation. They were too young and too selfish to question me about how I felt, what she was like or even how she'd died. Her death was just the way I was described, nothing more. I wore it like a badge. I would have avoided the subject, anyway, in case I accidentally revealed the way she'd spent her last months. She had been bedridden, soiled, forgetful. That version of her embarrassed me. Instead, I mourned, privately, the mother I'd scarcely known. I knew she'd loved me, though. I was almost sure I could remember that.

The first few pages of Sarah's diary seemed to be mostly lists of girls whose names I didn't know, ranked in order of importance as friends, with a few character traits added. *Molly Green (1) Nice nails. Isobel Huff (2) Likes Simon and Garfunkel. Vanessa Stewart (3) Two brothers.* There was a tiny clump of hair stuck to one page with 'Cut from My Fringe' written beneath it. Most of the entries were short. She'd written several times about wanting a part in the school play: we didn't go and see *Pygmalion*, so I supposed she wasn't successful. Then this longer, more confessional page. *Bruises where my bosoms will be.* It was odd to see her write about her body. It was a mystery to me these days. I'd known it so well for so long. I'd dried under her arms and between her toes, held and tickled her, squeezed her into coats and pulled vests over her head, the necklines tight enough to stretch her eyelids. I'd brushed her hair and cleaned her ears with a Kirby grip. She hides herself from me now. She'd yelped theatrically when I'd come into her room the other day, snatching up the counterpane to hold it between us. She's been steadily removing herself physically from me over the last little while. She closes every door behind her and grimaces if I even leave the bathroom door ajar while I wash my hands. As she retreats, so I shrink away, too. When she was small, I could distinguish her crying out to me instantly, among all the other children's babble. Would I even know her voice soon? Would I recognise her from any angle except straight on, while we confront each other? I glanced back over a few weeks of writing to see if I was mentioned. *Mum got cross, unfair* and *Mum said I could try coffee if I want to*, were all I could find. I wouldn't read her diary again, I thought. It was like having a strange, one-way conversation with someone I wasn't sure I liked.

I'd watched her carefully that evening, armed with my new knowledge. I expected to see her break her promise to Eddie. 'Were you and Eddie playing together earlier?' I said.

She frowned at the coincidence of this conversation. 'I've given him my farm set,' she said.

'Have you? Don't change your mind,' I said. 'It would break his heart.'

She glared at me. 'I won't,' she said. 'Unless I do, of course. It's up to me. If I want it back, I'll just take it. I don't care.'

Irritation flared in me like kindling to a match, quick and bright. She set these little fires all the time. 'Where is he?' I said.

'He's built a farmyard in the sitting room,' she said. 'An entire farm. Masses of it. That's annoying, isn't it? You don't like a mess in there, do you?'

I watched from the doorway as Eddie examined his

new kingdom, touching each animal in turn, as if they'd turn to ash if he ignored them for too long. He lifted a small, wide-legged plastic man tenderly on to the back of his rigid mount. The man's arms stretched forward for reins he couldn't possibly hold in his solid hands. *The horse can fly if it wants*, he said aloud, jiggling horse and rider across the floor. *But the boy just puts the man on its back and makes it walk. Do what the boy says. He is the master.* He lifted them above his head. *Whee, go up in the air before you're on the ground. Jump over the hay bales, sit tight, man, sit tight, you have a good seat. Go in single file, but the boy doesn't know what single file means, so it is just whee right up to the sky and down again. You are the champion horse. That was a clear round. Mummy might say is it hers, it is Sarah's, give it back, don't take her things, but the boy says*, *it is mine for ever now because she promised.* He clutched the horse and rider to him. *He is riding too*, he said. *He's not scared of horses. He doesn't think about the big fast feet and falling off then lying on the ground where they could tread on him. Do you want to go back to the farmhouse, man?* He trotted the little pair to a cardboard box on the floor and placed them tenderly inside. He leaned against the sofa looking bereft without them, even though he'd brought it on himself.

'Eddie,' I said.

He looked up. His face softened then tensed, as if he'd been dreaming and couldn't make sense of the real world as he woke. 'It's mine,' he said. 'Sarah gave it to me.'

'I know,' I said. 'She told me.'

'Will she take it away?' he said. 'Even though she promised?'

'No,' I said, 'I won't let her.' She doesn't want it, any of it, any more, I thought, but that won't stop her twisting his heart till it hurts, simply because she can.

Chapter 5

Eddie had actually seen a dead body but at first he hadn't known that's what he was looking at. He'd peered through the fence surrounding the big house's big garden because the man lay on his back on the grass. He was wearing a light yellow suit and the hat that should have been on his head had rolled away, to lie at an angle to its owner's prone form. Around him, a group of adults either stood or knelt. Someone was undoing his tie and another loosened his shoes. The man wasn't helping them. Eddie assumed he was asleep and they were doing things to him for fun. He wondered what the man would do when he woke up. His face was very red, perhaps he was only pretending to be asleep and was getting angrier all the time. They'd be really for it when he opened his eyes. One of the kneeling people was holding the man's hand by the wrist, the fingers drooped. He looked up at a large woman and shook his head. She began to make a funny sort of bleating noise. Then the man looked beyond her to where Eddie stood, his satchel at his feet.

'Oy!' he said.

Eddie winced. He sensed he was about to be told off but he couldn't think what he was doing wrong.

The man got up and came over to him. 'Bugger off,' he said.

Adults always said swear words so clearly. The woman's bleating was louder now. The man fished in his pockets and Eddie heard the jangle of loose change.

'Bugger off,' he said again, holding his hand out over the fence to reveal several coins.

Behind him, bumping over the pristine lawn, an ambulance came into view. Eddie was impressed by the fact that the vehicle was on the grass. It was clearly the sort of garden you didn't play in, let alone drive over.

'Don't you want this?' the man said. 'Not enough?' He rattled the change.

'No thank you,' said Eddie. 'Can I watch?'

The man smiled. He looked a bit like one of the prefects in the Upper House. 'How old are you?' he said.

People always asked him that. 'Seven,' said Eddie.

'Go home,' the man said. His voice was soft this time and kinder. He looked behind him to where the ambulance men were covering the man with a blanket. They pulled it right over his head. 'He'll be all right,' he said.

Eddie understood in that moment that the man wouldn't be all right at all. The crying woman, the kneeling and the ambulance all fell into place. He picked up his satchel and walked away, transfigured by knowledge. He wasn't afraid and that very fact amazed him.

Chapter 6

10.52. Beside Michael's bed is a timepiece that reduces each moment to a bald, numerical display. He'd noticed an actual clock above his bed as he was wheeled in but, unable to turn round, he can't see it now. He'd only heard its thudding tick briefly, too, before various machines were switched on and there was no more silence. The roar of the mask clamped to his face is so loud and intrusive it reminds him of dealing with a heatwave. There's no point in examining how hot you are, it doesn't cool you down. Similarly, fighting against the rushing in his ears gets him nowhere and he succumbs. He would like to see the clock, though, there's a kindness in knowing how each hour is measured. The circle of numbers is a comforting reminder of other times on other days. The digital display condemns him to a heartless present. His wristwatch waits in the locker, its leather strap curled and worn. He misses its face. Marion shoots furtive glances at the clock whenever she thinks he won't see.

Michael's world has reduced to the size of his room. Over the last few weeks, as his breath got shorter and people began to look much harder at him than they usually did and to insist on doctors and specialists, he felt as if he were being remodelled ineluctably in a simpler form. Matters that would once have preoccupied him now glanced off him, without leaving any impression. He noticed it first with the weather. He had always followed the forecast keenly; he based not just his wardrobe but his whole demeanour on what might happen. Knowing that the weekend promised sunshine would make him shrug off Tuesday's rain. If he knew storm clouds loomed a few days hence, he found it hard to enjoy being outside. Just before his last, catastrophic deterioration, a neighbour had called round. Her dripping umbrella bloomed from the end of her arm like a peony. It wasn't supposed to rain that day. That faulty forecast should have unnerved him. Instead, he felt joyful. He realised he was happy to leave others to deal with any unpredictability, meteorological or otherwise.

He tested this new state when Marion was with him. He could see how bored she was, fidgeting in the chair, getting to her feet whenever someone came in to tinker with the apparatus, although she could be of no use. He sliced into his old feelings for her, as if he were assembling a slide for dissection. Closer and closer he went, examining all the layers. He could detect a simmering tension, more to do with unfinished business than historic events. It buffeted him a little, like the wake from a distant boat hitting the shore. But when he thought of his home, he felt calm.

Beneath the thrum of the machine, inside his head, Michael listened again to the rhythmic sound of Sarah's young hands, meeting in a swiping clap then slapping one after the other on to her thighs, as she mimicked a horse's accelerating canter. Clap-ker-*thunk*. Clap-ker-*thunk*. Day after day, she guided an invisible mount over imaginary jumps or along unseen paths. Clap-ker-*thunk* as she sat at the dining table or in the back of the car. Clap-ker-*thunk* as she watched television or hesitated over her homework. She clicked her tongue against her teeth to urge speed and snorted through her lips in horsey reply. Michael closed his eyes and rode with her, gently, safely, over a sunny field under a never darkening sky.

Chapter 7

22 September

My nails almost reach the tips of my fingers. MUST stop biting the skin on my thumb. Got twelve out of twenty in the French test today, but Madame P said she'd sprung it on us so she didn't expect full marks.

I don't regret giving the farm set to Eddie because it looks babyish now and I can't remember ever wanting to play with it. He'll keep wondering if I'll change my mind and I won't let him off worrying. I have such power over him. Even if he's happy to start with, I can make him cry in seconds. If he's cross, I can make him laugh. Sometimes I get hold of his mouth and twist his lips up and down, making him look as if he's smiling or miserable, but I don't really have to touch him to do it. One time I was on my own with him, when he was about one and a bit. I wanted him to go to sleep. I put him in his cot and whenever he wiggled or tried to get up, I pushed my hand flat on his back. After a while, he sagged and closed his eyes. When he woke up, the first thing he did was call out for me.

The other day he was looking at his comic. A big splodgy tear fell on to the page. I asked him what the matter was and that made him cry more. I told him to stop before he made papier mâché which made him sort of laugh. He said the worst thing had happened to him in school and he didn't want to go back the next day. I said what and he said a boy in his class took his pencil case and ran off with it. I said that's not awful and he said it was because he tried not to cry but he couldn't help it and you should never cry in front of the other boys because they go on and on about cry baby and do you want your mummy and stuff like that. I put my arms round him. I smelled the sour waxiness of his hair and felt his woolly jumper warm up under my hands. I said they can't hurt you and they'll have forgotten all about it tomorrow. But I won't forget, Eddie, I said. I'll keep you safe. I meant it.

Chapter 8

'How's he doing?' the nurse says. She bristles with purpose. I suspect that she is different in the outside world. Timid, probably. Her uniform imbues her with confidence. It fits her tightly with no room to spare.

'Can you ask him how he is, please?' I say. 'Can he have the mask off, just for a moment?'

She raises and lowers her shoulders in an elaborate gesture of indecision. Michael's eyes are fixed on her, our Empress. Thumbs up or thumbs down, she will decide. 'Come on then,' she says. She lifts his head and undoes the strap.

He groans. The least movement disturbs him and this hurts, too. He relaxes against her hands as she eases him against the pillow.

She settles him and strokes the engorged skin of his cheeks, crooning as if they were alone. 'All right?' she says.

He mutters something but his mouth is dry, and the words don't form properly.

The nurse holds a beaker to his lips. She lifts both his legs together to straighten the sheet. It's no effort for her, Michael is as light as tissue paper now. He scarcely marks the bedding he lies on. He was always so solid before. He stayed upright, even when I pushed and then pushed harder to try to topple him. She picks up something from the floor. A card, drawn by a child. *Happy Mother's Day* with all the letters in different colours. She frowns. It's the wrong time of year.

'It's an old one,' I say. I open it before I put it back in the bag it escaped from. *From yor son,* it says. A large number of crosses start from under Eddie's name and continue to the edge of the page, as if he'd carried on writing them into the air.

'Excuse me,' the nurse says, squeezing past me.

'Sorry,' I say, resenting having to move. I begrudge her presence, her better knowledge of Michael's condition and her questions. When did he last go to the toilet, or have a headache, or cough? Not to know is to be negligent and uncaring. The nurse is passing me again, she looks puzzled at my not waiting, with my knees to one side, for her to make her way back round to the other side of the bed. 'Miles away,' I say.

In truth, I am decades away, watching myself buttoning up a fawn coat, with the dangling button I never remembered to sew on until I wore it, and fastening a paisley scarf round my neck. I am back over thirty years ago.

I had my shopping list shoved into my coat pocket. There were only four items on it, but I liked to write things down before I set out. It made me feel efficient, at least for a while.

The greengrocer said, 'Shepherd's pie? Nice big portions!' and winked, heaving the potatoes into my bag along with large clods of earth.

I blushed as my hands shook with the growing weight; there seemed to be a great many to the pound. He winked again. He saw the colour rise in my cheeks and kept his eyes on me as he took my money, rummaging for a long time in the front pocket of his apron for the change. I was almost tempted to ask for something else, so that he could see my face return to its normal colour, as it surely, eventually, must, but he had turned away and was already fondling a cucumber for the woman behind me.

I had to steel myself to go into the baker's, too. Five months earlier, I'd bought a fruit cake covered with stiff white icing and asked the woman behind the counter to write *'Happy Anniversary'* on it, so that I could surprise Michael. 'You're not a baker yourself, then?' she had said, raising her eyebrows as she'd noted the words on her little pad. 'It's normally only wedding cakes with messages I get asked for. Couldn't you rustle up even a coffee and walnut sponge for your hubby?' She looked up from arranging iced buns in a tower as I walked in. 'Ah, hello,' she said. 'Here comes the unbaking sinner of the parish.'

It was as I walked towards the church that I thought I saw Philip. The man wore a jacket like his; his hair was unruly and twisted, just as Philip's was when he pulled at it with both hands and it stayed upright on its own afterwards. While he was thinking. Or talking to me. Before he kissed me. This man was at quite a distance and facing away. I couldn't see him clearly, but I knew that it wasn't Philip. He would be in the classroom at this time of day, for a start, and not walking slowly down this village street in my part of Kent. And of course, it couldn't be him, because Philip was dead. He had been dead for eight years.

I wanted to sit down. I wished I could just sink to the ground where I was, drop my head to my chest and close my eyes. I didn't think I could make it home upright. If I tried, I thought I'd end up shuffling, martyred, on my knees for the last few steps. The man who wasn't Philip was so utterly not him by the time he was level with me that I wanted to laugh. My bag thumped against my shin at every other step, like a penance.

The recreation ground was an open patch of scrub. The grass was marked with white lines, faded to a line of dots after a summer of use. The goalposts sagged where they had struggled with the weight of dangling boys, testing their muscles and making their palms red with effort. The playground apparatus huddled in a corner. Underneath each swing was an aggressive swipe of dirt that puddled at even the lightest shower. The base of the slides was dark with dried mud, too. There was a shelter where mothers grouped by day as their children swung and slid. Their teeth were clenched against a permanently chilly wind that the three sides of the structure only seemed to invite in. At dusk, there would be a brief colonisation by the nearly-grown-up local kids, anxious to be elsewhere and making do with writing graffiti on the flimsy walls, sucking cigarette smoke into their cheeks and ignoring the playthings.

There was nobody there now. A woman with a child in a pushchair left as I approached; she looked relieved that she had served her time. I sat on the sloping slats of the bench.

I remembered Philip beside me, in the pub after the first rehearsal, sitting so close that his thigh pushed against mine.

I'd looked up at him quickly; he was talking to the woman across the table. He appeared preoccupied, but when I shifted my weight away, he'd moved again, renewing that pressure, his touch.

Was that the actual beginning? Don't things truly start long before you know they've begun? Philip and I had the kind of accidental meeting that some people would celebrate. Everything had conspired to make it happen, too. 'Yes, why don't you join the choir?' Michael had said, when our neighbour had tried to recruit me. 'Marion loves singing, it sounds fun,' he'd said, encouraging, kind.

The neighbour had beamed. 'Your husband's right,' she'd said, 'it's *great* fun. Nobody's really a *singer*,' she'd said, using the very phrase that could have condemned her.

What would be the point of going to *that*? I'd thought, singing with people who don't take it seriously, who'd turn the pages of their sheet music too slowly to catch the notes.

She'd turned to Michael. 'We have a little concert at the end of every term,' she'd said. 'So you'd be able to see what we've been up to.'

'I think you should go,' Michael said later. 'I can look after Sarah.'

The church hall was brightly lit with a fierce overhead glare. It illuminated the thick runnels of carelessly applied paint on the walls and there were no shadows to hide the scuffed chairs and peeling posters. People greeted each other with exclamatory glee. A woman in a tight orange coat made her way over as if she'd been specifically told to watch out for me. 'Subs!' she said in a bright, loud way. She held out an empty Farley's Rusks tin that rattled heavily with coppers. When she met my eye, she inhaled quickly. 'Oh, are you new?' she said. 'It's thruppence for tea and . . .' She waved at a table behind us. There was a knot of people around the choirmaster.

He was an earnest young man, who looked to be in his late twenties. He peered over his glasses at me as though I were much younger than him, which I clearly wasn't. 'We have a mixed repertoire,' he said. 'Some meaty choral pieces and a few popular tunes for light relief. We don't audition. Just decide on your range and off you go.'

The neighbour was nowhere to be seen. I went and stood beside a woman who settled herself into position like a large cat, her hands over her chest. She smelled of Vicks rub. I cursed myself for being persuaded to come, embarrassed for them all. I would feign illness, I decided, either my own or somebody else's, so that I could leave at the tea break. We worked through 'Rustic Song'. It was a laborious process; the pianist had to return to the same phrase again and again and everyone laughed at the mistakes.

Afterwards, they fell on the cups of tea and biscuits as though they were enormous treats. I looked for a way to leave without being seen. Philip came and stood in front of me. He wore a long black coat, unbuttoned to reveal a torn lining. There was a dab of yellow paint on his shirt and deep indentations on his belt. It had obviously been fastened more tightly as he'd grown thinner. I stared at him like a doctor examining a patient, half taking in what he said while listening for signs and clues to the real story. I can't quite see his face now. I remember the sensation of being with him, a delicious roiling and churning like being on a rollercoaster. A gulp of pleasure, the way illicit laughter catches in your throat as you stifle it. When he spoke, I knew his voice would become familiar to me. Someone brushed past him, and he turned away and raised his hands to his head and clutched his hair. I knew I'd see him do that again. I would touch the small wound where his razor had nicked his cheek and stroke the faint, black stubble on his jaw. He'd asked me about how I came to be there and who else I knew, while I learned the colour of his eyes and his high cheekbones and his wayward hair. Underneath his questions and my answers ran a steady, ostinato beat of desire.

He'd kissed me as we walked to his car. In the pub, he'd offered me a lift home. It was on his way, he said. He didn't wait to hear where I lived. He'd spun me to face him and kissed me. The collar of my coat lifted and pressed hard into my cheek, but I didn't want to move. He raised my hands and held them against his, palm to palm, all the fingers aligned. We'd left the next rehearsal early the next week, separately, trying not to laugh as we met in the car park. How on earth had we even planned that, let alone carried it through? It was such a risky thing to do.

It was just as perilous to go to his little flat, practically inviting the neighbours to spy on us as we left his car, a low-down frog-eyed Sprite I'd struggled to get out of and whose doors closed with loud, announcing clunks. He had two rooms on the first floor. Even though I'd never been there before, I could tell he'd straightened the eiderdown with extra vigour and put his clothes away. A pile of saucepans teetered on the draining board, still dripping. When I sat on his bed, a single, rolled sock sprang from underneath the pillow. He'd stopped my laughing by kissing my neck, my cheek, my mouth. He'd said he should put a record on, but I'd held him tightly because I couldn't bear him to take his mouth away from mine. We'd separated only for the time it took to remove clothing and made love so quickly that I'd felt embarrassed afterwards, like someone who has eaten too many bread rolls before discovering the rest of the banquet. The next time, the second time, that same evening, we'd stopped sometimes to look at each other, or touch somewhere, or say something.

I'd stroked the white weals that crossed his wrists, as if I were learning their configuration. I'd felt as if the rest of his life were an exam I didn't have time to prepare for. It would be useful, though, in the coming weeks, to remember where to put my cup to conceal the cigarette burn in the embroidered Indian cover on the table and the way to wrestle open the window catch, to take the milk bottle from the sill outside. I can recall the room quite clearly. The pictures he'd stuck on the walls were facsimiles of paintings on pages he'd cut from books. Sellotape glistened at their corners. If he'd wanted to, he could have removed every trace of himself from the room in seconds.

A few weeks later, Sarah fell ill with a heavy cold and fever. I'd defied Michael's worry about her rising temperature and insisted on going out. 'You'll only miss one week's rehearsal if you don't go,' Michael had said. I'd had to prise Sarah's fingers from me and ease myself away from that hot little head.

'Once she's asleep,' I'd said, 'when I've gone, she'll be fine.' I'd slipped away without thinking about either of them any more. Coming home, I'd set my life with them in motion again with the turn of my key in the lock, as if nothing had happened while I'd been gone.

Seven. That's all. That's the measurable total of our times together. Philip had looked at me the way small children or dogs do, with a clear, untroubled gaze. When we'd made love for the first time, I didn't even think I was being unfaithful. Being in bed with Michael had always left me feeling as if I were the runner in the relay team that never carried the baton over the line. I hadn't known that you could learn to make love. But I never took my lessons home. I lay beneath Michael as I always did. In my mind, I only betrayed myself.

I never once told him I loved him. Love was a ball he threw to me but I didn't catch it. I didn't try. At school, we'd all believed in love at first sight. We half expected a physical manifestation when it happened. Perhaps we'd be covered with stigmata or develop a huge, white-headed spot. Everything else showed on our bodies and our skin, after all. Falling in love, we speculated, must be something both pleasurable and painful, like getting into a too-hot bath. We knew about lust, of course, and practised intense looks on the hapless boy who collected our plates after school dinner. Phoebe had even written 'I Love You' in brown sauce, which he'd blushed to see.

When Michael had visited me after Sarah's birth, fresh from having had his daughter pointed out to him through the nursery window, one swaddled infant among many, he'd looked at me with admiration and not a little nervousness. It was as if producing a baby both elevated and enhanced me. I'd enjoyed the sensation. I'd allowed myself to think that what I felt in return – a sort of protective pride and an urge to pat him on the head and tell him that he was clever, too – was love.

Philip had a picture of Jeanne Hébuterne, one ear poking through the thick ropes of her hair, stuck to the wall. 'You can tell Modigliani loved the sheen of her,' he said, 'and adored that wayward strand of hair on her left cheek. The day after he died, she jumped to her death with their nearly-born child inside her. Such intense, consuming love,' said Philip.

I thought she was cruel and selfish. She would have ignored the baby's movements as she climbed the five flights of stairs for the last time. She and the baby would have tumbled together as they fell, neither concerned about knowing which way up the world was.

'I love you more than that,' Philip said. I only kissed him in return. He'd leapt on to his sudden plans for our running away together like someone clinging to a raft in rapids. Sarah, I said. I can't leave Sarah. He said that she'd soon adjust to my absence. I was at boarding school when I was her age, he said, and I didn't really care if I saw my mother or not. The boys I teach don't give their parents a second thought, either, I'm sure of it. We would send Sarah postcards and letters from wherever we landed, he'd said. She'll have her constant, glamorous reminders of you, my darling, until she's old enough to set sail herself and join us. Her friends will envy her, he'd said.

I'd humoured him as if he were playing a game. He was too young, too close to childhood himself, to understand. I'd laughed as he invented our flight, fantasising about long sea crossings and living in strange cities. I told him yes, I could sing while he played the piano on ocean liners, teasing him about the repertoire and the other passengers. But although he'd laughed too, I knew he was already imagining packing up his things. He would carefully remove the pictures to stick on other walls. Poor, painted Jeanne would have to do a little more travelling until she could rest. 'We'll make plans soon,' Philip said, his voice rising in excitement and I shushed him in case his neighbours heard us.

I wanted to leave his room earlier than we'd arranged. I was hot and sticky with a heavy cold coming. After he'd dropped me at the nearest, safest bus stop, I wept fat, rich tears of self-pity. Arriving home, swaddled by darkness, I'd encountered my neighbour on her doorstep. She was squeezing a rolled-up note for the milkman into a bottle's damp lip.

'Choir practice?' she said. I'd only nodded in answer. She stayed where she was for longer than her errand needed. 'They shouldn't make you sing such sad songs, should they?' she said. She stared at me. 'Not very nice for your husband, having you come home like that.' I didn't reply. 'He'll cheer you up, though.' She smiled in agreement with her own appraisal. 'Yes,' she said. 'Your husband's a very good sort.'

Chapter 9

Eddie watched Sarah through a sliver of open door. She was sitting on her bed and talking out loud, but there was no one else in the room. She spoke quickly and almost in a whisper. Bringing her hands to her face from time to time, she smiled and tipped her head. Although he risked stepping on the creaking floorboard, Eddie crept closer.

'A party?' she said. 'Yeah, I think I can come. If I'm free, I'd love to come. Yeah.' She laughed and patted her own arms, stroking as if to reassure herself. 'Let's meet up after school. Yeah, I love T Rex too.'

The floorboard under him squeaked.

Sarah looked over to where Eddie stood. Flinging the door open, she seemed almost boiling in her wrath while he cowered, frozen, in front of her. 'What the hell are you doing?' she said.

'Nothing,' he said. 'I wasn't listening.'

'You bloody were. I was going to set up a farm with you, but I won't now.'

Eddie's eyes filled with tears at this instant cruelty. She hardly ever wanted to play these days and he'd tried to enjoy just setting games up, as that was all she was likely to do before she stopped. He would settle for that. He would have liked even that.

'Go and play with your stupid truck,' she said. Her expression changed.

Eddie felt afraid for the first time. She was planning something, he could tell. There was a sense of purpose about her, and the redness that had coloured her cheeks when she discovered him was fading. 'I'm sorry,' he said, mentally planning his retreat.

She towered over him, pushing him against the wall on the landing and preventing escape. He watched, feeling weak with sorrow, as she went into his room. She emerged holding Truck aloft. Truck was a little metal lorry. A tiny faceless driver had once perched in his cab but was lost long since. Truck himself had a face, his headlights and grille styled to look human. Eddie loved him. Despite the toy's hard edges Truck was a source of comfort. He looked both ridiculous and brave as Sarah swung him above her head. Eddie didn't make a sound; he thought she'd twist the story until he was only and utterly at fault. She took her prize into the bathroom and held the toy down the lavatory, sluicing it in the water in the bowl. Eddie felt faint. He sat down in the doorway. He couldn't save Truck or himself. If Sarah had expected him to cry out or attempt to wrestle Truck from her, she was at first disappointed, then horrified, by Eddie's silence.

'It's okay,' she said, drying Truck on the bathmat. 'Eddie, for Christ's sake, have it back.' Eddie's arms stayed by his sides. She pushed the toy into his chest as though he'd take it in reflex, but he didn't move. 'Eddie.' Sarah knelt in front of him, put the toy on the floor and wrapped her arms around him. 'I'm sorry,' she said. 'I was just teasing you.'

It was too late. Truck was different now. He was reduced. I'm going to bury him, Eddie thought. Then I'll never have to look at his face again.

Chapter 10

Illumination in Michael's room is a choice between the glare from the single, central bulb or a weak puddle from the light above his bed. The overhead light feels unkind. I turn on the television. It contributes a cold, grey spill. He can't hear it; the breathing mask, replaced again without ceremony ('Here we go, Michael, it needs to do its job'), is noisy but he watches the screen. 'Do you want the volume up?' I say. He lets me know without much movement, just a tiny flicker of his eyes, that he doesn't need to hear it. The hospital is gearing up for visiting time, and there's a different energy to the rumble of trolleys and the conversations in the corridor outside. People who haven't spent all day here are adjusting to the pace, finding the right room, hoping to leave soon. Michael and I stare at some sort of quiz; people clap their hands to their heads in grief if they give a wrong answer or clasp each other in joy if it's right. The winning couple look pleased enough with their cheque. I wish I could leave. I don't want him to die but I wish he'd get on with it. In my head, I am explaining his death to his friends, to my colleagues, to Sarah, when she calls. If she calls.

I fish around in the bag. My hand closes over a letter without an envelope. I know this one, I don't need to read it.

Dear Mrs Deacon,

I enclose the leaflet about head injury complications I discussed with you. You may find it useful. Research is ongoing and we are always most grateful for donations.

The picture I retrieve is a wedding photo that I hadn't intended to bring. It must have stuck to another for the ride here. 'Look,' I say to Michael. His eyes swivel, he frowns. My brocaded dress was so stiff, it could have stood up alone. It was too big for my wardrobe so I'd hung it from the picture rail the night before our wedding. From underneath the gauze cocoon of its cover, it looked as if another woman was waiting to burst free and marry Michael in my stead.

How determined I was to see Philip that night. My cold, which I was loath to admit was more like flu, was closing my eyes and constricting my throat. 'There's no point in you going to the rehearsal, you're not well,' Michael had said, as I tried, unsuccessfully, not to splutter and stream. 'You can hardly speak, let alone sing,' he said. I'd even had my coat on, ready to leave. Michael put my irrational behaviour down to a fever. He'd bossed me into bed with a hot drink.

I see myself arriving at the church hall the following week. In my mind's eye, I look again, uselessly, for Philip, among the familiar faces and in all the corners of the room. I hadn't had any means of telling him I wasn't going to be there the week before; perhaps he was paying me back with his absence now. Everyone assembled into their groups; the cat-woman soprano smiled at me to acknowledge my return.

The choirmaster tapped his baton on the stand. 'Before we start,' he'd said, 'as I think we all know, very sadly, one of our tenors, dear Philip Moore, was killed in a road accident last week. His parents have asked that we dedicate our concert to his memory, which of course we are honoured to do.' Everyone murmured and sighed in unison. It was an impromptu madrigal of mourning. 'The funeral is next Tuesday,' he said, 'but as it's for the family and close friends only, I shall make a collection for some flowers. He was always . . .'

But I could no longer hear him. The layers of my skin felt as dense as clay. I only knew I was holding the sheet music because I saw it trembling in my hands. I mouthed the words of the songs because I didn't trust myself to sing. I had to concentrate on breathing, urging air in and reminding myself of expulsion. When did it happen? Why hadn't I felt a shock as he died, or lay dying? How much did he suffer? I should have felt a tremor at least, as twins are supposed to do if one of them is ill, or worse. For how long since he died had I been doing all the usual, stupid, pointless things, ignorant of his fate? As people jostled for cups of tea I hunted out conversations where Philip's name might be mentioned. A man and woman talked in low voices about shock and death and his family. I stood close to them.

'Where is the funeral?' I said. They separated, reluctantly, to admit me to their conversation. 'I'd like to pay my respects.'

The woman's eyebrows rose in the traditional arch of sympathy. 'Did you know him well?' she said. 'Away from here, I mean.'

'A little,' I said. 'He taught my friend's son.'

'He lived in Otsford, didn't he?' The woman sounded vague. She'd obviously hoped I had had a closer connection to him than that. 'I suppose they'll have it there.'

The man nodded.

'Was it sudden, do you know?' I said. 'Did he die at once?'

They frowned.

'Was he knocked down,' I persisted, 'or was he the one driving?'

The choirmaster began calling us to reassemble.

'Ah, there we are, off we go again,' the woman said. She looked relieved to be escaping my questioning. 'He was very young, wasn't he,' she said, busying herself with the next piece of music. 'Well, about the same age as you, I suppose. How old are—'

But I feigned a coughing fit and fled. When I'd discovered that my coat was submerged underneath several others on the peg in the cloakroom, I'd thrown them all to the ground to retrieve it and left them there.

Philip's death was outrageous to me. I was irate at his carelessness. I'd told Michael I had a doctor's appointment to explain my determination to leave the house early on that Tuesday and he'd frowned, because I knew he could see me crying. I was even furious at his concern. I remember standing opposite the church in Otsford. I had no idea what time his funeral would be held. I could be standing for hours, waiting. I'd wait for however long it took, I didn't want to leave. I found a tin of liquorice sweets in my bag and placed several of the tiny, fierce pellets on my tongue. When the first mourners began to arrive, they circled the porch and greeted each other in pairs and fours and sixes, then dispersed and reassembled, like the drones cast out of the ants' nests each summer. Eventually, they shuffled back together and formed a ragged line as the hearse approached. The coffin was squat and ugly. There were only two bunches of flowers on top. I'd wished I'd known exactly how long I'd been in the world without him.

I wept, ragged with anger. The mourners were still huddled in the porch outside the church. No one embraced. There were two older, rather smarter people I thought might have been his parents. A tiny woman in a brave, bright hat buzzed from one person to another, a bee on black flowers. And a man who looked a bit like Philip, but not unbearably so (a brother? or cousin? I'd never know), stared at a book in his hand, open at a page he would probably read from during the service. It was doing me no good to watch their grief, it only increased the distance between us.

I had lain in bed that night, awake, waiting, until Michael climbed in beside me, expecting me to be asleep. I'd touched him and sucked him, feeling his surprise at this departure from our usual routine. Before he could lean over to the bedside cabinet for what he needed, I moved above him, pinning him beneath me, so that he couldn't stop, wouldn't stop. He clasped my waist and although the room was dark, I knew he didn't take his eyes off me. With every movement, every tiny gasp and sigh, I was obliterating Philip. I was denying to myself that his hungry, furtive love had ever existed at all. The same body that had opened warm and wet to him closed around Michael, my arms held him tight until I was convinced that his shape was enough to fill them. As he groaned and reared beneath me, I stared at the ceiling, my eyes stretched wide and unblinking.

Chapter 11

23 September

<u>Dream Boyfriend</u>

Side parting, long fringe. Brown hair.

Floral shirt? Cheesecloth? (Just at weekends of course.)

Likes poetry, esp. ee cummings.

Knows the lyrics to 'Ride a White Swan'.

Has a sister (to be my friend).

Taurus.

Two years older than me. Doing English A-level NOT GEOGRAPHY.

Can play the guitar (but hasn't got yucky long fingernails to pluck the strings, like Izzy's brother).

Faithful.

Learning to drive.

Smokes.

Honey magazine says you can plan to be the girlfriend of his dreams. If his last girlfriend had long hair, for example, they say that you should get yourself a head of short, shiny bounce. I don't think I'd look very nice with short hair. I want him to have had a girlfriend before me, of course. But not be *too* experienced.

I'm going to have loads of boyfriends before I'm too old. Some girls fall straight out of their school uniform into a wedding dress. *That* is not enough experience *at all*.

I caught sight of her the other night getting ready for bed. She was in her nightie, bending over the basin. I could see the cheeks of her bottom wobbling as she cleaned her teeth. I have added *please do not let me ever have a bum like that* to my prayers.

I shouldn't have pretended to flush Eddie's truck down the loo but he's being all weird about it now and saying he doesn't want it any more. I told him it's only a toy, it doesn't matter if it got wet. I'll get him a new one for his birthday, if I can afford it. I read to him tonight. I opened *My Friend Flicka* at random. I didn't get very far because Eddie kept asking questions like what is sorrel and where is Wyoming. After a while I closed the book. I stared at the cover and the special blue of the sky behind the horses' heads. Eddie was fast asleep.

Chapter 12

I'd promised myself I wouldn't look at Sarah's diary any more, but her voice bubbled up from the pages, as unstoppable as a spring released above ground and I heard it whatever I did. Each word dripped. I wanted to snatch her hand away from Eddie's back and smack her, hard. Where was I while she squeezed and bullied him? How could she take Truck away from him, even for a moment? I saw myself in the kitchen, stirring or wiping something, while one floor above, Sarah held him down until he stopped resisting. If only to protect him, I'd read more of what she wrote. In some ways, this is a good thing to do, I thought, opening the pages and meeting her there again.

I sat on her bed, reading, beneath the shelves of china animals and wilting rosettes, beside her hairbrush, criss-crossed with hair, and some plastic pots of eyeshadow. I caught sight of myself in the mirror, hunched over the book. I examined my reflection as though I were still subjected to the unkind magnification of her gaze. She transfigured me, like a witch in a fairy tale, until my body was lumpen. My skin became as solid and pale as set milk. Forests of hair, dark and dense, grew on my arms and legs. I could feel the flesh swelling at my waist. I stood up with difficulty as if I'd begun to melt into the furniture and would soon be stuck fast.

Chapter 13

Through his bedroom window, Eddie stared hard at the field. He knew where Truck was buried but he couldn't see the actual spot. It was beyond the garden and the path and under the overhang of the wall. It had been hard to dig a hole in the ground. He thought it would give with ease like sand, but the first trowelling got him only as far as stones and gravel. Eventually, first crouching then kneeling, he made a large enough space to hold the toy. He left two white rocks to say where he'd been.

One day, he was going to find twigs to make a cross, replacing the stones. Next to the window frame, there was a strip of yellow paint. It was the colour of the room before it was the blue of his choice. His mother had let him decide what colour it would be painted, and he'd felt very grown up. Doing without Truck should have made him feel older, too; instead he pined like a little baby for his metal friend.

Chapter 14

'Do you need anything?' I say. Michael shakes his head; it's only a little movement but one that takes considerable effort. It's getting dark outside. How will he fall asleep, I think, when all he's done is lie here? But I've only walked from his bedside to the toilet or the cafeteria and my eyes are tight with fatigue. I could doze where I sit.

I go to the window and depress one slat of the blind. In the block of flats opposite there's a random pattern of dark and yellow squares, as the people living there return home. Each brighter shape represents a hand on a switch, a person in that room. I thought of Philip, turning the car into his road. 'My landlady's light will go on when she hears the engine die,' he said. 'She's like a dog, lifting its head from the carpet.' Sure enough, a glow suffused the dense curtain at one window. She'd moved a chair inside her room as we passed her door, squeaking it across the lino to warn us that she was listening. He'd made an exaggerated gesture to outline a large chest in front of his own. He'd put his hand over my mouth to stop me laughing and I'd licked his palm, watching his expression. In the rehearsal, we'd sung 'Sweet Gingerbread Man'. Lying on his little bed later, we'd quoted the words of the song to each other until I had cried with laughter, burying my head in his jumper and feeling my stomach muscles ache. *Nice sticky hands, sticky peppermint*. 'If you don't stop holding me so tightly,' he'd said, lifting my face from his chest, 'you'll go home smelling of turpentine.' He sniffed my hair. 'Too late,' he said. The wind howled in the chimney as if a storm raged outside. Even the littlest gust sounded fierce.

In Michael's room now, the window blind rustles and clicks as I let the slat go. I turn round ready to apologise for the unwanted sound, but Michael still sleeps. His mouth drops open and his lower lip sags to show his teeth. His lack of inhibition embarrasses me. I tiptoe into the corridor.

The nurse scuttles towards me; she has her coat on and knots a scarf dotted with sequins round her neck as she travels. She wears a short-strapped navy handbag across her chest, riding high on her bosom. For a moment, she looks disconcerted to see me, as if I shouldn't be here without good reason or her permission. 'Oh, Mrs Deacon,' she says. 'I'm off. Night Sister will be with you soon.' The sequins wink and flicker. They are too small to protect her from me, they are only a fairy's armour.

A woman appears, peering at each door's label and reading them aloud. 'Deacon,' she reads, stopping at Michael's door. 'Where on earth is Ward C?' she says, annoyed, as if the nurse and I are hiding it from her. We both point towards the far doors. She hurries away with renewed vigour and an admonishing tut, as though time matters more to her than to us. She is sharply outlined against the paintwork, the way that visitors to a gallery are defined by the bright lights. The clicks of her footsteps reverberate against the hard surfaces, as scattered and frequent as if she had more than two legs. A notice flutters on the wall in her wake. I have no one, and nowhere, to hurry to.

'I'm back,' I say to Michael's sleeping form. 'As if I never went away,' I say to myself. I seek out a particular letter from the bag, one I need to see. A palliative. Here it is, thank goodness. Its eau-de-Nil envelope and that familiar handwriting. I won't read it yet. I am picking up my memories like knitting from a basket, recognising their colour and shape.

I am trying to remember Philip's voice. The scattered fragments of our time together re-group themselves, the way the coloured pieces inside a kaleidoscope rearrange themselves into a new pattern when the dial's turned. There were songs, of course. The way he would catch one thumb and curl it back to touch the arm behind it, without thinking, as he spoke. There was a tin of meatballs he'd reheated on the Baby Belling. The tiny sketch of me he'd done while I was pretending to sleep. A conversation about how he hoped to inspire just *one* of the little boys he taught to really appreciate art. He'd said he wanted them to ignore the big picture to start with and concentrate on details. On brushstrokes. That was the way, he said, that they'd begin to understand about composition, form and colour. I had changed the subject, only too aware that the idea of the pupils in his class reminded me of the child I'd left at home. My child, whose pleas to me not to leave her I had willingly, easily ignored.

'Somebody telephoned earlier,' says the nurse, coming in

to Michael's room. 'I think it was your daughter?' Her voice lifts in question, as though the caller might just have impersonated a relative.

'Sarah,' I say. Michael is awake, listening. I don't meet his eye.

'That's it,' she says brightly. 'I told her Mr Deacon was sleeping. I asked her if she'd like me to wake him, but she said no, no, she'd call back. There was an echo on the line. It was very distracting.' She shakes her head as if she were still hearing her voice repeated back to herself.

I'd been tempted to email Sarah, but I couldn't frame my greeting or how I would sign off. Instead, I left a message for her, which only needed to begin and end perfunctorily. The spoken word was less dismissible. I'd never grown used to the twang of her answerphone's message, its flat, neutral Americanese. I always had to ring back, once I'd rehearsed what I was going to say. It's knowing I'm being recorded that unnerves me. I'd told her only the rudiments of this part of Michael's story. *Pneumonia. His heart. Not long.* I'd imagined her listening to it, pausing for a moment to absorb the implication.

Above the rim of his mask, Michael's eyes signal a query: Is she coming? *'She'll be here soon,'* I ought to tell him.

'Wake him if she rings again,' I say.

The nurse nods.

I catch the scent of boiled sweets as she passes me, some sort of indeterminate, sweet fruit. Her nurse's uniform clings to her as if she's upholstered. If I snipped at it, I suspect she'd leak horsehair. It's exactly what I used to think about

Sheila Turner. I haven't thought about her for years, but now she bustles into my thinking, her head still swivelling for information to be squirrelled away. She had a way of looking at a point just below my neck as though I had a mark there, something unpleasant like a fleck of the crusted yolk of an egg or a dob of sauce. Even thinking about her now makes my hands go involuntarily to my collarbone, checking and smoothing.

I'd seen Sheila that day, the day of seeing-not-seeing Philip. Hurrying, my eyes blistered with tears, nearly on the homeward path, I noticed her standing across the road, by the pond. She was in conversation with someone I didn't recognise, whose back was turned, but when Sheila saw me she stepped sideways from her companion and waved, mouthing 'Hel-lo,' in an exaggerated way. 'Wait a moment,' she gestured, holding up her hand with the palm flat to halt my progress.

Weighed down by my cargo of potatoes and bread and clutching my stiff handbag, I could only smile and shake my head, indicating that much as I'd *love* to chat, I really must press on. We were separated by a good twenty feet and a road.

'I'll pop round later,' Sheila telegraphed across the divide.

I was glad she was detained or I'd have had her alongside me all the way home, practically to the front door, as we lived so close to each other. I sped up, walking away without looking back and defying her to follow.

I walked carefully along the footpath, a rutted, uneven space next to the fences and the wall, speckled with stones and puddles. There was a quicker route, a flattened swathe across the middle of the field, but ever since I'd found a large beetle unexpectedly attached to the front of my shoe after I'd crossed there, I'd chosen the other way. You could see where you were putting your feet if you walked on stones. I'd screamed when I saw the bug, shaking my foot wildly to dislodge the thing. It took some doing – how did they cling so hard? – but eventually it fell off. I'd panted afterwards as if I'd fought a tiger and kept glancing behind me as I walked on, as though it might follow me home. Later that day, I'd realised that although I had screamed loudly – and probably more than once – no one had heard me and come running.

What time was it? I did a rough calculation. It must be about half past two. I didn't mind missing lunch. I always found it hard to decide on what to eat anyway, and it seemed extravagant to rustle up something especially for myself. Besides, it was better to go hungry and to feel the waistband of my skirt loose about my waist. In an hour and a half, Eddie and Sarah would arrive home from school. Later there'd be peeling and chopping and stirring. I wished I could make them all stand at the fridge in turn and take food straight to their mouths with their bare hands.

Chapter 15

The bedside clock announces 20.02. It flips its numbers at the last possible moment with one second to spare. Michael searches in his memory for what he used to say, as a child, to separate seconds if he needed to count them up to the minute. Madeira, was it? Madagascar? He feels a jolt of relief when he remembers Mississippi. He'll never forget how to spell it, either. His teacher, Miss Polder, her necklace swinging against her bosom, chants again in his head: *Mrs M Mrs I Mrs S S I.* He can't remember her face but her large, forbidden breasts are unforgettable. None of it matters any more. The time of day certainly doesn't. Somewhere, in places he's never visited, people have read his news and changed their plans. He imagines the emails hovering above a large atlas, the sort displayed on his classroom wall, before they swooped and landed. Pinned like coloured flags, they announced his departure and could not be removed. He is folding in on himself, shutting the world out, but it's a peaceful process and he doesn't feel the need to hurry it.

He regards Marion from underneath barely closed eyes. He is amused by her impatience at his slow demise. She is short with the staff; you wouldn't think she'd been in their ranks herself. He'd never asked her about that choice of career, but one of her friends did once. It might have been that big woman – Bridget, was that her name? The one whose hairline started high on her head, in the manner of a Restoration portrait. She'd asked why *ever* had Marion become a nurse? She was probably watching her manhandle a child into a coat or brush away the suggestion of a stomach ache. She was always robust in her treatment of childhood ailments. Marion had shrugged, as if the answer were obvious. 'I needed somewhere to live,' she'd said.

He likes it best when she is out of his room on some errand or other. He knows she is occupied, and she tells him where she's going. This is a change for the better. That was always the problem with Marion. Even when she was actually with him, he didn't really know where she was.

The very afternoon he'd met Marion's father for the first time, the old boy had told him to propose to her. She'd only been out of the room for a few moments when Stan issued his unexpected command. 'Look,' he'd said, 'I don't know what you're planning, but if you can't see any reason not to, I think you should marry my daughter. She's a nice girl.' Michael had thought he might have had more to say about her than that, but he seemed to think he'd said enough. 'No need to ask me for her hand now,' the old man said. 'Job's done.'

Michael had consulted a more worldly friend and booked a table at a restaurant in town. The same friend assured him girls wanted to wear an engagement ring straight away. It makes them feel special, he'd said. Marion, thought Michael loyally, was more sure of herself than that. He'd chosen a ring anyway, just in case the girls at the nursing home teased her about its absence.

By the time he asked her to marry him, he'd convinced himself he was doing the right thing. The thought of years of taking other women out and weighing up whether or not they were possible wives was alarming. He might well decide on someone, only to discover she didn't like him. Marion obviously did. The eight years between them allowed her to think he was more worldly and wise, too. When she accepted his proposal, although she got the whole thing over as fast as possible and hardly looked at the ring, she seemed as relieved as he did. And she seemed as grateful, too, that they'd found each other. Was there anything wrong with wanting safety? He remembered some moon-faced man, years ago, at a party, blowing out his cheeks in feigned horror when he'd asked Michael what he did. 'Accountancy? Wow, man, don't you go mad with boredom?' He'd understood the accusation; people often mistook having routine employment for a kind of punishment. If he'd wanted to, he could have pointed out all the ways in which his life wasn't dull at all. He envied himself his former innocence, though. It had been a long time since he'd been able to imagine an uncomplicated future, stretching ahead of him like a well-signposted road. 'Actually,' he wished he'd said, 'I love accountancy. It's people like you who are dull.' He wished, too, that he'd taken the two ends of the man's silly thin scarf and pulled them tight.

He is compiling a list of things that he has relished. It's short. It includes the births of his children. A new car he'd cherished. A couple of amorous experiences that had woken him to surprising possibilities. Getting into his bed at the end of the day, reaching for that other, warm hand. His body now is merely a collection of cells, mostly faulty. Eating and drinking provide no pleasure, sleep is functional. He lives with a series of dull pains that he only registers when the next dose of medication is due. He racks his brains for a defining physical memory, some sensation that he misses more than any other. Above all, he thinks, it would be hard to top the instant exoticism of a new toothbrush.

Chapter 16

After Philip died, grief had enveloped me like a caul. I could scarcely eat. I didn't sleep. I resented the fact I had to find secret places to weep, where no one could see me. I was tender and protective of myself, like a chaperone with a highly strung charge. 'Christ, Moo, are you all right?' Michael had said, as I'd hurled myself across the kitchen. I wanted to say, *Philip has died, he is dead, he is dead*, but instead I said, 'I can't bear this song,' and turned the wireless off. Michael had given me a quizzical look, but he didn't switch it back on.

'You're so lucky with Michael,' people said to me. 'Do you two *ever* row?' I said I sometimes wished we could. Michael never challenged me. If I was being irrational or too demanding, he'd simply smile at me and wait for me to calm down. They told me I was lucky that Michael loved me so much. He'd do *anything* for you, wouldn't he, they said. It felt disloyal to confess that I had begun to find his endless tolerance annoying. I tested his generosity deliberately: I'd ask him for a lift somewhere as soon as he'd settled down in his chair or suggest that he give me the very newspaper he'd opened to read, little things like that. It was more of a game than anything else ('Let's play When *Will* Michael Say No?'), but he never denied me. I told myself I had nothing to complain about. It was normal, I reasoned, to be annoyed by some aspect of your husband's behaviour and his was hardly offensive. But it was like spotting a crack in a glass. You could keep drinking from it, but you couldn't forget it was there and one day it would shatter. I knew that the more he met my demands with his soothing patience, the more I was in danger of sharpening the very knives I'd ask him to cut himself with. And, what's more, I knew he'd agree to do it.

'Isn't it your choir rehearsal tonight?' Michael had said the next week. I said I wasn't going any more, it wasn't really my thing after all.

'I'm sorry you gave us up. You missed a lovely concert,' our neighbour said later. 'Of course, it was very sad. Philip's mother cried all the way through.'

'Who's Philip?' Michael had looked at me.

'Young chap, tenor section,' our neighbour had leapt in. 'Killed in a *car accident*.' She'd mouthed the last words as though they were a curse. 'Everyone really liked him. He bought me a cider once.' People were always very keen to claim any sort of closeness to the dead.

'Did you know him, Marion?' Michael had said.

I said not really, that I knew him only by sight.

'Didn't he give you a lift home once? I thought you used to share a joke or two,' the woman said.

'No, no,' I said. 'Not me, I wonder what made you think that?' I was relieved to have got to the end of my sentence without screaming.

'Who did she mean, then, if not you?' said Michael afterwards. 'There can't be anyone else there like you, can there?'

When I was about five, I'd lost sight of my mother in a crowded shop. After only a few minutes, I saw her again and slipped my hand into hers. Except that it wasn't my mother's, it was a stranger's hand I held. She'd been kind and reassuring, telling me we'd find my mother any minute. But my heart had lurched at the wrongness of her, the sour smell of her perfume and the slash of dark blue eyeshadow on each eyelid that shuttered her eyes from me every time she blinked. I knew I should hold Michael's hand tight now, in case I was lost again. In case I reached for another hand. But this time, on purpose, I let go.

Chapter 17

23 September

Things I won't tell my boyfriend about.

I really like opening a Crunchie bar, taking a bite, making the end all spitty then leaving it overnight and eating it the next day, when it's sticky.

Last summer, some of us went to the rec with big bottles of cider. Tessa Wheatley's older brother and his friend brought them, because they'd gone to Tonbridge where nobody knew them in the offies and they wouldn't have known they're not old enough to drink. It was about a week before school started again. I don't like it then, it's when the time left is spoiled because you're thinking how soon it'll all be over. There were seven of us and five bottles, so I thought I'd just have to have a sip, but two of the girls squealed about going on to Guides and said they couldn't have stinky, drinky breath. They sat with us for a while, then brushed the dried grass off their uniforms and left. Tessa's brother said one bottle each ought to do it. He drank his very fast. His friend said cider made him randy. The other girl with us, Helen, giggled and said she knew what he meant.

That's when it changed. It was like switching channels on

the television. You're settled into one mood then suddenly all the pictures are different, and they sound wrong. The boy kept staring at her. Tessa said what time did we all have to leave, because she didn't want to walk home on her own if her brother was staying out. No one replied. Helen said could the boy help her look behind the shelter, because she thought she'd dropped something there. As they stood up, he looped his arm round her shoulder and pulled her towards him and squeezed her breast. When they were out of sight, we could hear them grunting and panting. Tessa's brother squirmed as if his spine was melting. Tessa and I looked away, across the field, anywhere rather than at each other. She said they should keep it down, they weren't in a soundproofed room, were they, but she whispered as if it was worse for them to hear us rather than the other way round. Suddenly, there was a kind of shriek. It was the most private noise I'd ever heard. It split me open inside as if it was sharp. It went right through me. It was like the joyful, yelping anticipation of pain you feel when you bang your elbow. It makes you catch your breath in gulps because you know you'll be in agony at any minute. I wanted to be there with them. The middle of me was hollowed out with envy and fear.

Helen emerged before the boy did. Her skirt was round the wrong way with the zip facing outwards. She looked as if she'd been winded. He followed her without looking at her and picked up his nearly empty cider bottle and swigged from it, but he couldn't make his mouth hard enough and liquid spilled down his front. Tessa's brother called him a dribbling baby, but his voice broke on the words. We sat there for a while until some woman came with her kids. She was giving them a holiday treat, letting them go on the swings in the last of the daylight when they should have been in bed. The little girl had her hair in bunches; they were pulled so tightly to the sides of her head it made her eyes look tilted. I suddenly felt weepy looking at her. I knew she was going to have to find out about all kinds of horrible stuff in her life. Even Eddie, who really would never hurt anyone, will have to suffer just for existing. It's really not fair.

Chapter 18

I must have dozed, because someone has cleared away the half-empty beaker of coffee and refilled the scratched plastic jug with water. The room is rudely impersonal. I'll give the nurses something when this is over. We used to love the sort of visitor who rewarded us with boxes of chocolates or biscuits. Make sure you share them with the doctors, they'd say, but we never did. I look at the clock above Michael's bed. Twenty to nine. His untouched meal lies on his table. I'd ordered it for him yesterday, when it seemed possible he might eat macaroni cheese. He'd been away on a business trip once and brought home a dark blue packet of spaghetti, about two feet long. He produced a little piece of Parmesan cheese to go with it. He'd described how the shop was hung with huge, red hams and dotted with baskets of biscuits and sweets in coloured twists of paper, as if he'd visited a place of worship. I'd wrestled the strands into and out of boiling water as best I could, but some of them stuck hard to the bottom of the pan. The raw sweat smell of the cheese clung to my hands for hours afterwards.

The doctor comes in, on his ward rounds. He's young, of course. 'Can I have a word?' he says. 'Outside?' We stand in the corridor. 'We'll have to make a decision,' he says. 'About the mask.' He looks at me then looks away quickly. He shouldn't feel awkward, this is all we have to discuss.

'Who has to decide?' I say. 'You?'

The doctor takes a step back from me, as if I'd challenged him. 'I'm not the senior registrar. He's the person who'll discuss it with you,' he says.

'I know,' I say. 'I mean, of course. I remember now. Sorry. I used to work in a hospital.'

He looks at me.

'I was a nurse,' I say. I can see him trying to take in this new fact. His hair is a faint ginger red, the sort that will go grey without leaving a trace of this fiercer colour. He has matching freckles. I want to ask him if he likes dancing, if he has a girlfriend and if she stays awake until he gets home, waiting to talk to him. Or to have sex. The expression on his face suggests he cannot imagine this old woman in front of him being either younger, or a nurse.

'Mr Deacon is sentient,' he says. 'He's aware of what's happening to him, he knows enough to express himself, to make decisions. But I can't be the one to ask him. I'll ask the registrar to pop in.' He looks back at his notes. 'Do you need to let anyone know what's happening?' He is trying to make sense of the situation.

'Everyone who needs to know is being kept informed,' I say.

He almost shrugs, but maintains his impassive stance.

This will be how it's done, then. A decision made first

in some office, confirmed in a corridor and completed in a bed. Paperwork made flesh. There's no suggestion of Michael leaving the hospital and going home to die, it's more efficient if he finishes here. The gap between his death and the parcelling of him to the morgue will be closed more easily this way. I think of his last cup of coffee with me, the last time he listened to the radio in our garden, turning the aerial to find the signal. When I go home, I imagine that I'll find his last, unfinished crossword puzzles and the last clothes he put in the laundry basket. 'I'll clear the room,' he'd said to me before, in that previous, terrible time of loss. 'You don't have to touch anything, Moo.' I'm filled with a dread of his absence now, made worse by the fact he still lives. I have always hated the bed half cold.

The house we'd moved to in those days, when the children were little and Michael and I were young, stood in a semicircle of identical houses, just far enough apart to be described as detached. The other owners chose the same type of flowers for their front gardens and kept their curtains pulled apart to the same distance during the day. There had been local objections to this development, Sheila had told me. It would take years before our houses looked as if they should be here. There was a prim nervousness to them, as if they knew half the village disapproved. She'd moved here from an old cottage on the other side of the village. 'Marvellous to have everything so neat,' she'd said. 'None of the walls in the old house were straight, Marion. It was full of character, of course, but you can't get rid of damp with character.'

Who lives there now? I wonder. We sold it to a man I didn't much like. I didn't meet his wife; he mentioned her in passing but never suggested she visit. I haven't been back since, not even to that area. Too much has changed and vanished. I do know that I couldn't wait to get home that day. I was in agony. One of my shoes rubbed at the heel. Their insides bulged with little pillows of padded fabric and caught my skin. When I'd bought them there was a cardboard advertisement propped up by the till, showing a woman gambolling through daffodils. She was attempting to point their blunt toes. At my last visit to Sarah's school I'd noticed that the headmistress, a woman of robust dullness, was wearing an identical pair. The saleswoman said they'd be as comfortable as slippers. She lied, I thought, practically counting the steps until I was home. I would have to save from my housekeeping allowance even to get a new pair. As soon as I got through the door, I'd slip the wretched things off. The last few paces were agony.

A car stood directly in front of the back gate. When we'd moved in, I'd thought that having a public footpath so close by was rather quaint. But people often left their cars at this last point before the road narrowed and the path began. It made opening our garden gate difficult and I felt observed as they clambered in and out, taking their time. There was someone standing next to the car as I approached, his hands in his pockets and staring at the ground. I braced myself for a small confrontation but then I realised it was Tom Spencer, not the car's owner at all. He looked up as I approached and, as soon as he saw me, his eyes flicked rapidly to one side and his head went down again.

'Hello,' I said, staring pointedly ahead. I'd now have to manoeuvre past both him and the car with my heavy bag and my painful foot. I was never quite sure whether to greet him or not; he looked uncomfortable if you even waved from a distance and he skittered away if your paths crossed. He was simple, that was all. People gave him odd tasks to do and he weeded or painted with a plodding obedience. He could be about to offer to do something for me now, of course, that might be why he was loitering. I had my answer ready. I put my shopping down, suppressing a groan of relief at being free of it and fished my key from my handbag. He followed me uninvited through the door. He wiped his feet on the mat outside, lifting his legs high behind him after each swipe.

'Car shouldn't be here,' he said, inspecting the soles of his shoes. His laces were heaped into an extravagant knot, the result of much looping and retying. Molly probably put his shoes on for him, making sure they stayed put no matter how much he jiggled or stomped during the day. He went and stood by the sink and examined the window above it with some care. I'd written a note, in letters large enough to be read from the path and stuck it on the kitchen window. 'Your note's gone,' he said. It was true, two torn strips of Sellotape were still stuck to the glass, empty of their instruction.

'Ah, well, it must have fallen off.' I kept moving towards him, hoping he'd move aside to let me past. He was leaving it very late. He rolled his shoulders back. His jacket was too tight. It stopped at his waist and wrists in bands of thick ribbing. The pattern, open checks in red, white and pale blue, reminded me of pictures of Canada, large pine trees and piles of logs. This thin fabric wouldn't have been enough to keep out an English winter let alone deep, piled snow.

Raising his head slowly and then too far, so that his chin rose, and I could see his Adam's apple move in his smooth, hard neck, he breathed in hard. 'Can I use your toilet, miss?' he said.

I hesitated. He could go to the downstairs cloakroom. I needn't apologise to him for the chaos of coats and boots in the hall on the way. He was waiting for my answer. I thought he was probably about fifteen years my junior, twenty-two or so, but it was hard to tell. When I was in my twenties, I thought anyone over thirty was ancient. I wondered what he saw when he looked at me. I was conscious of the fact that one button dangled on a thread from my unfastened coat. My cardigan hung open, too and my blouse was bunched up. He was looking at me with the watery, unfocused gaze of a newly-woken child. He had remarkably clear skin. Did he even shave? 'Of course,' I said. I spoke a bit too loudly, as if to suggest there was someone else in the house. 'It's just to the left,' I added, but he was already walking down the corridor.

I slipped my shoes off, both feet now aching in solidarity. My toes expanded painfully on the cold lino. The note had fallen into the sink below the window where the dripping tap smudged and blurred the words. I heard the door of the cloakroom open and close, then the lock sliding noisily in place. I thought of him concentrating as he negotiated the unfamiliar room. He would catch sight of himself in the little mirror. There was nothing outwardly to show how damaged his head was inside. Perhaps he was dropped as a baby. Sarah had rolled hard off the side of the bed once, and I'd found Eddie fallen at the bottom of a flight of stairs I hadn't realised he could climb. Apart from the endless pause each time, staring at their first white, then reddening, faces and waiting for them to cry, they'd seemed unharmed. The sort of hurt that bruised them but didn't rattle their brains in their skulls so that they'd never be able to hold a proper conversation or travel abroad alone.

'Thanks, miss.' He was behind me, close. I hadn't heard him come back. Distantly, the cistern clanked and refilled.

'You got any jobs need doing? Miss?' The boy put his hand on my shoulder and we both jumped, startled. I squealed. 'Sorry, miss.' He shook his fingers as though he'd burned himself. 'Thought you hadn't heard me. Sorry, miss.' He looked appalled. I couldn't think how to comfort him without touching him. I wanted to put a reassuring hand on his arm to pat or squeeze. My back was pressed up to the sink, there was nowhere for me to move. Despite his downcast eyes and the way he was trying to shrink away from me, he suddenly seemed to take up more room than he did before. I'd once found a bird trapped in the living room, which flew about wildly as it tried to escape. This boy had the samc frightened, ragged look about him. That had ended badly – I couldn't catch it and it never again found the open window it had flown in through. It had injured a wing as it battered itself against the walls and hard surfaces. Michael had carried it outside, placing it far enough away from the house so that we wouldn't actually have to watch it die.

'Don't tell,' he said, blinking back tears.

'Tom.' I was brisk with a mixture of annoyance and nerves. 'Nothing happened. Off you go.'

There was a pause, then he shook his head, as if to rearrange his thoughts, and left.

I rubbed my temples. My fingers found a little metal bar above my left ear. When I'd tidied this morning, I'd found one of Sarah's old hair slides on the sideboard. I'd pinned it in my hair to leave my hands free while I carried what I needed to take upstairs. I went into the hall and peered into the mirror on the hat-stand. The slide winked where it was fastened. I had done everything, talked to everyone, all day, with a child's decoration stuck on my head.

There was a spatter of dripped water on the floor in front of the basin where he must have shaken his wet hands. The bar of soap was sticky with recent use. I felt a sudden pang for his mother, doggedly instilling in her broken son these little decencies. The seat was still up, though. Michael always returned it to the closed position, and I was trying to train Eddie to do the same. It just seemed more *polite*, somehow. It gaped open now like a vulgar expression shouted aloud. The boy had left his mark. He would have stood here, holding himself, while I was only feet away. The door handle was wet. I went to the airing cupboard and selected a little flowered cloth. Just before I hung it on the empty ring, I sniffed it and inhaled Persil and fresh air. If he came back, I'd make sure he left with my scent on his hands.

Chapter 19

24 September

Sometimes I put Mum's clothes on, when everyone's out. There's a Chinesey sort of dress, with a mandarin collar and dragons on it, that I like looking at myself in. I go into the sitting room wearing it, like I'm the adult. It feels like a room in someone else's house when it's empty. I move the ugly black and white china cat, licking its chest with a large, pink tongue, from the top of the radiogram. The LPs are stored at one end, packed as close together as a pack of cards. I look for Julie Andrews. I love the way her pink skirt flies out on either side of her. She holds a travel bag in one hand and a guitar in its case in the other, swinging them up high as though they're both empty. I slide the record on to the turntable. I pull the stylus back till there's a click, to set it spinning. I like the hiss before the music starts. I feel as if the needle goes straight to my heart. What I want is for everything to stay just like it is and for everything to change.

Once, in the middle of a music lesson, I had sung middle C before Miss Mullarkey had played a note. It came so easily to me that I was surprised no one else could find it in their heads. I could do it over and over again. Miss Mullarkey told me I've got perfect pitch. It's a useless talent. We haven't even got a piano. Sometimes, I sing the note out loud all by myself and I know it's still true.

Chapter 20

Now, here's a thing. A postcard from Sheila. I didn't know I'd kept it. 'Do you remember Sheila?' I say to Michael, but only because he is safely asleep and will not answer. It's a view of Margate with a picture of two larger-than-life kittens superimposed over the top. Sheila was the last person to worry about the incongruity or the artistic gaffe. *September 1986,* it says. *It's lovely here today, Marion. It's an understatement to say I don't regret the move! Please come and stay again. I really do think the sea air did you good and helped you get over things. All the best.* I try to conjure her, solid and loud, as if she could walk in now and start examining Michael's chart or his medicines without permission, as was her way. She will not take proper shape, however hard I concentrate. But I often thought I saw Beattie Moore, out of the corner of my eye. For ages after her actual appearance as I went into the sitting room I would turn quickly, as if she still sat on the sofa, one leg bent. Or I might think I caught a glimpse of her beyond the wobbling glass of the front door. Beattie's beret and her pink coat flashed like fish scales under water in my peripheral vision. Can you be haunted by the living? Beattie's visit had been to the other, smaller house. The house I had been living in when I met Philip. After he'd died, I'd often stumbled into the furniture or tripped down the stairs, as if I were lost inside it.

When Beattie turned up, I was at that heavy, late stage of pregnancy, feeling comfortably full of baby. I'd spend some time each day organising and admiring a small layette of clothes and shawls. I was sorting these things, trying to persuade the sleeves of a tiny cardigan to fold, when the doorbell rang. I was tempted to ignore it. I was planning to listen to *Woman's Hour* later that afternoon and doze through the serial.

The woman standing there was tiny, her clothes would have fitted a child. Her coat was pulled in tightly at the waist with a black patent belt and fastened with enormous buttons. Her fingers were long, the nails painted dark purple. She held her hands to her chest, one folded over the other, the pose of a stone angel beside a grave. A ring with a large green stone flashed from her left hand. She wore a beret, pulled low over a sharply cut bob. She reminded me of someone, but the thought wouldn't crystallise into fact.

'Marion Deacon?' she said.

Her voice was unexpectedly low and slightly husky, as if she'd recently had a cigarette. I couldn't smell smoke. Her scent reminded me of my old French teacher's velvet perfume. I hoped my polite smile would last until I had some clue about who this person was. She was regarding me with what seemed like determined neutrality, neither returning my smile nor looking away. Perhaps she's canvassing, I thought, although I wasn't aware of anything that might need my vote.

'I'm Beattie Moore,' the woman said. 'I'm Philip's mother.'

Several possible options flickered in my head. Slamming the door in the woman's face competed with shaking her hand. I thought I could just say: 'Philip who?' Instead, I said, 'Would you like to come in?'

'Not really,' the woman said, stepping forward. The hallway was small, little more than a turning circle between the doorways on either side and the steep rise of the stairs beyond. My size forced us into sudden and awkward intimacy. The woman stared at my stomach. 'When's it due?' she said.

'In about two months,' I said, as if I didn't know exactly how many weeks and how many days away the date was.

'Not your first, is it,' Beattie said. It was not a question.

I wanted to breathe deeply through my nose, as if the lessons of the antenatal classes would carry me through this encounter, too, but the woman's face was too close to my own. Her features were disproportionately large and gathered at the front of her face, as if she'd been tipped forward while they set. She didn't look like Philip, I thought, although I was finding it hard to recall his face.

The floral curtains and three-piece suite in the sitting room looked too neat and domestic, like a childish riposte to upheaval and adult grief. I regretted the vase of tulips on the table. 'Would you like some tea?' I said.

'No, I wouldn't,' the woman said. She sat down and undid her coat. A released mass of floral fabric seeped over her knees. She crossed her tiny feet at the ankles and swung them as they hung over the edge of the sofa. On the road outside, someone rang a bicycle bell, then there was a clatter of thin tyres and a jangling frame as it passed by. On the windowsill stood a photograph of Sarah, aged about four, wearing a romper suit, her feet bare and partly buried in sand. 'She looks like you,' the woman said. She wriggled her long fingers into her coat pocket and held out a piece of blue-tinged paper, folded over twice.

I was beginning to feel dizzy, I couldn't take in enough air. The thought crossed my mind that this woman might be an impostor, not Philip's mother at all.

'Richard Matthews gave me your address,' Beattie said. 'I told him I was collecting anecdotes about my son from everyone who'd been in the choir.'

'Who?' I said.

Beattie looked amused. 'Not a choir member for long, then? He's the conductor.'

'Oh, yes, of course,' I said. The aged young man in charge. My name must still be on a list. 'I didn't really—'

'Did you love Philip?' his mother said.

The baby gave a lurch and I instinctively placed my hands to where its head or an elbow or a knee protruded, then receded.

'It's all in here,' Beattie said. She bent her head over the still-folded paper like a nun in prayer. I stared at the little stalk of fabric in the centre of her beret. 'I thought about not telling you,' Beattie said. 'I know it's not going to make me feel better. Or make any difference to what happened. Then I thought if I have to think about it every day, from the moment I wake until I try to sleep, you should have to think about it, too.' She half stood, pulling her coat taut and tucked one leg beneath her before she sat down again. It was a graceful movement.

I was still wondering what to say. I thought any answer I gave would be the wrong one. I don't know why I can't just tell her to go, I thought. But I stayed where I was and waited, mute and still.

'The thing is,' Beattie said, 'he didn't die in an accident.'

I felt a sharp pain in my chest, as if a thin slice was being shaved from my heart. Several images of him passed in a sort of unwanted slide show in my head: he bled, he hanged, he drowned. 'Was he murdered?' I said.

Beattie looked at me with scorn. 'Technically, no.' She unfolded the paper and scanned its contents. 'Ready,' she said. It was an instruction to herself.

Please don't think I'm a coward, she read.

At the end of a party in the nurses' home, I had been kissed by a junior doctor. I was unravelling pleasantly with drink, the edges of me loose and remote. He had leaned towards me as he talked and then put his mouth on mine without preamble, as if he were steadying himself after missing his step. I let him stay there politely, waiting for him to stop, when desire clutched at me like a hand through a trapdoor and I'd kissed him back. He'd pulled away and looked at me as though he'd thought he'd been kissing someone else entirely. 'Well, well, well,' he said. 'That was nice. What's your name?' He was close enough to see where each hair on his chin rose from its follicle.

I'd recovered from the effect of the kiss as if my veins had been cauterised, the alcohol no longer reaching my head.

Listening to Philip's letter, hearing first my name, then, horribly, Sarah's, as he wrote about ending his life, as he explained my part in his decision, was just as sobering. His choice of phrases: *I have no hope, there is nothing else to live for, the only woman I could love* struck me as clichéd. Did he sit on the little bed to write it, or at the table? It had one leg balanced on an opened copy of *Catcher in the Rye* to keep it steady. 'Have you read it?' I'd said, squatting on the floor and tilting my head to read the title. 'Yes,' he'd said. 'Once is enough. Page 16 is just right for this job.'

'Here.' Beattie held the letter out. 'Read it yourself.' I noticed that the green-stoned ring she wore was the sort with an adjustable clasp, like something a child would wear. The two ends crossed over each other to keep it in place on her thin finger. She twisted her mouth, tugging at the skin inside her cheek. 'Did he give you anything?' she said.

I felt suddenly panicked. How would I stop this woman searching for the drawing?

'I'd like it back, if he did.'

'No,' I said.

Beattie frowned. 'He always said he sketched *everything* he liked,' she said. 'That's very odd.'

'Perhaps he was planning to,' I said and cursed myself for saying so. I shouldn't have mentioned anything that hinted at Philip's plans for his future.

Beattie tucked the note back inside the pocket of her flamboyant coat. 'I suppose it wasn't about you, really,' she said. 'It's about who he *thought* you were. He thought you were special. He thought you really loved him, that you would leave your husband for him. He had no idea that you'd be able to just go on living your life without him.'

I could feel a small area of loose trim on the chair's upholstery. A pin was missing. I could easily repair it myself, if I could find one to match. Beattie couldn't possibly imagine Philip and me together or understand what had happened between us, however much she questioned or stared hard at every inch of me.

She pushed herself forward and stood for a moment on a single flamingo leg as she uncurled the other. 'He slit his wrists,' she said, cinching her belt.

I thought of the sealed, scarred wounds on his arms. Had he reopened them? *Just cut along the dotted line*. He'd tried to kill himself before, hadn't he? An attempt that couldn't possibly have been my fault. He should have mentioned that in his letter. He could at least have rescued me from listening to this woman. I began to cry.

'About time, too,' said Beattie. 'You can't weep for him in front of anyone else, can you? I'd say, "poor you", but your unhappiness doesn't really mean anything to me.' She paused, giving me a final once-over, then shook her head. 'I just can't see what he saw in you,' she said. 'You're so *ordinary*.'

After she'd gone, I went around the room picking up and replacing ornaments in turn, as if they needed to be exorcised of Beattie's low growl and her tiny, swinging feet. Philip lay deep in cold darkness. He couldn't ever hold me again, say my name or make me laugh. Whatever happened next, each new kiss or careless lie, was his fault. I would punish him until he was sorry about dying. Until he regretted every single moment he had deliberately left me to outlive him.

Chapter 21

25 September

Eng. lang homework: *Describe your environment, inside and out.*

My name is Sarah Jane Kathryn Deacon. My mother told me she always wanted to call her little girl Sarah Jane. She even had a doll called Sarah Jane, but she says she wasn't allowed to keep it because her father sold the house and everything in it when her mother died. I was called Kathryn after my mother's mother, who's dead. I wasn't given any name for my dad's mother, who's also dead. If I could choose my own name, I'd be called Emma. I have one brother.

The other night, Eddie woke me up because he was standing on the landing crying loudly. He said Alf the old window cleaner man had told him about our houses being built on fields. Eddie wanted to know what had happened to all the animals that used to live there. He was wailing about hedgehogs having no homes any more. I said they were all dead and one day he'd understand about progress. I swear his eyes changed colour with grief.

I am waiting, all the time, for things to be different. The other day in choir, I sat next to Bobbie. I always try to. We were singing 'The Silver Swan'; it's high and everyone wobbles on the long notes. Mrs W said that Gibbons would be disappointed in us. Bobbie did this thing, this tiny movement, tucking her hands under her arms and looking like a monkey. I couldn't stop laughing. Bobbie nudged me. I could feel the warmth of her in the small place where her elbow met my ribs and she was laughing too.

At least I got out of swimming yesterday. We hardly have any time to change afterwards and have to sit through French smelling of chlorine and with the backs of our necks damp. The first time I had to sign the swimming book, I could feel the ST between my legs, as bulky as a nappy. Mum had put a packet of bunnies and a belt on my bed, so I'd be ready. I'd never ever seen anything so ugly. I was convinced everything would slip round or slide down. Or that you'd be able to see the huge lump through my skirt. Bobbie told me about a girl in their class who got up to read in assembly and walked all the way to the front of the hall without knowing that the whole of the back of her skirt was bright red. I asked Mum for a packet of Tampax, but I haven't used any yet. Reading the leaflet about how to put them in always makes me feel a bit faint.

Eng. lit homework: *Puck says to Oberon: 'yonder shines Aurora's harbinger'. Use 'harbinger' in a sentence of your own.*

That is easy: Bobbie Cavanagh is a *harbinger* of my future.

Chapter 22

'Look at this,' I say to Michael. He squints and attempts to identify what I'm holding. The envelope reads *Mr M Deacon,* but there's no address. 'It was hand-delivered,' I say. I take out the card. A street scene, wobbly brush-strokes to look like the work of a renowned impressionist artist but fooling no one. 'There's a little verse,' I say. 'But we won't bother with that. Happy birthday and so on. Then it says: *Best regards, Rosalind Piper*.' I look at Michael. 'Why don't people hide things?' I say. 'Diaries and cards, for example. Much less trouble that way.'

Michael is impassive. Just as he was when I'd first found this. Lying in the hallway where it had fallen from his bag as if it were waiting for me. 'It's perfectly normal for one's secretary to send birthday greetings,' he'd said. I noted the formal sign-off and the way Michael took it from me, rather than add it to the mantelpiece display. 'Miss Piper always remembers,' he'd said.

Saying 'Miss Piper' was easy for him, it tripped off the tongue, but then she'd married an Unwin-Taylor which would have been a bit of a mouthful. Luckily she'd saved him from linguistic embarrassment by leaving. And it would be years before she was just 'Rosalind' to him.

I can picture myself long ago in that little kitchen. I was measuring out tea leaves from the tin with a pink plastic spoon. Sarah, coming home from school, rapped on the glass in the back door then swung it open. 'You made me jump,' I said.

'Sorry,' she said. Her tone was a long way from apologetic. She flung her satchel on to the table and kicked her shoes from her feet. They hit the bottom of the back door with two loud thwacks, making the key and bolt rattle with the blows. 'Oh, I forgot.' Sarah retrieved the satchel and unbuckled it, releasing a slew of exercise books on to the table.

I winced. Her every movement was too big and loud and brash these days. Her limbs seemed to enlarge hourly. The sleeves of her school cardigan were tight over her arms, her thighs bulged beneath her short skirt. In the days when I'd collected her from school, she used to rush up and fling her arms around me. The idea now seemed as incongruous and challenging as the prospect of hugging a seal.

'Here!' Sarah scraped the spilled contents haphazardly back into her satchel and handed me a large manila envelope. A used ink cartridge rolled across the table leaving a trail of blue dots and dashes on the Formica. The envelope was unaddressed and unsealed. 'School photo. Grotty.' Sarah made a face of elaborate distaste. She took off her blazer and picked up her discarded shoes, bundling everything together in a jumble of stiff wool and scuffed leather. 'Down in a minute! Strawberry jam, please!' she called out, sliding in her socks on the polished hall floor.

The room settled behind her, as if she had been a rapid swimmer making waves in a pool. I opened the envelope and pulled its contents free. Six photographs. In each image, bordered with brown card and sitting against a background of cerulean blue, Sarah was smiling and neat, her hair flattened and her eyes wide. She looked at once very young and strikingly mature. All I could remember of being fourteen was starting my period alone in the dorm and Sally Gibson having an epileptic fit. Those incidents must have been weeks, if not months, apart, but they were fused in my memory. The rest of that year was a blur of my father's extravagant, sobbing grief and the occasional sympathetic glance from one of my teachers. *Poor girl*, they implied, when I hadn't done well in a test or ran too slowly down the hockey pitch, *your mother died of . . . It was over a year ago, wasn't it, but you're still struggling, aren't you?* Easily the worst thing about my mother's death was my father melting into a puddle of alcohol and self-pity afterwards, but I hadn't thought the school staff would want to hear about that.

It was ludicrous to envy Sarah her untroubled adolescence. It was exactly what Michael and I intended, wasn't it? But something about her expression in the photograph made me want to grab her neatly folded hands and scrape them against a wall till her knuckles bled. I felt winded by the violence of my thoughts. I sliced and buttered bread and spread jam with resolute efficiency, in an attempt to cancel them out.

Where was Eddie? He should have been home by now. I was being punished for my attitude to one child with the absence of another. That was how fate worked. It watched you, waiting for your complacent remark or a slip in your way of thinking or a squeak of temptation, then pounced. There were many reasons why Eddie could be late, of course. He couldn't really tell the time, for a start. He was easily distracted, too, captivated by a particular stone or dead animal. 'Mark Wilson said a man waved his thing at him, in the woods,' Eddie reported one day, prompting a long explanation from me about why you should avoid strangers. Only a few days later, he'd brought a dishevelled tramp to the door, asking me to give him some food. I had produced a tea cake. I watched the man carefully unwrap its red and silver foil. He ate it in tiny bites, cupping his free hand underneath his mouth, rescuing dropped chocolate from his palm with a snakelike flick of his tongue.

'Eddie,' I'd said afterwards, 'do you remember what I told you? About not talking to strangers, or going anywhere with them?'

Eddie had looked cross. 'He's called Laurence. He's not a stranger. He's got a name. He told me his name.'

His generous logic could easily be undoing him now, I thought. I imagined him bundled against a grimy coat, his mouth silenced with a clasped hand. Should I go and look for him? 'He knows the drill,' Michael would say. 'And he knows the way home.' I could only think of Eddie's little arms and legs, his flesh still new over thin bones, too small and weak to resist anyone or run away fast enough.

I went to the drawer and tore a page from the little pad I used for lists and notes. It had a drawing of some owls on its cover and one of the children had filled in their large, circular eyes with a black pen. The ink was still sticky, it had never properly dried. I moved aside the ever-present pile of books and comics that were always waiting to be sorted through on the kitchen table.

'Please do not park here,' I wrote. As I fixed it to the window, I looked up to see Eddie approaching the house. He wasn't alone. A tall man strode next to him; he was carrying a large square folder under one arm, a battered leather satchel hung from his other shoulder and he held an empty, lidless jam jar in front of him like a torch. Eddie was talking animatedly although I could tell his companion wasn't paying much attention. I opened the back door and stood and waited for them.

As they got nearer, two things became obvious. The errant car belonged to this man. And he was handsome. His features were slightly too large for his face, giving him the cartoonish sensuality of an actor.

Michael and I had once been at a dinner party when an actor friend of our host's had arrived late, straight from the stage. Despite having 'scrubbed with the Pond's', as he'd roared in explanation (he was very loud), he'd seemed to be still made up, his features defined more clearly than anyone else's round the table. We had all watched him while he ate with gusto and noisy appreciation from a plated meal saved specially. 'This is so good,' he'd bellowed to the hostess, 'you're a wonder, Kate.' He'd affected a weary ennui with the play he'd just been performing: 'It's *not* one of his best,' he'd said. Michael said afterwards that the chap had given a virtuoso performance of *The Returning Actor Entertains Another Audience*, for the assembled company. He'd found him jarring, he'd said, but I'd liked the bounce of him, the way he'd turned his full attention to whoever he spoke to. When we'd both helped the hostess by clearing dishes, he'd brushed past me in the hallway, one hand resting for a while on my behind.

A single lock of hair hung over this man's forehead. If Michael's hair were not held in place with Brylcreem, I doubted it would fall over his face like that, as if it were meant to happen.

He opened the boot of the car, nodding towards where I stood without looking at me. He piled the satchel into a space already full of bags and boxes, balanced the jam jar against it, then placed the large folder on top with some care. I watched him, feeling like a teacher waiting for someone in the class to admit to a crime. He was in no hurry. Eddie jogged from foot to foot, obviously wishing that these two people would talk to each other, as they surely must, so that he could slip away.

The man finished his task and looked up. 'Oh my God!' he said, clapping his hands theatrically to his cheeks. 'I shouldn't have parked here, should I? Hell of a nuisance for you.'

'That's all right, I've only just replaced my note,' I said, aware that my bare feet trapped me in the kitchen. I could sense Eddie's disappointment at my letting this man off so lightly.

'I *have* been here a while, I'm afraid.' He furrowed his brows, pretending to be embarrassed. 'Until . . . ?' He gestured at Eddie.

'Eddie,' I said.

'Yeah, until Eddie discovered my lair and I became aware of the time.' His manner was breezy and light, as if he'd just arrived in this English village from a warm, foreign climate and he'd never encountered any clouds.

'Mum?' Sarah stood in the doorway. Her feet were encased in soft tartan slippers, trimmed all the way round with sheepskin. The fur had aged to a stiffened, grey band. They'd been a Christmas present two years ago. Sarah hadn't feigned delight when she opened the festive wrapping, she'd just put the slippers straight back in the box, refolding the tissue that protected them as carefully as if she were tucking a baby into bed.

She had loosened her long hair from its ponytail. It was parted in the centre and hung straight down on either side of her face. The man stared at her. Sarah stared back.

'A St Thomas's girl?' he said. Above the childish, cosy footwear – a long way above, her skirt was very short – Sarah still wore her school uniform. She came and stood beside me. She was taller than me now. It had been a long time since we had measured her growth against the kitchen door. 'Then you'll know my daughter,' he said. 'Bobbie. Bobbie Cavanagh.'

'Oh, yes. Bobbie. Yes, I know who she is.' Sarah looked awkward.

The man continued to stare, his expression one of pleasurable indulgence. Perhaps he was imagining Sarah and his daughter cheek to cheek or running about in the playground together. 'What do you make of it, then, your place of education?' he said.

'St Thomas's?' Sarah made a straight line of her mouth. She shrugged. 'All right,' she said, glancing quickly at me.

I felt uncomfortable. Sarah liked her school, didn't she? We'd never discussed it, of course, but it seemed to suit her. It would be disloyal if she said it didn't, especially to this virtual stranger. It cost Michael a sizeable sum to keep her there and she should at least pay him back with her gratitude.

'Pretty much what Bobbie says,' the man said. 'But I'd love to hear what you really think, when you girls are alone.' He smiled at me.

'Would you like some tea?' I said. I thought he'd say no. But he took off his large raincoat and came further into the room. I retrieved my treacherous shoes. He watched me as I pulled the heel of the shoe away from my ankle, trying to ease my feet into them without wincing at the patch of raw skin.

He was tall, the kitchen table and chairs looked too small for him. 'Here?' he said, not waiting for a reply and sitting down where Michael always sat, smiling at the plate of bread and jam. He hung his coat over the chair. It looked like a theatrical prop – a vast cape flung over a fake throne. I got an already opened packet of biscuits out of the cupboard and tipped them on to a plate. Several were broken. 'Chocolate!' Eddie said and grabbed one jagged, not-quite-half without asking.

The man held one large hand out over the table. Dabs of paint striped his fingers, and one thumb was tipped with green. 'Look at me!' he said. 'May I wash?' He got straight up and went to the sink, turning the tap on too hard so that water sprayed up at him and over the floor. Eddie giggled and the man laughed too. He squeezed a generous squirt of washing-up liquid over his hands and rubbed them together energetically, then cupped them and ran them from side to side under the flow. 'Towel?' He held his dripping fingers out in front of him.

'Oh,' I said, handing him a tea towel. Despite his enthusiastic display, he'd missed his coloured thumb and I watched him smear green paint as he wiped his hands on the cloth. He flung it on to the draining board and sat back down.

'What a feast,' he said. 'Bread and jam.' He reached across Sarah for a slice. They touched, his arm to her shoulder. It was as if I felt the pressure, too.

'Sorry, I haven't introduced myself,' I said, breaking the silence. 'I'm Marion.'

He nodded as if that were exactly what he expected me to be called. 'Adrian,' he said.

Eddie took advantage of the situation to help himself to another biscuit.

'Your boy Eddie came across me when I was just about to pack up,' Adrian said. He bit a chunk out of a crust as he spoke and chewed with his mouth open.

Eddie stared at him, as fascinated as if he were watching a wild animal wearing a hat and riding a bicycle. I hoped he'd leave before Michael got home. I didn't want to have to explain this oversized visitor to him. When Sarah was little, she would make a den out of blankets and chairs and invite me inside to share make-believe tea. We would crouch in the gloom, pretending to drink out of toy cups, miming eating invisible cakes from little saucers. Adrian looked as if he were playing house with us now. He sipped his tea with an exaggerated inward gurgle. Sarah sat watchful, her hands in her lap.

'What's your name, then, Miss Classmate?' Adrian brushed his hands together to remove stray crumbs, his fingers swished over his palms. His soft palms.

'Sarah,' she said.

'Hello, Sarah,' he said. 'I'll tell Bobbie we've met.' He regarded her carefully. 'Can I do something?' he said. He got up and stood behind her. He took her hair in his hands, gathering it into a mass at the nape of her neck, giving her the illusion of a shorter style framing her face. It was an imitation of my serviceable bob. He looked from each of us to the other. 'Like mother, like daughter,' he said. 'I'd like to paint you two together one day.'

He stood close to her. Both of them were looking in my direction, but it was her gaze I could not look away from. There was no plea for my help to free her from his hands or divert his attention. I understood the challenge of that moment and I thought she understood it, too. 'We'll see,' I said. 'Sarah has very little free time, though. She should be doing her homework now, really.' I knew she heard the brisk cruelty in what I said. I was reducing her to a little girl who had to follow my orders.

She blinked and shook herself away from him. He let her hair go. As it fell from his grip he looked as if he were going to touch it again, to smooth it flat.

'Paint me, too,' Eddie said. He scrunched his features.

'Could you sit still for long enough?' Adrian asked him. 'For even five minutes? I had better go.' He drained his tea. He pulled his coat from the chair, sending it rocking against the table. The china rattled.

'I'll see you out,' I said. I watched him walk to the gate with purpose, as if he weren't going to turn round. As if he were emptying his head of us as he left. I was overwhelmed with a need to prolong his departure, to think of a reason to hold him back before he slipped away.

'Can I see your paintings one day?' I said.

He turned round and tipped his head back a little and regarded me from beneath hooded eyes as if he hadn't seen me properly before. I recognised in my reaction a tiny, specific flash of desire. Attraction to someone else lies coiled, waiting, until the high frequency sound of its partner wakes it and it stirs. It can respond to the most unexpected, or unwonted call, shocking you with your reaction. That one, you think, that person, are you sure? But you have no choice. I had no choice. I stood rooted to the spot in front of him.

'If you want to,' he said. 'But you'd have to forgive the fact that they're frightfully amateur.'

'I'd forgive that,' I said. 'I'm sure I would.'

'We'll make it happen, then.' He frowned. 'Did I have a scarf?' he said, turning back. 'Wait here, I'll check.'

You didn't, I thought. I know exactly what you were wearing. Before I could say anything, he was turning away. I wanted to walk back into the house with him but instead I waited. My heel began to hurt again, as though the anaesthetic of his presence was wearing off. I watched them through the open door but I couldn't hear what they said. He mimed the swirl of a scarf around his neck. Sarah shook her head.

'No, it's not there,' he said, walking back towards me. His voice was suddenly bright and energetic, the way you speak to an anxious dog who has doubted you'll ever return.

I watched him fumble in his trouser pocket; his hand went in a long way. They must be very deep pockets to conceal such large hands, I thought. My arms would go in up to my elbows if I were to slide them in there. I flushed a little, as if he'd suggested I try. When he found the keys, he threw them a little way into the air, turning his hand quickly to catch them, closing his fingers round them like a claw.

'I'll knock on your door next time I'm here and if you're in, and if you want to, you can come and see what I'm up to.'

When? I wanted to ask. Soon? But instead I said, 'Well, I hope I'm here.'

He opened the car door. 'I hope so, too,' he said. He lowered himself into the car and was instantly distracted by the key in the ignition and the handbrake. When he looked up and saw me still standing there, he raised his eyebrows.

I watched him reverse all the way back down the lane.

Chapter 23

Eddie had had to revise his prayers. Once, they were as familiar as a nursery rhyme. He'd hardly had to think about their order, and they'd filled the space between lights out and his sleep very neatly. His mother used to listen to him while he prayed, but she was obviously reassured now that he'd mention her, his father, Sarah, his teacher, his toys, a contemporary crisis and anything he was especially bothered about – like not catching impetigo from the Johnson twins – without her prompting. She'd be yawning by the end of reading him his story anyway, and he suspected that his petition to God had a similarly soporific effect.

It had become more complicated now. His mother and father would always be included, of course. His faultless teacher. The famine in Biafra. But Sarah? He thought God wouldn't actually punish her, he knew that divine punishments were always harsh and fierce, but did she really warrant the Almighty's special attention? Eddie suspected God looked a bit like Alf who cleaned their windows, because he had first seen Alf on high, perched up a ladder. He used to ask God to look after Truck. After the burial, Eddie was determined to try to forget him, but his name often slipped into his list anyway, out of habit, and tripped him up, so that he'd have to start again.

Mostly, he did include Sarah. And he'd added the painting man in the big coat to his list, too.

Chapter 24

21.00 hours. Michael would much rather the time was written down in words, if it couldn't be told from a clock's face. *Nine o'clock* sounds a lot less clinical, less military, than its twenty-four-hour equivalent. He doesn't need Marion's carrier bag of photos to prompt his memory. Images, random and often unfamiliar, jostle into his thinking like a slide show. It isn't always pictures of people that appear. Sometimes, he sees objects: his fountain pen, the nib bent slightly to the left with the force of use. A pair of driving gloves, made of such soft leather that they held the curled shape of his hands when he wasn't wearing them, as if they were still holding the steering wheel. He wonders at such trivial things being offered to him from the entire repository of his memory. Today, it is a snatch of flowered fabric, a coverlet for Sarah's dolls. She used to put them in a little metal pushchair, bouncing its occupants along pavements at a frankly unmaternal speed. She'd accidentally run it into the back of his heel once and the pain was so sudden and savage he'd wanted to hit her.

He remembers bringing the wounded dog home. He'd found it lying by the side of the road. It was a long time ago, when Eddie was only about five, and it was Eddie who first saw him with the animal cradled in his arms. He'd pointed at the blood leaking on to his father's mackintosh and Michael had told him not to worry about the mess. The sounds of the dog's shallow breathing and Marion's voice, half-whispering, urgent, as she dealt with finding newspaper to lay on the floor and mollifying the children, looped over each other in Michael's head, tangling and fluttering like ribbons. *Hit by a car, I should think. Nothing you could do. Daddy found it in the road, Eddie. He couldn't leave it there. It's beyond help. No, no collar.* Sarah asked if it was a boy dog or a lady dog and Marion said that was the least of its worries. She'd spread the newspaper and the dog allowed Michael to place it on the floor without protesting. It shivered and lowered its head. The newspaper sighed underneath it. Sarah had retrieved the doll's old coverlet from a basket of lengths of cloth and spread it so that they couldn't see the red, wet pouch that protruded from its stomach. They'd all gathered round, kneeling like figures in the Nativity. The dog's eyes were as blank as eggs.

What Michael also remembers, an image that is accompanied by a sort of rushing feeling in his chest, is Marion's arm around his shoulders, her voice warm and his free hand on her knee. *You couldn't have done more, you're so kind to animals. I'll ask in the village tomorrow if anyone's lost a dog. It looks quite peaceful now, it knows you're caring for it; most people would have left it to suffer. Oh, darling. Poor thing. Oh, darling.* The dog died with its eyes open. Marion said it was the driver's fault. Who was driving the wretched car? that's what she'd like to know. Next time we have a bonfire, Michael had said, we'll put that little sheet on it.

He wonders how long Marion will continue to visit him here. The arrangement seems to suit them both, but it is hung from a flimsy hook. The presence of others could disturb it. The photographs she brought in move him, not so much the actual images but the way she sheds years looking at them herself. The letters and cards are a puzzle. He was brutal in his evisceration of the past, consigning everything to fires and bins. They had an unspoken agreement that they would not discuss what he destroyed, but she must have gone ahead of him, squirrelling things away so quickly she made no judgement about what she took. He recognises the occasional name, although he is surprised by their continuing appearance. He'd imagined a scything of all such connections. Among the few that resonate emotionally are many more mundane documents. Physical evidence of long-ago, long-forgotten appointments and acknowledgements. A history he has no part of – her attachments to local volunteer groups, the friendships that sprang from them and the plans made or broken – unrolls as she speaks. She has managed to sustain all this without any apparent break in her stride. It is impressive that very few of the letters refer directly to what happened to her. He knows that it is a matter of pride that no one can tell by looking at her, or even during a conversation, how wounded she is and how much she hides. He wishes he could convey what he feels about this achievement. Although, if he's honest, he's not quite sure whether to admire or pity her.

Chapter 25

25 September

I signed the swimming book yesterday. They hang it from a hook on the general noticeboard which means everyone can see you do it. It's weird how everything else about having the curse is all private, but if it's the reason you can't swim you practically have to shout out loud about it. The first day I signed it was the day Suze got the knitting needle stuck in her stomach. We all have to knit squares for Oxfam in domestic science. They are going to be sewn together to make blankets for Africa. Suze had taken to knitting in a big way, she was at it all the time and she managed neat, tight rows. Mine always gape and sag. I feel sorry for the Africans who get my squares; it would be very easy to catch your toenails in the loose threads. She was sitting on a bench in the playground, with a large ball of wool beside her. It followed her like a cat after a bird as she jerked the needles backwards and forwards. When the bell rang, she reached for her bag and one needle spun from her hand. As she caught it, she pulled it towards her and the pointed end slid right through her shirt and jumper. It was stuck fast even when she tried wiggling it free. She sort of laughed. There wasn't much blood coming out, just a red circle on her shirt. Obviously, they made a fuss and took her to hospital. When she came back to school next day she was pale and woozy, even though there wasn't a spike sticking out of her any more. She doesn't like talking about it now.

Eddie came into my bed last night. He hasn't done that for ages and I know he thought I'd kick him out but I let him curl up next to me. He said he felt sad but he didn't know why. I couldn't cheer him up, partly because I wasn't sure of what to say but mostly because I was crying and I had to concentrate on staying still so I didn't make the damp patch on my pillow any bigger.

Chapter 26

I had watched Adrian's car reversing away until I couldn't see it any more.

'You were ages,' said Eddie as I came back into the kitchen. He sat in front of an empty plate. He'd obviously eaten all the biscuits. 'That was em-barr-a-ssing.' He licked one finger and applied it to the plate to pick up the last sweet crumbs. 'Grabbing your hair. Ugh.'

Sarah tipped her head back so that she could actually look down her nose at him. 'Shut *up*,' she said, and Eddie heard the ice in her voice. He looked to me for a response.

I hadn't the energy to divert their quarrel. 'Right,' I said, sliding my apron over my head and wishing I was alone. I turned my back on them and opened the larder. 'I'll call you when supper's ready,' I said. I felt oddly nervous about Michael's imminent approach, sensing his arrival as if he were a giant, making the ground tremble at each step. Nothing was out of place, but I felt unsettled and light-headed. I couldn't make sense of the array of tins and packets I stared at. We'd just have to have a late supper, it wouldn't be the end of the world. I put potatoes in the sink, one each and one for the pot, flushing the soil from them, turning them over and over under the tap.

I heard the soft scuff of Sarah's suede soles in the hallway then the thump-thump as she ran upstairs, two at a time. I hacked more from the potatoes than I intended, slicing chunks of flesh away with the peel and gouging greater circles than was necessary to remove black eyes.

When Sheila knocked at the back door, I definitely frowned before I smiled, and I know she noticed. She wore a dark pink lipstick and the tips of her two front teeth were striped pink, too.

'Apologies,' she said, without a trace of sorrow in her voice. 'Still peeling?' She inspected the saucepans and tins lined up in readiness, laying a manicured finger on top of the can of peas. 'Do carry on,' she said. 'Don't mind me.'

'I'd better.' I heaped the potatoes on to the draining board. 'Running a bit late.' I slopped too much water, splashing myself.

'I won't keep you,' said Sheila, folding her arms and heading for a chair. A sliver of pale cream slip showed beneath her skirt as she sat down. I didn't think there was ever a time when she'd waited for an invitation. She had an uncanny knack of arriving when I was preoccupied, inserting herself into the proceedings with the air of a judge at a county show, marking my efforts. She had first appeared in our lives just as the removal van opened its doors to disgorge its load and as Michael was coming down the path, swinging the front door keys.

'Our new home!' he'd said.

Sheila was standing beside me, as close as if we were reunited friends. 'Welcome,' she said, her eyes on the furniture and effects being set down on the pavement. The chairs and cupboards, lamps and pictures exposed to the open air looked shabby and worn. 'Lovely,' she said vaguely. 'Sheila. I'm three down.' She gestured to her left, further along the crescent. She was probably about the same age as me, in her mid-thirties, but her hard perm and a certain expression on her face suggested she had long left playfulness and frivolity behind. She wore a neat jacket and skirt, not matching but still with the organisation of a suit. A large enamelled brooch, featuring some unspecific variety of flowers in a vase, glistened from her lapel. Her bosom was as solid as a bolster. Perhaps, I thought, she only has one, oval breast.

She came back later, unasked. Sarah and Eddie were upstairs; there were no carpets down yet and their footsteps were loud on the floorboards. She held out a china plate with a pale yellow cake on it; it was perfectly risen, neatly iced and already divided into slices. 'Lemon sponge,' she said, admiring her own handiwork. She glanced up to the ceiling, where the children now added a verbal fight to their stamping. 'Would they like some?' she said, smiling with tender sympathy at the ruckus.

I took the plate. 'How kind of you,' I said. 'And just as soon as we've found our crockery, that'll be devoured.' I put the plate down on a sideboard that sat in the middle of the room, as though it would never deign to sit flat against the skirting board.

'I've brought some serviettes.' Sheila fished in her pocket and produced five tiny squares of yellow tissue.

Just the right number, I thought. I had no desire to offer my fractious offspring up for this woman's further scrutiny.

'The children are settling themselves in, I'll call them later. Thank you.' I smiled, taking the little paper offerings and putting them with the plate. I held out both my hands for inspection. 'I'll need a good wash before I eat anything,' I said. 'And heaven knows where the soap is.'

Sheila seemed on the verge of arguing that a bit of dirt wouldn't matter. Or perhaps she was going to offer to feed me herself, holding the cake to my mouth. 'Pop the plate back when you can,' she said. She paused, casting a baleful glance at the twists of discarded newspaper that littered the floor, dropped carelessly as things had been unwrapped. 'I'll leave you to it, then,' she said.

We all slept straight on to the mattress ticking and without pillowcases that night. We'd woken the next day with feathers in our hair.

Sheila settled herself now with an exhalation, as if the journey from the door to the table had been a long one. 'Quick question,' she said. There followed a long explanation about some sort of petition involving traffic, while I clanged pans and opened tins. I hoped I offered the right sort of responses during Sheila's monologue, as I didn't stop to listen properly. Whenever I turned round, Sheila's gaze was fixed on a different area of the kitchen. When she eventually rose and said, 'I knew I could count on you,' I thought I must have missed something rather vital and wondered what I'd promised. Now Sheila was saying something about a car. And Adrian.

'I said, "No wonder you're running late. Adrian has no sense of time."' She had my full attention. 'That *was* Adrian

Cavanagh, wasn't it? If anyone was going to ignore signs, it's him. He's always been a law unto himself.' She had her hand on the door knob. 'Had you met him before?' she said.

I shook my head.

'No? He is charming, isn't he? Bit of a rogue, though.' Sheila smiled into the middle distance, as though she were flicking through a whole catalogue of Adrian's amusing misdemeanours.

I wiped my hands on my skirt. 'He's going to park there again, actually,' I said. 'I told him to ignore my sign.' I wished I could say his name as easily as Sheila did. 'He says he's found a very good place to paint.'

Sheila smiled. Her cardigan was buttoned to the top, where a small, tight circle of pearls divided wool from neck. 'Painting?' she said. 'That's the latest thing, is it?' She was still at the open door, unhurried in her departure. 'There's always a new craze for Adrian. And he likes to find new people, too.' The way she said *people* made it sound grubby. 'I've known him for years,' Sheila said. 'He's not to be taken too seriously. As many people have probably discovered. To their cost.' She looked hard at me. 'Of course,' she said, 'you don't have to worry about having your head turned by someone like him.'

There was a jangle of keys from the hall, the setting down of a briefcase and the loud, deliberate closing of the front door by a person who didn't need to creep in.

Sheila cocked her head, listening to the sounds of Michael's arrival. 'Was that the front door?' she said, knowing it was.

Michael called a hello cheerfully, but neither of us answered.

'Always got something going on, has Adrian. Or somebody.' Sheila was almost out of the door. She smiled at me. 'His poor wife. Well, I'm off, I'm afraid,' she said, as if I had been attempting to prolong her visit. 'Byee!' she yelled to the whole house, rattling the door closed without waiting for a reply.

I stood stock-still, feeling out of breath. I couldn't remember what I was supposed to do next. I stared at the door. I half thought Sheila would stick her head back round it and throw another dart. When Michael came into the room, I muttered about having promised things to Sheila without realising I was doing it.

'Backbone of the community, you.' He laughed, but when he put his arms round me, I stiffened.

'Good day?' I said, moving away. The saucepan lid rattled and spluttered as the water came to the boil. I turned the dial on the timer and wondered where Adrian was now. It would be twenty minutes until the potatoes were cooked; how many more lots of twenty minutes would there be until I saw him again? Jaunty music and singing floated from the television in the sitting room. Eddie must have put it on. *Light up the sky with Standard Fireworks. Dad brings surprises: Stan-dard Fire-works*. 'He should have asked if he could watch TV,' I said. The evening rolled away in front of me, as dull and predictable as a candlewick bedspread. I opened a tin of mince and tipped it into a pan and stirred it. The children were full of bread and biscuits and I was scarcely hungry, so only poor Michael would sit down with any sort of appetite. Poor Michael. *His poor wife*, I heard Sheila say again.

Sarah had seemed so confident with Adrian. Where did she get that from? I'd been unable to look adults in the eye at her age. They were awkward, too. *'Sorry to hear about your . . .'* they'd muttered, unable to articulate the awful fact. *'Let us know if you need anything.'* If they'd tried to help, they'd have been rebuffed by my father. He was a force field, defying anyone to cross him to reach me. The last time I'd seen her, I'd asked her about embroidery. I'd held my needlework up to her face and showed her the loops of chain stitch going awry. I said I'd done it all wrong and it was ruined. She'd said it didn't matter, that I could easily repair it. She was so pale that she made the white pillowcases behind her head look grubby. Give it to me, she said, and although she could hardly lift her hands, she guided the needle to and fro on the aida cloth. She was mine as long as she kept sewing. When she reached the end of the row, her hands dropped on to the counterpane and she closed her eyes. I waited for her to speak. She said nothing more. I took the cloth from her and left the room.

Years later, I remembered asking my father why I hadn't gone to her funeral. I hadn't even known when it was happening.

'You were too young,' my father had said, although his heaving sobs and actual wailing hadn't looked very grown-up to me. 'Oh Marion,' he said, 'I used to watch your mother suffering, in pain, and wonder why someone so good was going through such agony. I thought it should have happened to me, instead. If anyone deserved it, I did.' He'd paused to allow me to dispute this, but I said nothing. 'But then I realised something, Marion,' he said. 'I *was* being punished. I had to watch her suffer, didn't I? I couldn't help her. That was torture for *me*, wasn't it? I was the real victim.'

Sheila elbows her way into my thoughts once more. It's as if she's offering me that information all over again and observing my reaction, with her beady, fixed gaze. I could have ignored what she said. I could have dismissed it as irrelevant, even annoying. The odd thing is, many years later, it was to Sheila that I wrote, with my new address. And as soon as she had received my card, as if she'd had a stamped envelope ready, she had replied.

Chapter 27

I am still waiting to read the letter I put aside, savouring it like a treat. It will keep. But here is the letter with the blank window envelope. I know what it says, but when I open it this time I realise I have more than half a hope the contents might have changed.

1 November
Kent Hospital

For the attention of Mr And Mrs Deacon.

I note that we still hold several items here which remain uncollected by you, vis:

One pair of pyjamas, label reads: 'Age 8'

Two books, The Wind in the Willows *and* A Boy's Book of Stories

Various items (toothbrush, toothpaste, flannel) in plastic-lined wash bag

One colouring book and crayons (assorted) in red pencil case

Toy truck (boxed)

Please advise what you would like us to do with the above. I regret we have no facilities for further storage.

When Michael was admitted to hospital, three days ago, I was given a leaflet that made death sound like a procedure. It segued from *Signs That a Person May be Dying* to *Should You Be Worried?* to *How to Inform the Coroner*, without much interval.

Sometimes, there are no signs that a person may be dying. Sometimes, a person simply cannot hold on to life, because their hands are too small.

Chapter 28

I can still see that kitchen quite clearly. We'd left it pretty much as it was when we moved in, and after a while I didn't notice the cups and saucers wallpaper or the pretend pine cupboard doors. I wasn't the sort to tie a headscarf over my hair and start painting. Michael repaired things if he had to and, if the task was beyond him, we got a man in. After Adrian had left that day, it was the first time I'd felt ashamed of the decor and the silly little things I'd chosen to put on the walls. I was irked by the fact that Michael was still unaware of how gauche the room was.

'Reader's Digest,' he said, holding the day's post. He sat where Adrian had been, turning the pages. 'Shall I read "Life's Like That" out loud to you?' he said.

'If you want,' I said, digging the can opener into a tin of peas to get a purchase.

'What are we having?' he said. Seeing the side plates piled in the sink, he said, 'Oh, did you have visitors?'

I felt irritation rise in my throat, as sour as bile. 'Mince and potatoes,' I said, swinging away from him. 'No, not really any visitors. Just the father of one of Sarah's friends.' Not quite the truth, but not really a lie, either. Just something to distract him. It was like pretending to throw a ball for a dog and watching while it hunted for it in vain. I could tell him about Philip now, if I wanted to. I could change everything about our life together in a few sentences. I imagined Michael's puzzled expression at the realisation that I had betrayed him. He'd fill slowly with an unhappiness as sticky and dense as tar. My secret was as light as a feather as long as I held it in my heart, but if I were ever to throw my unfaithfulness at Michael, the words would become so solid in flight that he'd never get up again.

I turned to the stove, not wanting to look at him while I spoke about Adrian. 'He's a painter, an artist, he left his car here. Thought I'd better give him a cup of tea.' I speared a potato with a knife point. It collapsed under the pressure, breaking into a soft, uneven mush. I drained the potatoes and added milk and butter and mashed them as if it were a task that needed my absolute, undivided attention. 'Call the children, would you?' I said. When he left the room, I exhaled with a gasp, exhilarated at being alone.

I could hear Eddie's protestations about being summoned away from some programme or other, then he came and sat down. He regarded the flaccid meal with disdain. He knew better than to say anything. He bent low over the table so that he could transfer the food from plate to mouth across the shortest distance.

'Sit up straight.' Michael and I spoke at the same time. I felt him look across at me, but I fixed my gaze on Eddie.

'I'm not very hungry.' Sarah picked up her knife and fork without waiting for a response and balanced the smallest amount possible on the tines.

'Slimming?' Michael asked. It was not a question he took seriously, he didn't need an answer. He got up and fetched a jug then stood at the sink, waiting for the water to run cold. When I saw him standing exactly where Adrian had stood, I thought he looked foolishly small. His shoulders were narrow, and his thin neck bent over as if his head were heavy.

'What's that?' Michael pointed at the brown envelope on the sideboard. He picked it up before anyone could reply and slid the contents free. He held the photographs in front of him, looking first at his daughter, then at me. 'You two get more alike every day,' he said.

'That's what the man said.' Eddie raised his head from his plate, where he'd been working hard to combine everything into one pappy mess. 'That's 'xactly what he said,' he repeated, revelling in the attention. We were all looking at him. He pointed at Sarah. 'And he held her hair. Like this . . .' He extended his arms towards his sister.

He was too far away to touch her head but near enough for her to strike him, hard, on the arm. His yowl of pain vibrated round the room. Sarah lowered her head; her two curtains of hair closed in front of her face.

'Sarah,' her father said, turning to her, 'that's childish. Eddie's a little boy, he doesn't mean—'

'Shut UP!' She rose from the table with such force her chair upended behind her. 'He knew what he was doing. Leave me alone.' She couldn't stamp from the room in her soft-soled slippers and she couldn't slam the kitchen door because it was held permanently open with a wooden block, but she still exited with a flourish.

'Stupid cow,' hissed Eddie. Michael and I rushed to correct him to fill the silence. 'Please can I get down?' Eddie was half off the chair as he spoke, one leg lengthening, ready to run.

Michael righted the fallen chair. 'What did Eddie mean about her hair?' he said.

'I don't know.' I began to slide all the uneaten mince on to one plate; it seemed as if everyone had left a much greater quantity than I'd prepared. Only Michael had finished his portion.

'Need any help with that?' He offered every night.

'No, you go and sit down, leave all this to me,' I said, as always. I repeated a familiar litany in my head: *He's been at work all day, he shouldn't have to work at home, too.* I didn't know where I'd heard it said first, certainly not from my mother, who was dead before she could tie an apron on me. 'Won't take long,' I said, hoping I sounded bright. Michael still reminded me of a dog waiting for an instruction. He actually put his head on one side.

'Are you okay, Marion?' He stood in front of me and put his hands on my shoulders.

'Golly, Michael, careful.' I nodded towards the slippery contents on the plate I held between us. 'Yes, I'm fine,' I said. Then, to distract him, I said, 'Why don't you ask Don and his wife for dinner one night?' I'd met his boss once at a supper dance. He was wearing a large suit, the jacket flapping around him as he danced. I could tell he wore a soft, loose suit of his own flesh beneath it. I couldn't remember his wife at all.

'Right,' said Michael, sounding surprised. 'I shall. You just let me know when.' He waved towards the calendar, hung on a nail on the wall, where I wrote down our appointments.

'I could certainly squeeze Don and Patricia – or is it Priscilla? – somewhere among the dentist and school meetings,' I said. The discarded dishcloth, stained with green paint, still lay on the draining board where Adrian had flung it. It was like a relic of his visit.

'What are you up to tomorrow?' Michael said later, switching off one of several little side lamps balanced on thin tables. They all shook at the pressure of his hand.

'Bridget's coming,' I said. We'd been at school together; she visited about twice a year. I was fond of her, although our conversation never changed and, once we had exhausted the lives of people we both remembered and exhumed a couple of classroom reminiscences, time hung heavy. Bridget had the hearty vigour of a games teacher. In fact, she had continued to play hockey for some years after she'd left school. 'Oh, just with some girls from university,' she'd said. 'We're quite rough – the men couldn't cope.' I viewed taking part in organised sport of any kind with deep scorn, especially once you were old enough to vote.

Bridget lived in some part of the north. She liked to come 'down south' occasionally. The visits were one-sided. 'You're welcome to come and stay with me,' she always said. I mistrusted the long train journey it would involve and feared what I'd find when I got there. Bridget often boasted about how undomesticated she was. She and her husband had recently taken up breeding dogs. 'Little Westies. It's chaos,' she'd said. 'If you keep dogs, you can't expect to be tidy, of course.' I imagined her having to clear a gangway between her old games kit and a litter of puppies, just so that I could get into bed.

She'd called two days ago. 'It's awfully late notice, Maz, but could I come and see you? Don't cook anything, we can go to a pub.'

Sitting in the daylight gloom of the Swan with a plate of long, coiled sausages and gravy like lava didn't appeal to me. 'No, no, come here,' I'd said. 'That would be lovely. Which train are you getting?'

'That'll be nice.' Michael turned the last lamp off and plunged us into what was still surprising darkness. Only a sliver of illuminated hallway showed where the door was. 'You go on upstairs,' he said, as he always did. He'd have a cigarette before he came up, standing by the back door, keeping it open with one foot, just space enough to breath smoke into the night air.

Lying next to Michael later, hearing his regular breathing and not wanting to make him stir, I shifted on to my side, turned away from him. I slid my free hand over my upturned hip, feeling the dip at my waistline, the rise of my haunches. I imagined someone else's hand stroking there. Michael stretched and sighed. He smelled of toothpaste and tobacco and soap. I moved closer to him, slipping my arm under his shoulder to his chest, and gathered the folds of his pyjama top tightly in my hand.

There was a soft click from the door to Sarah's room. I heard her pad to the bathroom. Her body seemed to take up too much space in the house now. Last weekend, she'd sat down beside me on the settee and our thighs had touched. I'd almost cried out. It was a reaction of instant revulsion, like handling raw meat or discovering a dead insect in a cup. I'd got up quickly and moved away. She had a little laundry basket in her room, from which I collected her clothes. But recently I did it with greater care, putting only the tips of my fingers to the clothes, transferring everything into the twin tub as quickly as I could. Once, I could feel a stiff, dried ridge of fabric where she'd tried to wash a smear of blood from her knickers. I found even the things she'd worn and shed distasteful. She wasn't so much becoming a woman as bursting into adult life like a great pupa. The sheer, swelling physicality of her made me grit my teeth.

Chapter 29

'This one,' I say to Michael. 'It's from Bridget. Do you remember Bridget?' The letter is a scrappy thing. The edges of the page are bordered with flowers. The children used to write their thank you letters on stationery like this. By the time they'd expressed gratitude for whatever they'd been given, there was no room for any more information, which suited them fine. This handwriting is small and cramped, the writer is well aware of the need to condense their message. I read it aloud.

May 1990

Dear Maz,

Thank you for a wonderful weekend. I know you'll think it odd I'm saying that, as you stayed with us, but it was so nice of you to come after all this time. Trevor and I really enjoyed ourselves (a bit too much sherry taken though, he says!) and are delighted to see you looking happier. You're an inspiration to both of us in how well you've coped. You can't beat a long friendship, can you? The offer of a puppy still stands, by the way.

'Do you want to spend the night?' the nurse says, coming in with the bustle of her timetable. 'We can make up a bed.'

I've avoided the little fold-away they produce for visitors till now. Hospital nights aren't like the real thing, are they, there's too much noise and there's always someone checking on the patient, putting the lights on and speaking in a loud, sing-song voice, whatever time it is. I'd be no use to him, anyway, I'd be getting in the way just to lie beside him. 'I don't live very far away,' I say. I realise that I've made myself sound singular. 'I can get back here very quickly, if . . .'

The nurse adjusts his pillows and mask. She doesn't need the rest of my sentence. She is small and dark. Younger than Sarah, by the look of her. I lean over Michael and put my mouth to his forehead. It is scarcely a kiss, but it is one thing I can do that she cannot. I am no more important to him here than the people who tend to him. Life outside these walls is meaningless, absent, irrelevant to them, beyond my owning up to being his next of kin.

'See you in the morning,' I say.

The nurse turns round. 'Oh, I might not be here,' she says. 'I'm off shift at seven thirty.'

I catch Michael's eye. I mouth *I was talking to you*. He smiles the faintest of smiles, but it's so direct and intended for me that I feel rewarded.

Chapter 30

28 September

I hit Top C in choir today. Lizzie H must have heard me, because the altos have to stand next to the sopranos. I think it put her off because she came in very late for the chorus. The sound seemed to come out of the top of my head as well as from my mouth. Mrs W says you have to go higher than the note in your mind then swoop down on it from above, then you can sing it easily. She says we should think of it like climbing on to a diving board. I don't think I could reach it if I had to sing anything solo, so I didn't put my hand up when she asked who wanted to try out. Bobbie didn't volunteer either. She caught my eye and made a sign of sticking her fingers in her mouth and pretending to retch.

Because we rehearse in the hall, everyone who did get up to audition on their own sounded small and weak, the sound hardly reaching over the sheet music they were holding. It must have been hard to read the words anyway, their hands shook so much. That's probably why their voices trembled. Mrs W looked sad. I'm sure she hoped all that stuff about the glory of God would be heard in heaven, not just reach the level of the noticeboards.

When I tell Mum I've joined the choir, she's going to think it's because she wanted me to. She always cries in the carol concert; she cried even when I was an Upper Third and we only sang 'The Cowboy Carol'. I would have thought twenty of us yoi-yippee'ing about riding the trail would have made her laugh, not weep. She sang 'And the Glory of the Lord' to me in the kitchen when we got home. She made me hot chocolate and warmed my dressing gown on the radiator. She could get the high notes really easily. She said that all flesh shall see it together, so I ought to go and put my pyjamas on. I remember I laughed till I squeaked.

In biology we had to look at our own blood under a microscope. We put elastic bands around our thumbs, squeezed them till they swelled, then pricked them with a sterilised needle and smeared the red dot on to a glass slide. I didn't think I could do it but when it came to it, I wanted to. I wanted to see inside myself. All my billions of cells jostling together in that one tiny drop. It made me feel fizzy and tingling, I could feel my blood moving about in me as if it were charged with energy, making my veins swell as it flowed. I wished Bobbie was there. I would have suggested we mix our blood and make a pact.

Mrs D says your blood can reveal a lot about you. It can prove your father isn't who you think he is, for a start. Or who he thinks he is, more like. She says since the war there'll be a lot of people only really half belonging to their parents. Molly put her hand up and said can blood tell what sex someone is, but that's only because she got dared to say sex out loud.

Lynne said seeing her own blood coming out made her feel queasy. But as she told me at break yesterday that she has a boyfriend and that she's done it with him, I think she's just a liar. Her hair is so greasy that it needs washing by the end of every day. No boy is ever going to fancy her, let alone do *that*. Unless he's got as many spots as her, I suppose. Mum is always telling me there's someone for everyone. I suppose that must mean even for a greabo like Lynne.

We got our school photos back today. Helen snatched mine away from me. She said you look like a virgin and what does a virgin have for breakfast? I said I thought I'd known the answer to that once, but I couldn't remember it now. I meant I'd forgotten the punchline, but she went on and on about me claiming I'd already lost my virginity. She is a real slag, so she was probably just trying to deflect attention from herself. My photos are awful, I look like a swot and a prig. I'd tried to make a proper photo face, but it didn't work.

I wanted to wait and see if Bobbie was walking to the bus stop, but her class comes out later than ours on a Tuesday and Miss M was doing a hem check on the way out of the cloakroom, so I had to leave straight away. Otherwise I'd have hung around pretending I needed to be there until I heard her speaking. I undid my skirt in the lavvy and tugged it down a bit lower, so I could pass the test. Once, they actually used a ruler to measure everyone's skirt length, but it took so long and the cloakroom was so crowded that Isobel Huff fainted. Now they do it by sight alone. Miss M looked over her glasses at me and said fine. She seemed tired. The queue behind me was quite long, so she'd be there for a while, staring at girls' knees.

Tom Spencer was hanging around by the post office when I got off the bus. I once told him that if I thought he was following me, I'd scream, and it's funny to watch him trying to stare at me now without getting caught. He looks as if he's trying to go through everything he knows, all at once. What he wants to say is in there somewhere, I suppose.

I could hear Mum talking to someone downstairs but I didn't recognise the man's voice. He sounded smooth, like someone on the wireless. She sounded nervous, her voice was all high and bright. I was going to wait until whoever it was had gone, but I was hungry and anyway I was halfway down the stairs by the time I'd thought about turning round. When I saw him, I wished I wasn't wearing my slippers. He was very tall. He was wearing the sort of shirt that needs cufflinks, but he hadn't done the sleeves up. The edges were all frayed, even though he sounded like the sort of person who could easily afford new clothes. He had hair below his collar, and he ran his hands through it quite a lot. I think it was because he liked the way he looked when he did it; he made his hair fall through his fingers and flop over his forehead. He looked comfortable in our house. He spread himself out, so that we'd have had to climb around him to get anywhere.

He asked me which school I go to, but I could tell he already knew because of my uniform. When I answered, he smiled, as if he had won a prize. He asked if I knew Bobbie Cavanagh. It was weird hearing someone saying her name aloud. I say it silently to myself all the time. I acted very calm and kind of pretended I didn't really, or only a little anyway, but my tummy was flipping, and my heart raced.

The bread and jam looked like baby food. She emptied a whole packet of biscuits on to a plate in front of him, as though that's what she always does. Eddie couldn't believe his luck – she wasn't even counting how many he ate. The man came and stood behind me. He was so close that I could smell a mixture of incense and tobacco, like a room after a party. He held my hair up to make it seem short and he said it made me look like Mum and he wanted to paint us together. But as he was standing there and saying stuff, he stroked his fingers against my neck. I could feel his soft hands there all the time. He kept talking to her as if there were nothing going on and he wasn't touching my skin. He sat back down at our table as if we were lucky to have him there. Mum actually told him that he could park his car outside the gate whenever he likes, which is ridiculous after the fuss she's made about anyone else doing it. If me or one of my friends was as full-on about fancying a bloke as she was being, we'd just laugh at them. She's almost forty – she ought to pull herself together. I watched her standing in the road for ages after he'd driven away, as if he was going off to war or something.

She made a disgusting supper, watery mashed potatoes and vile tinned mince. I bet Daddy had to force it down. No one said anything of course, because we'd have got her usual martyred look if we had. She didn't even notice that I hadn't really eaten anything at tea, so I said I wasn't hungry as if I'd wolfed down bread and jam like Eddie did.

I am determined to lose seven pounds by the end of next week. Helen told me that if you eat toothpaste last thing at night, it fills you up all the next day. After everyone had gone to bed I sneaked into the bathroom and squeezed some Colgate into my mouth, but it was really hard to swallow very much of it. I got back to my room before the cistern finished emptying, anyway, so tomorrow should be a lucky day.

Bobbie once said that she thinks that people are meant to meet. We were looking across the playground, watching some Upper Thirds. They were playing Buzz, chasing each other from the benches to the netball posts and the fence and then yelling when they reached home. I said I can't believe that was me three years ago – they look like babies. Bobbie said this is our slice of the world and whatever happened before, even on this very spot, is nothing to do with us. And what's happening anywhere else doesn't matter, either. Just this moment, in this place. I tried to imagine our house with Mum in it but I couldn't. I have no idea what she does all day.

28 September

The thing is, he came back. He came back into the kitchen and asked if he'd left his scarf and told Eddie to go into the hall and find it. I started to look, too, but he said it's not here, I came back for you. He said he wanted to paint me, could he pick me up from school sometimes? I had this sensation of growing taller, my spine tingled. I looked straight at him. I said yes, he could. He said he'd be in touch. He went out to where she was waiting.

Chapter 31

I'd slept heavily that night and woken in a panic. For a moment I didn't know why I was alone in the bed. Where was Michael? I could hear the clink of china bowls and the growl of the radio; they were already downstairs in the kitchen. I watched from the doorway as they chattered and circled.

'Mummy!' Eddie sat in front of a bowl ringed with a sticky mixture of cornflakes and milk.

'Are you ill?' Michael said. 'You didn't wake, I thought I'd better leave you.'

'No,' I said, 'I just went back to sleep by mistake.'

'Perhaps you're coming down with something.' Michael looked solicitous. 'That would explain it.' He had his shirt on, but no tie yet. It made him look unqualified to give any sort of opinion.

'For God's sake,' I said, 'does an extra ten minutes upstairs need this much analysis?'

Sarah was catching her hair into a ponytail, unlooping an elastic band from her wrist and securing it in three deft twists. 'I'm going to be a bit late home,' she said.

'How late?' I said. Sarah rolled her eyes. She often did. She has the luxury, I thought, of openly finding me ridiculous.

'I dunno. Seven?'

'I *don't* know, not "dunno". I'll keep your supper warming.'

'Don't bother, if it's anything like last night's.'

I registered the warning shot but decided against retaliatory action.

Sarah pushed back her chair with her behind as she stood up. 'Did you choose a photo?' she said. She swung her open satchel on to one shoulder. The books moved against each other without falling out.

'Not yet. I haven't had a chance to look at them properly. Eddie. Hands. Teeth. Wash. Now.'

'Mum!' Sarah stood at the door. 'Do you want to know why?'

'Why what?'

'Why I'm going to be late. I've signed up for choir. We've got a rehearsal in the church, after school.' The choir always processed up the darkened aisle at the beginning of the Christmas concert. They held lighted candles. Their hands shook with the intensity of their task. All you could see of the girls were their faces, solemn and full of concentration in the quivering lights. A parade of virgins. Mostly.

I watched them leave, Eddie half walking, half skipping, six paces to Sarah's one. Whenever I imagined a telephone call, the voice at the other end breathy with horror, it was always Eddie whose fate I feared. I saw myself opening the door in the middle of the day to someone with terrible news to impart about Eddie. Only Eddie lay immobile, in front of the too-late-to-brake car. It was Eddie whose description I gave to the policeman charged with finding him. *When did you last see your son, Mrs Deacon? What was he wearing?* In my mind's eye, he constantly fell from unknown heights or drowned in unspecified water and I rehearsed over and over again my distraught, unknowable reaction to the news. Beside Eddie, Sarah was an Amazon, striding through her day in full armour. I suspected that if anything *did* happen to Sarah, the worst thing about it would be having to tell Eddie.

I slid open the drawer of my dressing table and checked the contents, running my hands over the old letters and cards, lipsticks, safety pins and a copy of *The Naked Ape* that I'd hidden, in case Sarah found it. I retrieved Philip's little sketch of me from between its pages and unfolded it. 'Philip,' I said aloud and looked at myself in the mirror. My dressing gown was ruched at the waist and made me look pregnant. I tucked the drawing away again. It was impossible to imagine being with him, it was like trying to remember the light, long days of summer when it snows.

Reading Sarah's diary had become habitual. I should stop, I told myself. But it was too late, I was opening her bedside locker every day, moving her things aside to pull it free, as deftly as a dancer performing remembered moves. The book was like a living thing. I half expected it to be warm.

He didn't go back for his scarf, he went back for her. I gasped aloud. *He said he'd be in touch.* I went downstairs and washed up with vigour and too much noise, but I couldn't escape what I'd read. I put the wireless on and tried to distract myself. Her words throbbed in my head, as painful and inescapable as toothache.

The more I thought about it – and I could think of nothing else – the more I became convinced that *her* interpretation of events was wrong. Twisted, even. Young girls don't tell the truth all the time, do they, not even to themselves. She would only have *wanted* to believe he came back to speak to her, that he'd even noticed her. I remembered his studied carelessness, his unbothered shrug as he walked towards me. 'No, my scarf wasn't there. I must have left it in the car.' He was genuinely seeking a lost item of clothing. He was distracted, and she'd said *Paint me*, emboldened by my absence. It wouldn't have been his idea. She had sensed our quicksilver, subliminal attraction to each other and it had woken something in her. She was like a Sleeping Beauty opening her eyes, too soon, to see the wrong prince.

To believe otherwise was to think badly of him. My desire for him was like an arrow in flight, I'd taken aim and I couldn't call it back. With too little concern about my building materials, I began to create who I needed him to be.

Chapter 32

21.54. The mashed potato Marion has ordered for him wrinkles on the tray in front of Michael. He has no appetite. Food has never been a priority, anyway. He has eaten what was put in front of him, without complaining, his whole life. He has never expressed any particular appreciation, either. In the early days of their marriage, Marion struggled with recipes and ingredients. He hadn't said anything, he knew she'd believed she was doing her duty, but he would much rather she'd just opened tins. He remembered a dessert of some sort that had struck him as particularly silly: it involved great clouds of sweetened froth and submerged mandarin segments. He wouldn't have minded if she'd just mixed cream and sugar together and offered him that.

Most of the nurses come into his room without knocking, but this girl pushes the door open gradually into the space. She inclines only her head round the door, the rest of her body hidden. He's reminded of a puppet show. 'Mr Deacon?' she says. 'Just need to do your checks. Can I come in?' He can at least nod. He's grateful for her courtesy. She bends down to pick something up from the floor. 'Oh, what's this?' she says, holding out an envelope for his inspection. 'I think it's been sitting here for a while, there's a footprint on it.'

Michael's heart lurches. The letter must have slipped from Marion's cache. Addressed to M Deacon, the nurse would have imagined it was meant for him. Behind his mask, he makes a sound, though neither he nor the nurse can tell what it is.

'Okay?' she says.

He can tell he's frightened her and tries to speak. His strangled sounds alarm her more.

'Shall I get someone?' she says.

He shakes his head, a gesture that seems to tear at the skin of his face. His hands are not his to take the envelope from her, they are pricked and clamped and lie useless by his side. Clips and tubes proliferate.

'Would you like me to open it?' she says.

Michael is presented with a quandary. To have her read it might reveal far too much; he prefers the neutrality of being just a patient. But he is curious about its contents. She is already sliding a pointed thumbnail along the flap.

'Lovely,' she says, examining the card. She holds it out to him. It's the sort you buy in the gallery gift shop, a proper copy of a painting. *'The Blue Boy,'* she says, squinting at the small print. 'Dear Marion,' she begins. He does not stop her from reading.

Michael listens to Sarah's brief, anodyne message, the sort that doesn't need an answer, but in his mind's eye he sees her at seventeen. Taller than him. Standing in front of a set of bare shelves. They'd been like that for months. They stayed like that for ever. She wore a short, suede skirt that was too big for her, which remained in position like armour while her tiny waist twisted inside it. On her feet were multi-strapped sandals, which encased her lower legs up to the knee as if she were displaying her own skeleton outside her body. She'd made holes in both sleeves of her jumper and stuck her thumbs through them. She always kept the scars covered. What she said then is louder to him now than the words the nurse reads. *'I can't be in a place that has her in it.'* He had set things in motion without demur. He and Marion had parted noiselessly. He was reminded of skaters, letting go of each other's hands to glide and spin on different parts of the ice. Sharing a house with Sarah rearranged his thinking and soon he couldn't imagine his life with anyone else. When she left she had put, first, a town, then an entire ocean between them. 'It's not an exorcism,' she'd said, folding the few clothes she took with her into a rucksack. 'It's a baptism.' Her absence was not unkind. She had prepared the way for his last, magnificently tender pairing.

'I'll put it here,' the nurse says, propping the card on the locker beside him. There is something furtive in her expression. 'Mr Deacon,' she says. 'May I have the stamps? Would you mind? My brother collects them.' She gazes at the envelope. 'America,' she says. 'Your daughter's in America.' She smiles at Michael, marvelling at him as you would at a baby that liked olives. She examines the postmark. 'This was posted a while ago, wasn't it?' He tries to speak. She looks around to make sure she's not observed and then removes the mask. 'Just for a moment,' she says. 'So you can say what you want to say.'

'Do have the stamps,' Michael says. She smiles. 'But could you put the card away?'

'Pardon?' She leans towards him, tucking her hair behind her ear.

He can see that she wears only one little stud in her lobe but there are many more piercings. He imagines her sticking all manner of earrings through the holes on her nights off, in defiance of the rules here. Great hoops and outrageous sparklers. 'In the drawer, please,' Michael manages.

'Not on display?' she says, disappointed. She gives him a moment to change his mind, holding the card towards him.

'No,' says Michael and regrets that he hasn't even the strength to say: 'thank you'.

He admits to himself that things may not end as he wishes. The thought is both unnerving and satisfying. It's as if he were completing a crossword puzzle only to discover that, although they are correct, some of the answers are not words he knew.

Chapter 33

29 September

Bobbie's father, Mr Cavanagh, is called Adrian. I tore a page out of my Page-a-Day diary and wrote his name on it and folded it over until it was small. I put it in the Jesus box, with the others. It's got a picture on the lid of Him with mighty beams behind His head and a massive halo. The names rub against each other in there. There are seven now.

Number 1 is *Greg*, who I met at a party. He told me my breasts were SBHs, which is Standard British Handful.

2. *Daniel*, who came round door-to-door selling pictures on velvet he'd painted himself. He said they were inspired by Africa. He didn't say if he'd been there. He had very beautiful eyes, but he didn't come back, even though my parents said they were quite interested in buying something.

3. *John*, who is Lizzie H's cousin. He had grown much taller the last time I saw him, which made him attractive.

4. *Neil*, who went to the same holiday swimming club as me. It was only for a week and I hated most of it, but on the last day he made me laugh until my tummy hurt.

5. *Anthony*, who is the son of one of my parents' friends. He shouldn't be in there really. He's a bit gross but he asked for my phone number.

6. *Kev*, who goes out with Izzy in my class. He's a biker. She says when they go round the bends on the roads together, he leans the bike so far over she nearly scrapes her knees on the tarmac. I've never spoken to him, just seen him with her after school.

7. *Adrian*. I've never called a grown-up by just their name, so I added *Mr Cavanagh*.

After a while, I tore out another page and wrote *Bobbie*'s name on it. It had my New Year resolutions on the other side:

Be nicer to Eddie.

Stop biting my nails.

Get a boyfriend.

I've nearly stopped biting my nails.

Chapter 34

'Mrs Deacon?'

The young doctor is hurrying after me. I'm by the lift. We both glance up at the display: the number three is illuminated and will be for a while; these lifts are very slow. His white coat flaps open. He wears this official garment without ceremony. Nearly fifty years ago, I stood in front of the full-length mirror in the outfitters. It was the first time I'd seen myself dressed as a nurse. The little cape hung heavily, and I could feel every pin anchoring my cap. It suited me.

This doctor's face is anxious, he looks as if he'd like to hand this encounter to someone else. 'The registrar can pop in tomorrow,' he says. 'The morning round, I think. It'll be at about—'

'It doesn't matter what time,' I say, 'I'm going to be here all day.'

He looks down at his shoes. They are plastic, round-toed, the sort of shoes small children would wear on the beach. He smiles. 'Practical,' he says, shrugging.

'Ugly,' I say.

'The thing is,' he says, ignoring my remark, 'the thing is, it would be a good idea to get the family here. Soon. Would that be possible?'

I don't answer. I don't want to make this easy for him.

'Do you have children?' he says.

I nod.

'And grandchildren, I expect?' He thinks he is being kind.

'Yes,' I say. 'But not in this country.'

'Oh,' he says. 'Well, it's just that whoever wants to see him should come, to say—' He stops.

I know he means well, but I also know he'll have to have this conversation many more times, with many more people, over the years. He is gauging how much truth I can stand. He deems me a practical type, able to assimilate what's happening without hysterics. I'm not even crying, am I? 'Thank you,' I say. 'I'll tell everyone who needs to know.'

I negotiate the agonisingly slow lift and the car park's obstructive exit without irritation, as I'm rehearsing the calls I must make. I wish I didn't have to speak to anyone else. I don't want to hear their voices. I turn off the car radio and drive home in silence.

I'm affronted by the stillness of the house. Only a couple of circulars on the mat indicate there's been any change at all. I switch on the lights in all the rooms, to defend myself from shadows. I turn on the television. Instead of concentrating on what's on the screen, I can only see, washed up from the past of thirty years ago like wreckage from a storm, that other life.

Reading Sarah's list of boys was comical, until I got to his name. Next to where she'd written: *'Adrian Mr Cavanagh'* there were stars and an open-petalled flower, the sort you draw in a big, lazy swirl without taking your pen from the paper. I opened the Jesus box and examined the other contents. Two baby teeth and a badge saying, *'Tower of London'*. Some silver charms tarnished without use. A tiny phial of Ma Griffe. An origami swan. A small glass monkey and a postcard of a Spanish dancer, her skirt made of real ribbon. Sarah had tried to hoard these things in secret, but children have no power. While everyone was out, I could roam through every inch of the house, opening all the cupboards and drawers at will and undisturbed.

I put on my coat. I willed the space where his car might stand to stay empty until I returned. It was only half past nine. I didn't like to think of his bed somewhere, and him either in it or not in it, or about who else might be there with him. I pulled the notebook from the drawer and wrote 'biscuits' on the little sheet of paper, as if I might forget the task if I didn't.

Almost as soon as I'd shut the front door behind me, Sheila walked down her own path. When she caught my eye, she waved and increased her speed. We were separated by three front gardens.

'Going out?' she said.

'Just as far as the corner shop,' I said. Had she been waiting for me? She wasn't wearing a coat, so she hadn't intended to leave her house for any length of time. She had her handbag. She probably picked it up whenever she left the house, even for a moment.

'Marion' – she put one hand on my arm – 'come and have a coffee. Just for half an hour.'

'I've got a friend coming later. I can't—'

'When's she coming? This morning?'

'Midday.' I couldn't fib. Sheila probably clocked me on and off, anyway.

'Super. Who's that, then?' It didn't occur to her not to ask.

'Bridget.'

'Ah, your old *school* friend. Lovely.' She implied that people you'd known at school didn't really count as chums. Michael had a Rolodex on his desk. Its little cards would flatten apart at the name he needed. I imagined Sheila must have a similar system, only hers was in her head. It had just whirred and stopped at Bridget's name.

I'd only been to Michael's office once. We were going to the theatre and I'd been in town already, both of which were unusual. We'd had to make quite a complicated plan involving Michael actually taking a small suitcase of my clothes with him on the train, so that I could change for the evening. Michael's secretary was a tidy young woman, whose clothes fitted her as neatly as if she'd been sewn into them. Miss Piper. I didn't know her Christian name then. She sat at a little desk outside his room, like a sentry, and she indicated the door for me with a slight hesitation, as though it were private and I shouldn't really be admitted. The suitcase sat in the middle of the room; it must have been stowed somewhere else all day. I knelt on the floor and opened it. My clothes, slightly dishevelled after their incarceration, looked as dear and familiar as old friends. The room was not overlooked – the only window gave on to a nondescript inner area of the blank, windowless walls of other offices – but nevertheless I'd felt conspicuous and exposed at the thought of taking my day clothes off there. I went and stood behind Michael's desk, on the same side as his chair and next to the wall, as though that offered privacy. Curled up next to the chair's leg was a crumpled apricot tissue. It was the sort that came out of a cardboard box decorated with flowers. I remember, too, that the room smelled of lavender.

'You've got ages,' Sheila said, steering me along the pavement. 'Coffee. Shop. Home.' She made a bouncing motion with one arm as she spoke, as though you got to each appointment by hopping. She retrieved her purse from her handbag, opened it and took out a key, dropped the purse back and closed her handbag's clasp with a loud click. 'Now, in you go.'

Our houses were similarly sized but the builder had had some fun ordering them slightly differently inside, making hallways wider or narrower, or putting kitchens where you might be used to a dining room. In Sheila's house, the stairs veered sideways to a little platform before going off at a different angle to continue upwards. The platform looked like a tiny stage. There was no room for any performance, it was half taken up with a nest of tables, topped with green leather held safely under glass. Beside it was a box full of medical supplies. It looked like a little field hospital of bottles, dressings and pills. Sheila's mother lived with them so I supposed they must all be to do with her care.

I had met her mother at a Christmas drinks party Sheila had held for the neighbours. 'Shared locality, shared friendship,' she'd said. She had placed all the chairs against the walls. The old woman had perched on the same one all evening, glaring into the space in the middle of the room and refusing vol-au-vents and any attempts at conversation. 'This is Marion, Mother, she lives down the road,' Sheila yelled.

The old woman looked at me. Thinning strands of her hair formed a lattice over her pink and barren scalp. 'Don't they all?' the woman said.

She'd sounded quite, what, exactly? Cockney? She certainly didn't have Sheila's clipped vowels. She'd looked quite healthy, as robust as she could behind the wrinkling and trembling of her years. She hadn't looked as if she'd needed much *treatment* of any sort, anyway. I shivered. If you had to do all the sort of things for old people that you had to do for babies, wiping and dressing and helping them eat, then Sheila must be some sort of saint. It was hard to reconcile that notion with Sheila's four-square, earthly demeanour. It was more than likely that she just left the box outside her mother's room and told her to fend for herself.

'Come in.' Sheila opened the sitting room door wide and gestured to me to go through. 'I'll get coffee.'

She continued to talk to me as she went down the hallway and as she reached the kitchen, she raised her voice to a high shriek to cover the distance between us. I couldn't match her volume in return, and anyway I felt foolish yelling back from the settee, but Sheila didn't appear to mind the conversation being one-sided and carried on. It seemed to be to do with objecting about the removal of a zebra crossing. Or possibly the instigation of one. When the kettle began to whistle, Sheila got louder still. I sat on the edge of a seat so hard and ungiving I thought it might bruise me. Cushions of stone-like inflexibility were set at precise intervals along its length. Sheila hadn't suggested I take my coat off, but it tightened at the sleeves and collar as I sat, so I stood up and undid the buttons.

'Sit down, sit down,' said Sheila, coming back in – as though I'd been standing, waiting for her, all that time. She carried a small tray and tiny cups tinkled on their saucers as she set it down.

On a matching plate, three plain biscuits were arranged in a fan. 'Sugar?' Sheila held out a bowl of coloured crystals.

They seemed larger than the usual sort and were difficult to persuade on to the spoon. The teaspoons were miniature, too, making my fingers feel large and imprecise. I thought of Adrian's hands, making the cup he'd held look small.

'So,' Sheila said, 'how nice your friend is coming. She lives in the north, doesn't she?'

'She does, yes.' I took a sip of the coffee. It was extremely hot. The thin china burned my lips. I had to set the saucer down before I could replace the cup, balancing the doll-sized spoon in case it fell. The shock of the heat made me too quick and careless and the liquid spilled over one side, a little Vesuvius erupting on to the table.

'Never mind!' Sheila said loudly, obviously minding very much. She rushed out of the room, hissing, 'Cloth!' as she went.

I stared helplessly at the spreading puddle. I thought I'd better move whatever might be in its path, picking up first a porcelain flower arrangement with a disproportionately large kitten investigating the blooms. Next, a heavy frame.

It was a wedding photograph. Sheila and Alan, her arm looped through his, her gloved hand hovering so that it wouldn't crease his jacket. They stood in the middle of a group of smart people, seven or eight of them, caught in the act of throwing confetti over the couple. I stared at the faces. One of them was Adrian. Unmistakably him, although the picture was a good fifteen years old, if not more. The other people were turned towards the newly-wedded pair, he was looking at the photographer. He wore a wide, double-breasted jacket. A little handkerchief, neatly folded, peeked from his pocket and he held a trilby in one hand. Even in black and white, he was the most colourful person there.

'Right, here we are.' Sheila was at my shoulder. She dabbed with a cloth. The table top was a shade lighter where the coffee had been spilled. The room smelled strongly of lily of the valley. There were no real flowers anywhere. I felt as if I'd been caught writing a lewd poem on the wall. 'There we are.' Sheila set the ornament back in its place. 'The crime will go undetected.' She followed my gaze as she replaced the picture. 'There he is again,' she said, 'Adrian. Before domesticity sprang its trap.' She smiled at his image.

Had he ever been here, in this room? I tried to imagine Adrian sitting on the Dralon covers. You didn't stand close enough to someone to throw confetti at them without being quite a good friend. He'd look very untucked beside her, if he stood here now, with his uncuffed shirt and voluminous coat. Sheila's clothes behaved themselves. I suspected they weren't placed in a wardrobe, but stood waiting for their wearer in rows in her bedroom, still assuming her shape.

'May I use your . . . toilet?' I asked, cursing myself for my hesitation. I hated the word, but lavatory seemed rather personal.

Sheila looked momentarily annoyed, as though she thought I should have gone home to use my own facilities. 'Yes, of course. Pop upstairs,' she said, after too long a pause. 'Alan's re-tiling the cloakroom, so it's out of bounds.'

'Thank you. It's – um?' I pointed to the ceiling. I didn't want to open any door but the right one.

'Round to the left at the top.' Sheila put the coffee cups on the tray and plumped a hostile cushion.

The bathroom was entirely pink. There were enough towels to dry a cricket team. A packet of Radox sat beside the bath taps, but other than that there was nothing on display. I was tempted to open one of the mirrored cupboards and examine its contents, but I thought Sheila might be acutely aware of how long I would – and should – be gone for, so I sat down and regarded the back of the bathroom door instead. A man's striped dressing gown, the only sign of Alan anywhere, hung from a fish-shaped hook.

The bar of soap on the basin was so new that the little raised label on top was pristine. The towels seemed to absorb no moisture and left a fluffy rime. When I came out, Sheila's mother stood on the landing, so close to the door that I almost collided with her. 'You were in there a while,' she said. There *was* something slightly cockney in her delivery.

'I'm sorry.' I tried to step round her, but she took up quite a bit of space. She seemed to be wearing several dressing gowns at once. 'Have you been waiting?'

'I got me own facilities,' the woman said, still not moving. 'I'm just having a wander, that's all.'

Close to, it looked as if several different pieces of creased flesh had been applied over existing folds and wrinkles on her face. Her eyes were deep-set, and the lower lids sagged to reveal a pink, inner curve. She blinked constantly, to clear tears that gathered and spilled in the corners.

She leaned towards me. 'Want to hold hands?' she said. She extended one arm. 'You could be my friend,' she said. She took my hand in hers. Her skin was soft and barely warm. She closed her fingers round mine in a tight grip and raised her arm. 'Look,' she said, forcing her fist close to my face, 'nice and red.' Each nail was scarlet and filed into a neat oval.

'That's lovely,' I said.

Her grip relaxed. 'I'm allowed,' she said. 'Because I'm a big girl now.'

I stroked my thumb against each glossy tip. 'You are,' I said. 'And you're a clever girl.'

Her expression changed. It was as if the years unwound from her like wool from a spool. 'Am I?' she said.

I nodded. I squeezed her hand. 'Very clever.' I could see her struggling, clutching at her thoughts as a swimmer surfacing on to wet stone gropes for a purchase.

'I am,' she said eventually. She dropped my hand. 'I was.'

'Now, Mother.' Sheila took the stairs at a surprising trot to reach us. 'What are you doing out here? It isn't lunchtime.' She turned to me with a small laugh, one hand on her mother's overstuffed elbow. 'She doesn't know what time it is.'

Her mother undid one of the many sashes and cords at her waist then retied it, grunting with effort. 'I'm a prisoner,' she whispered to me. 'They won't let me out. I shouldn't be here.'

'Oh, Mother, really,' Sheila said and raised her eyes at me, not letting go of the old woman, shuffling nearer to keep hold of her. They clung to each other like boxers at the end of a bout.

'What have I done with my life?' The old woman crumpled where she stood. Sheila dropped her mother's arm, which hung down at once, as if it were only loosely fastened at the shoulder. They stared at each other.

'Mother,' Sheila said, 'come back to your room. Let's look at your photograph albums. You'll see exactly what a marvellous time you've had. *Again!*' This word was flung at me, with another eye roll.

The old woman gathered herself, pulling flapping material and sashes into place. It was like watching a marquee buffeted by high winds.

'The only thing I've achieved,' she said, to neither of us in particular, 'the only thing I've achieved is not dying young.'

I watched Sheila guide her along the landing. The way to the stairs – my escape route – was clear.

'Just a moment, Marion,' said Sheila without turning round, as if she read my thoughts. 'I'll see you out. Two secs!'

It was not negotiable.

'Where are you off to, then, did you say?' Sheila came down the stairs brushing her hands together as if they'd been dusty. The little box of medical wares was gone. Perhaps she'd been performing some sort of procedure.

'I need to get some nice biscuits.' I thought of the uneaten trio Sheila had offered. 'Bridget's coming.'

'Oh, well, I don't think I'll come with you on *that* outing,' Sheila said, as though we'd made a plan. 'But next time you're off to town, let me know. Once I've got things sorted here' – she gestured towards the ceiling – 'I'm a free agent. I'll tell you a funny thing . . .' She took two steps towards me, glancing about her as if all the rooms nearby were full of people. 'You know that little coffee bar in the middle of Temple's?' She paused to give me time to imagine it. It was a functional, plain space on the ground floor. 'Do you know who loves going there?'

I shook my head.

'Adrian Cavanagh. I know!' she said, seeing me react. 'Imagine him and all the ladies. Usually it's just somewhere for a drink and a bun when you've finished buying bras, isn't it?'

I felt hot. Why did Sheila want me to know that? It was odd enough that he chose to spend any time in the rather gloomy café in the middle of the entirely gloomy department store. It was even stranger for Sheila to tell me this with such glee. 'Does he?' I said, as lightly as I could. 'I only really go there for school uniforms. It's not very glamorous.'

'Adrian doesn't mind *that*,' Sheila said. 'I don't think *glamour* is high on his list of attributes.'

I couldn't tell which was more upsetting, the ownership of Adrian's desires or his choice of location.

'Anyway,' she said. 'Next time you're in there, pop in. See if he's there. Say hello. And if you fancy company on the train, let me know. We could have lunch at Wooller's.' She rubbed an invisible mark on the glossy paintwork. 'I'll be round for you to sign our petition as soon as it's printed.' She opened the door. 'I meant to say,' she said, 'Sarah's growing up, isn't she? I saw her setting off the other day – I presume she was meeting some of her friends, she wasn't wearing her uniform. In fact, she was hardly wearing anything at all. If skirts get any shorter . . .' She turned to face me. 'It must be a bit peculiar to have a young woman about the place; she's not a little girl any more, is she? My mother didn't like it at all, when I started growing up. Too much like competition. Anyway.' She brushed her hands together again, dismissing the topic and me. 'Anyway, mustn't keep you.' She opened the front door and hurried me out.

I wanted to get on a train, right away, and go to Temple's and try to find him. 'For goodness' sake, Marion, stop it,' I said aloud. 'Just go and buy your bloody biscuits.'

Chapter 35

30 September

There's a little drawing of Mum tucked inside the cover of *The Naked Ape*. She's hidden the book in her dressing table drawer because it's got some dirty stuff in it. I don't know why she's hidden the picture. It's a small sketch of the top half of her – you can just see her bare shoulders. Her hair is spread out to one side; it's long and wavy. I don't remember her ever having long hair. When I first saw the picture, I put it away quickly. I felt as embarrassed as if I'd seen her naked. You can sort of tell whoever drew it couldn't stop looking at her. Her eyes are closed. Properly closed. Like if you're really sound asleep. Or when you're dead.

We did levitation the other day. Isobel volunteered. We stood in a circle round her and chanted all the usual stuff – you shall rest, you shall sleep, you shall rise – then slid our hands underneath her. We managed to get her about a foot in the air before she wriggled and laughed and fell. But when she was lying down with her eyes shut, it made me think of that drawing of Mum. I suddenly thought she was waiting to be lifted, too. I don't know why but it made me feel sorry for her, which I didn't like. I think I broke the levitation spell because I was holding up Isobel's fat bum and that's the first place that hit the ground.

I didn't see Adrian Mr Cavanagh until he stood in front of me. I was reciting the list of enzymes for the stupid test and I'd just got to maltase when he said hello. I jumped. He said I was obviously deep in thought and he was sorry he startled me, but he didn't sound sorry. Some of the Upper Sixth girls came past us and he turned and watched them walk away. That made me feel cross, because he wasn't concentrating properly on me. I said are you waiting for Bobbie and he looked at me for so long I went red. He said no, I'm waiting for you. He set off down the road and I had to walk quite fast to keep up with him. He said let's get in the car. It was weird sitting there. I felt very close to him, as if I were actually breathing in air he'd just breathed out. He asked about stuff I did after school, if I'd got any day when I could meet him. We'd just do a sketch, he said. Wouldn't take long. I said maybe Wednesday. My voice sounded high and wobbly, like those girls who flunk the Bible reading in assembly. He said okay, next week then and leaned right across me to open the door. I didn't want to get out. I wanted his weight on me for ever, his hair almost touching my chin. Afterwards I felt as if I were separated from something that had been keeping me upright and I leaned against the bus stop so I wouldn't keel over.

Chapter 36

23.03. Michael raises his arm as instructed by the nurse and holds it aloft as she wraps the cuff around it. His gesture is not without effort. He can't remember a time when he could make any movement without preparing for it and working hard to carry it out. They wait together as the cuff inflates; he watches her note the numbers. It doesn't matter what she writes down, he thinks. Unless it's a matter of a slight acceleration of proceedings or – less likely – a slowing down, he's aware of exactly where he's heading. She takes his hand and replaces it on the cover, as if it had become out of place. He feels a perceptible jolt at the contact; it is rare that someone touches him now without medical purpose.

He thinks of Eddie, aged about six, falling from his bicycle. Running behind him, Michael accelerated towards his sprawled figure and had begun exhorting him to get up, telling him he was fine until he reached him and saw the blood running from his knee. Even then, Michael had chanted phrases about bravery and getting back in the saddle. Eddie cried with increasing vigour as he watched the red stream flow. Michael was crouching beside him, inspecting the damage to the bicycle as much as to his son, when Eddie flung his arms round his father's neck and clung to him.

Michael had held him before, of course, but only by arrangement. The baby Eddie was put briefly into his arms, just long enough for Michael to register the combination of wool and warmth and to feel slightly shocked, horrified, even, by his son's tight, red face. The toddler Eddie had squirmed on his lap before someone – usually Marion – took him away. It seemed to him that he'd never before felt this chosen embrace, the texture of Eddie's skin, his breath. Michael had felt grateful for his son's unhesitating, uncomplicated need. It was one of the few moments in his life when he knew exactly who he was. Being this boy's father was enough of everything. The way his small, slight body fitted alongside his own completed him. Eddie only let go when he wanted to examine his wound more closely. Michael didn't hurry them home.

He will cut loose from this eking out of his days soon. He has really only himself to consider, after all.

Chapter 37

Sheila's words repeated in my head. I had no reason to go to Temple's. It was an expedition, involving trains and fares and plans. If I went and he wasn't there, that would be half a day gone. If he *was* there, what would I do? I had a sensation of heightened tension, as if I were being watched. Or as if I were the spy, waiting for my quarry to reveal himself.

There was no one behind the counter of the Terrible Shop. The bell that sounded when the door opened was very loud. I looked without any appetite at the packets of biscuits. Did Bridget like plain ones or prefer chocolate? I'd better get both. Chocolate rolls in little foil wrappers and some digestives.

The shopkeeper emerged from somewhere in the far reaches of the space behind the counter. He was chewing a generous mouthful with elaborate circles of his cheeks. He wiped his hands over his mouth, one after the other like a cat. He was more bulldog than feline, his head large with full jowls. 'Do you want a bit of light on the subject?' he said. He reached for a switch on the wall and a neon bulb above him flickered into life. The shop's contents looked no more appealing under this light.

'Thank you.' I handed him the packets.

He slid one hand the length of his brown overall before taking them. 'Right,' he said, continuing to retrieve food from his teeth with the tip of his tongue. The sound of it was unnerving, wet and sticky. The strip light buzzed. He wiped his other hand against his chest, then keyed in the price very slowly on the cash register in front of him. Each key pinged loudly as he depressed them, his index finger sticking out straight and pink. The numbers bobbed up behind the glass.

'Plus VAT,' he said sonorously. 'Anything else?'

I shook my head. I was glad I had the exact money in my purse. I could drop the coins straight on to his palm. I was reluctant to touch his skin. He turned off the light as I left.

Bridget arrived with a flourish. She kissed me on the cheek, which I couldn't remember happening before. She wore a fitted lime-green dress which stuck stiffly out at the hem, and her fringe was flattened across her forehead in little rows, like corn. 'You haven't seen me in a dress since for ever, have you?' She hung her coat over the banister. 'That's what you're thinking, isn't it, Maz?'

I laughed. 'It's nice,' I said, 'to see someone dressed up. Nobody bothers much in the countryside.'

'You need a reason, don't you,' Bridget said. She breathed in sharply and bit her lip. 'Oh, Marion.' She looked away quickly towards the kitchen and the back door beyond, as though she thought she heard other visitors. I waited. Bridget seemed about to say something else but instead she went to the mirror and turned her head this way and that, examining her rigid hair.

'Lunch?' I said brightly. 'I thought I'd just do a salad.'

'Fine. I'm not very hungry.' Bridget tugged at the waistband of her dress. It gripped her tightly; a little roll of flesh circled just above the belt. 'This is new,' she said, still wrestling. 'Do you like it?'

I had the distinct impression my approval was not required. 'It's such a lovely colour,' I lied. 'It suits you,' I added, heaping another falsehood on to the pile.

'I'd never normally wear this colour,' Bridget said, her cheeks flushing, which didn't help. Again, she seemed on the verge of saying more. 'Anyway, I brought you this.' She fished in the bottom of a carrier bag and retrieved a box of Terry's All Gold. We both stared at it. 'Oh, God, I'm sorry, Marion. I really meant to get you something proper, but I'd left it too late and there was only this awful shop next to the station. I actually had to dust this packet with my scarf after I'd bought it. It must have been on the shelf for ages.'

'I went to a terrible shop to buy biscuits, so we're quits,' I said. 'The shopkeeper was very greasy, so I might have to clean the packets before I even open them.'

'Marion.' Bridget stood with her arms by her sides as though she didn't trust herself not to make a sudden movement. 'It's no good. I've absolutely got to tell you something.'

'Here?' Standing in the hall felt awkward. Where was the best place for a confidence? 'Shall I get lunch while you tell me?'

'I can't eat!' Bridget flung her head back towards the ceiling, her little blonde bob tipped back in a solid clump.

Just as well, I thought, that I'm not hungry either. 'Come in here,' I said. The sitting room was untouched since last night. The *Radio Times* lay opened at yesterday's page and some of Eddie's toy farm animals were still in their knitting-needle-fenced enclosure on the rug. He'd raided the sewing box to create the farm: the little horses drank from a darning mushroom and there was a copse of bobbin trees. I knelt and gathered them up. Eddie would be angry when he found I'd moved them. 'Sorry, I meant to tidy in here,' I said, but I could tell from Bridget's expression that even if we'd discovered a corpse, or the aftermath of a small fire, it wouldn't have distracted her.

'Marion.' Bridget smiled. 'I'll just plunge in. And I'll understand if you disapprove.' She smiled again. 'I'm having an affair.' Her large face was bright with achievement. She shone with pride. She regarded me with a kind expression. 'Are you shocked?'

'It wasn't what I expected,' I said truthfully. 'How long, I mean, when? And . . . who?'

'I didn't expect it either.' Bridget leaned back against the cushions. 'Oh, ouch,' she said, sitting forward at once and holding a small plastic pig. 'I mean, I thought I was happily married . . .' She leaned back again.

I tried hard to imagine Bridget's husband. Trevor, wasn't it? Had we even met? I seemed to think he had glasses and not much hair.

'And Richard was the last person I'd thought I'd notice.' Bridget seemed to relish saying his name. 'Or who would notice me. Oh my God,' she said happily, 'it's such a cliché.' She paused and sighed.

I wonder, I thought, who is looking after the dogs?

'Are you being careful, Bridget?' I meant about everything.

Bridget sat up straight, sober after her dizzy reverie. 'Oh Marion. You *do* disapprove.' Her eyes filled with tears. She ran from one emotion to the other, like a child playing tag. Even through her tears, Bridget seemed airborne with pleasure, her toes only lightly on the ground.

'I don't disapprove,' I said. 'I'm sorry, I just don't think you've ever told me anything like this before.'

'I've never said it aloud.' Bridget sniffed and shook her head, like a wet dog. We both looked in different directions, in silence, till we caught each other's eye and began to laugh. 'Oh God,' Bridget wailed, pulling a cushion from behind her and burying her face in it. When she looked up, there were two mascara trails down her face. 'I'm so happy,' she sobbed. 'It's ridiculous and difficult and he's married and so am I and I don't know what will happen and I don't care!'

'Well,' I said, after a pause. 'You are a one.'

'I am. I am a one. I'm such a one!' Bridget gasped and blew air into her cheeks, exhaling with a loud rush of air. 'I never thought I was the sort of woman who . . .' She laughed, still short of breath. 'I don't know who I thought that was, really. But I suppose I didn't imagine she'd be someone like me. Everyone thinks I'm practical and a bit plain, don't they? And they'd have looked at me with my awful hair and my fat calves and thought no one would think I was in the least bit fanciable.' She looked straight at me. 'I bet you thought that, too, didn't you?'

'No.' I tried not to fidget under her gaze, feeling found out. 'You've never said anything about you and Trevor being unhappy.'

'Trevor!' Bridget clapped her hands to her cheeks. 'Oh, Marion. Trevor is so dull. He's so boring. He hardly says anything. He doesn't *see* anything. He hasn't even noticed my hair.'

'Really? It's very different.' Perhaps Trevor thought that Bridget's new look was a big mistake and was ignoring it out of kindness.

'Do you like it?' Bridget fiddled with her fringe. 'Richard just sort of pushed my hair to one side like this' – she exaggerated the sweep of her hair – 'and he said it really suited me.'

The jury, I thought, was still out about that. And I was pretty sure that Michael would notice if I suddenly cut off half my hair and then used a can of Elnett on it every day.

'Richard thinks I'm beautiful,' said Bridget. 'He says I'm the most interesting woman he's ever met.'

Something in her tone, half wistful and half proud, silenced me and smudged every mocking thought. Bridget seemed redefined by her lover's appraisal. Had Michael noticed me gleaming like this, when I was seeing Philip? I shut the thought down. This was different. This was flippant and casual. This time next year, it would all be over. And Richard would still be alive.

'Marion,' Bridget said solemnly, 'I want to ask you a favour.'

'Wait a minute, I'm going to tidy you up. Just in case . . .'

'Is someone coming?' Bridget started back in her seat.

'No, no, but I don't want you to say something important to me while you look like the wreck of the Hesperus.' I pulled a tissue from my sleeve and scrubbed at the black streaks on her cheeks.

'Thank you,' she said, stroking her face gingerly. 'All gone?' She laced her fingers together. 'Would you mind saying I'm staying with you for one night, Maz?' Her fingers tightened in her lap. 'Just for one night? Richard and I have only been able to meet in the daytime, but he's got to go away on business soon. I could stay at his hotel with him. I could tell Trevor that I'm with you. Could I? Would you do that for me, Marion?'

'I suppose so,' I said. 'When?' I thought of a sullen hotel and an anonymous bedroom. I imagined Bridget waiting there for hours, in new underwear. Richard would race through a meeting to get to her. The room could be stale with another occupant's cigarette smoke, there might be ominous stains on the wall or the bedding and the noise of the bar might carry on past midnight, but the lovers wouldn't notice. If they did, they wouldn't mind. Jealousy, unexpected and violent, flooded through me like water through an open sluice gate.

'I think it'll be soon,' Bridget said. 'Probably next week. I'll telephone you. You are a dear. Are you sure?' But she didn't need my answer, she had already jumped over any obstacles to the open field beyond. 'Shall we have lunch now? I'm suddenly starving.'

Bridget chattered while I washed lettuce and chopped tomatoes. She talked about the little Westies and her new front door, but the main topic of conversation was Richard. How he noticed everything about her, how he made her laugh. How he'd managed to smuggle a birthday present to her: 'Ingenious! It was a book, Maz, so that anyone could have given it to me, but he'd written a little code on a slip of paper and it corresponded to the initials of certain words on specific pages and it spelled *"I love you"*.' He didn't live nearby, she said, so meeting up was difficult. Neither of them had children which, Bridget said, looking at me with pity, would have made it all much worse. But his wife wasn't well, so he couldn't just leave. 'And I don't know what it would do to Trevor, either,' she said. 'His mother died last year.'

The whole thing sounded like quite hard work. What obviously redeemed it, although Bridget didn't say as much, was that being in bed with him made all the secrecy and lying worthwhile. 'A whole night!' Bridget said from time to time, then: 'Thank you!' as if she needed to keep being grateful to ensure that I kept my word. 'It's just if Trevor calls, that's all,' she said, to reassure me that there'd be no more role-play required other than a quick, simple untruth.

'I'm off to a gallery,' Bridget said, putting on her coat. 'Well, *we're* off to a gallery. That's why I'm all dressed up. Richard's in town and he likes that sort of thing. I'm just happy to do whatever he wants. Trevor thinks I'm going to be with you all the time today.' She caught my eye and looked guilty for the first time. 'It's not really a lie, is it? I'm here now,' she said, as if one of her lies was worse than the other. I'd stopped short of asking for a physical description of

Richard, but Bridget supplied the occasional detail ('he's got such lovely blue eyes,' or: 'he's much taller than me,' and: 'I adore his smile') so that he'd shifted about in my mind's eye, like someone in a hall of mirrors.

Bridget took the top off her lipstick and painted her mouth with a thick layer of peach frosting, spreading the colour well outside her lip line. She gazed at her reflection in her powder compact. She saw me watching her and made an exaggerated, kissing pout for my benefit. 'I owe you,' she said, placing a hand on my arm with a grave expression. 'And I'll find a way to pay you back. Why don't you come up and stay or something? I'd really look after you.'

I imagined me and Trevor sitting together without speaking, counting the hours until Bridget returned. We'd both notice that she was still flushed.

Bridget's antics were all rather stupid, really. It was hardly the stuff of romance. It was more the content of newspaper articles about husbands who discover their wives' affairs and then murder them as a consequence. Bridget would be jolly hard to do away with, though, she had the sort of bouncy resilience that would repel any attempt on her life. 'Don't be daft,' she'd say, while undoing the rope at her throat or taking the gun from Trevor's hand, 'I'll go and feed the dogs, then we'll chat.'

After she'd gone, I could smell her scent everywhere she'd been. I hoped she never had cause to visit Richard's house, because the invalid wife would be tormented by the perfume of infidelity, drifting to wherever she lay, too weak to move. If he had such a bedridden wife, of course. He was lying to whatever wife he *actually* had to see Bridget, wasn't he, so he could well be deceiving her, too. People want to think you're telling them the truth, after all. It's not so much that anyone is a good liar, I thought, but that most of us are good believers.

Chapter 38

1 October

I walked the long way round, through the field. I wanted to rehearse what I was going to say to Bobbie, so that I could seem really not very bothered when I told her about her father coming to our house. I wasn't going to tell her about seeing him after school. I felt swollen with information, my stomach actually ached. The pony trotted over as usual. I picked some long grass and held it out to him. He rubbed his velvet lips on my skin as he ate. He licked me and his huge emery board tongue filed my palm flat. I leaned my face on his neck and breathed him in. It was the smell of the only thing that used to matter to me. I laced my fingers through his tough mane and leaned into his flank. He swung his head and looked at me with one kind, brown eye. Whenever I walked anywhere – along the lanes, going to the bus stop, even through the school corridors – I'd be thinking about riding. If we drove anywhere, I'd sit in the back of the car and look at fields to see how good a gallop you'd get there or size up gates for a jump. Whatever I was doing, wherever I was going, I'd pretend I was still riding. I was half horse and half myself. I'd shake my neck as if I had a mane. I'd paw the ground and snort. I'd canter along the paths and snap sticks to make short crops, slapping my thighs as I ran. It made me feel as if I could run anywhere and leap over any obstacle. I was wild and strong. Tom Spencer saw me once and he started giggling. 'Why are you running along hitting your own leg?' he said. I was a bit frightened of him then. I didn't know that he is just a bit soggy, like overcooked veg. I'd dropped the stick and walked away from him, as fast as I could.

Being near the pony wasn't the same any more. It was as if a magic spell had worn off.

Eddie used to keep Truck on a little doll's house chair next to his bed. It's not there now. I asked him why and he said he'd buried him. I said dig him up, he's metal he won't dissolve. But Eddie said Truck was happy where he was. He said he doesn't have to think about him any more. He said you can look after me now, instead. I said I would. I think I mean it. Last summer, we caught freshwater shrimps in the stream by the castle. We took them home in jam jars, even though they hardly ever survived even one night. Eddie half filled his jar with stones and twigs and the little dead shrimps would catch on them and wriggle about if you shook them. He thought they were still alive. There's a complicated sadness inside my chest, all the time. If I poke at it, it wriggles like they did. When Eddie was born, Mrs Owen from the next-door cottage told me babies come to the right parents. She said your little brother is exactly who they need. He's like glue, she said. They'll stick together now.

Chapter 39

Michael is being ministered to when I arrive. Three nurses, as attentive as geishas, bob and bend, moving over and beside him, adjusting and checking. There's nothing for me to do. 'I'll go and get a coffee, shall I?' I say.

One of them pauses and looks up. 'Oh, hello, Mrs Deacon,' she says. 'Mr Kazmi will be here soon.'

I raise my eyebrows in question.

'The senior registrar,' she says.

The other two exchange glances, as if I've stumbled upon a secret. I remember how nervous those sorts of visits made me, once.

'Should I wait?' I say.

Another ripple of embarrassment. 'Probably best to wait, yes,' she says. 'We don't want to miss him.'

I stand next to Michael. 'Better not skive off, then,' I say, 'you stay right here.'

He smiles, his mouth flattened against acrylic.

Two hours pass, in spite of the alleged imminence of the registrar's arrival. I have no appetite for the letters today. They keep up a constant clamour for attention but it's as ignorable as a party in a distant neighbour's garden. I retrieve a newspaper from underneath a pile of unopened books and skim old news without concentrating. Time slows. I have a circular conversation in my head about a broken fingernail. I explore it with the tip of my thumb and I remind myself, over and over again, to buy a file, to smooth the edge.

When he finally comes in, Mr Kazmi is preceded by a phalanx of nurses and the young doctor. They form a guard of honour as he approaches me. 'Mrs . . . ?' He glances at the whiteboard above Michael's head. 'Deacon, yes,' he reassures himself, as if I couldn't be relied on to give the right answer. He is small, plump, unhurried. Around him, the others are in perpetual motion. They look at him for only the briefest time before twitching away, as though he is too bright to be gazed at for long. 'How are you?' he says to Michael.

Still dying, I think.

'Let's get this mask off, shall we?' he says.

This galvanises everyone, and a job that would have taken one of them only a few minutes is shared out between them. The room stills afterwards. I miss the machine's hiss.

'Now, then, Mr Michael.' Kazmi speaks too loudly. His voice is clipped, and he lifts the end of his sentences, as though everything is in doubt. The nurses shift from foot to foot and stare at a blank space above the bed. The young doctor avoids looking at me. 'Do you know, Mr Michael,' Kazmi continues, 'that this machine cannot let you live for ever? It breathes for you now. Without it, you cannot breathe.'

Michael nods. His mouth is dry, and his lips are cracked. I want to let him sip some water, but the space between us is guarded by this small, loud man.

'You must decide yourself, Mr Michael, sir, to stop using it. When you do, you will not live.' He pauses. 'You are in control,' he says. His words swoop upwards, regardless of the fact that this is not a question.

Michael hasn't taken his eyes off his interrogator. You do realise, I want to say to him, that this man is telling you to decide when to die.

'Just one thing,' Kazmi says. 'It's Friday today.' He looks at the nurses. They nod in agreement. 'I am not here tomorrow. Or the next day.' He raises his eyebrows at Michael, as if he wants him to confirm the fact, too.

'I don't think the days of the week matter now,' I say.

Kazmi looks at me in surprise. 'But, Mr Michael,' he says, though he aims what he says at me, 'there will be no one here to supervise over the weekend. I am not here until Monday. The machine will be very uncomfortable for you by then.'

I know only too well that if a doctor tells you something will be *very uncomfortable*, they are warning you of intense pain. Or of procedures that feel worse than what they're trying to treat. This time, they mean they are predicting nothing else mattering except getting through to the end.

'Shall I leave you to decide?' he says, still as loudly as if he needed to reach the back of a lecture theatre. 'It is best that you decide soon.'

'I don't want the mask any more,' Michael says. He hasn't looked away from his strange confessor. I realise I haven't heard him speak above a whisper for some time.

'You are sure?' Kazmi has begun to assemble himself to leave. His work is done.

'Yes, I am sure,' says Michael.

'Then, Mr Michael, sir, I'll leave you,' Kazmi says, an operatic flourish of farewell.

The young doctor hovers in the doorway after the cortège has left the room. 'Do you have any questions?' he says.

How long? I want to say. After this struggle, will he have some days in peace? Or only hours? Can you actually *see* him? I want to ask.

'I'll be on the ward for a while,' he says.

I open two slats of the window blind between my finger and thumb. 'It's a nice day,' I say to Michael. 'In some ways,' I add.

He smiles. He seems brighter now, as if making the decision has freed him of the need to ration his energy.

'Are you afraid?' I say.

'Not of this,' he says. I sit down and take his hand. We never hold hands. The pose is awkward.

'Go and get your coffee, Moo,' he says huskily and although I prevaricate, I leave.

Two nurses walk down the corridor, just behind me. We're separated from time to time by people coming in the opposite direction but come together again without losing pace. It's as if we're all dancing, knowing the steps without thinking, keeping to the rhythms of our steady, living hearts.

I sit in the cafeteria. I'll get a drink in a moment. The queue snakes back past the biscuits and almost to the magazines. It vibrates with tension. Everyone who joins it comments, with or without words, on its length. Progress, I think, has not affected how frustrating it is to stand one behind the other, waiting. We have not evolved to cope any better than we did. I certainly have no more patience now. I remember how waiting to see if Adrian would appear later that day was tortuous. Ennui had settled on me like snow. It filled every corner of the house and my head. I went from room to room without purpose. I sat at the kitchen table and stretched my arms above me, feeling the discomfort as my spine lengthened, grateful for a physical response. If I had to be energetic, I hoped I could manage it. If Eddie was marooned halfway up a cliff, or too far out to sea, surely I'd be able to get to him, wouldn't I? If I needed to, surely I could swim. Or climb. Or run. I concentrated on making a fish pie, glancing out of the window from time to time to see if the car had arrived. To see if Adrian had come. I grated cheese and arranged sliced tomatoes on the mashed potatoes and tried to stop thinking about Bridget and whoever Richard was, going round a gallery supposedly gazing at the pictures, but really just looking at each other.

Even if Bridget's choice of dress was an odd one, it had perked her up. I couldn't remember the last time I'd shopped for frivolous clothes for myself. Michael had been amused to see me darning the elbows of an old jumper and he'd given me some money to get a new one before I'd even asked, but that was months ago. I looked down at my slacks; the knees protruded at an odd angle. I ought to get new trousers before buying anything prettier. Sarah and Eddie outgrew their uniforms before each term was out – I should consider that, too. I'd once come home with a little turquoise dress for Sarah, which I'd bought on an impulse from the charity shop by the bus stop. When she'd realised it was second-hand, she'd refused to wear it.

The telephone rang. Who on earth would be calling now? It wouldn't be Bridget this quickly, surely, unless she wanted to put in a date for her tryst and had stopped to find a call box. Or perhaps she was going to ask me if I'd mind covering up for her for an entire month, or even two.

'3262.' I stood in the hall with the phone wire stretched to reach my ear. I twisted the loops, threading them round each finger.

'Marion?' It was Michael. Had something happened to Eddie? Why else would he call me? 'How is your day?' he said.

I've made a fish pie. I bought some biscuits. My friend wants me to say she's with me while she stays the night with her lover. And I've been thinking about someone else all the time. Another man. 'Oh, fine,' I said. 'Nothing much to report.'

'I'm going to invite Don and Priscilla over, as you suggested. It's a good idea,' Michael said. 'What about Saturday week? It doesn't clash with anything, does it?'

'Just some bullfighting and a visit to the undersea world of Jacques Cousteau,' I said.

Michael laughed.

'No,' I said, 'it doesn't. Michael, can I get a new outfit to wear then, do you think? I know it's a bit daft, minding what I'm wearing when they come, but I haven't had anything new for ages.'

'Of course, you don't have to ask, Moo.' Michael cut across me. He sounded embarrassed by the request.

'I'll take myself into town, I think.' I felt my throat constrict with excitement. 'I'll probably go to Temple's.' In the musical of my life, I thought, the orchestra would come in here with a big, triumphant anthem.

'Good idea. See you later.' He hung up without saying goodbye. He'd never liked using the telephone, he regarded it only as a means of passing on and receiving basic information. He couldn't understand how Sarah could chat for hours with her school friends. 'What on earth do they talk about?' he'd say. 'They've been together all day.'

I wrote D and P in the little square for that Saturday's date. We'd eat at the dining table, I couldn't have them bunched up in the kitchen. That made me think of Adrian, his knees against the table. Everything made me think of him now. If Adrian hadn't come today, there would be reasons: good, solid reasons. It couldn't be because I hadn't been in his thoughts as much as he was in mine. I could not admit that he might not even have thought of me at all. I felt a clutch of panic at the image of him and Sarah in even a brief conversation. I inspected the sensation, gingerly edging towards the most appalling conclusion. Supposing he wanted her? With relief, as if I'd turned off the timer on a ticking bomb, I dismissed the idea. She was a child, only just past the age of hopscotch and stuffed toys. That's what he would see, too.

'Right,' I said aloud. 'Hair wash.' The bathroom cupboards were an assortment of shapes and sizes. Rubber things – hot-water bottles, the suckered mat for the base of the bath to stop babies slipping – were stuck together on one shelf.

There were spots of black mould on each surface. I squeezed the shower's little cups on to the taps and bent over the bath. I gritted my teeth as cold water pricked my scalp. Supposing Adrian came now? I covered my hair with a towel when I'd finished, twisting it like a turban, and hurried to the bedroom window. No car. There was someone standing there, though, looking up as if he'd been waiting for me. I darted my head back instinctively, but I knew I'd been seen. I looked out again, as if I meant it this time, and Tom Spencer waved and smiled. He put both hands in the pockets of his flimsy jacket and felt in them till he found a tightly folded piece of paper. He unfolded it carefully and held it up, but of course it was too far away to read. 'I'll come down,' I mouthed, pointing to the door below.

He nodded.

When I opened the front door, he was already on the step. He hesitated, holding the paper against his chest. 'Oh, Tom, what is it?' I said. He looked past me, obviously wanting to come inside. I sighed. 'Come in for a moment, then. I can finish this later.' I gestured to my head.

He looked at me as if he'd only just noticed the towel arrangement. 'Did you wash your hair?' he said. He followed me into the kitchen and sat down at the table.

'I'm being sponsored,' he said, looking hard at his paper. 'I'm going to walk ten miles and then I can give the money to the dogs.'

'That's a long way.' I extended my hand for the paper. He smoothed it out on the table before giving it to me. *Miles for Mates*, I read. *Support a Sponsored Walk to raise money for Man's*

Best Friend. It was illustrated with cartoon dogs walking on their hind legs and wearing hats. Below were several columns, detailing miles it was hoped would be achieved and the amount promised and by whom. So far, only his mother had added her name.

'Have you got a dog?' I said, getting up to look for a pen.

He shook his head. 'They're a lot of work,' he said. 'They need exercise every day and you can't just leave them and who's going to look after it if we go on holiday?'

I smiled at his recitation; someone had taught him well. 'That's all true,' I said, sitting back down. 'It's extra nice of you to raise money for them.'

'They're abandoned,' he said, without emotion. 'It's to find them homes.'

'Right, well, let's help then, shall we?' I wrote my name and matched his mother's offer. It was very low, but it would have seemed presumptuous to exceed it. I looked up.

He was staring at me. 'Is your hair all wet underneath? Can I see?'

I unwrapped the damp towel and ran my fingers through my hair. He watched passively, as if I were on a screen. Then he stretched out his hand and placed it on the top of my head. He held his palm flat against my hair. I stayed still for a moment, for several heartbeats, then I moved backwards in my chair. He pulled his hand away. He looked as fearful as when he'd touched my shoulder.

'I expect your mother does this,' I said. 'Washes her hair, then waits for it to dry.' I shook my head as if that would speed the process. My voice sounded too loud and too bright.

His nervousness made me feel sorry for him. I didn't want to pity him. I thought there were probably enough people feeling sorry for him already.

'Yes, she does,' he said, but I wasn't convinced he knew if she did or not.

'I'm going to make a cup of tea,' I said. 'Would you like one before you go?' The chair's legs scraping against the floor as I stood sounded aggressively noisy.

'No, thank you.' He began to fold the paper, carefully obeying the creases.

I shouldn't have invited him in, but he seemed so lost, somehow, and trying so hard to behave as he should. We listened to the kettle's accelerating roar together and he watched in silence as I ladled leaves from the caddy. 'We've got that spoon,' he said.

'What?' I looked down at the pink plastic spoon with a little teapot instead of a handle. 'Oh, this. It was a free gift,' I said, then hoped it wasn't offensive to suggest Molly Spencer didn't pay for things. 'Useful!' I said brightly.

To my relief, Eddie came in through the door in a whirlwind of flung blazer and dropped school bag.

'Can'avesomemilk?' he said, as if it were all one word. 'Hello,' he said to Tom, sliding on to the seat opposite him. He took the unexpected appearance of this person in his stride. Tom had the wary but tolerant look of an old dog with a puppy.

'How was your day?' I said. It was pointless to ask Eddie, really. When I asked him what he'd been doing, or even what he'd had for lunch, he could never remember. It was as if the school gates scrubbed away his day when he left, like a car going through the wash. Besides, he didn't connect the outside world with anything that happened at school. He knew he had to be there each day and that was enough.

'Fine,' he said.

He accepted my proffered glass of milk and bread and jam without comment. 'Thank you,' I said, putting my hand briefly on his head as though I were blessing, not correcting, him. When he set the glass down, he had a thick moustache of milk on his top lip. He wiped it against the sleeve of his jumper. He stared at Tom, the milky beads still shining on his arm.

'What's the matter with your head?' he asked conversationally.

Tom frowned. 'Eh?' he said. He twisted his jaw from side to side and each joint creaked.

'Mummy says you've got something wrong with your head. What's the matter with it?'

I felt as if the entire surface of my skin were being exposed to heat. Embarrassment flamed against my chest and head, scorching my back and burning the tops of my limbs. I knew my face was scarlet. The kitchen was entirely silent, except for the faint 'tock' of the clock on the wall.

Eddie breathed in as if he were about to ask something else, but Tom said, 'I'm slow,' before he could speak. 'I'm just a bit slow. I can manage.'

'Can you do sums?' Eddie ran his tongue over his upper lip to catch the last of the milk stain.

'I'm good at sums,' Tom said. 'And that is always a *useful skill*.' His slight emphasis on the last two words suggested he wasn't quite sure of their meaning.

'Can you read?' Eddie propped his elbows on the table, rested his chin on his hands and tugged at the skin below his eyes, exposing the pink inside his lower lids.

'Course. I'm not stupid. I'm only slow.'

'Have you read *The Wind in the Willows*? It's a chapter book. Miss Cargill is reading it to us at school. But I've got that book at home, too. And it's at school, as well,' he added, in case there was any doubt.

Tom shook his head.

Eddie looked gleeful. 'Would you like to borrow it? You can take my book. Mummy?' He looked enquiringly at me, animated by his plan. 'You can take it. It's quite long,' he warned. He was still in the habit of measuring his reading by density.

I watched Tom's face. His expression was neutral.

Eddie was not deterred. 'I'm going to get it. Stay here,' he instructed, including me in his last sweep of the room.

'Have you got time to wait?' As soon as I'd spoken, I felt foolish.

'I can wait a minute,' Tom said, as if he might well be busy later.

Eddie was gone for longer than was comfortable, but I didn't want to begin another conversation or start any task. I couldn't think of anything to say without referring to Eddie's embarrassing statement. I took tiny sips of tea from my mug, making sure I didn't empty it. Once or twice, I caught Tom's eye. His gaze was steady. I was the one who looked away. I was on the verge of offering him something to eat, to break the silence, when Eddie returned. He held the book close to him. I could tell he was reluctant to let it go now and that he was regretting his earlier generosity.

'Tom will bring it back as soon as he's finished it,' I said, sounding as positive as I could. 'Won't you?' I said.

'Yes, miss, I will,' he said. He took the book without a word and got up. 'Thank you for sponsoring me.' He put the slip of paper back in his pocket and went to the back door.

I watched him go. He held the book with no particular reverence. I looked round for Eddie, but he'd left the room. Moments later, he howled with disapproval as he discovered the dismantled toy farm. I heard him chatter to himself as he reassembled it.

I felt exhausted. Adrian obviously wasn't coming now. I thought of his coat sweeping the floor, his large presence. I wanted him. It was so long since I had felt desire that when it first fluttered, then swelled, I placed my hands just below my stomach as if I could actually feel something through my clothes. The stout Crimplene of my slacks was as effective as a muffler. I was being ridiculous. It was only happening because I hadn't really had a proper conversation with a man for ages. I was out of practice, that was all. Michael didn't count. Husbands didn't. Unless, apparently, they were someone else's.

With renewed enthusiasm, I set the table and put a pan of water on to boil. We'd have frozen peas with the pie. And I'd let everyone have as much tomato ketchup as they liked.

Chapter 40

Eddie climbed on to the sofa. He still had his shoes on, but it wasn't raining when he came home and he hadn't trodden in anything, so that was okay. He sat down facing the wall and shuffled until his bottom was against the cushions and his legs towards the ceiling. He lay on his back for several minutes, enjoying the different view of the room from that angle, then he raised his arms above his head and wiggled backwards until his hands and head touched the floor. With a grunt, he swung his legs over, too. Then he pushed his legs back on to the sofa in a clumsy headstand. It was close to doing a real one, he thought. Lots of people at school spent the whole of playtime tumbling against a wall, the girls' dresses falling to reveal their knickers. He couldn't imagine being brave enough to swap the soft cushions of this landing for real concrete.

You could still see tiny brown dots where the dog died in the hallway, if you knew where to look. Although his mother had scrubbed at it, gaps in the parquet flooring held on to the dried blood. They'd called the RSPCA, who'd come and rolled the little body into a blanket and carried it away. Eddie had felt a sense of privilege that he'd been in the same room as a living thing that stopped breathing. He'd elaborated on the story at school, until he'd almost come to believe his father had tried to save the dog's life – not just with his care and concern, but with actual surgery. The inevitable ending was still too sad to bear. He'd gone to the dustbin later and torn a strip from the bloodied newspaper the dog had lain on. From time to time he examined this trophy, noting with forensic concentration the way the colour deepened to a dark brown.

He tried not to believe in ghosts but his grandparents, long dead before he was even born, moved things in his room or troubled the hours before he fell asleep. He'd seen some pictures of them. Even though they didn't look much fun – in fact, they looked either sad or a bit cross, as if they knew they weren't going to be alive much longer – they looked normal in the photographs. But at night, they had skulls instead of faces and bleeding wounds which were visible through their clothes. He chanted times tables or sang hymns in his head to try to dislodge them. He whistled for the dead dog's ghost as he walked, though, in case dog ghosts were real, too.

Chapter 41

'How was choir?' I asked.

Sarah regarded me coolly. 'Okay,' she said.

'Nice pieces?' I said.

'I suppose so.' Sarah pushed some peas on to her fork with her knife. 'Something for prize-giving. 'Agnus Dei'. Then we start Christmas stuff. Descants for carols. Handel.' She lifted her mouthful carefully, keeping everything balanced.

'Handel?' Eddie seized on the word. 'Like door handle?'

Nobody answered him.

'I need a cardboard box,' he said, wiping one finger in the pool of tomato sauce on his plate and licking it. 'I've got to take one to school tomorrow.'

'What for?' I said. 'Don't do that, Eddie.'

'A project.' Eddie examined his finger for traces of flavour. 'I don't know. Making something.'

'You must have known before now, Eddie.' I sighed as I opened a cupboard to inspect the contents. I picked up and shook several packets in turn. 'Nothing's nearly finished.' I regarded a half-full cereal packet. 'I suppose you could take this and I'll find something to put the cornflakes in.' I pulled the cellophane bag free.

'You've definitely got some Tupperware,' Michael said. 'In fact, you bought enough from Franny to get her a car.'

'Yes, I did,' I said. My friend's brief sojourn as a saleslady meant that I'd bought pretty much every shape of container from her, out of loyalty.

'Here.' Michael carried several assorted, yellowing boxes. They were as scratched as if they'd been used for target practice in a quarry and smelled strongly of plastic.

'Cer-e-al,' Eddie said in a sing-song voice, examining the empty box. 'Do you 'member the pony contetition, Sarah?' Eddie upended the box and shook it. Fragments as fine as dust fell on to the table.

'Com*pet*ition. Stop making a mess.' Sarah stood up. 'Can I leave the table?'

'You were going to win a pony, 'member?' Eddie persisted. 'You said you were going to keep it in the garden. You said you were going to teach me to ride.'

Sarah ignored him. 'I've got homework. Can I leave the table, please?' She moved towards the door.

'Oh yes, I remember that.' Michael turned from the draining board where he'd been piling crockery. 'I'm surprised you do, though, Eddie. You must only have been about three. That's right, isn't it, Sarah? You were about nine or ten. That was pretty much a gymkhana summer. You wore a riding hat all the time, squashed over your plaits. Have you still got all your rosettes?'

'I suppose so, somewhere.' Sarah was almost out of the room.

I used to like doing her hair then, choosing ribbons, tying them tightly to stay in place over elastic bands. I was never very good at cutting fringes; Sarah's always ended up skew-whiff. Michael took Eddie to his barber these days, practically scalping him.

'I'm going to win one,' she'd said. 'All you have to do is answer some questions and then say why you love cornflakes. P'easy.'

'That can't be right,' I had said. 'Where does it say that?' And Sarah had shown me the carton, pointing at the leaping horse and the starbursts proclaiming 'Win' and 'Competition'. I had read the small print. 'It's just six riding lessons,' I'd said, watching her deflate with unhappiness. 'Not the whole horse.'

Sarah had burst into tears, utterly desolate.

Were my children having happy childhoods? I wasn't sure exactly what one looked like, but at least theirs didn't involve early death or drink. I was as kind to them as I could be. Keeping them fed and clothed was kindness, wasn't it? They seemed to be getting bigger and learning things without me having to do much about it, except not get in the way of their education and replacing their shoes as their feet grew. When was the last time I'd combed Sarah's hair?

'I want to learn to ride *now*,' Eddie said.

'Do you?' Michael said. 'You've never said that before. This one practically lived on a horse for a while, didn't you?' He smiled at Sarah. She didn't respond. 'More expense.' He rolled his eyes at me. 'Hey, Sarah, why don't you try winning us another horse?'

Sarah scowled, but she looked tearful, too.

'I'm teasing you,' Michael said, wounded. He looked across at me.

I ought to say something to support him and appease Sarah. I didn't speak.

'I don't want a horse any more,' Sarah said quietly.

'Sarah could teach me to ride.' Eddie turned to his sister, looking victorious.

'I'm not a bloody teacher,' Sarah said. 'I don't even go riding any more, in case you hadn't noticed.' She glared at Eddie.

'Language, thank you,' said Michael mildly. 'Maybe you could just pop Eddie on a horse down at the stables, so he can see if he likes it. You still know people there, don't you?'

'You *pop* him down there, if you want. I'm not doing it, I haven't been there in months.' Sarah left the room without waiting for a reply.

Eddie put both hands inside the box and waggled it from side to side.

'Careful,' I said. His turbulent hair seemed to grow from four different crowns, goodness knows how the barber coped. His uniform was scabbed on one sleeve where he habitually wiped his nose. His face shifted from baby to boy even in the seconds that I examined it. I couldn't see a man there, yet. 'Careful.' I took the box from him and bent to kiss the top of his head.

He ducked and slipped from the chair.

'Come and watch the telly with me, Eddie. Special treat,' Michael said.

I stood at the sink and ran the water too hot to put my hands into. I felt as though I were about to sit an exam I hadn't revised for. Michael hadn't induced this sort of trepidation in me. We'd met quite by chance, sitting side by side in the theatre. I was on a nurse's night out: productions that weren't selling well gave free tickets, on spec, to the nurses' home to fill out a sparse audience. I grabbed them when I could; it was fun seeing something unexpectedly and I liked dressing up and going out anyway. We'd watched a silly farce and caught each other's eye a few times as we'd laughed. He'd bought me a drink at the interval and then taken a telephone number before parting. My friend Ginny had knocked on my door a few days later and told me there was a call for me downstairs. 'Someone called *Michael*,' Ginny had said lasciviously, as though his name were synonymous with naughty behaviour. I had stood in the draughty corridor outside the housekeeper's office and, because the housekeeper doubled as both chaperone and prison guard, I'd tried to keep my answers short and unexciting. We'd arranged to meet for a walk, then went for tea at the Kardomah.

The next few weeks progressed along similar, chaste lines. I remembered feeling safe. The fact that Michael arrived when he said he would, commented pleasantly on my clothes without indicating he'd like to remove them in haste and delivered me back to the nurses' home well before my curfew, strengthened me. A port in a storm. If Michael was more of an English fishing village out of season than an exotic continental harbour it didn't mean I felt any less pleased to be on dry land. The years between us were comfortable, even approved. I had no curiosity about how he'd spent his youth. I imagined there had been other women, perhaps even other promises, but I felt no jealousy. I liked the way he seemed fully-formed, a grown man, by the time we met. He was well-groomed without any vanity and always dressed appropriately for the weather. He had the sort of easy-to-look-at face that you couldn't quite remember after you'd said goodbye.

He'd been courteous to my father, when I'd finally persuaded Stan to meet him. 'I just want to introduce you, that's all,' I'd had to yell into the telephone one afternoon. 'Yes, I *do* like him, Daddy. It's already been six months. No, of course I'm not pregnant.' I could feel the housekeeper's ears pricking up; my father's deafness was a great aid to her eavesdropping. Stan had arrived well before the required time for the assignation, which I knew was so that he could settle himself in my one and only armchair and remain there, otherwise he'd have to walk in and reveal how stooped he was, and how frail. He hadn't been that old then, but what the war had started the alcohol had nearly finished. Michael had understood the situation instantly, persuading him to stay put: *'This room's too small for all of us to stand!'* and talking at length about his own prospects, although I felt pretty sure Stan wouldn't have questioned him about them if he hadn't. I'd felt so grateful to him. We'd opened some whisky and used tooth mugs to toast each other. I had had to be quite vigilant about the amount my father wanted to pour.

When Michael proposed, after dinner at the Trocadero, I remembered being more concerned he got it over with than concentrating on what he said. He didn't go down on one knee, thank God, but the way he'd leaned across the table and proffered the Garrard's box had all the waiters circling.

Did he mention love? Surely he did, he must have done. He'd already asked my father for my hand (which must have happened when I went to the lav, as they hadn't been left alone apart from then) and then, a few weeks later, I'd met his parents over a Sunday lunch in Orpington. It was a good thing, I thought, pulling on rubber gloves and coaxing stiffened fish and potato from the plates, that I hadn't tried getting to know them – or indeed Orpington – any better than I did, as they'd both died within a year of each other and not long after the wedding.

There must have been grief, but I could only remember the practicalities of their deaths. There was a day after his father had died when we went straight from choosing curtain fabric for our new house to selecting a coffin. It was true that Michael had wept when he'd told me his mother had been found dead in the garden, but he was more full of saying how marvellous it was that his parents were together again than empty with his loss. My father had finally given up on life a few years after that. I had a photograph of him holding Sarah, as stiffly as a Victorian grandparent, the baby in a long christening gown. But even his death had been muted, like a sound from another room. I'd felt relieved rather than bereaved. He'd been a constant irritation in his premature old age, like a floating speck in the corner of my eye. We were both only children, Michael and I, and we'd benefitted from neat wills and savings in his parents' case and a surprising sum of money in my father's.

We'd blown some of it on a holiday in France. I remembered walking down a street there. It was after lunch and I'd eaten soft cheese on bread with a hard crust and a dense centre and curled, aromatic meat. I'd been wearing a kind of sundress, so it must have been quite early in our stay, because I'd got sunburned later and the straps had chafed. I'd felt entirely continental, which was remarkable to me. I'd never encountered foreigners in large numbers before. And that afternoon, in my light dress and with my belly full, I'd imagined I had acquired a sort of Frenchness. Until I caught sight of my reflection in a window, that is, and saw a plodding girl looking overcooked in unforgiving cotton. Even my gait was English. Michael had got food poisoning a few days later. We hadn't known you shouldn't open any reluctant mussel shells.

'All done? Well done,' said Michael, coming into the kitchen just as I dried and stowed the last dish. 'Thought I'd have some cheese and biscuits. You?'

I've just bloody washed up, I thought, annoyed at the prospect of more crumbs and dirty crockery.

He shook crackers on to a plate and cut himself a large slice of cheese. He smiled at me, ignoring the shavings of cheese on the work surface. 'These are a bit soft,' he said, biting into one as he went.

I folded over the waxy packet inside the box of biscuits as tightly as it would go.

France had smelled different. The cigarette smoke, the coffee, the scent of cooking that drifted across the pavements in the late afternoon: you'd never smell anything like that in England. It changed us as we inhaled; we'd even stayed in bed for most of one day.

We'd left Sarah with Michael's aunt for the duration of the holiday. I hardly knew the woman, but she'd been so insistent ('Oh, you don't want to travel abroad with a *baby*,' she'd said) that, despite the fact she hadn't had any children herself, we'd left our infant daughter in her care for two whole weeks. I'd never have left Eddie like that. I thought of how Sarah had clung to the aunt when Michael and I returned. 'Now, now,' the woman had said, disentangling the baby's little fingers from her cardigan, 'Mummy's home.' She didn't repeat the offer to care for her again. In fact, she'd got a dog soon afterwards and then claimed that Target or Tricket, or whatever it was called, couldn't really be trusted with children. We'd gradually stopped seeing her altogether.

Chapter 42

The telephone rang. I heard the television's volume increase as Michael opened the sitting room door and then, just as loudly, Sarah hurtling down the stairs and shouting our number into the receiver. She was still talking when I crossed the hallway, hunched away as I passed her then looked over her shoulder, waiting for me to leave.

'School friend?' Michael asked.

I shrugged. 'I suppose so.'

'What *do* they talk about?' he added, as I knew he would.

'You always say that,' I said.

'Do I?' said Michael. One wing of his shirt collar protruded over his jumper. He looked crumpled. I should go to him, tidy him, put my arms round him and say nothing. I felt as if I couldn't reach him.

'They rang us. It's not going on our bill, is it?' I said. 'She's not doing any harm.' I watched him react.

'But no one else can get through,' he said.

'Are you expecting an urgent call?' I said.

He looked puzzled and shook his head.

'Exactly. In fact,' I went on, 'I can't remember the last time anyone even rang here for you.' I could keep this up easily, and for hours.

'All right,' he said, after a pause.

'You don't even like talking on the phone,' I said. 'That's probably why you get so worked up about Sarah chatting away. It must be like hearing a language you don't speak.'

'It might well be, I'll have to listen more carefully,' Michael said.

'She's just young and having fun,' I said. 'Do you remember how that feels?'

'All right, Marion,' he said again. It was always his tactic, this way of calming me down by agreeing with me, not rising to the bait.

I felt infuriated. I also knew how ludicrous it was to make so much of something so trivial, but it was too late. 'You always sound so disapproving,' I said. 'No wonder Sarah never tells us anything.'

'What are you talking about?' Michael had a trace of anger in his voice.

'You still treat her like a little girl. All that teasing about cornflakes and horses. She's going to be into boys soon. You need to face it.'

'I don't think I'm avoiding anything, Marion,' he said quietly.

'You are,' I said. 'You never notice when she rolls her eyes at you, you look embarrassed when she's dressed up to go out. It was always going to be awkward for you when she started growing up, but you're going to have to admit she's not a child now.' It was like plucking a chicken: the more the feathers came away in my hand, the more I wanted to see of his pale, vulnerable skin underneath. Fight back, I pleaded silently. Save yourself. Save me, too. His expression was that of a parent who waits for a fractious toddler to exhaust itself. I felt as if I had been batting and swiping uselessly at a fly that buzzed, infuriatingly, just out of reach. Now I opened my hand to discover that I'd caught it with no effort at all.

We sat in silence until closedown. Michael got up and pushed the television's switch. We both watched the white dot disappear from the screen. He was coldly polite as we prepared for bed, filling a glass with water and setting it on my bedside table and wishing me goodnight before he turned off his light. He lay straight and stiff, as if there were a channel of deep water between us that he'd fall into if he shifted even a little. I felt buoyed up on a tide of my own irritation. I couldn't sleep. Michael was already snoring. I got up and tiptoed to the bathroom. Eddie's door was open; he had a nightlight, but he also liked a spill of light from the landing. I could hear the whistle of his outgoing breaths. I peered in at him. A floorboard creaked beneath me and he stirred, flinging one arm out across the blanket. I stood still, in case he'd heard me and woke, but he was as deeply asleep as if he were drowned and didn't move again.

I waited until the bathroom door was closed before I felt for the dangling string above the basin. The light was grey and spare. My face in the mirror was out of focus. The shadows made my mouth appear hollow and toothless. I gathered the brushed nylon of my nightdress and held it tight against my waist, outlining my breasts and hips in a parody of a screen siren's dress. I heard the click of a door opening nearby. I hesitated, alert and cautious. I switched off the light and felt for the door handle. Sarah stood on the landing; she looked surprised to see me.

'Night,' I whispered.

Sarah pointed towards Eddie's room. She held her finger to her lips in an exaggerated instruction to be silent.

'I know,' I hissed. I crept back into bed, where Michael maintained his board-like position, even in sleep. I heard the lavatory's flush, then Sarah's quick footsteps as she rushed back to her room. She'd want to be back under her covers before the cistern's final filling *clunk*. I knew it was one of her good luck charms.

Michael was still aggrieved the next morning. I countered with my own detachment. I saw Sarah hesitate in the doorway of the kitchen, registering the skirmish. I used to wait like that, to see if my father had already been drinking by this time in the morning. I'd watch for the tremor in his hands and if he held his cup steadily then I'd know he'd started. If he shook, trying to disguise it with careful and deliberate gestures, then he was sober. But we both knew that all he'd be wanting to do, all he'd really be thinking about, would be having a drink.

Michael and I hardly spoke to each other but Eddie chattered, oblivious. He was like a fully-wound clockwork toy that kept moving forward, despite any obstacles in its way. Michael got up and stood behind him, squeezing his little shoulders and bending almost near enough to him to kiss him on the top of his head, if he'd wanted to. 'Have a good day at school,' he said and let go. Eddie hunched his freed shoulders to his ears then pushed both his hands through his hair, leaving it upright.

Michael had nearly left the house when I hurried after him. 'Could I have some extra money, please?' I said. 'I thought I might go shopping today.'

Michael felt in his trouser pocket for his wallet. Taking out several pound notes, he counted them first to himself then into my hand. 'Enough?' he said, replacing the wallet without waiting for an answer. I blushed. He must have intended it to feel like a transaction. His thick, neat hair was combed and creamed into obedience as usual and his short, practical coat was his armour against the day.

'I'm sorry,' I said. His hand was on the door handle and he wasn't looking at me. 'Michael, I'm sorry. I was a pig.'

He turned round and I saw relief flood through him and soften his features. 'It's all right, Moo,' he said. There was a pause. 'You were probably just tired. Was Bridget good company yesterday? Did she have much to say?'

Bridget's round and glistening face bobbed in the corner of my memory like a happy balloon. 'The usual. Not much. There are some more puppies.'

'Oh, the puppies. *Never* agree to having one.'

'I won't. I've my hands full with you lot. I'll see you later,' I said, brushing at the shoulders of his coat.

When I was finally left alone, it was as if I'd been holding my breath till then, my ears bursting with effort and my lungs aching. I had a superstitious hunch that I had to earn any pleasure to come by doing what needed to be done first, but I was tempted to leave everything as it was, the plates unwashed and the milk bottle out of the fridge, like a domestic *Mary Celeste.*

Chapter 43

2 October

For once, I had a real reason – more than choir practice or being in the same lunch queue – to talk to Bobbie properly. It made me feel nervous and excited at the same time. Sometimes when I think of her, she's like the Jesus figure on my box, holding her arms out to me with streams of light behind her head. It was her hair I noticed first: it goes right down her back in thick, shining waves. When I was little, I often used to sleep with my hair wetted and rolled up in strips of cloth so that it would be curled by the next day. The rags circled my head in big lumps. They hurt whenever I turned over in bed. Mum told me that everyone suffers to look beautiful, but my curls only ever lasted till lunchtime.

Bobbie was standing in the front row of the Senior Choir when I first saw her, facing away from me. When she turned round, she was singing and smiling at the same time because the girl beside her had made her laugh. I'd never thought a girl was attractive before. Me and Lizzie make loads of lists of boys we fancy but we wouldn't ever dream of writing down any girl's names. I didn't fancy Bobbie, either, I just thought that I wanted to be her friend. I knew that I'd like to make her laugh like that. Now I can't remember when she didn't matter to me.

If you want to be with someone enough, you can make it happen. I started looking out for her, waiting to see which classroom she left at what time and where we crossed in the corridor. I didn't even want to speak to her, but I liked the silvery feel of a day with her in it. If she was away from school, if I didn't see her dark head in assembly, I felt as if everything were smudged and spoiled. Even Lizzie noticed after a while. She asked me if I actually wanted to be in the Upper Fourth with all those snobs. I said of course not, but I made sure I was more casual about getting closer to Bobbie after that. It was like playing Grandmother's Footsteps, no one could know I was creeping up.

Eddie was so annoying on the way to school yesterday morning, as usual. He's always dawdling or singing to himself or running ahead of me. Today he kept going on about wanting me to teach him to ride. I said I'd think about it, to shut him up, but then he wouldn't stop saying when and asking which pony I'd put him on. He yelled out that he wanted to ride Caramac or Nell. I said I'd put him on Rebel, which would serve him right. That pony hates everyone. When we got to the crossing, I walked off really quickly without saying goodbye. Then a car honked its horn behind me, and I turned round and saw it was because he'd nearly stepped into the road without looking. I ran back and really shouted at him. I know perfectly well that if anything happened to him, she'd never, ever forgive me.

They'd obviously had a row the other night because Daddy was looking very upset the next morning. The softer he seemed, the harder she got. She acts as if she's his mother sometimes and as if he's always in trouble. It's really easy to imagine him as a little boy. I've seen pictures of him and he still has the same round face as he did when he was young. His hairstyle hasn't changed either. He wouldn't need to look in the mirror when he combs his hair because the parting probably makes itself, even when he's just got out of bed. The only time I've ever seen him without it was when he went swimming on holiday. He dived under the water and when he stood up, his hair was slicked off his face, flat as sealskin.

I can't imagine her as a child at all.

I'm glad I didn't hear them arguing. What's worse, though, what's the absolutely vilest of all, is when I have to listen to them together. The first time it happened, I was reading in bed when I shouldn't have been. I was supposed to have my light out, so I flicked the switch off really quickly when I heard them. At first I had no idea what the noise was. I actually thought she was in pain, she made this little whimpering noise like an injured cat. Then I heard piggy grunting. When I realised what they were doing, I felt as if I were going to explode with embarrassment. No matter how hard I stuffed my fingers in my ears or hugged my pillow to my head, the sounds got in. Even thinking about it now makes me feel sick.

She nearly caught me reading once. I didn't have the light

on because I'd heard her coming upstairs but she held her hand over the top of the lampshade so she could feel the heat from the bulb. She didn't say anything, but she was looking as smug as if she was the cleverest detective, solving a crime.

Chapter 44

I took Michael's route to the station. I suspected that he followed exactly the same path every single day. His footsteps would wear a groove in the pavement by the time he retired. He had hardly ever taken a day off work. I could clearly remember the only time he'd been really ill. He'd shaken with cold one morning as his forehead burned and he keeled over on to the sofa, without saying a word. I was unnerved by his decline, he was so seldom unwell. I'd nursed him without much tenderness, tiptoeing into the bedroom to replace jugs of orange squash or provide aspirin. He was an undemanding patient, even as he convalesced: he didn't request so much as a newspaper and just lay staring at the ceiling. When I'd asked if he wanted anything, slightly exasperated by his passivity, he told me he liked just being in the house, listening to me go about my tasks or chatting to the children. It was delightful, he said, he could feel it doing him good. Perhaps he was trying to tell me that he loved me. Neither of us would ever have said it aloud.

The station platform was almost deserted. One other woman sat on the wooden bench, making her way through a large sandwich. The greaseproof paper on her lap was dotted with dropped tomato slices. You shouldn't eat anything in the street, I thought. Ice-cream cones or lollies were the only exception and then only in high summer. The woman compounded the breach by licking each finger in turn when she'd finished. She caught my eye and returned my gaze with some hostility. Beside her sat a small, plain child. My father would have said she had the sort of face that even the tender appointments of youth passed by. He had a good way with words before he drowned his conversation. There was one open carriage, already quite crowded, but I headed for the partitioned coach and found an empty compartment. I wanted to sit alone.

Walking through the town in the still-early morning made me feel as if I hadn't been there before. No one really knew where I was. Normally, I was so *accountable*. I hummed under my breath and walked quickly, ignoring the fact that I was wearing headmistress shoes and had a plaster on one heel.

The escalator to the first floor of the store was absurdly slow, moving at less than a walking pace. It was also narrow. I couldn't move past the two women already in front of me. They chatted loudly, undeterred by the restriction of being one behind the other. From time to time, the escalator stopped for a second then resumed its unhurried climb with a jolt. The women squealed in delight as they were jerked and thrown about. They thrust their hands dramatically on to the handrail and gasped with relief, as though they were being rescued from a shipwreck.

The racks of dresses looked as if they'd given up on ever being worn. They slipped low on their hangers. Two assistants stood near the till, engaged in conversation. Their voices were several notches above *sotto voce*. They registered my presence with a small shrug of their shoulders. 'I said to him,' one said, pressing on the already flattened edge of a ream of tissue paper, 'I'm going to look the length of the counter before making my selection. You're practically the first person I've had it off with, so I'm not going to stick with you, am I? Can I help you?' she said.

I was trying to prise a reluctant hanger from its moorings. 'Can I try this?' I said.

Like a successful miner, I'd spotted the golden seam of the dress beneath the silt. It had a print of tiny yellow flowers without stems. The front was ruched and smocked like a child's party dress. It was the new longer length, falling to mid-calf. The girl had a thick swipe of frosted brown eyeshadow on each lid, which gave her the look of an animal recently roused from hibernation. She gestured with half-hearted weariness to an area of little cubicles, their curtains held back on hooks. She hung the dress on the rail. The sense of sleepy despondence was infectious. The task of taking off my coat, never mind my skirt and top, now seemed Herculean, but I put my bag on the small stool and unhooked the curtain. The curtain stuck to my elbows as I shed my clothes. The girls' conversation sounded louder from in the cubicle than when I'd stood next to them.

There wasn't a mirror. I padded about in my bare feet to find one. I'd shucked off the headmistress shoes. The only mirror was in a far corner next to some wilting anoraks, but I stood transfixed the minute I saw myself. The gathering of the fabric over my chest had an extraordinarily flattering effect, which both softened and enhanced my shape. I was reminded of a book of fairy tales I'd had as a child. One of the stories was illustrated with a young woman, half fairy, half flower, rising out of the ground as though she were growing in a field. And here I was, half fairy myself, in a corner of Temple's, smiling at my reflection.

The girl approached. 'It looks lovely,' she breathed, but I didn't need her approval.

I thought of the other, the real, purpose of my visit. He wouldn't be there. I could have a cup of tea in the café, anyway, couldn't I? The whole store was covered with a layer of gloom, as if it had been draped with cellophane, as shop window displays are protected from harsh light. People moved without purpose between the counters and rails. It seemed ridiculous that Adrian, who could choose anywhere at all, would decide to come here. Perhaps I had misheard Sheila.

There were plenty of free seats. I chose a little stool right against the counter; it felt less obvious that I was alone if I faced the cake stands and sandwiches instead of an empty chair. There was a menu positioned at an angle in a small metal stand, its cover featuring a sketch of a cup with an elaborate rising coil of steam. 'Tea, please,' I said to the woman. She wore a green nylon overall. Embroidered over her left breast was the same cup and steam motif. She was large-bosomed, the cup was prominent, but the steam went backwards towards her sternum at an acute angle. I tucked the carrier bag against my ankles. I didn't really want to put it down. I held my handbag to my chest. The only other customers, a mother and daughter so alike it was comical, sat at a distance from me.

The overalled woman produced a small, stainless-steel teapot and miniature jug of milk, then clattered a cup and saucer in front of me. 'Cake?' she said, waving a pair of tongs over the Victoria slices and jam tarts.

I shook my head. The handle of the teapot was already too hot to hold. I gasped and rubbed my fingers in pain.

'Marion?'

When he spoke, I felt the world lift and settle, the movement of a small earthquake. Nothing was broken. It was awkward twisting round on my small stool with my bag clutched in front of me like a shield. Adrian seemed on the point of leaving, as though he had been looking for something he didn't expect to find. I blinked; it was hard to focus on him, since the fluorescent light behind his head made a halo of his hair. He looked at once in the right place and entirely at odds with it. He was wearing the same large, loose coat as before.

He spun the little stool beside mine and sat down. Our knees touched. 'Who is this tiny furniture made for?' he said.

I could smell the scent of him, sweet patchouli mixed with soap and smoke.

'Have you had any of this tea?' He peered theatrically into my empty cup. Then he looked at me. 'Have you had any lunch?'

'No. But I have to go soon,' I said.

'What time is it?' he said. 'I don't wear a watch.' His coat sleeves were pushed back from his wrists, rolled up into a thick band. He was wearing a watch.

I flushed, embarrassed for him.

He looked amused, seeing my quick, awkward glance away. 'This?' he said, extending his wrist and twisting it to show every side of the watch. 'This was my grandfather's. It hasn't worked for years. I wear it because I like it. It's right twice a day.'

I wanted to touch his arm, to turn the watch's face towards me. His knees were still against mine. 'It's twenty past twelve,' I said. 'There's enough time for lunch, if we're quick.' I gestured towards the counter. 'A sandwich or something?'

Without answering, he waved at the woman in green and beckoned her over. 'The bill,' he said. 'You are coming with me. We're not going to have sandwiches.'

'Where?' I said. 'I've got to get a train later, so I can't go too far.'

'What time do you need to be home?' He counted coins on to the saucer and added a tip so generous that I winced.

'Half past three,' I said, offering the absolutely latest time I could. 'The trains are every half an hour, so—'

He actually put one finger to my lips, to silence me. I felt the slight pressure.

'I am going to give you a lift,' he said. I thought of the return ticket in my bag, his extravagant tip. He spun his stool away from the counter with a flourish. 'Come on,' he said, taking the carrier bag from me. He feigned an effort, as though it were heavy. 'What have you got in here? Coal?'

I laughed. Outside, the streets were almost empty. 'Is it far?' I knew I sounded nervous.

'It's just beyond the ends of the earth,' he said. 'Or – it's just here.' He halted in front of a café. It was covered in scaffolding. Through the window, partly covered with a whitewash, I could make out chairs covered in dustsheets and pots of paint on trestle tables. A large banner reading 'Business as Usual' hung over the door.

'Good name for a caff, isn't it?' Adrian went in ahead, full of a confidence that suggested he'd been here many times before. 'Graham!' he said to the man approaching us, which dispelled any lingering suspicions.

'Mate.' The Graham man clapped Adrian on the shoulder. 'Hell-oo,' he said to me, rolling his eyes and drawing out the words in a Terry-Thomas sort of way.

'This is Marion,' Adrian said. Did he even know my surname?

'Marion. Oh, hello!' This time, he was more Kenneth Williams. 'This way, stop mucking about,' he said, steering us to a table. The surface was covered in a fine layer of white powder.

'Flour,' said Adrian, seeing me inspecting it. 'The whole place is quite tediously themed. Isn't that right, Gray? Random ladders and poles dotted here and there, pots of paint with their lids off scattered about, that sort of thing.'

'Oh no, oh no no no.' Graham offered this as Frankie Howerd. The chair was mercifully free of dust or nuts and bolts, at least. I sat down. The menu looked as if it were written on a jagged piece of torn cardboard. I picked it up. It was.

'Two omelettes, old thing,' Adrian said, not looking at the menu. He cleared a space on the dusty table in front of him and planted his elbows. 'And some red wine,' he said, without asking.

I smiled at him, not wanting to let him know that I seldom drank alcohol in the daytime. One other couple sat at a nearby table, their arms entwined in front of them. The man stroked the woman's bare elbows in large, sweeping circles. The white powder speckled their clothing. Adrian shucked his coat backwards off his shoulders, heedless of how it fell to the floor. Underneath, he wore a velvet jacket with bone buttons. The collar of his shirt was huge and spread out wide to his shoulders. The two top buttons were undone. He leaned back in his chair and swept his hair off his face with both hands.

'Have you been painting?' I said. I regretted the question instantly. Of course not, he'd hardly have wandered into Temple's dressed for a party if he'd been out in the woods.

He rubbed his scalp with his fingertips. 'No, I haven't,' he said. 'Ask me something else.'

'How many children have you got?'

'Unexpected.' He laughed. 'Three. You?'

'Two. You met them. Eddie. And Sarah.' I watched him, to see if he reacted to her name. Nothing changed in his expression. He stretched his arms behind his head and the fabric of his shirt clung to him. Sarah was miles away, trapped behind a school desk, imprisoned by timetables and rules. I am here, I thought. I am here.

'Course I did. My turn. What did you want to be when you grew up?'

'A teacher.' I wished I had a more exotic answer, but the truth would have to do.

He ran his tongue over his top teeth. 'That fits,' he said. 'And were you?'

'No. I was a nurse. For a while. Until I got married . . .' I said. 'It gave me somewhere to live, because . . .' I hesitated, wondering if I should tell him anything he hadn't asked. 'Because my mother had died when I was thirteen and my father sold the house.'

'Marion.' He righted his tilted chair and leaned towards me. 'The poor little motherless nurse. There *is* something of the orphan about you. Or are you still fathered?'

'He's dead now, too, but I don't think you're really an orphan when you're adult, are you? Are both of your parents still alive?'

'God, yes,' he said, sitting back again. 'Horribly. Both sides of the family seem to go on for ever, worse luck. Ah!' He greeted the arrival of our food with an expansive opening of his arms. 'Omelette, *merveilleuse*. *Merci*. *Scusi*.' He got up and went to the entwined couple's table. 'May I? Thank you so much.' He took their salt and pepper without waiting for a reply. I watched them enjoy his charming carelessness.

When I sliced into the omelette, its centre was still wet and raw. I separated a small cooked portion from the very edge and chewed it nervously.

Adrian put a dripping forkful into his mouth. 'Ta,' he said

as the wine arrived. 'Cheers,' he said, holding up his glass. 'Let's drink to – adventure.'

'Adventure,' I said, clinking my glass to his. 'What sort of adventure?'

'Ours.' He looked straight at me. 'We're going to have one.'

'Are we?' I felt light-headed after only one sip. I watched him demolish his food with gusto. I swallowed some more wine, trying to keep up with the rapid tempo he set. My head already buzzed.

'I think we are. Don't you?' Adrian tore a bread roll in two and swiped one half over his plate; strands of clear albumen swung from it as he lifted it to his mouth. 'You've hardly touched yours,' he said, seeing me flinch.

'The only thing I can't eat is . . .' I pointed at the viscous yellow pool. 'It's too raw.'

'Oh, God, I'm so sorry. I never even asked! I'm terrible. Do you forgive me?' He clasped his hands in mock penitence, bowing his head and looking up at me. His hair fell forward over his eyes.

'Stop it, you silly thing,' I said. I wanted to reach over the table and touch his face. He finished his wine in two more gulps and signalled for more. Graham was leaning against the bar; his cheesecloth shirt had ridden up, exposing his pale stomach as he waved back. I needed the lavatory. Where was it? I stood up quickly, feeling pleased that I didn't sway as I walked away.

'Wee girl's room?' Graham seemed to have a Scottish accent now, but I wasn't sure who he was supposed to be. He pointed to the far corner. 'Doon the stairs,' he said. 'Mind yer heid.'

There was no banister, but the stairway was narrow. I spread my arms and patted the walls on either side as I went. I descended with care, planting both feet together on each step before proceeding. It reminded me of Eddie, learning to walk. There was only one cubicle, marked with the signs of the zodiac. The building site theme hadn't reached this far. 'Oh well,' I said aloud. When I sat down it seemed a good idea to bend forward from the waist because my head was very heavy. I righted myself with difficulty. I leaned back and gasped as my spine met cold plastic behind me. Someone had written: *'There are a lot of cunts in here'* in tiny, neat writing on the back of the door. Adrian was a long way away, up a lot of troublesome stairs. I peered into the little mirror above the basin. In the dark space, I could barely see my face, but I thought I had a film-star glow; my lips looked fuller and my eyes seemed brighter than usual.

'Find everything you need?' Graham's own speaking voice was light and colourless. I half smiled, looking past him to where Adrian sat, the second glass of wine already half finished. 'He's still here, don't worry.' He jerked his head in Adrian's direction. 'You are a lucky girl. He doesn't always stay.' His face had an unnaturally smooth patina, as though it had been oiled. He was very narrow, and his thin shirt had two raised points on either side of his neck where it had been hung on a wire hanger. The triangles of his bony shoulders and the lifted fabric made me think of a lizard.

As I walked past Adrian, he brushed one hand lightly against my hip.

The bill sat on a saucer, weighted down with a screwdriver. He picked it up then made the face of a bashful child. 'You won't believe this,' he said in a stage whisper, 'but I've come out without enough cash.'

I thought of the large amount he'd given the tea bar waitress. Was this a fib? Or some sort of test? Couldn't he have asked Graham to put it on tick? 'Don't worry, I've got some,' I said. I opened my bag, momentarily worried about how much money I actually had. Despite all the mateyness, Graham had charged us quite a lot. The uneaten food was congealing into plasticity. I hadn't touched my second glass of wine, but it was now empty.

Adrian followed my gaze. 'Didn't think you'd want it.' He had a little-boy simper. 'You're already quite pink. Sorry about the cash, sweetie. My turn next time.'

I counted out the money on to the plate, reluctantly giving up a five-pound note. The other couple had left the café and Graham was on the telephone by the bar, dipping in and out of Ted Heath and Alf Garnett as he spoke.

Adrian reached over the table and caught my wrist. 'I'm sorry,' he said, his voice serious and quiet. 'I know you've got to get home. I was just having fun. This has been a bit of a disaster.'

'No, no,' I said, 'I had fun, too. It's just I do have to get back and I'm sorry I didn't like the omelette. I'm sorry that wine makes me go red.'

'When we've finally stopped saying sorry to each other, we can have a proper conversation, can't we?' He still held my wrist. 'Marion, Marion' – he was leaning very close to me now – 'you're gorgeous.'

I looked round, fearing Graham's further scrutiny and his comments. This would be a perfect opportunity for his Danny La Rue.

'He's not here,' Adrian said, following my gaze. 'Probably gone out the back to pour vinegar into the wine bottles. You know what,' he said, 'I'd like to paint you.' He held my gaze. 'I want you,' he said.

Cold liquid sluiced through my veins. My fingers tingled. Adrian was outlined in sharp relief against the draped and shrouded chairs and battered tables. His words were as light as air. They settled and shook like a bird on a branch. I swayed with pleasure where I sat. When I stood up I was taller, stronger. I would kiss him soon. I would hold his gaze as I touched him, until the only name in his head and on his lips was mine.

Chapter 45

3 October

I didn't want Eddie to tell Mum about the car that had nearly hit him. I couldn't help imagining him all mashed and broken and me not even being allowed to cry about it, because it would have been my fault. I said why don't we play with the doll's house together. I moved it into his room ages ago. He said it was a girl's thing, but I know he likes arranging the rooms and sitting the figures on the little chairs. He didn't even pretend not to want to, so I sat cross-legged next to him while he made the doll's house people talk to each other. Sometimes, he just turned round and grinned at me. His two front teeth on the top and bottom are huge next to the baby ones beside them. It makes him look extra happy when he smiles.

I keep thinking about Bobbie walking across the playground towards me last week. I can still see her swinging hair and the way she looked as if someone had just told her a funny story and she was going to burst out laughing. She said it was groovy that her dad came to my house. I wanted to say it was amazing when he said her name. I wanted to tell her that my mother had made me want to blow up at her because of the way she carried on about him after. Bobbie told me that her dad had a habit of collecting people. She said he likes to make connections. She made it sound as if they'd slot together as easily as Lego bricks.

It wasn't like that. The more they'd stared at each other, the more I could see that they shouldn't ever be alone. They made each other look jagged and awkward. They were the exact opposite of a perfect fit. But all I could do was open and close my mouth like a fish, while Bobbie went on as if it was normal for our parents to fancy each other.

I wanted to say if he collected anyone, he'd collected me, instead. I'm the one who could stop him getting to my mother. And I will.

Eddie made a terrible smell. He laughed loudly when I scrambled to my feet waving my hands in front of my face. He said he was King Pong and started jumping from his bed to the floor like a monkey, beating his tiny chest.

Chapter 46

I sit with my coffee in a corner of the hospital café. I feel guilty at being away from Michael. I am failing to make these moments count. The coffee is bitter and thin, barely concealed under a layer of temporary froth. Someone has left a magazine. I flick through the pages, trying to find a story I could discuss with Michael. Something simple and uninvolving. It's as if he's a tourist I need to entertain but we don't share a common language. I reach back over the years to that street, to where Adrian and I are walking together, him half drunk with wine and me full of wanting him. Look at me then, as full of purpose as a novitiate nun, with only one idea in my head: to be standing between this man and any other woman. Obscuring his view. Keeping my own daughter out of his sight. I note that I wore selfishness next to my skin and a matching coat of unkindness. I whisper in my own, young ear: *Wait. This won't last. Wait. It will all resolve without you. Don't you see what will happen?* The young woman who was me answers, as I know she will: *Yes. But I will not stop. Can't you feel how alive I am? Do you want me to walk away from all of this now, from the rush and roar of possibilities, the energy and dazzle of desire?* Everything will run away from me later, as fast as a ball down a hill, but I can't deny I set it in motion. And if I held my life in my hands again, knowing the steep curve of the slope as well as I do, I know I would still let it go and watch it roll.

Just that one glass of wine was enough for me to have to concentrate hard on even simple functions. When Adrian opened the car door, I had to pause to remember exactly how to get in and where to tuck my feet. I sat holding my bags on my lap, feeling awkwardly folded. Adrian leaned his arm across the back of my seat as he reversed. The gesture had an extraordinary effect: it was as if his arm and my insides were connected, and there was a pulling sensation above my thighs that melted hotly upwards. I wished we could go backwards all the way to my house. I clutched my possessions. He frowned slightly each time he changed gear. He drove fast, hardly glancing at junctions, not pausing before he turned. As we got nearer the house, I felt a sudden panic. 'Just here,' I said, two roads before my own. He looked over at me but slowed down without replying.

'Thanks.' I fumbled for the handle. He leaned across me; his arm reached over my bag, but it was in the way. 'Sorry,' I said, pushing everything to the floor.

He smiled. 'It's a bit fiddly, isn't it?' He released the catch, and as I bent forward to retrieve my things, he collided with me and for a moment I felt the warmth of him, precise as a brand.

'I could come over tomorrow,' he said. 'Can I see you then?'

When I was little, I had a doll with a long dress and a happy face. When you pulled up its skirt, instead of a pair of legs it had another body and a face with a sad expression. I have a choice, I thought, between my two selves now: under one skirt I was entirely neat, my future mapped and bland, under the other I was becoming a little unravelled. 'Yes. Yes, you can,' I said. And I smoothed my skirt over my married life until it was completely concealed from view.

'Tomorrow, then,' Adrian said. He looked away from me. 'Oh, hello,' he said.

I followed his gaze. Sheila was walking towards us. She was still quite a distance away, but I knew that she'd be taking in the stopped car, the open door, the two of us side by side. Adrian put his hands on the steering wheel and raised his fingers in a small gesture of greeting. Sheila waved back.

'Oh God,' I said.

Adrian laughed. 'Mind if I leave you to it?' he said. He started the engine.

I scooped my things from the footwell then got out, holding my bags to my chest. He closed my door. He didn't mouth any goodbyes or even look back as he drove away. Sheila turned to follow the direction he travelled and waved again. Then she swivelled swiftly round to where I stood and started walking towards me.

'Temple's!' she yelled. She was still too far away for conversation. She pointed at my bag. 'You went by yourself! Although I see you didn't come home by yourself.'

I felt the beginnings of a headache behind my eyes.

'No, I bumped into Adrian. Which was lucky, as I'd missed my train. And he was already planning on driving this way.'

Always tell the truth, my mother used to say, *it's so much easier to remember*.

'Was he? That *is* lucky.' Sheila plucked at the carrier bag. 'What did you buy?'

'A dress.' I held the bag closer, as if Sheila were about to grab it from me.

'Let me see,' said Sheila, and she snatched it away, just as I had feared she would. She peered into the bag. 'Lovely colour.' Sheila looked at me then back at the bag's contents. 'I think it's very brave to wear floral prints with English colouring. Did you show it to Adrian?'

'What? No, no.' I tried to take the bag from her, but Sheila was pulling the dress half out of it. It looked very flimsy. Had it been that translucent when I tried it on? I decided not to wrestle with Sheila in case it tore. 'I thought it looked pretty, but I only tried it on very quickly.'

'No need to worry,' Sheila said with the briskness of a nurse completing an examination. 'You'll fill it nicely.'

'I'd better go . . .' I said, nodding ahead of me.

'Oh yes. Mouths to feed.' Sheila suddenly jabbed at my face.

Clasping my bags to me, I couldn't defend myself and recoiled.

'Steady!' Sheila said. She sounded cross. 'You've got something white on your cheeks.' She sniffed at her fingers. 'What is it? Flour?'

'I don't know,' I said, trying to free a hand to brush away the evidence. I wouldn't put it past Sheila to spit on a hankie and scrub me clean.

Sarah was already sitting at the kitchen table. She looked up briefly when I came in and grunted a greeting but looked up again quickly when she spotted the bag.

'Your reaction just then was pure Lucille Ball,' I said, shrugging off my coat. I noticed a patch of powder on the top of each sleeve and rubbed them together surreptitiously to disperse it.

'Who?' Sarah continued to stare at my shopping.

'Lucille Ball. She's queen of the double-take.' I had done the best I could with the rubbing, I couldn't see any white marks any more. 'Eddie not home yet?' I tried to sound casual.

'You've been to Temple's. Christ! Couldn't you have waited? I *said* to you I wanted to go there and get a proper bra. I *said*.' Sarah's face was childish with annoyance. It was true. 'I'm still wearing a stupid training bra,' Sarah had hissed from one side of the airing cupboard door as I folded towels on the other. '*Please* will you buy me another one? A proper one?'

I had said of course I would but had done nothing about it. It would mean looking at Sarah's breasts in the confines of a changing room. I'd recently caught sight of her by accident, when I'd gone into the bathroom without knocking. 'Get out!' she'd said, sitting up abruptly, sending waves splashing over the side of the tub. She'd reached for a flannel and held it over her chest, but I had seen her nipples, as pink as raspberries, and her breasts set high on her creamy body.

'I will get you a new one. This weekend?'

'What did you get, then?' Sarah eyed the purchase with suspicion.

I didn't want to confess. 'I'll show you later, shall I? I'll put it on after supper.' I tried to leave but Sarah was on her feet.

For the second time that day I tried and failed to prevent someone taking my precious parcel from me.

'What's this?' Sarah held the dress aloft. If it had seemed fragile in Sheila's hands, now it looked shrunken, too, a doll's garment. Sarah held against herself. 'A midi dress? Is this for you? Tragic,' she said. 'If I wore this, you'd tell me I was going to attract the *wrong sort of boy*. When are you going to wear it?' Sarah still sounded pitying.

'Dad's boss is coming to dinner. I thought it would be nice to—'

'You're not going out in it, are you?' Sarah cut me off. 'I suppose you could wear something over it.'

'Good idea.' I took the dress away.

'What's that stuff?' Sarah wiped her index finger against my neck. 'You've got some powdery stuff on your neck.' My hands flew instinctively to my throat. How on earth had the flour spread so much?

'I was going to do some baking,' I said. 'But then I decided to go into town instead.'

'After you'd weighed the flour?' Sarah said, still investigating my skin.

'All right, Perry Mason.' I wanted to move away but Sarah leaned in further.

'Breathe out,' she said, frowning.

'What?' I tried not to exhale.

'Breathe at me,' Sarah commanded, her nose close to my mouth, then she said, 'Alcohol!' She sounded both triumphant and perturbed. 'You've been *drinking*.'

'I bumped into a friend. She was shopping, too. Just one

glass. It seemed like a good idea.' *Tell the truth,* my mother said, *it's easier*.

Sarah looked incredulous, as if I had claimed I'd been dragooned into working a shift as a barmaid. When she sat down at the table again, I thought I saw, unaccountably, the bright flash of tears.

Eddie arrived home. He shrugged his blazer and bag to the floor, his gaze fixed on bread and jam. I watched him eat with the same pure pleasure that he took in clearing his plate. The straight lines of piping on his blazer and the stripe of his jumper were at odds with his crumpled socks and tangled tie. 'What did you need the box for?' I said.

'Dunno. What's kwontine?' Eddie arranged the crusts to form a letter. 'E for Eddie,' he said, looking pleased with his creation, then he ate it.

'Kwontine? I don't know, haven't heard of it.'

'It's a place. Paul Thorpe's there. It means he doesn't have to be in school. I want to go.'

'Oh, *quarantine*. That's when you're not well, Eddie. You don't want to go there.'

'A Roman fort,' Eddie said. 'That's why I needed boxes. I made a good one.'

By this time tomorrow, I'd have seen Adrian again. I wanted to say his name, shape the word in my mouth and hear it aloud. Sarah was reading, the book held close to her face. She hadn't looked at me since Eddie's arrival, she'd made a show of getting a textbook from her bag and studying it.

'Let's go to Temple's this weekend,' I offered. Sarah didn't look up.

'I can't. I've got a shift at Orion's, then Lizzie's party. No time.' She spoke from behind the book.

I heard the snub. Every other Saturday, Sarah sorted stock or weighed dog biscuits at the grocer's at the far end of the village. 'Next weekend, then.' I waited for a response.

Sarah shrugged. 'Okay,' she said, at last.

The carrots in the vegetable basket were limp with age. I peeled them with difficulty as they bent away from the knife. I separated a string of pink sausages from each other with scissors and pricked their casings with a fork.

My headache was worse.

'Sausages!' Eddie said at suppertime and prodded one. 'They're a bit black,' he said, revealing a charred side.

'Never mind,' I said.

'What's that?' Michael said as I got up to clear the plates. He came and stood beside me, holding my hair to one side. 'You've got flour on your neck,' he said.

I was so thoroughly marked, I might as well have been tarred and feathered.

'It was probably because she'd been drinking.' Sarah waited for both of us to turn to her. She didn't have to wait long.

'Drinking?' Michael said, just as I said, 'Hardly!'

'When?' Michael said. He sounded disbelieving.

'I bumped into a friend,' I said. 'By chance. She suggested we just have the one.'

'Who?' said Michael, which was a reasonable question. They were all staring at me.

'Ginny.' I named an old nursing friend. 'She always liked a drink.' Poor, blameless Ginny. We were on Christmas card terms at least. *Another year gone!* we'd both write. *We must meet up!* We hadn't actually seen each other for years.

'What was she doing round here?' But just as I was searching for an answer – perhaps Ginny could have been visiting a relative? – Eddie clattered his plate to the floor where it broke. The pieces spun away from each other over the lino.

Thank God, I thought, kneeling at once and busying myself with collecting fragments of china.

After supper, I made a mug of tea and took it to Michael. I put a couple of the biscuits I'd bought for Bridget on a little saucer. Of course, I could have told him that I'd bumped into Adrian. I could have made the whole episode sound foolish – *You know how much I hate undercooked omelette. And his awful friend kept doing terrible impressions. Then I was really worried about being home on time so I had to get a lift in his silly car* – but instead I hugged what had happened to myself, breathless with excitement. I felt as if I were only superimposed on my life and could be peeled away. I could be lifted from everything that suffocated me. I could be placed somewhere else, somewhere more exciting. The carriage clock wheezed eight o'clock with a trill of little bells. I'd hoped it was later. Time had slowed to a crawl. Adrian still wouldn't be here in twelve hours' time.

'Not like you, drinking at lunchtime,' Michael said. His tone was mild. He kept his eyes on the television. 'Where did you bump into Ginny, then?'

'Near the station. I was on my way home.' Was my voice trembling? I didn't seem to have quite enough breath for normal speech. He pulled at the sleeves of his jumper. It was as if we didn't know each other very well.

'Going for a drink on a weekday is a bit odd,' Michael said. 'But I suppose it's because it makes me think of your father.'

By the time Michael and I had met, the story of my father's drinking was in the past tense. Michael hadn't had to put up with his weeping self-pity, his staggering steps as I attempted, once again, to walk him home, after every cab had refused us. I had hidden empty bottles in various bins and skips round London and tried to conceal plenty more full ones from him, too. He'd resented my interference and mocked my sympathy. I'd told Michael something of what had happened, of course, but I'd edited my account. No one else needed to know about rinsing vomit-soaked sheets in hotel basins or hearing my father wailing my name outside my boarding school gates when he'd turned up, angry and dishevelled, insisting that I let him in.

Coming home late after one glass of wine was hardly in the same category. 'Shorry, Michael,' I said, slurring like a stage drunk, 'it was only one lickle drink, I shwear.'

'Which one is Ginny?' Michael said, unsmiling. 'I don't remember her. I didn't know you'd kept up.'

'We haven't, really. Christmas cards and the occasional letter.' I felt as if I were shrunken, scuttling round in the corridors of my own head, trying to find a safe door to open.

'How is she, then?'

'Oh, fine. I don't think I'll see her again, though. We don't have that much in common. She's – a bit lost. Actually, I think she's having an affair.' Why on earth had I said that?

Michael frowned. 'Did she tell you she was?'

'Not in so many words. She hinted at something. I wasn't really listening, to tell you the truth. I wanted to get home.'

'Sounds grim. Poor you.' Michael was back on solid ground, reassuring me. Behind him, the doors of my secrets rattled, but stayed shut.

'Lesson learned,' I said brightly.

Awake next to Michael that night, I felt him shift on to his side. He leaned over and pulled my shoulder, turning me to face him. He muttered something. I didn't want him to speak. I slid my hand down on to him, my eyes still closed. I loosened the cord at his waist then, as I always did, I let go at once. He moved away, and I waited for the soft click of the bedside cabinet as he fetched what he needed. He rose on one elbow and I heard the packet tear. He breathed out hard as he rolled above me. His cotton pyjamas were at half mast. He finished what he had started and afterwards he lay on his back, one arm draped across me like a sash. The awful thing wasn't that I'd lied to him, I thought. It was that I'd wanted to.

Chapter 47

4 October

Bobbie was late to school today. I was looking for her when we all lined up at first bell and when I didn't see her, it made me shake with nerves in case she was away. Miss Mertaugh shouted at me for being dozy and when I turned round my form queue was miles in front of me and I hadn't noticed them move. When I'd told Bobbie yesterday about her father coming to my house, she was okay with it. She might decide that she isn't, after she's had a chance to think about it. I'm not going to tell her about sitting in her father's car. I need it to be a secret from everyone. The way he looks at me is different from anyone else. It makes me feel funny, like something squirming inside me. Last night, when the phone rang, I nearly broke my neck to get to it because I thought it might be Bobbie, even though I haven't given her my number. She might have got it from someone else. It wasn't, of course, it was Debbie, trying to find a party to go to on Saturday. She kept saying do you know Greg and can you get us into his?

Bobbie was there at lunchtime. I bumped into her accidentally on purpose and acted all surprised to see her, as if I hadn't been wishing the day away because she wasn't there. She was with her crowd. They roll up their skirts at the waistband and wear knee-length white socks over their tights. Bobbie has these shoes that are dark blue and shiny, with white piping all the way round. She said that I should come to a party with her and her boyfriend Jeff. I could see her lot all thinking why does she want to hang around with a Lower Fifther? She said that our parents are friends which was so much bigger than the truth. They separated a bit to let me in then. There were five of us, sitting round one of the tables in the dining room.

One of the girls looks as if she'd run into a hedge of red hair and her face had got stuck in the middle of it. She said she'd seen me in Orion's and was that my Saturday job. When I went in about the Assistant Required card in his window, Mr Jobson asked me if I was sure I wanted to work there. He said surely I'd rather be somewhere more glamorous like Chelsea Girl. Nothing cheers him up. He greets everything from deliveries of seed to people buying dog food with equal sadness. Mrs M says the Brontë parsonage was full of *dolour*. Mr Jobson is *dolorous*. You could weigh *dolour* out like grain at Orion's, there's so much of it around. I like the brown and grey of the shop. My overall and the walls and most of the stuff on sale are all the colours of mud. There's no need for me to do anything except weigh things accurately and count out the right change. I don't have to chat to Mr Jobson. We always work together in silence. He never asks me any questions. He gives me my wages in little dun envelopes.

I said I just did it for the money and it's really boring. I felt very disloyal. The hedge-haired girl said she understood and she felt sorry for me, maybe I'd get to work somewhere more funky soon. I took up my space among Bobbie's friends as if I really belonged there. I joined in the conversation as if I always did and pretended I knew all the boys they were talking about.

I think Tom Spencer might actually be waiting for me these days. He was at the parade of shops again, his big hands in the tiny pockets of his check jacket. I ignored him, of course, but he came up and hissed that he'd seen them in the man's car. I said I didn't know what he was talking about. I called him a cretin and I gave him a look that made him run away like a mouse disturbed in a larder.

Not only did Mum go to Temple's without me, although I'd *specifically* said I needed to go, but she'd bought herself a dress, too. It's really tarty, covered in flowers and smocked tightly all over the chest and it's midi length, which she's way too old for. I felt like asking why she hadn't gone to the charity shop to get herself something, which is what she'd thought was good enough for me. The idea of someone else wearing something before you wore it is gross. Another person could be eating and farting and having arguments and worse while they had it on. If you put the cloth under the microscope afterwards and examined the fibres, you'd probably see their whole life there, still clinging to the fabric, wriggling around.

I could hear her bashing saucepans and crashing china while she was making supper. She'd met a friend in town and gone drinking with them, which is tragically pathetic. She had dots of flour all over her too. She only uses a cake mix, if she ever bakes at all. She sang: 'You Are My Sunshine'. It sounded naked without any harmony. I thought of Eddie in the bath with a white wig of bubble bath, holding his notes against mine with all his might. You couldn't see yourself in the little mirror on bath nights, it was always completely steamed up by the time we were dry.

I'm going to try on her dress. I'll whirl around in it as if I'm the little ballerina in my jewellery case. Or I'll clomp about with my hands on my hips, like a farmer's wife in a field. Whatever I do, it'll look better on me. Fact.

Chapter 48

At playtime, Eddie went and sat on the bench that had the girl's name on it. *Stella Lincoln. She loved this school*, it said. Neil Piper said she'd died in an accident, but Eddie couldn't think how you'd be killed falling off a bench. Neil said it was haunted. It would take a really noisy ghost to be heard above the noise of everyone skipping and running, being as free as possible before the bell rang. His class teacher Miss Cargill was on duty. She was holding a mug of tea, her fingers folded round it as though she was cold. Her actual name was Esme. He'd heard his mother say it. He worried he might call her Esme one day, by accident, instead of Miss Cargill. It was a huge responsibility that sometimes stopped him saying anything at all, just in case.

He thought of the horses. His horses. He could hear the beat of their plastic hearts and the clop of their hooves. He'd only been on a real pony once, at the fête. He'd sat there obediently as the pony was guided round a small circle by a bored girl in a green all-in-one suit, but he was willing her away, wishing he was alone. His father had lifted him off at the end, after only three short circuits, and he'd grabbed at the dense, grassy mane in an effort to stay put. The girl had shouted a lacklustre instruction to let go. The pony had turned its beautiful head towards him and snorted. He closed his eyes so that he could remember the animal moving underneath him and between his legs, swaying him from side to side in a great, rhythmic roll. His fingers ached now to grip leather reins. Sarah had only wanted to jump neatly over red and white striped poles and stick another rosette on her wardrobe door. But Eddie was a cowboy. He thought, with some certainty, that he already knew how to ride.

He examined a scab on one knee. He traced an outer ring of new, pink skin around the stubborn brown centre with his forefinger then hooked his fingernail where the crust loosened. Although he could feel pain as he lifted and pulled at it, the edifying spectacle of the gummy crater he was revealing was enough reward. A single dot of blood emerged where the scab had stuck most firmly, like a small, red protest, but it congealed at once in the open air. Sitting back on Stella's memorial, Eddie chewed on his trophy. When the bell rang, he slid it into his cheek for later.

Chapter 49

Michael's room is warm with a dry heat. The skin on my face prickles. He is asleep again. I sit beside him, examining his expression. He is beyond dreams, lost in a dense fog of oblivion. It's as if he were practising for his death. I select another photograph at random. Sarah. She wears one of those curious poncho blanket things. The front hangs low in a fringed point and her hands are hidden. The picture is in black and white, but I know that it was striped orange and brown. She will have posed under sufferance. When she was this sort of age – sixteen perhaps? Not much older, certainly – she was only really animated in other people's company. Michael could make her smile, but even he had failed this time. There are no pictures of her beyond this point, at least not in the pages of the albums. I don't doubt she stood in front of other cameras, sometimes held in Michael's hands, but not for me. 'It's better if it's just us from now on,' she'd said. 'Dad and me.' Chilly as an automaton. You're supposed to be able to let your children go, aren't you? You're constantly told it's an important part of child-rearing. But what if they're wrenched from you? Or supposing they just drift away? The current doesn't seem that strong at first, but when you try to reach them you quickly realise its power. Better to lie back and stare upwards than swim, helplessly and fruitlessly, against the tide. After a while, you'll find you relish the easy sway of the water beneath you and the unquestioning sky above. And should you glance at the riverbank from time to time, you'll see her. Your daughter. Safe and dry. You'll realise that she didn't need rescuing, after all.

'Shall I read another letter, Michael?' I say. 'This'll make you laugh. *Dear Mrs Deacon, I am delighted to confirm your place on our course. Everything will be supplied, so no need to bring anything – except your appetite!*'

An entire day has slipped by without much demarcation. At three o'clock I ate a sandwich but I struggle to remember its contents. I realised I hadn't eaten anything until then because the physiotherapist made her daily, unnecessary appearance. I can tell the time by the various arrivals to his room. The trolley bearing papers and magazines means it's mid-morning. The League of Friends offering, random items like hand-made spectacle cases and books of crossword puzzles, arrives at four. They all rattle along regularly, even though we've never shown any indication of wanting anything from them. Now that Michael has made his decision, there's an ambivalence in everyone's attitude to him. He must be cared for, drugged, investigated by rote, but they know the end is in sight and their attention is elsewhere.

'Mrs Deacon?' The nurse who bustled out last night bustles in again. I can't read her name tag unless I go too close to her. It's odd that nearly all the people who gather at this intimate time are anonymous. Only Mr Kazmi, the executioner, has a name. 'Mask off, I see,' she says. She catches my eye. 'Are you all right, Mrs Deacon? Are you staying tonight?' she says. 'I can make up a bed.'

Should I, this time? The nurse and I are both weary at the idea of the fold-up bed, the ill-fitting sheet and flattened pillow. 'It's better if I go home, I think. I ought to get things ready for the family,' I say.

She nods. 'A daughter and two grandsons, that's right, isn't it?' she says. She is choosing her tone and her words with care, sounding neither too involved nor too judgemental.

'That's right,' I say. 'Yes, they're on their way.' I let her picture them, negotiating airports or stations, pulling their cases and glancing at clocks and watches, hurrying to be here.

'See you tomorrow,' she says, gazing into the space above my head and dismissing me.

Chapter 50

3.02. It is not a time you can do anything useful with. You cannot steal a march on dawn at this hour, relishing the creeping light. If you haven't yet slept, it taunts you with how little night is left. Michael stares at the numbers until they fall and reveal 3.03. He is bored. It is an uncomplicated boredom. It reminds him of how he felt as he turned the page of the hymnal in assembly to see yet another page of interminable Victorian verses. Or during the Sunday afternoons of his childhood, saturated with the unpleasant anticipation of the week to come. The darkness, milky and warm, punctuated by spots of noise and dashes of light, seems ladled around him in heavy dollops. He observes the lengthening intervals between each breath with anticipatory pleasure, as if he were merely waiting for a conductor to tap his music stand and summon the orchestra. He does not need anyone here. He is grateful to them all for their absence. Even Marion, especially Marion, has left him free to go. 3.04. Let other people measure the days from now on, he thinks. He has an appointment to keep. He will never again be as punctual as this. 3.05 arrives without him.

Chapter 51

I had lain in bed that morning and let the anticipation of the day ahead seep into my head. It was sweet and rich, like the fug of candyfloss near a fair. I suddenly wondered if it might rain. The possibility hadn't occurred to me before and I felt a rush of pure terror. Adrian wouldn't come if it was raining, would he? I flung back the sheet and blankets and got out of bed.

Michael sat up. 'What is it?' he said, seeing me at the window holding the curtain aside.

'It looks like a nice day,' I said. 'I thought I might do some gardening.'

'Really?' Michael said.

Neither of us were keen. Michael cut the grass, cursing at the blades of the cylinder mower when they encountered something stubborn. Next door Derek had offered us a borrow of his hover, a phrase we repeated to each other in ever more exaggerated tones for a long time afterwards. The flowers from the borders lolled on the grass like heavily set women after too much sherry. In the centre of the lawn was a neglected circular bed of straggling roses.

'I could attempt a bit of weeding,' I said.

Michael put on his dressing gown. He made an elaborate

show of listening at the door, pantomiming one hand cocked to his ear. Sarah was spending longer and longer in the bathroom these days and Michael liked to pretend he found it wearingly female of her. 'All done? Finished primping? Tony Blackburn approve?' he'd say as she emerged. She took her little transistor in with her, you could hear Radio One tinnily over the running water. 'Coast is clear,' he said.

I wished I could push time with a bulldozer, sweeping away their toast and jam and cereal and tea, their teeth-cleaning, their coats and satchels and briefcases, leaving the way clear. After they'd left, I went out into the garden. I was never quite sure which were weeds and which weren't. Someone had once told me that what loosened easily when you tugged at it was what you should throw away. I pulled at some untidy fronds but they stayed put. Everything looked quite happy where it was. I moved a football, caught in low planting and glazed with mud.

There were some nice little blue flowers; perhaps I could put them in a vase. They weren't difficult to pick. They might be flowering weeds, for all I knew. I went and got some scissors and snipped away at some other blooms, intending to make a spray. It would prove I'd been outside, anyway.

Adrian's knock at the window startled me. I was washing up, turning cups and bowls under the running tap. He opened the back door himself before I could get to it. 'I always like a woman in Marigolds,' he said. 'Carry on, I'll finish this.' He waved a lit cigarette and then sucked on it, making a circle of his mouth as he exhaled and watching thin smoke rings rise and dissipate. When it was finished, he extinguished the cigarette on the draining board and threw the stub into the garden.

'Rubber things are hard to deal with, aren't they?' he said, watching me prise the gloves from my hands. 'I love the way you blush so easily.'

'I don't,' I said, holding my palms to my cheeks. 'Yes, I do,' I said.

He laughed. 'It suits you.' Adrian leaned back against the kitchen counter. 'It's very sweet and natural. Just like you. You're very wholesome.' He opened the nearest cupboard. 'You got any food?' He examined the contents. 'No more biscuits?'

'You must have been to a public school,' I said. 'Public schoolboys are the only people who think it's all right to forage. Here.' I handed him the box of crackers. 'They're a bit soggy. Sorry, sir.'

'Minor public school,' he said. 'Kicked out at sixteen.' He sprayed crumbs as he spoke.

'What did you do till National Service?'

'Didn't do that.' He looked affronted. 'Couldn't see myself getting up early every day and putting on a uniform. Luckily, old pater agreed. He's a shirker, too.' He smiled, ferreting bits of biscuit from between his teeth with his tongue. 'Quick letter from the family medic and that was the end of it.'

'Saying what?'

He sniffed. 'Probably confidential. Can I trust you?' He looked around theatrically. 'Bed-wetting,' he whispered. He sat down where he'd sat before, as if from habit. 'Your old man sign up, then?' And there it was, a casual reference to my real life.

'Yes,' I said. 'He didn't talk about it. Just something he did, he said.'

'Oh, did he have a *difficult war*?' he said, imitating an old man's cracking and trembling voice. 'Right, playtime,' he said, without waiting for me to answer, as if he'd reached the end of a dull exercise. 'Painting fun. I hope you won't be bored.'

'Are you trying to put me off?'

'Certainly not. I want you there. I want you there very much.' He opened the cupboards again. The contents shrivelled as he moved them around. 'Have you got a Thermos?' he said.

'A Thermos? Yes, I think so. We had a couple of them, but I think one's broken, so—'

'We'll only need one. Put some tea in it, there's a good girl. With plenty of sugar.'

I don't take sugar in tea, I thought. Sure enough, one flask sounded like a hail of gravel when I shook it. I undid the top of the second one and sniffed at a sour mixture of curdled milk and bleach. Rinsing it with baking soda didn't seem to have worked. Anything you drank from the little plastic cup always tasted odd, anyway, however carefully you washed it. I made the tea in a Pyrex jug, adding several generous tablespoons of sugar before I poured it into the flask.

'We'll need a blanket, have you got one?' Adrian said, looking around as if he expected to find one draped over the back of a chair or on the windowsill. 'Or something to sit on. I don't want you getting wet.'

'I'm sure we have,' I said, not very sure at all. When was the last time we'd had a picnic? There must be an old blanket in the airing cupboard I could use. I felt a momentary flicker of irritation that Adrian hadn't come better prepared. 'I'll go and look,' I said.

Towards the bottom of a pile of rather stiff sheets I found a thick, beige blanket, bordered with a wide satin trim. As I tugged at it, one hand slid between the layers; a piece of cloth caught in my fingers. It was a lace mat, dobbed with rust stains. The corner was embroidered with my mother's initials. It was the sort of thing you'd use to line a breakfast tray or place beneath a plated meal for an invalid. I had so little left of her that I could never have thrown it away, but I had no immediate use for it, either. Was it a sign? What would she say to me now? I had no real recollection of how she sounded and I had never invented her voice, either to console or inspire me. She was a collection of half-memories and anecdotes. She was this little cloth and three jewelled hat pins. An old doll with one closed eye. I was now a year older than she'd been when she died. I was already living beyond her having any possible experience of this dancing excitement, this wanting and aching. I imagined Adrian waiting, one floor below. I felt like an astronaut regarding the distant earth with tenderness, able to ignore for a moment all the roiling complications there.

'Found it?' Adrian was on the landing.

'Yes,' I said.

He took the blanket. 'Looks too good to be put on the ground.' He ran his fingers over the binding. 'Nothing a bit more ragged?'

'It's ancient,' I said, closing the airing cupboard door. 'Pretty sure it's been pressed into service before.'

'What were you thinking about?' Adrian was looking at me carefully. 'You were absolutely lost. I was watching you.' He touched my cheek. 'Maid Marion,' he said.

He handed me the blanket and flask. He left me to shut the door while he got his painting things from the boot. I watched him heave a large canvas bag and a drawing pad under one arm and hang the broad leather straps of an easel from the other. He crooked an elbow to the tailgate to slam it shut, then set off at quite a brisk pace down the footpath. It was too narrow for us to walk side by side. Adrian strode ahead without looking round. At the end of the path, we had to climb over a stile. I struggled with the different heights of its steps. The blanket was an awkward thing to carry and I was gripping the flask so tightly my hand hurt.

In the field, Adrian threw his bag to the ground. It reminded me of the way cowboys in films slung their horse's reins over a wooden bar, untied, when they dismount, assuming the animal would stay put. He took off his coat. He was only wearing a shirt underneath. He kept his scarf on. 'Blanket here, there's a poppet,' he said. He set about assembling the easel and arranging paints and brushes.

I looked around. There wasn't much to see. I didn't know why he'd chosen this particular spot. I could see the ruin of the old castle keep in the distance. Local youths hung about in it after dusk, smoking or snogging or climbing on to its broad window ledges and setting off fireworks. There was not much left of it but, even so, it was more scenic than this part of the field. I opened the blanket. It had several dubious brown marks in the centre. I took off my coat and placed it, neatly folded, in one corner.

'Would you be an angel?' Adrian said, imitating the high, sing-song voice of an old man. He held out two empty jam jars. 'Could you fill them up from the stream? Ta ever so.'

Although it wasn't steep, the bank was covered in long grass with what looked like thistles and nettles protruding from it. He saw me hesitate.

'There's a path there,' he said. He gestured to where someone or something had flattened the undergrowth.

It still looked challenging. I squatted and extended one arm gingerly towards the stream. The water was about a foot from the top of the bank and still out of reach. I'd have to kneel down to get anything into the jars. I glanced over my shoulder: Adrian was frowning as he made marks against the paper, tilting his head back to look at the view, half closing his eyes. Not for the first time, I had the impression he was playing a part.

I knelt down. At once, wet, cold earth and what felt like a thousand tiny, sharp pebbles stuck to my skin. I stood up abruptly. I brushed the debris from my knees. My hands were covered with mud.

'I can't reach,' I said.

Adrian crouched down and undid his shoelaces. He held on to my shoulder with one hand, while he shucked his shoes and socks. The pressure of his grip loosened and tightened as he swayed. He rolled both trouser legs up to underneath his knees. His long toes were splayed wide; his second toes were longer than the first. His pale, bare feet made him seem as exposed as if he were naked from the waist down.

He walked towards the bank and then straight into the water. He splashed up and down for a moment, then bent over and let clear water fill the jars. He balanced them on the bank and waved to me to join him.

'Come here,' he said. 'Come in. The water's lovely.'

'I can't,' I said.

'Will you dissolve?' he said. My tights were stuck to my knees with dried mud. His trousers darkened where the water lapped. He held his arms wide apart. 'It's only a few inches of water,' he said.

'All right,' I said, 'turn round.' I took off my shoes and placed them in a pair. Adrian put his hands over his eyes and looked at me through his parted fingers. I hitched up my skirt as little as I could and wriggled free of my tights.

The pebbles underfoot had been washed into a soft smoothness by the running stream. Cold water raced round my ankles and tugged between my toes. It pricked and tingled on the raw skin of my heel. I clung to his hand. He laced his fingers through mine. Each step felt strange and new. The current hurtled past me and rooted me to the spot.

He bent down in front of me and splashed my legs. 'You've got dirt on your knees,' he said. 'You can't go home like that.'

I couldn't see beyond the edge of the field. It was possible to imagine that nothing existed beyond the stile. Adrian climbed out on to the bank. He held out his hands and steadied me as I got out but, at the last moment, he pulled hard, so that I staggered and fell into him. He put his arms round my back as if he just wanted to keep me upright. He felt very warm. He released his grip, but I stayed where I was for longer than I needed to. 'All right?' he said.

I busied myself with pouring tea, because I knew if I looked at him at all I wouldn't stop. He had left a kind of physical stain on me, I could still feel his hard chest and encircling arms.

'Nectar,' he said, draining the little cup. 'Oh, wait, come here, I've missed a bit.' He slid his hands on my legs. 'Very nice,' he said, his fingers spread wide on my thighs.

'Am I still muddy?' I said, knowing I wasn't.

'Oh, very,' he said, stroking me, not even pretending to do anything necessary. 'I could,' he said, looking up at me, his hands still on my thighs, 'be very naughty with you.'

'You sound like Leslie Phillips,' I said.

He frowned. It was like the sobering moment when you emerge from the cinema after watching a matinee, back in an instant to daylight and real life. I resolved to leave. The fact that he kissed me straight away and then went on kissing me for quite a long time completely changed my mind.

He retrieved a packet of cigarettes and a lighter from his bag. He bent his head and cupped his hands, concentrating on the connection between his cigarette and the flame. It seemed to be a gesture of delicious and deliberate tenderness. I looked up, to where the clouds made shapes above me. If you were high enough, you'd reach a point where you could see Sarah and me at the same time, even though we were miles apart. He tipped his head from one side to the other, sizing me up.

'Who was your favourite, Katy Carr or Mary Lennox?' he said. 'I won't judge you on your answer. Well, I will, actually, but tell me anyway.'

'Very specific choices. Why were you studying books like that?' I said. 'Shouldn't you have been reading *Treasure Island* or *Tom Sawyer*?'

'The men were away at war when I was at the prep,' he said. 'All my teachers were women. They only ever read us books about girls. I don't think I even realised that boys could actually be the heroes in a story until I was in my teens.'

'Which one am I, then?' I said. 'The one who needs to be taught a lesson by falling off a swing or the one who has to have a child of nature wake her up? Is that you?'

'Oh, no, I'm not Dickon,' Adrian said. 'When I read those books, I was Katy and Mary. Actually, I think you're more Heidi than anyone else.'

'I don't think we've got anything in common,' I said. 'I don't drink milk all the time, for a start. Didn't she just want everyone else to be happy?'

He took a long drag of his cigarette and blew smoke out of the corner of his mouth. 'I've got it,' he said. 'Anne of Green Gables. That's who you are. No arguing.'

I watched a ladybird totter over the mountainous fibres of the blanket. 'What's your earliest memory?' I said. 'Mine was during the war. My father was away, and my mother didn't seem to mind being on her own with me. I think she forgot that I was so little. She used to forget to put me to bed most nights, anyway. I'd wake up on the sofa to find the room full of her friends. I'd pretend to be asleep, so I could listen to them.'

'I can remember sharing a room with my little brother.' Adrian lay back on the blanket. 'He cried all the time,' he said. 'Then they took him off to hospital and it turned out he had meningitis. No wonder he cried.'

'How old was he?' I said. 'What happened?'

'Two? Three? That sort of age. But I didn't feel sad he'd died, just rather relieved I didn't have to share a room with him any more.'

'He *died*?' I stared at him. 'Oh my God, that's awful. Your poor parents.'

'Yeah, I suppose so.' Adrian frowned as if this were a completely new thought. 'Never really thought about it. Didn't miss him, or anything. Plenty of other brothers. Have you got any brothers or sisters?'

'No.' I was still struggling with the crying child, his sudden illness, a tiny coffin.

'Look,' Adrian said, 'I think there's something you should realise.'

'What?' I said.

'You don't have to *approve* of me,' he said. 'That's not what this is about. You fancy me. You can't help it, you do. And I fancy you, so let's have fun. For a while.'

I suddenly remembered Michael carrying the wounded dog into the house. I'd started going through the Yellow Pages, looking for a vet, but he'd said it was too late for that. He knew it wouldn't survive, he said, but he couldn't leave it dying on the road. He'd soothed the poor thing as it faded. It lay quite still, as if it didn't want to take up any more space than the rectangle of paper spread beneath it. We'd watch it die its small, soundless death together. It was the first time I'd seen Michael weep since his mother died.

'We'll have to be careful,' I said to Adrian. 'So nobody finds out. I don't want to hurt anyone.'

'Yeah, right. Course. Don't look so worried. Look,' he said, 'supposing . . . ?' He opened his hands, palms upright, in a gesture of ignorance. 'Christ, sorry, I don't know your husband's name.'

'It's Michael.' I didn't like telling him. It sounded like someone small.

'Okay. Michael. Would you care if Michael kissed someone else?'

'Who?' I said. I couldn't imagine how that would happen. It didn't seem relevant to bring the possibility up. 'No, I wouldn't,' I said, but really I didn't like the idea at all. It would be unreasonable of him. 'Would your wife mind?' I asked.

'No, no, she wouldn't care,' he said. 'She thinks restricting people in any way is very bourgeois. Aggie's very clear on what's bourgeois and what's not.'

'Am I bourgeois?' I asked.

He looked at me. 'If you want to be,' he said. 'But I don't think you do.'

'I don't think I do, either,' I said.

'So that's okay then, isn't it?' He closed his eyes.

There were dark hollows underneath his cheekbones and his mouth looked even larger in repose. His lips turned up slightly at the corners. No wonder he found everything amusing, he was designed to. The physical fact of him, the way he lay in front of me without minding whether I was watching him or not, made me hesitate to speak. I held my breath for a moment. 'Do you really want to paint us together?' I said, with a lightness I didn't feel.

He half opened his eyes, shielding them against the bright sky.

'You said you wanted to paint her and me. Sarah.' The very sibilance of her name was a gasp.

He muttered something indistinct.

'I'd feel too self-conscious, posing with her for you, I think,' I said. 'So would she. Why don't you just paint her?'

He sat up, alert now.

'That might be better,' I said. 'Don't you think? Would you do that? Would you just paint Sarah, by herself?' The risk of it! What if he said yes, that's a good idea? As if it were my suggestion.

He lied at once. No, he said. That wouldn't be his thing. 'I don't think so,' he said, and I watched ribbons of untruths flutter from his mouth. I loved the way they caught the light. 'Why would I want to do that?' he said.

I answered his question by kissing him. He put his arms round me then twisted his hands in my hair so that I couldn't move away. I didn't want to. I knelt over him, my mouth on his, as if I were reviving him.

'Jesus,' he said after a while, moving awkwardly as if he

had cramp. 'Give me your hand,' he said, and when I did, he pressed it to his groin. The fierce hardness of his erection was startling. He closed his hand over mine and the muscle beneath my fingers twitched. 'Can you help with that?' he said, sounding drugged.

When I was small, a bomb fell on the corner of our road. It sliced the house in its path in half, revealing rooms and staircases. A lavatory was propped against only open air and a wardrobe dangled over a new precipice. It had seemed impertinent to stare, as if you could suddenly see the house's underwear. The open space around us widened and gaped in the same way now, exposing us to the elements. 'Later, not here,' I said.

Adrian got up without saying anything and without looking at me. He went back to the easel. I lay down and tried to cope with the ground's assault. It seemed to get harder and more lumpen by the moment.

Adrian turned round. He opened his arms wide in exaggerated exasperation and came back to where I lay. 'What are we like?' he said, burying his hands in his hair in mock despair. 'I can't concentrate, I keep remembering you're here.'

'I'm glad to hear it,' I said. He wanted me. I felt sharper now and calmer. It was like stepping off what looked like a cliff to discover it was only the height of a kerb. I picked up the blanket and shook it, sending grass and little twigs into the air. He took the other side and we began to fold it together, like two washerwomen taking sheets off the line. We got closer together at each folding until we stood toe to toe and then we kissed for quite a while. We didn't speak after that. He packed up his things and I emptied the last drops of tea from the cup.

'Were you surprised to see me in that funny shop?' he asked, as we neared the end of the path.

'Temple's?' I said. 'Yes, I was. It didn't seem like the sort of place you'd go.'

'Sheila told me you might be there,' he said.

My stomach contracted. 'Did she? Is that why you went? What did she say?'

'Just that I might bump into you, that you liked the little café there. It looked ghastly, but just as I was going to leave – there you were.'

'She told me *you* liked it there too. Why would she do that?' I said.

Adrian shrugged. 'Does it matter? We'd have made things happen on our own. At least we needn't go back to that grim little place again.'

I didn't feel reassured. 'Has she done that before? Told you where to meet someone?' I said.

He didn't answer.

'Adrian?'

We'd reached his car. He put everything down while he reached for his keys. 'Better not kiss you goodbye,' he said. 'Just in case the witch is watching.'

'Don't be ridiculous,' I said. I kissed him hard, holding the Thermos against his back as I squeezed my arms round him.

'Oh *kay*,' he said. 'Don't get reckless.' He disentangled

himself, pushing me away. I saw him glance upwards at the windows of the house as if we might be observed.

There's no one there, I thought. I know exactly where everyone is. Including Sarah. Especially Sarah.

When I got to the door, I realised he hadn't answered my question. I picked up the milk bottles. They'd been on the step all day, like beacons, advertising my absence.

Chapter 52

5 October

Of course, I *have* actually been kissed. Three times. Although two of those times were by the same boy. It was all right at first. We were lying down on his single bed and we had to keep changing grip, like those wrestlers on television. We paused between each hold and grunted into the next position. But the longer it went on, the more bored I felt. I opened my eyes in the middle of the kissing. His face looked like a different landscape. His forehead loomed over the wide prairies of his cheeks. His nose ploughed furrows into my face. His lips were soft then hard, like excavators looking for a spot to plant his tongue. He opened his eyes and sprang away from me, leaning backwards, but his pelvis stayed fused to mine, as if we were Siamese twins joined at the hip.

I practised kissing last night. I lay on my bed and folded my pillow in half. I closed my eyes. He said you are beautiful, and I said how beautiful and he said very. So I said do you want to kiss me and he said yes and he did. His hand was on my shoulder and he stroked me. He kissed me and I said don't stop don't stop don't stop. The pillow man had Adrian Mr Cavanagh's face.

Chapter 53

Eddie had made good plans for when he was grown up. Most adults wasted their opportunities and that wasn't going to happen to him. They ate food that didn't seem to excite them and they went to bed too early. He wouldn't have to be hurried out of Young's Toys when he was big. He'd spend as long as he liked choosing things from the glass cabinet, without an adult yawning and hurrying him up. He felt under his desk for the lump of chewing gum somebody had stuck there. On cold days it was solid, but if the weather warmed it up even a little, it softened and smelled.

The painting man in the fields was good at being grown up. He'd greeted Eddie without any fuss, instead of asking him what he was doing there. He'd let Eddie sit with him while he held his drying picture in one hand and a cigarette in the other. He'd waved both as he spoke. Eddie knew he was late home afterwards and had braced himself for his mother's ire. He was puzzled by her soft response. He was even more puzzled by her failure to tell the painting man he oughtn't to park his car outside the gate, because she'd been going on and on about people disobeying and when there was someone she could *actually* be cross with, she let him off. When he was big, he'd say what he meant, then do it.

Chapter 54

I haven't been home long when the telephone rings. It is probably the hospital. I'll wait a moment, to gather myself. It seems vital that I don't go to pieces. I am relieved to have set myself a goal. I have no other plans. The answerphone clicks into action, my recorded voice sounds clipped and shrill. I hear an inhabited pause as the caller waits. I imagine Sarah breathing in, ready to speak. She says nothing. She hangs up.

The next call rouses me in darkness and I wake to find a magazine over my face. I'm infuriated by the lapse, because it feels undignified and elderly to slide into sleep under whatever I'm reading. This time, the caller is hesitant, stumbling over my name and the information she must deliver. She's sorry. Her apologies pepper her speech. It was very quick, she says, but Mr Deacon has passed. *No, he is dead*, I think. I reassure her that I'm calm, that I'm coming, that I'm grateful. It's an awful call for you to make, I say. Thank you for being so understanding, she says. She tells me about what I must do next without pausing and I wonder if she's reading the instructions from a card. We say polite goodbyes to each other. I put the phone down and howl into the room. I have no choice but to make the sound. It is loud and overwhelming, as impossible to prevent as being sick or fainting. It occupies every inch of me until I am out of breath. I am not frightened, I have been this powerless before. It will let me go soon.

I write the emails and leave the messages I must. The description of what has happened sounds cold and spare, as if these are words that shouldn't apply to someone I knew. When I see Michael's coat on the hook in the porch, I am puzzled to see it there. Surely, I think, he should have taken everything with him, when he left. I look more closely. It is my coat, of course.

After I'd watched Adrian leave, I saw myself in the hall mirror. I'd caught the sun, even that late in the year. My cheeks were pink and the freckles across my nose were darker. I took a half-finished tin of baked beans from the fridge. I couldn't remember how long it had been in there. It was sealed with a rubber lid, another purchase from Franny's selection. Underneath, the contents gleamed orange and glutinous. I sniffed at them but they didn't seem to smell of anything at all. I ate from the tin. I've become feral, I thought. In a few more weeks, I'll be going through dustbins. When I was little, my father had come home with a kitten. I must have been about seven . . . I'd wanted to be with the kitten so much that I'd got out of my bath and gone, naked and dripping, to where it slept in a cardboard box. That was exactly how I felt now, I wanted to run to Adrian at once. Whatever had happened to that kitten? My father had got rid of everything when my mother died. I couldn't remember a cat in the house at all.

I stood on the little pedal then widened the bin's lid with one hand as the mechanism creaked. There were some bits of paper at the bottom, which I'd swept out of the drawer when I hunted for a pen. Old bus tickets and dry cleaning receipts and a torn letter with a familiar heading. I read *Dr Mosley* and felt a rush of alarm. I dropped the tin and watched the thick sauce leak and obscure it. This was only a routine letter from the surgery, but the sight of his name wounded me all over again.

I'd thought I only wanted one child. The baby, her pink newness and the smell of her, was enough. I read *The Reader's Digest Book of Childcare* so often I almost imagined the family in the photographs was my own. I'd even planted marigolds because that mother knelt beside a bed of them, her pudgy knees indenting the grass, holding out her arms for her baby's next step.

I couldn't quite tell when it wasn't enough. Certainly by the time I was putting away matinee jackets or consigning bootees to the ottoman, I knew there was an empty ache in my arms that Sarah's toddler shape was too large to fill. I began to crave being pregnant, feeling the rolling waves of a baby inside me. I wanted to run my fingers over its unknown shape, trying to make out a head or hand as an odd hardness pushed at the skin on my stomach. The space beside Sarah was filled with a smaller child that no one else could see.

When I tried to tell Michael how I felt, I failed. Or he only heard the possibility of saying *no* when I said, 'Don't you wish you'd had a son?' or 'Do you suppose Sarah will mind being on her own?' He asked me why I was keeping all the outgrown clothes and walking reins, each little blanket or bonnet folded with tissue in the chest of drawers. I muddled an answer about somebody else wanting them some day. He seemed to accept my response, although I made sure I put my treasure trove somewhere he wouldn't see it. Months later, stirring porridge for Sarah, I felt suddenly repulsed by the sight of it and a rush of sweet saliva filled my mouth. I counted up weeks on my fingers several times as the porridge stuck to the bottom of the saucepan. I had to wait all day to tell Michael what I suspected, almost walking around on tiptoe to keep my secret and my baby safe.

'I think I'm pregnant,' I said and wished at once I hadn't, because he snapped back in his chair with a whiplash of disappointment and horror.

'Are you sure? How? I'm so careful,' he said.

'It happens,' I said, thinking that the dialogue in the scene I'd rehearsed in my head contained a great deal more joy and delight.

'Have you been to the doctor?' he said.

I shook my head. 'I'll go tomorrow.'

'Right,' Michael said. He was obviously hoping Dr Mosley would diagnose indigestion or wind and I wouldn't have to mention the subject again.

I didn't want to go to the surgery. I disliked the way no one spoke in the chilly waiting room. They looked disapproving if you made any sound at all, even a cough, and I had to keep shushing Sarah as she played with the tired toys they kept in the basket by the door. Dr Mosley laid his hands on my stomach as he looked out of the window on to the tiny, unused garden outside. His flesh was white and swollen, as if he'd spent too long under water. It made me think of the sunken contents of specimen jars in a museum. When he stuck his fingers inside me, he caught my eye.

'I think so, yes. I'm pretty sure,' the doctor said. 'We'll take a drop of blood to confirm.' He looked across to Sarah, piling scuffed wooden blocks into a tower. 'A nice gap between your children,' he said. He took the last block away from Sarah's hands and finished the tower himself. 'Off you go, missy,' he said.

When I told Michael, he only said, 'Right, then.'

The *Reader's Digest* woman probably got flowers.

The first pain flicked, present then absent, so quickly that I could almost have pretended I'd imagined it. I was through queasiness by then, beginning to feel the waistbands of my skirt tighten and a heaviness in my breasts. I was hanging washing on the line. I wasn't doing anything strenuous, I thought. It was a comma of discomfort, that's all, no more than that. But it left a mark on me, like a thumbprint in wet clay. It was shaped like fear. Several hours later, I felt it again. It grew. At first it was a small, curled fist, then the fingers spread until its sharp nails even reached to my shoulders and shins. I knew that I would see blood mingled with the water in the lavatory bowl, but even so, when I did, I gasped, because it was an unarguable fact. I took Sarah to a neighbour. We were still living in the cottage then, and the woman living next door was old enough to be my mother. She absorbed my distress as if she were a plump, worn cushion.

I lay on the bed as hope turned liquid and leaked from me. At one point, I rose in pain and cried out in the bathroom as I expelled the last of what I had tried so hard to hold on to. Michael found me in darkness and didn't even ask what was happening. He brought me a boiled egg and cold toast on a little tray I didn't recognise. I cleared it away myself later, uneaten. By the time I had made my appointment with Dr Mosley, three days later, Michael had assumed a confident bluster. He hugged me and kissed the top of my head with some force. I felt bruised by his wooden limbs. The doctor had the same breeziness as he informed me of my commonplace loss and my youth. Michael at least knew better than to throw me platitudes or jolly comfort. He just waited. I was bleached by grief. When I looked at Michael, I couldn't see him. The edges of him were soft and out of focus. He was camouflaged so effectively in the rooms he stood in, or against the streets through the window as he drove the car, that I could barely make him out.

When I'd discovered I was pregnant again, I waited to be afraid. I steeled myself, expecting a tide of panic. It never came. Instead, I sank into that pregnancy like fruit into jelly. Though Dr Mosley had long since confirmed Eddie's beginning and peered more frequently into the children's ears or throats than he ever had at my burgeoning stomach, I could not forgive him for witnessing my failure, all those years before.

The doorbell rang, two harsh notes. It'll be a salesman, I thought. The bell sounded again and was followed up by loud knocking as whoever was there tried another approach. I stiffened. I'd like to have crept upstairs, but you could see movement in the hallway through the circle of distorting glass in the top panel and I couldn't trust whoever stood outside not to press their face to the window and catch me sneaking away.

I stood stock-still, as if any move I made would reveal me, even though I was two rooms away from where the visitor stood. When Sheila rapped on the back door, I actually shouted aloud in panic.

'Good grief, Marion.' Sheila looked alarmed, too. 'Didn't you hear the bell?' she said. 'I knocked, too. What were you doing?'

'Planning a menu,' I said.

'Were you?' Sheila looked around suspiciously for evidence. She was tightly trussed into one of her not-quite-suits. Her legs were capped with little black patent shoes as if otherwise her feet would fray. The top of her head was edged with a tight perm. A row of large beads glimpsed beneath her scarf threatened to perforate her neck.

'I won't stay long,' she said, 'but I have got time for a cup of tea. If you're having one.' She put her handbag on the table, then started to take off her coat.

I felt just as I did when I was recovering from flu. I'd had to concentrate hard on even the simplest tasks, as if I'd forgotten how everything worked. 'Of course I am,' I said.

'I came round earlier. Where have you been?' Sheila settled herself, sitting sideways from the table so that she could watch me more carefully. Her scarf was a hectic pattern of yellows and browns, secured at her neck with an enamelled clasp. She undid it and folded the scarf up into a neat square.

I thought of Adrian folding the blanket in the field and shivered.

Sheila continued her inspection. 'Been out all day?' she said. Her expression changed. 'I saw Adrian's car,' she said. 'Further up the lane. Did you see him?' She left a little space round her question, sending it airborne to hover above us, waiting for a reply.

'No,' I said.

'What a *shame*,' Sheila said, putting her head on one side with an exaggerated expression of sympathy, as if she'd just been told that I was very ill. The room filled with a high piercing whistle. 'Kettle!' She gesticulated towards the cooker as if I might not recognise the source of the noise.

'He was looking for you,' Sheila said, still watching me. 'He said he was going to take you with him, if you wanted to go. Honestly, I think he imagines it's some sort of treat. Sitting about while he paints. What on earth would you do? You could hardly get on with anything useful, could you?'

I didn't answer.

'You oughtn't to be missing each other all the time,' Sheila said. 'One in, one out, like that little couple in the weather house. A mug's fine,' she said, as if conferring a kindness. She pulled the pile of magazines and papers towards her and sifted through them as she spoke. 'St Thomas's School,' she read aloud, examining the envelope on the top. 'School report?' She held it up.

'School photo. Sarah's,' I said.

Sheila took this as assent. 'Of course, it's all individual photographs now, isn't it?' she said, shaking the pictures out on to the table and squinting at them. 'In our day, all you got was a picture of the entire school, didn't you? It was hard enough to find your own face among everyone else's, let alone recognise your chums. She's lovely.' She picked up one of the photographs and showed it to me, as if she were reminding me of what my daughter looked like. 'Adrian said he thought you two were very similar, but I can't see it.'

'Yes, he told me that,' I said. Why did they discuss me? Did he say anything else?

She tugged again at the pile of papers. It was utterly mystifying, I thought, how she could be so nosy.

'Finished with this?' She held up a copy of *Argosy*. 'I hardly have time to read. But I'll try to get through it.' She rifled through the outgrown children's books, reading their titles aloud. '*Puppy Tales. Judy for Girls. The Adventures of Binkle and Flip.*' Sheila replaced each one in turn. 'Oh, look! A paper doll book. I used to *adore* these. No one's cut you out, have they?' she said, addressing the pictures in a baby voice. 'Look at all your lovely clothes. Who's giving you away?' Her eyes glistened with pleasure as she turned the pages.

'Would you like to take that, too?' I said.

Sheila hugged the book to her. 'May I?' she said. 'Silly, isn't it, but I would.'

We sipped our tea in silence. A bird twittered loudly outside. 'Isn't that pretty?' Sheila said. 'It's like the one on *Going for a Song*. I love Arthur Negus, don't you? Better let you get on.' She stood, smoothing her skirt, although it would have taken a Chieftain tank to crease it. She picked up her handbag and wiped one hand along its underside. 'I expect you and Adrian will see each other at the party, anyway, if not before,' she said, still brushing away imaginary crumbs.

'What party?' I wished I needn't ask, but how could I not?

Sheila clasped her hands together. 'Oh, silly me. That could have been quite a faux pas, couldn't it? But I'm *sure* you'll be invited. Adrian and Agnes are having a big do in a couple of weeks. Hasn't he mentioned it?'

'I don't really know him that well. There's no reason for them to invite me. Invite *us*. Our daughters are at the same school, of course, but I've never met his wife.'

'Haven't you? She's *looovely*.' Sheila breathed the word languorously, as if short vowel sounds wouldn't do the woman justice. 'And she's the very definition of "long-suffering". Although "turning a blind eye" might be more accurate.' She smiled and leaned so close to me that I could see tiny red veins snaking across the whites of her eyes. 'Family money,' she whispered. 'Adrian knows which side his bread is buttered on.' She inspected me carefully, her snake eyes narrowing. 'Of course he'll invite you,' she said. 'He invites everyone. Last time I went to one of their dos, I met his *butcher* there, for heaven's sake! He throws invitations out left, right and centre. And you two have a real *connection*, after all. They live in an absolutely lovely house.' She gazed wistfully into the middle distance.

It was easy to imagine Adrian in the centre of a riotous throng, the butcher capering beside him like a jester, garlanded with a string of sausages.

'I don't expect to be invited,' I said. I opened the door. Cold air rattled the glass in the window frames.

'Oh, I'll have a word, I'll make sure you are.' Sheila pulled the edges of her coat together over her solid frontage and forced its large buttons through the small holes. 'Thank you for the tea. It's fun to keep it casual, isn't it? Oh, by the way' – Sheila scampered back towards the table and held up one of Sarah's photographs – 'I think this one's the best. Just my opinion. I expect it's hard to be objective, isn't it, when it's your own child?' She wound her scarf around her neck, looping and doubling the fabric, as though she were practising for a Girl Guide badge.

'Bye, Marion dear,' she said. She smiled and her pink teeth shone.

After she'd gone, I filled in the form and ordered the pictures and wrote a cheque and swept everything into the envelope without looking at Sarah at all.

Chapter 55

6 October

Bobbie actually came and found me today. I was in the furthest part of the rec, right by the rhododendrons. We used to play ponies there, when I was in the Upper Third. Every break was a gymkhana. We had lots of branches set up as cavaletti, and some little sticks driven into the ground. We weaved in and out of them as if they were several feet high, not a few inches. Of course, they're all gone now. She said she'd been looking for me. I was so happy that I could hardly look at her. She asked if I'd got a boyfriend. I was going to fib, because Neil had taken me to the cinema last Christmas and I could pretend that counted, but she said that she didn't have a proper boyfriend till last year, so I didn't have to say anything. She asked me if I'd been kissed, and I said I had. The first time didn't really count. Neil had to bring me home on the bus, my parents made him. We got to the end of my road and I was just about to say goodbye when he put his hands on my shoulders and sort of collided his mouth with mine and moved about from side to side. I could feel his teeth behind his lips and it made me think of his whole skull beneath his skin and under his neat brown hair. Bobbie said was it properly with tongues? I shrugged as if it didn't matter either way.

We walked back towards the school buildings together. She opened the back door of the changing room, the one that's supposed to set off an alarm but doesn't and pushed me inside. It's odd being in there when it's empty. I told Bobbie that I always think that the coats are waiting to escape with us at the end of the day, like accomplices. You're always being watched in school, I said. Someone always wants to punish or make fun of you. You can't talk back, or run where you shouldn't, or cry or shout without someone knowing about it. You're all together, all the time, all day, so no one ever forgets if you were ever vain or clumsy. They always remember when you were sick or when you walked about without knowing that your skirt was tucked into your tights. If you get given a nickname in school, it's as permanent as a tattoo. But the moment you leave the building, it's like you're set free.

Bobbie said she felt pretty free all the time. I wished I hadn't said all that.

She sat me down at the far end so we could see the door, and then we could hide, or say we needed the toilet, if someone came in. A games bag kept bashing me on the head, which seemed to be full of hard shoes. She said I needed to learn about snogging and she'd be my teacher. She told me to stick my tongue out. I wanted to ask her why she'd chosen me for this lesson, but when I looked at her, she was just waiting for me to do as she said, so I did. It's weird that the minute your tongue's out of your mouth, it makes you feel naked all over. She leaned towards me. I was giggling, so she told me to close my eyes. She touched the tip of her tongue to mine. It felt huge. Without being able to see her, I couldn't tell where that warm, wet, solid bit of Bobbie came from. She could have been someone else, too. It was only because I could smell her scent that I knew it was her. It was like that bit on *Ask the Family* where you have to identify an object from looking at a close-up photo of part of it. It's hard to recognise a cheese grater or a lemon squeezer like that.

When I opened my eyes, Bobbie was killing herself laughing. I didn't know what to say, so I got up and tucked a stray plimsoll into the wire locker under the bench. Bobbie said it's okay to be a virgin. She said she lets Jeff touch her under her knickers, but she hasn't gone all the way yet. She said he wants to, of course. I want a boy to want me like that. The last party I went to, the music was really loud, and this boy kept talking to me. He had to get closer all the time, shouting into my ear above the noise. Eventually, I could make out what was he was saying. It was only did I know Debbie, and could I tell her he fancied her?

This party was going to be different. I'd walk with Bobbie, as if I was arriving at a wedding. In fact, it was just as if she was going to be giving me away.

She told me that Jeff was going to meet her later. There's usually a little group of boys from the grammar waiting around by the gate after school. They move in a clump, like seaweed under water. When they see the girls coming out, they always look at their own shoes or take a few steps backwards or put their hands on their heads. The girls talk loudly, laughing and clutching each other's arms and ignoring them. But you only have to walk a few yards away from the school to find them all divided into twos, standing as close as if they'd been glued together. I peeked out of the window of the library and saw Jeff waiting. I couldn't see his face, but he's got quite long hair. As they walked away, Bobbie tucked her hand into the back pocket of his trousers and he held on to her waist, lifting her blazer.

Adrian Mr Cavanagh was waiting for me in his car. He sounded the horn which made me jump. When I got in, he drove off fast, without saying anything. He parked outside a house, which was enormous. It must be where Bobbie lives too, of course. I couldn't help looking around. He saw me looking back at the house. He said don't worry, no one's in. I followed him into a sort of studio at the end of the garden. He gave me a dress and told me to put it on, he said he'd wait outside while I changed and he wouldn't look. It was a blue velvet dress with a lace collar. I know it was one of Bobbie's: it smelled of her. He kept saying are you ready, are you ready, which made me clumsy and slow. The dress was a bit tight. I struggled to do it up.

The room was almost bare, as if he'd only recently collected all the things he needed. I wondered if Bobbie had been in there. I stood as still as I could while he drew me. I didn't say anything. I could see my school uniform on the floor where I'd left it. I wished I'd been allowed to keep it on. After a while, Adrian Mr Cavanagh said he'd got enough to work with. He said okay, get changed, I'll drive you back, but I wondered if he wished I could just leave by myself. It took me ages to take off Bobbie's dress. I was reaching behind me for the zip and wriggling to get out of it until my arms ached.

When I came outside, he was smoking, leaning up against the wall. He offered me a cigarette. I took it, although it was only the second time I'd ever had one. He said, of course, really, he liked to paint a woman nude. That was the real challenge, he said, getting the flesh tone and the expression in the eyes right. I looked up at him quickly but he wasn't looking at me. I leaned against the wall beside him. He seemed to be more himself than any of the boys I know. Their arms and legs are spindly and new, like those baby animals in films, struggling to get to their feet. He says what he wants to say straight away, instead of leaving awkward gaps or coming out with the wrong thing. He wasn't practising what he said. It wasn't a rehearsal for someone else. It was all meant for me. I felt as if I was filling up with something rich and sweet. I wouldn't be able to stop having more, even though it made me sick.

You could paint me like that, I suppose, I said. He turned to look at me. Yes, he said. Yes, I could.

He didn't say anything on the way back. I looked out of the car window all the time. He dropped me outside the school. As I got out, he leaned over and said I was a nice kid. I kept thinking if he's with me he can't be with her.

Chapter 56

I won't wear my canvas sneakers to the hospital. I'd left them by the bed last night and slipped them on when I got up, but it seems very important that I change my shoes before I go. I need to put on a more a substantial pair, I think, something with a proper heel. I survey all the shoes in the wardrobe with increasing distress. I can't remember buying any of them. How did I walk around the narrow aisles in shops, scrutinising my feet and ankles in the small mirrors, then choose to buy any of these? They seem out of character, as if I were auditioning to play another version of myself. I select a pair of brown courts. Headmistress shoes.

Michael is still in the world. As long as his body takes up space, he exists. You can claim he is making a *substantial contribution*. He is still the sum of himself. When he is gone, in his new, past tense, I will become his interpreter. He will be *Michael was* or *Michael always did* or *Michael never could*. He had his own ideas and opinions, things that made him angry or amused him but I will have to explain and filter him from now on. He lies – where? I can't remember when they remove the body. I used to do it, of course. It was routine, just a response to an instruction. It wasn't a person I helped to heave from the bed, but a heavy and uncooperative object. I must have ignored all the photos and the unfinished books, the cards and children's drawings. I can see myself then, in my uniform, pushing a gurney along a corridor to the morgue. There was only a sheet between me and the new death but I chatted to the orderly, catching up on gossip, laughing because we knew no one could see us. Michael is about to be consigned, first to memory, then to a future without any of us. He will become a figment of repeated anecdotes or the sudden finding of his name on a book's flyleaf or an opened letter. These glimpses will substantiate him briefly, flickering to illuminate one moment in time. Without him to give voice to his point of view, who owns it?

Rosalind Piper was very tall. I'd only seen her once before, when I was hurrying to change. There was no indication then of her height. In the doorway of our house, she seemed out of proportion to her surroundings. Not least because her visit was entirely unheralded. 'Mrs Deacon?' she said. 'Miss Piper. Rosalind. I'm so sorry to catch you unawares. I should, perhaps, have telephoned ahead.' There was a slight clip to her voice, as if the vowels were flattened between her teeth. I had an impression of what my mother would have called *good breeding*. She held Michael's wallet out to me. It was something so familiar that to see it in someone else's hand made me physically recoil. 'He left this in the office,' she said.

'I know,' I said. 'He was cursing this morning. He's not here. In fact, he's away today. Overnight. In Rome. Of course, you of all people will know that.'

'Indeed,' she said.

'Would you like to come in?' I said.

She shook her scarf free from her neck and handed it to me. It was warm and light. She passed me her coat next, but there was no assertion of rank in her manner. She followed me into the sitting room.

'Would you like a cup of tea?' I said.

'Oh, I would, please,' she said. 'I'm skiving, really. But I did think Mr Deacon would need his season ticket when he travels into work tomorrow. It's nice to get out of the office, actually. Oh, how lovely!' She reached for a little china figure. 'Royal Copenhagen, isn't it?' she said, turning it upside down like an auctioneer.

'It was a wedding present,' I said. I didn't think I'd taken much notice of it before. 'Why don't you wait here while I make the tea.'

'May I come with you?' she said.

I watched her take in the kitchen furniture and the pictures and ornaments on display. She wore a belted, checked dress. Its wide collar framed a maroon polo neck and a string of pearls that hung at the level of a mayoral chain. I thought she was the sort of girl who would receive pearls on a significant birthday. And who would expect to, as well. Her pleasant face was neither too pretty nor too plain. She looked as if she'd happily make up a four at tennis at a moment's notice. You could hand her anything – a parcel to post, a small child to care for, the route of a walk in Cumbria to follow – and she would undertake the task cheerfully and in the right shoes. I wished I had a cat. I'd like to have watched it settle on her lap. She wouldn't have fussed about the fur it shed.

She clasped her mug. Her nails were frosted with a perfect pink. We regarded each other. The silence was unusually comfortable. She pulled a crumple of apricot tissue from one sleeve and dabbed at her nose. There was a faint smell of lavender.

'What were you going to do if I was out?' I said.

'Oh, I had an envelope ready,' she said. She patted her handbag. 'To post it through your letterbox. Or I'd have left it with Mrs Turner.'

'Sheila?' I said. 'Do you know her?'

'Oh no.' She looked fleetingly guilty. 'Mr Deacon has mentioned her, that's all. He tells me she is always around.'

I couldn't imagine Michael talking about his life here to anyone. 'So am I,' I said. 'I'm home all the time as well, I suppose. It's never really occurred to me until now, but it's true. I don't – I mean, I can't drive. I go on errands but I hardly ever leave the house for very long. For the most part I'm just – *visited*.'

She smiled. 'Mrs Deacon,' she said, 'if I lived somewhere as cosy and lovely as this, I wouldn't want to leave it, either.'

I looked at her quizzically, waiting for some spark of spite or condescension. There was none. The house relaxed under her benevolent gaze, the objects stood proud on their shelves.

'To be honest,' she said, 'I really wanted to see where you lived, too. Mr Deacon speaks so fondly of his home and you and—' She stopped abruptly. 'I'm sorry, I don't mean to imply that – or he – Sorry, I don't mean to be forward. I suppose I just hope I'm as happy as you are when I'm married. That's all.'

I stared at her. She radiated a kind of unassailable assumption she would never be made to feel unwelcome anywhere. 'Any plans to be married?' I said.

'Yes, I'm engaged,' she said. Her left hand fluttered as she resisted the temptation to proffer her ring on splayed fingers.

'Congratulations,' I said. 'When is the wedding?'

'Next year,' she said. 'I'll be Mrs Unwin-Taylor. Preparations are all in hand though, courtesy of my mother. I think I'll feel more like a guest on the day than the bride.' She smiled happily. 'I don't think Jock will want me to carry on working much after that, though, of course.'

I frowned. 'Won't he?' I said. 'Will you mind?'

'Oh goodness, no,' she said. 'I love working for Mr Deacon but once I've got a family, that's it.' She inclined her head. 'Did you work before?' she said.

'Yes, I was a nurse,' I said.

'Marvellous!' she said. 'Such a useful thing to do. I'm really not in the same league.'

'I'm sure you're very useful,' I said. 'Especially today. After all, you've returned the wallet.'

She smiled again. It came so naturally to her to smile. I thought how comforted Michael must be to see her smile every day.

'I did, didn't I?' she said. 'Even if my motives weren't entirely pure. It was so nice to meet you properly, Mrs Deacon. Forgive my barging in.' She rose to her feet, confident that I hadn't minded. At the door, she paused. 'I'm so glad I came,' she said. 'Now I can imagine Michael being here.'

I closed the door behind her. I realised that she'd finally said his name. I gave her a Royal Copenhagen china figurine some years later. 'You can call it a wedding present,' I'd said.

I am used to order. I keep to a routine. I know where everything is. If I were blindfolded, I could move around my house quite easily without coming to harm. Not much disturbs my equilibrium. I usually recognise the writing on anything that comes through the door. Once, in an entirely unfamiliar hand, there was a note, from Bridget's cousin, informing me of her death. She had attached a little sticker with her address on it to the back of the envelope. Printed, to avoid error. I'd noted it, but I couldn't think what would cause me to contact her again.

This discipline, this torpor, has been my satisfactory state for a long time. At first, my grief left me raw and naked. Even other people's sadness, however slight – the boy running to the stop just as the bus pulled away, the woman stopping in her tracks and searching anxiously in her bag for her lost purse, the eyes of the forlorn dog tied up outside a shop – wounded me. I learned to inure myself until I could listen to the old people's sadder stories or read someone's bad news without hurting myself. Michael's death seems to have punctured my defences. I feel on edge, as if I have forgotten something vital. My shoes clatter on the bare floorboards in the hallway. 'It sounds as if I'm clog dancing,' I say aloud. 'Don't you agree, Michael?' When I fetch my coat from my little porch it feels chilly to the touch.

Chapter 57

I reread the pages of the diary again and again, until they blurred. Its cheap leather stuck to my hands. I could not undo that day. I was heavy with its blue velvet and cigarette smoke. It spread like spilled ink, staining my thoughts. I slid the diary back into its hiding place, but her words did not lie quietly. They whispered like a Greek chorus. I saw how she twisted what he said until she heard what she wanted to hear. She'll be hurt and confused when she realises he's only playing. I can't blame him, this little display of adoration must be flattering. If I try to stop her from seeing him, I think, she'll want to know how I knew she would. And I'll only postpone what she must discover at some point: she won't get what she thinks she wants. It's for the best. She needs to be taught this lesson and I persuaded myself that I was being generous in letting her learn it while I watched. *If he's with me he can't be with her*.

I had been standing at the bedroom window for some time before I realised someone was waving at me from the street below.

I opened the front door. The little figure of Sheila, leaning on my garden wall, got larger and more resolute the closer I got.

'I've something for you,' she said. She grinned like a naughty child. She opened her handbag as far as its hinge would allow and wriggled her hand inside. 'You *shall* go to the ball,' she said, putting a large envelope into my hand. 'Aren't you going to open it? It's a beautiful invitation.' I wanted to open it alone, away from Sheila's possessive stare. She smiled. 'He had a whole pile of them,' she said. 'Oh, you *must* come.' She smiled again. 'You've bred the babysitter, haven't you? That's what my mother always says about big gaps like yours. That'll keep Sarah out of harm's way, anyway, won't it, being on duty. I expect she's got all the boys after her. And the men, too, if Adrian's anything to go by.' Her smile was as sharp as steel. 'He's very taken with her. With you both. *I want to paint them together, Sheila*, he says. He's confusing himself with Picasso.'

'I'd better go and make supper,' I said.

'See you soon,' Sheila said. It was a threat she'd certainly carry out.

I slid the embossed invitation out of its silky, mauve envelope. It was lined with purple tissue. There was a coat of arms on the card. I read the sideways gothic slant. Then I reread it, to make sure. I got up and looked hard at my own handwriting on the calendar. It confirmed what I already knew: that we'd asked stupid Don and silly Patricia or Pauline or Pam or whatever her name was to supper on the same day. What could I do? Michael wouldn't want to change the date. He hadn't even met Adrian and I couldn't imagine explaining him, without betraying myself. It was hopeless. I sat with the card in my lap, like a suburban Cinderella.

'Chow mein. Is it a special treat?' Eddie said, beginning to eat before he'd even sat down, placing one of the little curls of noodle on his tongue to feel it contract.

'Sit up properly. Put your tongue away, please. No, it's not a treat,' I said. 'I just thought it would make a change.'

'*Nice* change,' Eddie said.

'What's this?' Michael picked up the envelope. 'It's a bit fancy,' he said. He turned it over and then back, looking for clues and then, because his name was on the front, too, he opened it. He read it to himself, pursing his lips, then looked up at me. 'Someone's party. Do we know them? They've spent a bit on this,' he said, frowning at the lined envelope and glossy card. 'Adrian,' he said. 'Agnes.'

Across the table, Sarah sat immobile. I stared at my plate. There was a rushing in my ears, as though I'd been under water for some time.

'Right,' Michael said. 'And we're invited to' – he squinted at the address – 'Lynwood Hall because . . . ?'

'Because his daughter's at Sarah's school, I suppose,' I said. I avoided her eye. 'He's a friend of Sheila's, too.' The table seemed to ripple in front of me.

'And any friend of Sheila's is a friend of ours, is that it? God help us.' Michael examined the card again. 'Oh, Marion, isn't this when we've already invited . . . ?'

'I know,' I said.

'Can I have a party?' said Eddie.

'Your birthday isn't till April, stupid,' Sarah said.

'When's April? Is it soon?'

'Ages and ages away. Past Christmas. Months,' she said, swinging the fact to hit him hard.

'April the tenth,' said Eddie, screwing up his eyes as if the date dazzled him.

'Well, it's up to you, Marion,' said Michael. 'We can change the date, if you like. If you'd rather go to this.'

'Yes, let's put them off,' I said, too quickly.

Michael raised his eyebrows. 'You're not usually a party person,' he said.

'I can't actually remember the last time we went to a party,' I said. 'I suppose it was your works do, wasn't it?'

'You wore your red dress,' Michael said.

I felt stung that he'd remembered. 'Did I?' I said. 'Well, I'm wearing a new one for this.' It was as if he'd thrown something fragile to me and I'd made no attempt to catch it.

'Let's hope it lives up to expectations,' Michael said, getting to his feet.

'Crappy invite,' said Sarah, putting the card on the table.

I looked at her at last. I willed myself to see only a little girl. I kept my gaze fixed, as if I could make her years younger if I concentrated. 'Careful,' I said. The air between us buzzed.

'Didn't know it was so precious. You're hardly going to forget the details, are you?' Sarah tilted her chin. 'I'm out then, anyway, so don't ask me to babysit.'

'Where?' I said.

'There's a party. A really *good* party,' she said, as she retreated. 'Not just a lot of old people jigging around.'

I heard more than what she said. Something was being revealed, little by little, until the whole picture became clear. When I realised what it was, the joy of revelation made me want to shriek. Sarah sounded *childish*. She was like a paper doll. She was trying on various ways of being a woman, but they could only stay in place until their flimsy hooks gave way. She'd snatch them away herself if they hampered her or made her feel unsure. Before too long, she'd fidget behind his vision of her. She couldn't sit at the grown-up table for too long, she'd soon want to go back to the nursery. I felt as if I were growing and taking shape. There was something elemental in my strength. I wouldn't read her diary any more. I didn't need to. The only story that mattered now was my own.

'Sarah didn't say: "Can I leave the table?"' said Eddie, always on the lookout for transgressions. 'I'm seven and a half,' he said. 'Can I have a half-birthday party?'

I pulled a piece of writing paper from the pad. The top sheet was still indented with my last letter, so I used the one beneath it. *Michael and Marion Deacon are delighted to accept*, I wrote. A prim, formal acceptance. I left it propped up on the table in the hall. *P.S.*, I wanted to add, *when can I see you? I want to see you. I want you. I want you. I want you.*

Chapter 58

7 October

My favourite clothes so far in my life: (1) my Ladybird dress, which I chose myself from the catalogue. It had an elasticated waistband and a stretchy band on the end of the sleeves. If I'm honest, it was a bit scratchy. (2) My cardigan with the angora front. I saved it for best because Mum said it would probably need dry cleaning and nothing I'd ever worn before has needed that. I haven't worn it much at all. The last time I put it on, I could hardly do up the buttons. (3) The pink top Mum gave me. It has a polo neck and no sleeves.

When I walked past the building site on the corner of Shepstone Road last week, the men there called out hello darling. One of them shouted could I walk past again, only faster, and they all laughed. At Tessa's party, Greg put his hands on my breasts as if they were cricket balls he'd just caught.

For my birthday, I am going to ask for hot pants and wet-look boots. Bobbie came into my classroom just before register today. Everyone stopped talking. Her waterfall of hair swung behind her as she came up to my desk. Some of the girls followed her; they were all in line as if they were doing country dancing. She handed me a bag and said it was for me, for Saturday night, and then she walked off without turning round. As she shut the door behind her, everyone started shouting LEZZIE at me. Lynne asked me what she'd given me. Luckily the bell rang, so she couldn't say anything else.

It was a dress. It wasn't made of blue velvet, thank God. I'd peeked into the bag on the bus to see a swirl of purple and pink. It released a burst of Bobbie's light, soapy perfume. I took it out of the bag and waved it gently round my room when I got home, so that atoms of her scent would land everywhere. I thought I'd sleep with it under my pillow before I gave it back. Facing away from my mirror, I slipped it on and then waited till the last moment, till I couldn't bear not to see what I looked like, before I turned round. It was baby-doll shaped and very full. The sleeves were really long and edged with tiny bobbles that bounced and swung when I moved. It smelled of Bobbie, but it made me look completely and utterly like me.

Chapter 59

A faint scent came from the dress as I shook it from the bag. I held it to my nose. I didn't recognise it; it was sweet and floral. The girls in the shop probably tried things on after hours. It was a brighter yellow than I remembered. Kneeling in front of my wardrobe, hugging the dress, I rocked gently to and fro.

'Mummy?' Eddie stuck his head round the door. 'Is it true you're going out? Is Daddy going too?'

'Yes, sweetheart, but a lovely lady is coming to babysit.' I hadn't actually met the girl, but she'd sounded all right on the telephone.

I could tell Eddie was anxious because he didn't correct me with: 'I'm *not* a baby.' Instead, he said, 'Isn't Sarah looking after me?' His face was contorted with worry.

'She's going out, too. But we won't be long.' I waited, watching him decide between sorrow and anger. 'Do you want to see Mummy's new dress?' I said, holding it up.

He looked doubtful. 'Why is it yellow?' he said.

I laughed. 'Because it's not green,' I said. 'Look, choose me a necklace.' I held out my costume jewellery box. He inspected it as though he were being lured somewhere he didn't want to go. 'I'll put on my dress and you find me something nice to go with it.' I held the box over the bed and upended it recklessly on to the counterpane.

He regarded the tumble of sparkling stones and bright beads without enthusiasm. When he was very small, I could distract him for ages with a tin full of buttons, a random assortment for ever waiting to be sewn on to clothes. He was too old for that now. He went to this new task reluctantly. 'This?' he said, holding up a bracelet fashioned like a curled snake with red jewel eyes.

'No, my dress is flowery. Look carefully, Eddie,' I said. 'You're good at that.'

I pulled off my jumper. I'd have to change my underwear. My everyday bra was simply chosen to keep everything where it should be. Should I wear a roll-on? I looked across at Eddie, who was now lying on the bed, concentrating on a convoluted tangle of chains. I pulled everything out of the drawer to search.

Eddie stopped what he was doing. 'Can I do that?' he said. He let a handful of glittering gold and silver fall on to the floor.

'No,' I said. I found exactly what I wanted.

Eddie looked perplexed. 'Why are you 'cited?' he said. 'Can I go downstairs?' He was planning to leave me with a mess of his making.

'Go on, then,' I said. When he'd gone, I stood in front of my reflection timidly, as if waiting for an announcement. 'Good,' I said aloud. I patted foundation over the little hills of my cheeks and chin. I spat on the cake of mascara, concave with use, and leaned close to the little mirror in the compact, widening my eyes as I scrubbed the black ink on to my lashes.

'Mum?' I heard the clunk of Sarah's platform shoes stopping outside the door. 'I'm off now,' she said. She pushed the door open. 'I'm getting a lift,' she said. 'Oh.' She stopped abruptly, seeing me reflected in the mirror. 'Is that your new dress?'

'Yes. It's the one I bought the other day.' I smiled at her without turning round. 'Have a lovely time,' I said. I opened my mouth and flattened my lips against my teeth as I applied a coating of dark pink lipstick. I glanced at Sarah. She was wearing a short floral dress that stuck out from underneath her bust. It looked like a doll's party outfit. I frowned. 'Have I seen that before?' I said, twisting round to face her.

'This isn't mine. I borrowed it.' Sarah tugged at the hem, situated at a point not far below the top of her thighs. Little tassels swung and tangled from voluminous sleeves.

I felt as if I could hold her in my mouth like a cub and shake her until she dangled, limp and still. Despite the brown frosting on her eyelids and the apricot smudge on her mouth, despite her swelling breasts and the swing of her hips as she walked, she was still a child. Like fruit picked too soon, she'd taste bitter. I was ripe and swollen with sweetness. The slightest touch would burst my skin.

Chapter 60

I drive through the grey dawn. I observe every traffic light and slow at every junction, although the roads are empty. When I was small, I used to imagine that scenery unravelled for me as I travelled. I thought that forests or houses were dragged into view only moments before I saw them. The people I saw through train windows or from the back seat of the car had been summoned to appear. Everything would be folded away once I'd gone past. The waking town has the same sense of recent assembly. I wind down the window. I want to hear more than the car's engine. I want to be sure everything exists.

I remember sitting beside Adrian as he drove that last time, the unfamiliar landscape making me tense. I willed the miles to pass. I didn't know they were taking me further from so many last times and lost chances. I can't remember his face very well now. Catching a glimpse of the back of his neck or his wrist then was enough to make me want him. I was so hungry for him it obliterated all my other appetites. I examine this memory without emotion, I cannot remember the taste of it. With care, waiting to feel again the pulse of panic that became a roar, inching along a precipice of memory with nothing but a sheer drop on every side, I make another journey in my head, to another hospital. I had a violent need then not to make haste, I didn't want to arrive at all. As long as I was still on my way, I couldn't hear any bad news. I could still have hope. There was no hope.

I will tell Michael now, again, that I'm sorry. I will hold his cold hand and whisper for his forgiveness although from now on I will wake every day without that possibility. I stretch against the fact of my loss, the way you force air into your cheeks. I feel the sharp darts of cold air from the open window. Two people walk past; their muffled conversation swings into my thoughts. Between them, dragging his feet, a small boy yells in protest. They are ignoring his cries, their smiling and chatting at odds with their charge's red-faced anger.

I want to be wanted again. Beyond the pincer grab of desire, I want to be held. To be needed. To be where nothing else is possible but warmth and safety and the smell of lavender. I have felt like this before. It will pass.

Chapter 61

'Is this it?' Michael stopped at the gatepost. In the distance, I could see the lights of a large house. As a general rule, I thought, places called Something or Other Hall tend not to be bungalows, but this place was huge. As we reached the end of the drive, a boy in an oversized military greatcoat came to Michael's side of the car and circled his hand to tell him to wind his window down. As he bent towards him, I could smell his cigarette: the smoke was rich and sweet. 'Over there, yah?' he said, waving laconically to where other cars were parked. His hair fell forward over his face in irregular lines.

'Fat lot of good,' Michael said, winding the window up as he drove. 'What regiment is he supposed to be in?'

'It looked a bit naval to me,' I said. I hoped that I sounded calm. My heart was racing. If I saw even one person I knew, I planned to cling to them like a limpet. Anything rather than watch Adrian talking to anyone else. Although if the only other person in that category was Sheila, I might have to make another plan. 'We shouldn't stay long,' I said.

Michael pulled the key from the ignition. 'It's a party,' he said. 'You might enjoy it.'

I thought I heard a sliver of sharpness in his voice. I wondered whether to leave my coat in the car, rather than face the ignominy of having anyone take it from me. They were bound to have staff, even if it was just for tonight, weren't they? But a cold wind hit as soon as I got out of the car and I wrapped my coat around me.

Next to the doorbell was a handwritten sign, instructing the visitor to: 'pull hard'. It was an old-fashioned affair, the sort of bell that you couldn't hear yourself as you pulled the lever. It must ring somewhere deep inside the house. I could hear chatter without words and music with a thudding bass, but no discernible tune. It was the unspecific background noise of any party. No one came.

'Good start,' said Michael. He pulled at the lever again. 'Come on, someone.' He turned to me with an expression that confirmed he'd expected this sort of thing.

'S'open.' The boy who'd directed the car came past us and pushed at the door. In the hall's light I could see spots on his chin, a crop of the livid pinks and yellows of rhubarb and custard sweets. There was an assortment of people in the hall, in groups of two or three, engaged in urgent, quiet conversations. They looked across expectantly at us as we came in, then resumed their pairings, disappointed. It reminded me of the way cows looked at you if they thought you might be bringing hay. I didn't know any of the parents at Sarah's school well enough to recognise them in party civvies, but I suspected that none of them would have worn quite so much velvet all at once. Under the high ceiling, a pall of cigarette smoke already clouded the air.

There was no evidence that any special effort had been made to prepare for a party. There were no large vases of flowers or trays of drinks in sight. The hall light blazed brightly, a bare, unshielded bulb. The family's own coats, an assortment of weather-proofed jackets and anoraks interleaved with dog leads and skipping ropes, took up all the hooks. Two chairs nearby were already overflowing with outer garments. People had started putting their coats on the floor. I placed mine gingerly on top of one of the piles on the chairs, prompting an eruption of sleeves from all the coats underneath it.

'Hi.' A man stood beside me, holding out a drink. 'Punch,' he said. 'God knows what's in it. Probably emptied the cupboard and just threw some sliced orange in at the last moment. Hello. Are you bride or groom?'

'Sorry?' I took the glass. It smelled of Christmas and something woody caught in my teeth.

'Adrian or Aggie?' The man wore a paisley jacket. He seemed to have borrowed his trousers from a smaller sister. 'You *might* be both, I suppose. Which one is your friend?'

'Oh, well, Adrian, I suppose. My daughter—' But he had gone. Where was Adrian? I wanted to see him, and I dreaded it, too. Wasn't the host supposed to greet the guests? The party seemed to be happening somewhere beyond this room.

'God, what is this?' Michael held his glass at arm's length, looking for somewhere to put it down.

I drained mine and handed it to him.

'I'm impressed,' he said. 'I think it had lighter fuel in it. I'll keep an eye on you, in case you burst into flames.'

The music was suddenly louder. 'All along the watch tower!' a woman sang. 'Love it, but you can't really dance to it, can you?' She moved her arms, sweeping the sleeves of her dress against her face. Her eyes were ringed in purple and maroon, like a bruise. She moved her hips as if she danced unobserved.

'Our very own Pan's Person,' the man beside her said to me. 'She'd like to think so, anyway.' He watched the woman; her dress was fluid and bright. Cut low at the neck, it revealed the circles of full breasts when she bent forward. My free hand went involuntarily to my chest to check that my own bosom was securely stowed. 'What is this dress supposed to be anyway?' he said. 'It looks like an explosion in a fabric factory.' He grabbed the woman's skirt and pulled it, walking away from her so that it extended quite a long way into the room.

'Get off! It's made of scarves. Different silk scarves. Careful! It's fragile.' She batted his hand lightly, then held it. They embraced and danced together to a different rhythm from the insistent thumping above their heads.

Michael put our glasses on the windowsill. His was nearly full. 'It'll probably strip the paint if it spills,' he said. 'Hadn't we better find either of the Cavanaghs?' He walked towards the music. The noise came from above; the living room must be upstairs. The house had an instant exoticism merely by having rooms on unexpected levels. On some of the steps we had to step over piles of books or children's discarded clothing. There was a basket of dry washing in the middle of the landing but I couldn't tell if it was destined for, or returning from, a wash. Nobody moved aside to let us past, they simply carried on their conversations or their canoodling on either side of us, like an undisciplined guard of honour.

A man with a large woolly head of hair leaned both his arms against the wall, pinning a woman between them. His face was very close to hers, as if he were choosing between interrogation or kissing. I thought I recognised her from somewhere; she had the long blonde hair and sticky, plum mouth of a magazine model. Pictures, actual real paintings, of many different styles and subjects, were arranged higgledy-piggledy above the dado rail, many more of them than I had ever seen hung together. There were plenty of them propped against the skirting, too. As we went past an open doorway, I caught sight of a large bed. The sheet and blankets were only loosely pulled up, the pillows still dented. It was an unwanted glimpse of intimacy.

'Marion?' Michael jerked his head for me to follow him.

The music crashed against my chest as I walked through the wide doorway into the room beyond. Someone had rigged a flashing light that pulsed red and green, but it was rather dark otherwise. Too many bodies were squashed on to each available piece of furniture. People danced, either pressed together or wriggling apart. In the gloom, I could just make out Adrian. He had a cigarette in one hand, the other was resting on a woman's lower back. They were both turned away from each other, talking to someone on either side of them. I registered a tumble of thick, dark hair, hanging loose. From a broad sweep over her shoulders it thinned to a little curl at the base of her spine.

'I'm going to get us a drink,' Michael yelled. 'There's a table over there.'

Adrian's hand stayed specifically, gently, on his wife's back, on the pale green of her dress, on her hair. I stared at the spot so intently that I thought Adrian must have felt it, because he looked up and saw me. He bent to his wife's ear and whispered something. I braced myself for the woman to look around, to look straight at me to see who he'd meant. *That's Sarah's mother – you know, Bobbie's friend.* Instead, she shook her head and carried on with her conversation.

As Adrian came towards me, several people grabbed his arm or shouted something at him. He responded, smiling, but didn't stop. 'The parting of the Red Sea,' he said, reaching me. His shirt was very fitted and although his trousers didn't look in any danger of falling down, he'd threaded a large and complicated belt through the loops.

'You got a drink?' he said.

'Michael's getting one,' I said. I had to shout my answer, which made me feel foolish.

'Where is he?' Adrian said.

'Over there.' I pointed to where Michael was picking up first one bottle, then another, reading the labels. I knew he was trying to find what he thought was something decent.

'Blue jumper?' Adrian said. Michael seemed to be the only person in the room wearing a jumper of any colour.

I nodded.

'I want to talk to you.' Adrian took my elbow. 'But we'll get him sorted first.'

I felt a bit sorry for Michael, heading towards us triumphantly carrying two glasses, happily unsorted. He handed one to me.

'This is Adrian,' I said, and took a large gulp of whatever was in the glass so I couldn't say anything else.

'How do you do?' Michael extended his free hand.

'Jolly well, old bean,' said Adrian unkindly, although I didn't think Michael had heard him. They shook hands; only one of them was aware of the incongruity. 'Now, Michael, I want you to meet' – he swung round, with one finger circling, playing lucky dip with his guests – 'Malcolm!' he said, guiding Michael towards a rotund man with a thin, striped scarf wrapped many times round his neck like a cloth serpent.

I watched as Adrian described them to each other; I couldn't hear what he was saying, but both men seemed mollified by the other's credentials.

He took my hand, leading me from the room. I wondered if his wife had seen us leaving. I looked for Michael over my shoulder, but the space between us was now filled with people and noise. Adrian didn't let go of me, he didn't seem to care how it looked if we were hand in hand. 'Going to get some more glasses,' he said, extricating himself as someone caught his arm. We went down the stairs as if we lived in the house together, as if it were our party. There were fewer people here, although a larger number clustered in the kitchen.

A tall man wearing a cloak was standing at the open fridge, glumly inspecting the contents. 'Isn't there any bloody food?' he said. He picked up something from one of the shelves.

'What the fuck's this?' he said, holding what looked like a very old roast potato between finger and thumb. I was less shocked at his careless expletive than by his rummaging, uninvited, through someone else's leftovers.

'Where are you going, man?' he asked, as we went past him.

'Getting wine glasses,' Adrian said, and repeated it several times, miming drinking in explanation, as people clapped him on the shoulder or shouted a greeting. At the far end of the kitchen he opened a door into a corridor.

'Where are we going?' I said. I hoped I wouldn't have to find my way back alone, I hadn't been concentrating on the route.

'In here,' he said. He still held my hand. He flicked a switch and a single bulb under a flat metal shade made a small yellow pool of light, revealing a long room full of empty stone shelves.

It looked like the sort of place where you'd store drying apples or leave a blancmange to set. It was cold. I shivered as he closed the door behind us. 'Where are the—' I started to say, although I couldn't finish my sentence because he kissed me and that was obviously what he'd planned all along.

I kept thinking about Michael and then noticing things like spiders' webs. There were a great many of them, festooned with trapped insects and dust. I didn't feel guilty about Michael because there wasn't any room to feel anything else apart from how lovely the kissing was and how much I wished I could only think about that and not how hard this room would be to clean. But it was like swimming, whenever I put my head under the water and started to dive lower, I'd have to come up for air.

My shoes pinched and I swayed unsteadily on the thin heels. He stood with his back to the door, close enough to prevent anyone coming in, and pulled me towards him. I could smell his dark and musty scent. It was the sort of dense perfume that would cling to my skin and clothes. After some more kissing which also involved his lips on my neck, which was pleasant, and his tongue on the general area round and inside my mouth, which was particularly nice, he stopped and looked at me. Without looking away, he put one hand under my dress and wiggled his fingers into my knickers and then further. I began to think that it might be a good idea if he didn't stop what he was doing. It occurred to me fleetingly that it was a shame that, at this angle, with this poor lighting, he couldn't see the pretty sprays of flowers on my underwear or that it matched, but soon I couldn't maintain any coherent line of thought at all. There was something just out of reach I wanted to get to. It was like being a mouse in a mixing bowl, the slippery sides sending it repeatedly back to the bottom. I knew he was watching me as I scrabbled and slid. I put one hand over his and forced my heels into the floor, to keep myself earthbound.

I wanted to lie down afterwards. I wondered if the wide, empty shelves would take my weight. Adrian was still breathing hard. He undid his belt. Releasing the buckle was as unwieldy as lowering a drawbridge. His trousers took some unpeeling. He curled my fingers round him, frowning and closing his eyes. I listened to his laboured breathing and felt his frantic movements as I held him. It was very repetitive. It made me think of feeding my infant children, the way you had to keep scooping the same spoonful from their cheeks and chin back into their mouths over and over again. When I felt him spill, I relaxed my grip, but I thought it would be rude to take my hand away. He stood panting, holding on to my shoulders as if he'd just run up a hill.

He wrestled the thick leather of his belt back through the oversized buckle. The pockets of his trousers were entirely flat. 'God, I need a cig,' he said. He looked at me as though he'd just remembered I was there. 'You're great, you know that? I thought you'd be good.' He ruffled his hands through his hair. 'Let's go away together. Soon.'

'What?' I said. 'What do you mean?'

'I mean, a night. A bed. A few hours together.'

'I don't know if I could,' I said. 'How could I?'

'Haven't you got a friend you could say you were staying with?' he said, patting his chest pockets as if they really could contain a packet of cigarettes.

I looked at him, seeing the way he was rearranging his hair into just the right state of unkempt and tucking his close-fitting shirt even more firmly into his waistband. There was Bridget, of course. 'I may have someone,' I said.

'Really?' he said. He grabbed my arms, not quite looking me in the eye. 'It would be brilliant. Think about it and let me know,' he said, as if he were a salesman and I was a persuadable client. 'Ready?' He opened the door. 'You go first. I'll follow you out in a minute.'

Nobody looked at me as I made my way back through the kitchen. In the hallway, the round man we'd left Michael with was talking to a semicircle of people, one arm across his big chest and the other gesticulating, as if he were addressing the Senate. As I got closer I could see that the reason for their grouping was a large joint, being passed between them with careful regularity. I wondered what had happened to Michael. From the tone of the man's voice, I could tell he was dull. As I walked past them, one of the group turned round. He held the joint out wordlessly to me. I took it.

'Have you seen my husband?' I said to the orator.

'Do I know him?' the man said, not quite looking at me.

'Michael,' I said. 'Blue jumper. He was upstairs with you.' I felt suddenly desperate.

'Is that his name? Oh yes. Something in accountancy, isn't he?' He took the joint from me. 'He was *fascinating*. Lucky you.' The man smiled, revealing uneven teeth. 'He told me *all* about his job,' he said, his voice heavy with feigned boredom. 'Anyway,' the man said, 'your daughter arrived and, *sadly*, we had to part.' He turned away, dismissing me.

I felt transparent with fear. Sarah? What was she doing here? I looked round the hallway. Where was she? Where had Michael gone? There was no sign of either of them. Perhaps they'd already gone home? I thought of Michael searching for me. Someone might tell him we were last seen fetching some glasses. I felt as if my insides were calcifying, it was hard to move or speak.

'Still here?' Adrian touched me lightly on the shoulder. If I hadn't seen him moments before, fused to me and breathing hard, I'd hardly have believed it was the same person. He was calm and steady, as if this was the first time we'd spoken that night. He'd found a cigarette somewhere and he sipped from a full glass of wine. His gestures looked deliberate and larger than life, and he held the cigarette and glass as if they were props that had been set for him before this entrance.

'Marion, there you are.' Michael appeared at my other side. I hoped he wasn't going to ask where I'd been. I didn't want Adrian to hear me lie.

'Michael!' said Adrian easily. 'Did Malcolm tell you all about his fish?' he said, raising his eyes. 'He breeds koi carp. They're more important than family to him. Isn't that right?' He slid one arm around the large man's shoulder, dangling his wrist and the lit cigarette. 'Doesn't seem to realise that they're the most boring things on earth. Or in water.' He squeezed the man to him and kissed him loudly on one plump cheek.

'No, he didn't,' said Michael, politely answering Adrian's question. 'Marion, Sarah's here. She arrived with – with your daughter,' he said to Adrian. 'Sorry, I don't know her name. I think they're both a bit drunk.'

'Bobbie went to a party tonight, so I sincerely hope she *is* drunk,' said Adrian. 'But if her boyfriend's pissed too, I'll kill him. He was supposed to be driving her home in his silly little car.' Adrian was loud, addressing the whole room. I realised with a start that he was probably quite drunk, too. 'It's a bubble car.' He laughed. 'What sort of a bloke gets into a bubble car?'

'Where is she?' I said, standing close to Michael.

'Upstairs,' he said. 'I think we ought to get her home.'

The flight of stairs looked higher than before. I could see Sarah at the end of the landing. The girl beside her must be Bobbie. She was wearing a blouse with huge leg o' mutton sleeves, a long purple skirt and shiny black boots that laced at the front like a Victorian housemaid's footwear. Both girls were holding full glasses of something that definitely wouldn't help them sober up. Sarah watched me advancing towards them and, as I drew level with her, she laughed.

'Did you just nearly fall upstairs?' she said. 'I didn't know it was you, you looked so funny staggering about. You shouldn't bloody wear heels if you can't walk in them.'

'Let's go home,' I said. Sarah's cheeks were spotted with bright pink, as if she were flushed with fever. She blinked hard as if she needed to clear her vision and I turned round to see Adrian coming towards us.

'Who's this?' the Bobbie girl said, pointing at me.

'Hello, Bobbie darling.' Adrian leaned across and took the glass from his daughter's hand. 'I'll take this. Say a nice hello to Sarah's mummy and daddy.'

'Nice hello to Sarah's mummy and daddy,' she said in a baby voice.

'Jeez, drunk kids are so dull.' He came closer to her and sniffed theatrically into her face. 'Just hooch? No weed?'

Bobbie rolled her eyes. 'Just al-co-hol,' she said carefully. 'Lots of it. That's why she's pissed herself.' She spun Sarah round to reveal a long stain like a dark, wet tail.

Sarah continued to revolve in an unsteady circle until she faced us again. Her hands went to her face, she held on to her chin and breathed hard.

Adrian put his hands on her shoulders. 'It's okay,' he said.

She closed her eyes and leaned against him. He moved his arms around her back.

I felt hot tears swell behind my eyelids. I wanted to pull the two of them apart with great force, scratching at their hands. 'Michael,' I said angrily. 'Get hold of her. Take her home.'

Michael put his head on one side and looked at them as if separating them was a difficult puzzle.

Adrian whispered something in Sarah's ear.

'Sarah?' Michael said. 'Sarah, come along. Let's get in the car.'

She didn't respond. The party swirled around us, people continued conversations and yelled goodbyes across the landing and down the stairs.

'Sarah!' I said loudly. Everything seemed to have gone into slow motion.

Eventually, Sarah raised her head. She looked very young. Michael took her hand and prised her gently away from Adrian's embrace. She smiled at him, but she didn't look at me at all. With her father on one side and Adrian on the other, she allowed herself to be led down the stairs.

In the hallway, our progress was impeded by a knot of people attempting to leave. We were mired in a tangle of retrieving coats and last-minute conversations. Adrian's wife extracted herself from the crowd. She looked as if she had spent the evening somewhere else, drinking only cold water. If you were choosing features out of a box to assemble a face, you would never have put that long nose under those wide, slightly protruding eyes. And if you had, you might have hesitated to include that small mouth. She regarded us through enormous glasses, as square as little televisions. Round her neck was a black velvet choker, studded with little cloth flowers. She was beautiful. Sarah suddenly slumped forward at the waist and I had to use both arms to stop her from falling.

'Hello everyone, how marvellous to find you!' Sheila greeted us as if we were all assembled for her benefit. In the dishevelled unravelling of the evening, she was preserved intact, like a fly in amber. Her husband hovered behind her, a satellite in the orbit of its large planet. 'It's been such fun,' Sheila said, ignoring the way I held Sarah in a wrestling grip. 'How lovely that the children came, too.' She smiled at Sarah as if she were a four-year-old in a velvet party dress. 'Now that you've all met,' she said, clutching her bag to her bosom with both hands, 'I'll arrange a dinner party.'

This is how she does it, I thought. There's no subtlety, no cunning. She just bosses the world into the shape she wants it to be.

Sarah leaned so hard against me that I had to take several quick steps to keep my balance.

'Goodbye, Adrian. Thank you,' said Michael, polite to the last.

I felt a pang at the niceness of him. What a useless quality it was, like a silk scarf when you need a fur coat or an umbrella in a hurricane.

We lumbered out of the front door like an awkward, six-legged beast. We had to half drag Sarah up the drive, her shoes ploughing deep furrows along the gravel, then force her onto the back seat. Her inert limbs stuck straight out in front of her as though she were in the first stages of rigor mortis. Circling the car to climb in, I looked back to see Adrian holding something large and shapeless out towards me.

With a gasp of grateful recognition, I leapt away from the car. 'My coat,' I said over my shoulder to Michael, who was still coercing his daughter's legs into bending. I ran up to Adrian so fast I almost tripped.

'Hey,' he said, catching me by the arm. The gesture seemed so tender that I couldn't speak. 'Isn't this yours? I thought I'd seen you wear it.'

'Oh, yes, you have, it's mine,' I said. I was ridiculously pleased that he'd remembered.

'Is she going to be okay?' He pointed into the dark drive to where Michael and Sarah wrestled unseen.

'Sarah?' I said. 'Yes, of course. As long as she isn't sick everywhere. Adrian, listen,' I said, standing on tiptoe to whisper to him. 'You know what you said? About going away?' I thought he looked momentarily bemused, but it couldn't have been because he'd forgotten. Perhaps he hadn't heard me properly.

'Yeah?' he said and began to help me on with my coat.

'Yes, I will!' I said. 'I'll come away with you. For a night.' Saying it aloud made it seem entirely possible.

'That's great!' said Adrian. He made a move towards the door. A man with beads and a Jesus beard forced us apart by hugging Adrian, rocking him from side to side in his embrace.

Adrian looked surprised to see me still standing there as they separated.

'Come over on Monday, so that we can plan,' I said.

He hesitated. In that split second, I felt as if I were out of my depth with miles of deep water beneath me. He nodded.

When I got back into the car beside Michael, I was breathless. 'You okay?' he said, but I didn't reply. I began to feel the sadness of impending sobriety.

'God,' said Sarah, registering us both. 'What *is* that smell? Something stinks of hippy stuff, it's like being in Ken Market.'

'Could have been any number of suspects,' Michael said, glancing at her in the rear-view mirror. 'Quite a few leftover beatniks there.'

'Beatniks!' Sarah snorted.

I sank lower in my seat. The dark lanes swallowed us up. I could only see Michael's face when it was revealed in the occasional flash of an oncoming car's headlights.

The hallway was in darkness when we got home. The babysitter emerged blinking; she had no shoes on and had obviously been asleep.

'I'll take you home,' said Michael.

I went to fetch the girl's things. I wanted her out of the house as fast as possible. There were discarded biscuit wrappers on the sofa. 'Here!' I handed her the shoes and a floppy velvet bag. Sarah slunk past us and went up the stairs without a word.

'Nice time?' said the girl, putting on her shoes and not looking at anyone in particular.

I crept past Sarah's closed door and into Eddie's room. His nightlight wasn't on. I flicked the switch to let the china rabbits sit round their fire. Eddie lay asleep with his eyes closed. They were as smooth as if they'd been drawn on his skin. His mouth was open. In one hand, he held something that caught the light. I bent to examine it. It was a necklace. It was mine. He must have chosen one for me, after all. I'd run from the house earlier, so eager to leave that I hadn't even said goodnight. I looked at him, taking in the tiny chaos of his rumpled sheets and bitten fingernails, waiting for my heart to break. I felt as if I was testing the sharp point of regret with the tip of one finger. There was nothing, everything was worn smooth. I had filed all the splinters of my guilt away.

Chapter 62

9 October

Jeff has a tiny bubble car. Instead of having doors, the front of it opens up. When we sat inside and he closed it, it was as if he were pulling a bedspread over us. Bobbie was giggling in this really annoying way as he drove. She talked to him in a baby voice and I thought that if we'd only just met, I probably wouldn't bother to say anything to her. Even though he was wearing a cheesecloth shirt and his hair curled over his neck, Jeff made me think of the boy who sits in the front of the accountant's office on the high street. We have to pass him every week, on the way to the hockey pitch. We're already in our games kit. Some of my class walk really close to the window and mouth 'hello' or flick their skirts at him, to tease him. He's probably the same age as we are, but he ignores us and gets on with his work. He looks dull. If you put Jeff in a suit like his and cut his hair, he'd look boring, too. I had to sit behind them, squeezed on to a little ledge where you could hardly fit a suitcase, let alone a whole person. I had pins and needles in one leg when I got out.

The music was really loud. I could see the silhouettes of the people in the neighbouring houses close to their windows, getting ready to complain. Bobbie grabbed my hand. 'We've got to find Adam,' she said. I wanted to get my bearings first and see who else was there, but there was no escape. She held on to me all the way into the kitchen and grabbed two bottles of cider. She told me to drink it straight away. I tried, but it's hard to get fizzy stuff down you quickly. She watched me carefully, but she wasn't drinking the second one herself. It was for me. She was saying something, but the music drowned her out.

She mimed to me that the boy called Adam had arrived with big, rolling eyes and fluttering hands like a silent movie star. He was really little, not much taller than me. He was wearing a huge white shirt, so long that the cuffs completely covered his hands. The sleeves on Bobbie's dress hung over the ends of my arms, too. If we went out together, we'd be like those characters in the fairy tale who are doomed to manage without the use of their fingers. He wore a pair of army-style trousers. They were turned up so much at the bottom that he had to stand with his legs apart. His skin was really pale and his wide-set eyes were a bright, glassy blue. Above them, his brows were permanently raised at the top of his white forehead. It made him look very surprised all the time, as if he'd just been told something awful. He said hi to me and then Bobbie shoved him in the back and he took several steps forward and said hi again, right into my face.

I drank another cider, because the more I had, the easier it was to swallow. Adam tried to hold my hand but there was too much fabric in the way, so he put his arm round me instead. That was quite awkward too, as he wasn't tall enough to reach my shoulders comfortably. I could feel the cider muddling my thoughts and making me stumble as I walked.

The rest of the evening isn't very clear; it's like leafing through an album of fuzzy pictures: there's me and Adam in the garden, him smoking and me feeling quite cold. Here's Bobbie dancing, twisting her tummy round in circles as if she's balancing a hula hoop. This is Jeff and Adam taking us up to a bedroom to snog. It was a boy's room, full of football stuff and a poster of *The Godfather* on the wall. Bobbie and Jeff sat on the floor and kissed with their eyes tightly shut. Adam found a guitar, rolled up his sleeves and sang 'Lay, Lady, Lay' to me, which was excruciating; it has hundreds of verses and I didn't know where to look. When I did catch his eye, he was doing a kind of smirk. It didn't go with his startled expression and made him look about four years old. We lay down on the little bed and he slid his mouth around on top of mine. He put his hand on where my breasts were concealed underneath Bobbie's dress and the training bra. He squeezed one as though it would make a sound. I felt sick, so I concentrated on not being and didn't move much. Adam gripped various parts of me from time to time, as if he was checking I was still alive.

The music downstairs stopped suddenly and the next thing we heard were loud, grown-up, sober voices. Bobbie said that someone must have called the police. I looked out of the window to see everyone filing out into the night, as if it was a fire drill. There was no police car in sight, but all the downstairs lights were on and there were a couple of adults marshalling people on to the pavement. I wanted to get my coat, but Bobbie said that was a bourgeois response. When I got downstairs, the first person I saw was Mrs Edgecombe. She was wearing a pink twin set and a peeved expression. I was at primary school with her son, although he was just a name between two others on the register as far as I was concerned. We must have been in his bedroom, lying on his Leeds United duvet and kissing. She said hello, as if it were quite normal for me to be drunk in her hallway at midnight. She said she was sure I wasn't one of the troublemakers.

I wanted to go home. I didn't want to get back into Jeff's stupid car. But I did really need the loo. We were all standing in a circle – me, Bobbie, Adam, Jeff, Mrs Edgecombe and someone I suppose was Mr E, but he didn't speak. The hall light was really bright. Mrs E told her husband I used to be in Malcolm's class. I hoped she wasn't going to ask me any questions about where I was at school now or how my parents were. No one was moving, it was as if we were all daring each other to leave. Bobbie looked bored and restless. Jeff kept on yawning, showing all his teeth and exhaling with a kind of groan. Adam's permanently startled expression was appropriate, for once.

Bobbie suddenly made a dash for the door and Jeff grabbed my arm and pulled me after her. The car door yawned open like his mouth had done and he flung me in clumsily. I wet myself at once with a great surge of joy. I closed my eyes and lay on the little ledge as if it was my bed. I thought they'd take me home. I'd hoped that, if they didn't, I could sleep where I was till morning, but the car stopped and Bobbie yanked me upright in darkness next to a big house I didn't recognise. She yelled as her hand found the patch of cold liquid. I felt very heavy and stiff. It took me ages to turn my head to speak to her and, by the time I had, I'd completely forgotten what I was going to say.

Chapter 63

I wanted to phone Bridget. I'd rehearsed in my head the conversation I needed to have with her. She'd be delighted to welcome me into the fold. I could imagine her saying, *I thought you'd realise eventually that Michael was a boring old codger – you just sort of know, don't you, especially when you see the alternative.* I positioned myself on the little console and looked up Bridget's telephone number. There were a lot of eights in it and when I started dialling, I wished I could hurry the dial's return to its starting position each time. It retraced its circle agonisingly slowly. Eventually, I heard the click and whirr of connection, then the telephone rang wherever Bridget lived. There was no answer. With rising dread, I began to realise that Bridget might be out. Or even away.

'Burley 8788,' said a man's voice.

I hadn't expected that, either. It must be Trevor. I asked for Bridget without preamble.

'Who's calling?' said the man.

'Amanda,' I said. Everyone knew an Amanda, didn't they?

'Hello?' Bridget said a moment later, sounding cautious.

'It's me, Marion.' I kept my voice low, as if I were the one being overheard.

'Marion? I thought Trevor said "Amanda". I don't know anyone called Amanda.'

'Can you talk?' I said, hoping that Bridget would understand that the phrase was shorthand for: 'talking without anyone listening'.

'What is it?' Bridget sounded very suspicious now. Of course, she probably thought I was going to bale out on agreeing to cover for her.

'Everything's *all right*,' I said, stressing the last words to reassure her. 'But I need to ask you a favour.'

'What sort of favour?' She still sounded wary.

'Well.' I twisted the plastic curls of the cord through my fingers. 'You won't believe it. But you'll understand completely. I'm going to go away for a night. With someone. A man. And I want to tell Michael that I'm staying with you.'

There was a great chasm of silence, as if Bridget had suddenly simply let the phone dangle from her hand. Perhaps Trevor had struck her, after all.

'Bridget?' I said, several times, fearful that I might be calling her name into thin air.

'Are you joking?' said Bridget eventually, her voice brittle with anger. 'Is this a sort of blackmail? Because if it is, it's not worth it. Trevor knows. He knows everything. You're too late.'

'Of course, I'm not joking.' My thoughts raced away and collided with each other. I felt as if I were trying to gather spilled marbles. 'Bridget! What do you mean? Are you okay?'

'No.' Bridget was crying now. 'Marion, I'm sorry, it's been awful. It's not your fault.'

I know it isn't, I thought, wondering how I could ever have thought phoning Bridget was a good idea. I'd have to tell Adrian that I couldn't come away after all. I wanted to weep, too.

'Look,' Bridget said, through a chorus of sniffs and snorts, 'I'm not being fair. I asked you and you said yes. So I'll do it for you, if you really want me to. But I'm telling you, Marion, I wish I was dead.'

'Bridget!' What on earth had happened?

'I'll call you back,' Bridget said, before hanging up. I sat with the phone in my hand, inert with disappointment. It wasn't the end of everything, I told myself. But Bridget's distress lingered like the aftermath of a headache, an echo of remembered pain.

Chapter 64

It's both predictable and strange how ordinary everything is when I arrive at the hospital. There is no one on the desk. The nurse who comes into view makes no attempt at transition from whatever kept her out of sight to address me. I remind her of why I'm there and she looks at me with a querying archness. It's as if she registers my grief on an internal meter and measures her response accordingly. He was an ill, old man, she calculates, and this old woman is his match. We must both have expected his death. I had made those assumptions myself, in her place. I would not have thought his seventy-eight years an unreasonable span. She types with her young fingers and tells me where the computer has assigned his belongings. 'His effects,' she says. She fetches a bag and hands it to me. His bag. For the first time, I cry. The nurse looks satisfied. This is what I should be doing. 'You'll want to see him?' she says. I follow her to where he lies. For a moment, she waits with me. I'm about to plead for solitude when her pager bleeps. She rushes from the room, apologising, as though the intrusion of the modern world into Michael's ancient state was a faux pas.

His grey, grave face betrays no final agony or resolution. He is just – *not here*. Someone has folded his hands one across the other. It's not a pose he'd ever have assumed in life. He does not look content. He does not simulate sleep. He is absent. His body seems irrelevant. He looks neither old nor young. He looks like Eddie.

The nurse hurries back in. She slows her pace as she approaches the bed, as if he could be disturbed. 'It was peaceful,' she says. She probably thinks I should have been here.

I know Michael waited till I'd gone. He was a private man, after all. He kept all his feelings from me, even his grief. Especially his grief. Not for him the last-minute confession. He had nothing to tell me. I would not have been forgiven, either. Not even at the end.

'Did he say anything?' I say. 'Did he ask for his mother?' She looks startled. I'm flustered and embarrassed for us both. 'I mean . . .' I begin.

'He didn't . . .' she says; both of us are speaking at the same time. 'It was very peaceful,' she repeats.

'He was tired,' I say. 'He wanted to go.'

She cocks her head at my choice of words. 'I'll leave you for a while,' she says.

'No.' I gather my things, pick up his bag. 'That's enough,' I say. I turn to Michael. His inert, passive form doesn't need anything from me now. I took too much away from him, a long time ago. *'Did Eddie ask for me?'* I'd said. *'Did he say he wanted his mother?'*

The door flies open and yet another unfamiliar nurse appears. Red-headed and pale-skinned. 'Mrs Deacon? You're here?' she says. 'I asked them to let me know when you arrived.' She shoots an accusing glance at the other nurse, who begins an explanation to do with rotas and sickness. The red and white girl cuts across her. 'I had all this ready for you,' she says. It's a sheaf of papers. 'You'll need these, I'm afraid,' she says. 'The certificate and so forth.' I have seen papers like this before. *Cause of Death: Post trauma haemorrhagic shock. Age: seven.* 'And there's this.'

I recognise Sarah's familiar handwriting. When I picture her leaning over the page, it is still her teenage self I visualise, one arm crooked to conceal her work.

'It's the drawings she sent, from your grandchildren. Cards and so on,' she says. She isn't looking for the effect her words might have.

I peer into the package. There's an unopened envelope. I pull it free. It's addressed to me.

'It's such a shame she couldn't come and see him,' the nurse says, 'but of course you can't fly that late in a pregnancy, can you?' If she sees me flinch, she doesn't let on. 'These things happen. She rang, of course. We held the phone close to him. He heard her. Did she tell you?' She looks at me with more suspicion now.

'Yes,' I say. 'I'll look at these later.' I want to leave the room in case tears spill. 'Can I wait somewhere?' I say. 'Until the others arrive?'

I see a flash of annoyance. We're done here, she wants to say. There's nothing else we need from you. 'Of course,' she says. 'There's a family room at the end of the corridor.'

We are a family of sorts. You'd find it difficult to fit our description on the door, though. The nurse sees my smile, but she does not return it.

Chapter 65

10 October

When I woke up the morning after the party, I thought I'd died. I couldn't open my eyes properly and when I did, they hurt. Bobbie's dress seemed to have shrunk overnight; it was lying on my floor looking very small. It was still wet. I tiptoed downstairs and put it in the dustbin. The ground was moving as if I was on a boat, which made me feel sick. It's a good thing I was already outside when I was.

I hate going into their bedroom. I don't like inhaling the scent of her talc or seeing his collar stiffeners in the little dish. When I opened her dressing table drawer to find the Alka-Seltzer, everything rattled about loudly. Lipsticks clunked against powder compacts. Tins of pins and tacks rolled into sunglasses. At least she wouldn't know if anything had been moved, it wasn't exactly laid out like Kim's Game.

I looked at myself reflected three times in her dressing table mirrors. You can position them to see the back of your head and check your hairstyle, but I just wanted to watch myself cry. I seemed to have an endless supply of tears. I saw my eyelids swell and felt them tighten till I could hardly see.

My eyes were puffy for the rest of the day, but nobody said anything.

Adrian Mr Cavanagh whispered into my ear last night. He held on to me. He squeezed me tightly because I was swaying. He said I'll wait for you. I'll be there the day after tomorrow, don't forget. And even though it was hard to concentrate, because everything in my head was rearing up and kicking like wild horses, I knew I wouldn't forget. I would walk over broken glass with pins in my feet to get to him.

Chapter 66

Adrian didn't arrive until late afternoon. He switched the engine off and let the car roll the last few feet. I was at the door before he'd cranked the handbrake.

'Oh God,' he said, sliding on to a chair in the kitchen and clutching his head. 'Still recovering. Bloody punch.'

'Have you been thinking about our plans?' I said. I meant to sound flippant, but my voice was as high as a child's.

Adrian looked at me as if I was just coming into focus. 'Of course,' he said. 'Silly girl, course I have. Come here.' He buried his face in my midriff. I put my hands on the top of his head. His hair felt greasy. He moved his head from side to side against my stomach, the way you do when you want to make a baby laugh.

'Adrian,' I said, letting his name be everything I wanted to say. He was here, his hair under my fingertips and his big coat trailing on the kitchen floor.

'I'm going to tell M—, everyone, I'm staying at my friend Bridget's,' I said.

He put his hand over my mouth. 'Not too much information, honey,' he said. 'I'll leave all that to you, it's better if I don't know. When did we say we'd go?'

'Next Wednesday,' I said. I ignored the chilly breeze of his forgetting. He read the entries on the calendar on the wall in a monotone, tracing my handwritten notes with his forefinger, like a child with a reading book. 'Den-tist. Par-ent/tea-cher mee-ting, brackets Ed-die. Sure you can fit me in? You're pretty busy.'

'Don't tease me,' I said.

He put his arms round me and kissed my neck. How sharp desire was, when it pricked you.

'Marion,' said Adrian, turning me to face him and sounding serious, 'I think it would be a very good idea if you and I went upstairs. Now.'

In my mind's eye, I saw Michael's dressing gown on the back of the bedroom door and his slippers standing guard on his side of the bed. 'We can't,' I said. 'I really can't. But it's lovely that you want to,' I said, as if I were refusing some unexpected hospitality.

'Don't you want to? I'd sort of imagined this was a mutual thing.'

'It is. I absolutely want to,' I said. 'It's just that the children might be home soon. I wouldn't be able to concentrate properly.'

'You're very sweet.' Adrian didn't appear to mind my refusal. We kissed for a while. There seemed to be enough time for that.

'Would you like some tea?' I said. I thought it would be a good idea if he had a reason to be there when Eddie appeared.

'God, I'm dehydrated. I'd better just have some water,' he said, opening the nearest cupboard. He took out a jug and held it under the tap.

'Let me get you a glass,' I said, watching him raise it to his lips.

He shook his head, still drinking. 'Nah,' he said at last, and wiped his mouth with his hand. 'That'll do. Bye, honey. I'll be in touch.'

After he'd gone, I tipped the jug to drink from it myself and the last inch of water missed my mouth altogether and spilled copiously down my chin. I heard the tremulous ring of the doorbell. I pressed a cloth to my chest. It was amazing how wet such a little bit of water could make you. Through the wavy glass, I could make out a tall shape. Tom stood on the doorstep.

'Hello,' I said.

He hesitated. He was half turned away from me, as if he needed to include someone else in the conversation. There was a woman at the end of the path, standing outside the gate. It was his mother.

'Molly!' I called to her and waved, but the figure didn't respond. 'Wouldn't your mother like to come in?' I said.

He shook his head and held something out to me.

'The Wind in the Willows,' I said. 'Gosh, have you finished it already?'

He shook his head again.

'Then keep it.' I pushed the book gently back towards him. 'We don't need it back yet, Tom. Eddie's got a copy, he told you that, didn't he, and—'

'Mother says I don't want it,' Tom interrupted me. 'She says we don't need your charity.'

'What?' I looked towards his mother. She was too far away

to see clearly but I could feel her fury, even at this distance. 'It's not charity, Tom. Eddie just wanted you to have it. He's enjoying it at school, you see, and he thought that you would, too.'

'Mother says you think I'm an idiot. I told her you said my head's not right, and she said we shouldn't talk to you any more and we should certainly give you back your perishing book.'

'Tom.' I felt weak. 'I didn't mean . . .' I couldn't finish the sentence. It was like trying to translate my thoughts into a foreign language. 'What about your sponsored walk?' I said. 'Have you done it? Shall I give you your money?'

'She says you're very high and mighty for someone who goes gallivanting about in the fields with strange men.'

Molly Spencer stood at the end of the path with her arms folded and her face set. There was no point in striding out to confront her, there was no point in trying to defend myself, either. I must stay calm, I thought, that was the best thing to do. 'Please tell your mother that I never meant to upset either of you,' I said. 'I'm really very sorry if I did.'

He stared at me, his hazel eyes unblinking.

'Tom,' I said quietly, standing directly in front of him so that he blocked his mother from my view. 'Did you like the book?'

He nodded his head with the tiniest movement.

'Look,' I said, 'I'll leave it outside the back door. There's a little ledge by the window. You can take it and read it whenever you want. Just put it back there afterwards, instead of taking it home. If you say anything to anyone, though, I'll be in trouble and I'll have to stop and then you won't be able find out how the story ends.'

I took the book from him, making sure his mother could see me do it. 'I'm sorry,' I said.

In the kitchen, I sat down and leaned back in the chair. I wanted Adrian. He'd said nothing about what I meant to him. Had he even looked at me when he idly picked the date? It didn't matter. When I was a little girl, I'd been picked to play a party game by the birthday girl's older brothers. 'Watch carefully,' they'd said, and they'd put a pile of cushions into the middle of the room. They added a waste-paper basket on its side, an upended chair, a glass vase. Then they'd blindfolded me. In my muffled, woolly darkness they'd guided me over the obstacles. 'Careful, you need to take a really big step now,' they'd encouraged, holding my arm. 'A high jump here and you'll be safely over,' they'd said. I'd obeyed. I'd finished panting and dizzy from holding my breath in fear. But I was elated that I hadn't tripped and fallen or broken anything. When they'd undone the blindfold, giggling to each other, I saw that they'd removed all the hurdles. Nothing was really out of place. I had been leaping over empty spaces. They'd howled with glee at my humiliation.

I had my eyes open this time. I could step over everything in my way, whether it was there or not.

Chapter 67

11 October

Adrian Mr Cavanagh was leaning back in the car with his eyes closed. I watched him for a while because I wasn't sure what to do. In the end, I knocked on the window. He wasn't startled, he just stretched like a cat. He looked as if he had been woken in the middle of an especially satisfying dream. He wound down the window. He said he was going to ask what I was doing here but of course it was my school, too. I had this shivery feeling, like when you're asked a question in class but you haven't really been listening and everything goes quiet. I felt big and small at the same time. I said I thought we were going to the studio today. I thought you were going to paint me. I said you told me to be here. My voice was getting high and wobbly. I felt stupid, standing in the street, wishing he'd behave like he did before. He shook his head as if he needed to clear it. He said, honey, listen, people get drunk and say things, right? Then he said some things so terrible that I can't write them down.

Bobbie came up behind me. I jumped away as if I'd been caught doing something wrong, which was unfair because he was the bad person. She said are you feeling better but she didn't look as if she really cared one way or the other. Adrian Mr Cavanagh said do you want a lift and I said no. She said just as well, it wasn't really on their way, was it. I said I was just saying hello. Bobbie got in and slammed the door shut. As they drove away, she waved at me as if she was pretending to be the queen, her hand flat and stiff.

I wished the car would crash into something in front of me. I am too weak to punish him alone. I am too powerless to stand in his way. I'll find someone to help me. I know exactly who that person will be.

Chapter 68

'I think I might stay with a friend next week,' I said, as we sat at supper.

Michael frowned. 'Who?' he said, just as Sarah said, 'Why?'

'Nobody expects the Spanish Inquisition!' I raised my hands as if I was being held at gunpoint. I turned to Michael. 'Bridget,' I said. 'Friends do stay with friends, you know.'

'You don't,' said Sarah.

'Apparently I do.' I sliced a chunk of meat from a pork chop. 'Any more questions?' I looked round the table as if it were a classroom.

'When are you going away?' said Eddie in the ensuing silence.

'I'm going away on Wednesday,' I said.

'Wednesday is when Mummy leaves us.' Sarah reached across the table for the ketchup.

I said, 'It's all right, Eddie. Mummy's only going to be away for one bedtime.'

'One night?' Michael said. 'I thought she lived miles away. Yorkshire, isn't it? One night isn't long enough, is it, if you're going all that way?'

'Now Daddy wants me to leave for ever.' I felt stupid as soon as I'd spoken, it was too much.

Michael put one hand over mine, something I thought people only did in films. He smiled at me gently, as if I was armed and he needed to remove the weapon. 'You go,' he said. 'We'll be fine. All I meant was that if you did want to go for longer, we'd understand. Wouldn't we?' He looked across at Sarah. She glared back at him. 'Eddie,' he said, still holding my hand, 'Mummy is only going to be away for one bedtime.'

'And one bathtime,' Eddie corrected.

Inexplicably, I wanted to cry. I'd have preferred them all to be angry with me. Instead, Michael seemed to be suggesting I'd been overwrought and that some brief time away from my duties might restore me. I pulled my hand out from under his.

'Thank you,' I said. 'I'm glad I'm allowed to make one decision for myself, at least.' Michael had his puzzled puppy look again, which made me feel better.

'You are so selfish,' Sarah said. 'Have you any idea how unhappy you've been making Daddy?'

'Sarah,' Michael began, but she got up and left without speaking. 'She doesn't seem to be able to leave the room in any other way,' Michael said.

'Why's she cross?' said Eddie.

'Oh, she's just a bit tired,' Michael said.

'Why doesn't she have a bedtime, then?' Eddie said. 'I have to have a bedtime, why doesn't she?'

'Because she's fourteen and you're seven,' I said with some force. 'Shut up and finish your supper, Eddie. It's nearly your bedtime, whether you like it or not. You stupid little boy. Shut up.'

It was harsher than smacking him. He began to cry. 'I don't want it.' He pushed his plate away.

'Come on, Eddie,' said Michael, looking helplessly across at me. 'Mummy didn't mean it.'

'I'll go and talk to Sarah,' I said.

Eddie collapsed into his grief, hurling himself away from the table. He looked at me as if I were a changeling, a cruel simulacrum of his kinder parent. I stood outside Sarah's room for a long time before knocking. The silence from within was enormous. I wondered if she was close by, just on the other side of the door, listening to my breathing and waiting for the sound of my departing footsteps.

'Sarah?' I said. I heard the squeak of bedsprings then the door opened a crack.

'What do you want?' said Sarah. I could only see a sliver of her face. I heard the thickness of recent crying in her voice.

'Bolting out of the room is no way to finish a conversation.'

'I hate the way you talk to Daddy,' Sarah said. It was unnerving to hear the same measured politeness in her voice as in mine.

'That's up to me and him,' I said. 'I wouldn't criticise the way you talk to your friends.'

'You would. And anyway, it's not the same. You're always banging on about being polite and listening properly and respecting people, but you talk to Daddy as if he's stupid and he doesn't matter and as if you don't even like him.' Sarah's voice rose and broke.

'Don't be silly,' I said. Sarah didn't reply, but her visible eye reddened.

The shrill of the telephone startled us both. In the second that I turned towards the sound, Sarah closed her door.

'Marion?' Bridget said at once, without preamble. 'I just wanted to say that you need to give me the address of where you'll be staying.' She wasn't crying, thank goodness. In fact, she sounded practical and efficient. 'And the telephone number. I do need to be able to get in touch with you, if anything happens. When are you going?'

'Wednesday,' I said. 'I will. And thank you, Bridget.'

There was a pause. I heard her draw in her breath and braced myself for more of her misery. 'Goodbye,' I said, to prevent it.

'Was that Bridget?' Michael was standing by the kitchen door.

I nodded.

'Why did you need to tell her it's Wednesday? I thought it was all arranged,' he said.

I blushed as if I'd been slapped. 'She gave me a choice, actually,' I said. 'Wednesday or Thursday. I thought Wednesday would be better. For all of us.'

'Right,' said Michael. He paused for a moment, looking at me. 'Right,' he said again.

I felt a little twist of guilt. 'I'd better put Eddie to bed,' I said.

Eddie's antipathy dissolved in the bathwater. He had forgiven me by the time he brushed his teeth and forgotten his anger completely when I read to him. I glanced up from the book from time to time, to see if his eyes were closing. His gaze stayed fixed on me. It was as if he were committing me to memory. I remembered looking out of the window, when I was about his age, to where my mother sat in the garden. She was wearing yellow sandals and her skirt reached almost to her ankles. She wore a hat with a wide brim. When I called to her and she looked up, it shaded her eyes. What colour were her eyes? I couldn't remember. Eddie concentrated hard as I read.

My mother had made me a daisy chain, biting holes in the stems to thread the flowers through. When she put it round my wrist, I'd been afraid to move; it seemed too fragile to survive even the beat of my pulse. It broke when I brushed a strand of hair from my face. 'Nothing lasts for ever,' she'd said, when I cried at its loss.

'Will you always be here?' I'd said.

'Of course. I'll never leave you,' she'd said, lightly, impossibly.

'I'll never leave you,' I said to Eddie.

'Me neither,' he said.

I could not know then just how soon one of us would break the promise.

Chapter 69

12 October

I was so nervous about seeing Bobbie again this morning that I gave myself hiccups. I couldn't sing in assembly. I wanted to look preoccupied when she arrived, to prove I was capable of having fun without her, so I talked to Lizzie about the party for ages. I told her about everyone being drunk and I demonstrated how people were dancing. She said she didn't care, because she wasn't there, was she. All the while, I was looking for Bobbie out of the corner of my eye. She headed straight towards me. Her crowd surrounded her as she made her way over, keeping close together. It looked as if they were carrying her in a sedan chair. I was terrified she was going to ask about her dress or tell everyone what I'd done. But she just said why didn't I come over to hers tomorrow. She said we could do our homework together. Lizzie looked as disapproving as if we were planning a robbery. Bobbie said that we needed to discuss the party, too, and I said yes, we did. She said wasn't it great and started singing: *She flies like a bird* . . . and I joined in. The song was just right, because I felt as if I was floating above the playground like the girl in the ad. If Adam asks me out I'm going to say yes. I can always chuck him if someone better comes along.

Tom Spencer was actually standing right by the bus stop when I got off. 'Hello, Sarah,' he said, sounding as hoarse and hesitant as if it was the first time he'd spoken all day.

I didn't reply but that didn't put him off. I walked away quickly. He followed me, and even when I started to walk a bit faster he kept up. I stopped and asked him what he wanted. He took his time, counting out his words in his head to make sure they added up. He said I should know that his mum had seen my mum in the fields with a man. He told me that they were snogging. I said, 'So what?' but I felt like screaming. He kept saying she shouldn't do that, she shouldn't be kissing. The pavement was solid under my feet and all the books in my satchel were slipping down on one side as usual, so I knew it was real life and not a film. I wasn't going to ask him what he meant because I didn't want to hear it out loud. I knew it was true. I knew who it was.

He said he'd given the book back. I told him I didn't have a clue what he was talking about. He said he'd wanted to read it, but his mum said he mustn't and he looked so pathetic I thought he was going to cry. He got so close to me that I could smell his breath. I didn't know whether to run home or back to the shops. I wasn't afraid, I just didn't know how to get rid of him. It was as if I'd stepped in something I couldn't wipe off.

Then Old Sheila came trotting round the corner and for once I was almost glad to see her. That feeling didn't last long, though, because as soon as she'd sent him packing, shooing him like a dog, she started telling me about her mother not being well. I muttered that I hoped she'd be all right soon and I said poor thing whenever there was a gap, but Old Sheila didn't leave many. There was no escape, of course, because she lives so close to us, so I had to walk the whole way home with her. She puts a ton of lipstick on every day, which is a complete waste of time as no one's going to be looking at her. She wears really strong perfume, too, you can almost see it swirling around her like a swarm of bees, looking for a queen.

Mum was sitting in the nearly dark when I got home. I could see her at the kitchen table with her head in her hands as if she was listening to the radio, but I couldn't hear any music. She didn't see me. I stood outside, next to the little alcove where the milkman puts the yoghurts. I had to peer inside it, the way you feel compelled to open the drawers of an empty chest. There was a book pushed to the back. It was *The Wind in the Willows*. I recognised it, because it was an old one of mine. Mum was reading it to Eddie now. I gave her a fright when I barged into the kitchen. I asked why Eddie had put my book outside. She said that it wasn't him, that she put it there. She told me she was lending it to Tom Spencer. I said that giving my books to a mentally defective person was out of order. I said he wasn't safe and he might hurt someone or steal something. She said he wasn't dangerous, just dim. But I could tell she was rattled. I told her that he sees things, he's nosy and he follows people. I told her that he's been watching her. I said he saw you in the field.

She went red and then white. She didn't ask what I meant. I wished I hadn't said anything. It was just like the time when I'd caught Eddie drinking evaporated milk out of a jug in the fridge, without asking. He'd giggled when he saw me, but I'd said I was going to tell on him. He went from being happy to sad as quickly as the sun goes behind clouds. His eyes scrunched shut then opened to release tears. He kept saying please don't tell Mummy. I felt as if I was holding a flaming torch to him that was burning me, too, but I couldn't stop hurting him. I told on him. When I heard Mum smacking him hard later, I wished that the weals would come up on my skin instead of his, like stigmata.

I said are you still going away and when she said yes her voice was hard and sharp.

When I got upstairs I put the book right at the back of my wardrobe, underneath my old riding boots. I hope I'll forget where it is.

Adrian Mr Cavanagh is the worst person I know.

Chapter 70

Eddie had forgotten his anger but, even so, he was unusually subdued in the morning. I put the radio on. George Harrison sang *Give me hope, help me cope.* I wished I was listening alone or, better still, with Adrian. 'I like this one,' I said, turning the music up louder. 'We should get this record.' *Give me love, give me love, give me peace on earth.* 'I might go into town later,' I said, feeling full of unused energy when the song ended. 'Shall I come and meet you two after school? We could travel home together.'

'I'm not coming straight home,' Sarah said. 'I'm going to Bobbie's.'

I shivered. I didn't want to think of her in that house. 'Are you? What for?' I said.

'She's my *friend*,' she said, with the tiniest stress on the word. 'I might not be in for supper. I'll ring you when I know.'

'You're going to stay there for supper? Do you really want to? You hardly ever do that,' I said. 'In the holidays, perhaps, when you can stay a bit later, it's all right then. Are you sure you should do that now? What about your homework?' I tried to think of one fact that might stop her going.

Sarah lifted one corner of her mouth in an expression of extravagant condescension. 'We're doing it *together*. That's the *point*.'

I thought of her tearful accusation: *you speak to Daddy as if he was stupid.* I felt like pointing out the similarity here.

'Yes, well, let me know, then. Eddie? Shall I come and fetch you?'

'What day's it?' said Eddie, wrinkling his nose.

'Oh, yes, Eddie, you're right,' I said. 'It's swimming day.'

'I go on the bus then Mrs Wimbourne gets me,' he said, reminding me of my own arrangement for him.

'Right, well, I'll just take myself home on my own,' I said, with a squeak of fake laughter. I didn't meet Sarah's eye.

I knew where Adrian lived now, of course. I could look up the bus times and go and stand outside his house, just to wait for him to drive past. Of course, the actual house was miles from the gate, and the place was so isolated I could hardly have turned up by chance. He would be pleased to see me, but his wife might find it odd to find a leftover party guest in the lane. His wife, with her glassy gaze and long, coiled hair.

I had plenty of things to be doing, but I felt weary at the thought of tackling any task at all, even the smallest thing. I washed up as if the water were treacle and my arms were made of lead. I pulled the bedclothes into shape. They were hardly disturbed. We'd slept at a distance, side by side. Michael had folded his pyjamas before he went downstairs.

Outside in the street, I heard the rumble of a large engine, the sigh of brakes and then the metallic clunk of opening doors. I looked out of the window to see an ambulance. There was no flashing light and the driver was leaning against his door with a cigarette cupped into his palm, so there was obviously no great emergency. I waited to see whose house they visited. Sheila appeared. She looked up at once. When she saw me, she clasped her hands to her chest as if she needed to stop her heart escaping. There was a commotion just out of sight and I recognised her mother's voice. She seemed to be protesting and, as she came into view, I could see she was being firmly escorted towards the ambulance. The uniformed men on either side of her had the look of people for whom this was all in a day's work. They spoke loudly to her as they walked, a chant of reassuring, unspecific comfort. *'It's all right, dear. This way. We'll look after you. Nearly there.'* The old woman's bundle of clothing was topped by a pink quilt, which slipped from her shoulders like a stole. I'd better go down, I thought. But I didn't hurry.

By the time I got outside, the men were closing the doors without ceremony. They turned their cheerful attention to Sheila. *'She's in good hands, don't you worry, love.'* We watched the ambulance drive away together. Its shuttered back doors reminded me of a horse box. The old woman would be tethered inside, whinnying uselessly.

'What's the matter with her?' I asked.

Sheila was staring at the retreating vehicle in a trance. She wasn't wearing lipstick and her perm was beginning to drop. She shook herself as if emerging from cold water. 'It's her heart, I think. We had a bad night.' Sheila turned her attention to a bush that overhung the wall. 'That needs cutting back,' she said briskly. 'It's all go, isn't it?'

I was thinking about the call from the hospital, years ago: *Your father's very ill, can you get here as soon as possible?* and how I had deliberately taken on a new task, ironing sheets with unusual care, determined to finish it, hoping it would be too late by the time I got there. It wasn't. I'd squeezed his chilly hand and gazed over his head at the rows of shrivelled old men in the beds beside him. Everything was in the past tense on that ward. You couldn't tell what sort of people the other patients had been at all: it was difficult to imagine them upright, let alone see them as young men. All you could see were their heads, sticking above the bedding. Most of them were balding but some had a sparse roof of hair. From time to time, one of them got up and walked slowly down the corridor on unsteady legs. I couldn't remember when I'd ever seen my father in bed before. He had his eyes closed and his hand stayed cold and inert under mine. *He knows you're here,* the nurses had lied to me. I'd done the same, when it was my job. There was no point saying anything else to patients' relatives, they'd only turn their needy attention to you, if you did.

'I said, what will be, will be,' Sheila said. 'Goodness, you're miles away.' She looked as if she were going to say something else. 'You look a bit pink,' Sheila said, getting closer. 'Are you all right? The ambulance will be coming back for you at this rate.'

'I've got to do some packing,' I said.

She raised her eyebrows.

'I'm going to stay with a friend. With Bridget. For the night,' I said. I felt annoyed at how easily I gave up the information.

'Are you?' she said. 'With Bridget?' Her gaze was direct, even a little disapproving. 'Wellingtons,' she said eventually.

'She's in the countryside, isn't she? You'll want to wear something very stout.' She continued to stare at me. 'Very stout indeed,' she said.

'Let me know if you need anything,' I said.

Sheila shrugged as if she couldn't imagine what help I'd be. I felt both relieved and rejected.

I regarded my clothes in despair. Nothing looked right. I didn't even know if I should pack something smart. What would be best, I decided eventually, was my suit. It could pass for Jaeger and I could wear a plain blouse with it, one that would look nice without the jacket. At least I didn't have to worry about my monthly, I wasn't due for a couple of weeks yet. Moving aside the assortment of things in the dressing table drawer, I found a lipstick. I applied it with care, leaning into the mirror and flattening my lips. The room had become gloomy. Switching on the bedside light, I looked at the little travel alarm in its leather case, worn to the metal in places with age. The tiny luminous dots at the tip of each hand clearly showed that it was long after the time Eddie should have arrived home. Where was he?

The Wimbourne family lived several roads away, but the boy's mother had assured me that it was no trouble to scoop Eddie up from the pool, like a frog in a net, and bring him home each week. She'd stopped at the bus stop after the session one week and offered us a lift. 'You don't drive?' she'd said to me. 'No? Let me take him to and from.' The car was full of children. I couldn't tell which was hers, as she always seemed to have several small people on the back seat. 'Oh, once I've got one on board, I might as well cart round some others,' she said. She took them back to the Wimbourne house for tea. 'Boys get very hungry after a swim, don't they? I'll feed him.' Even allowing for some dawdling along the streets afterwards, he should have been home by now. I'd been preparing my clothes, as eagerly as a bride inspects her trousseau, while Eddie was alone in the dark.

I stared out of the window, as though I could make him appear by willpower in the speckled, low light of the late afternoon. Fear began its snaking path through my body, even my ears began to ache with it. I sat on the bed, beside the pile of clothes that I'd imagined taking with me. I won't go, I thought, beginning to sway backwards and forwards. If he comes home safely, I promise I'll never see Adrian again.

The back door rattled open and slammed shut. 'Eddie!' I yelled, rushing from the room, ready to punish and hug him. Sarah stood in the hall.

'It's me,' she said. 'What's the matter?'

'I thought you were going to Ade— to the Cavanaghs.' I knew that I sounded angry. I was having difficulty forgiving Sarah for not being her brother.

'I changed my mind,' Sarah said. 'I said I'd call you if I was going to have supper there.' She held my gaze for a moment as if weighing something up. Then she shrugged and opened her satchel. 'Bobbie gave me this to give you. I don't know what it is. It can't be a thank-you letter, can it, because you'd be sending one to them.' She handed me an envelope.

I didn't recognise the handwriting. It only had my Christian name on the front. It must be from Adrian. 'Why should I write to them?' I tried to sound casual. I put the letter down on the hall table, then promptly picked it up again. Michael shouldn't see it, whatever it said.

'Because of the party, of course,' said Sarah. 'The *massively successful* party. Aren't you going to open it?' She was watching my awkwardness with an odd expression. 'Why have you got lipstick on?' she said.

'Eddie's not home,' I said, ignoring her question. 'I was just beginning to worry.'

'Telephone the Wimbournes,' Sarah said. 'He probably hasn't left their house yet.' She started to go upstairs, then turned round. 'If you're really worried, do you want me to go and look for him?' Her tone challenged me not to panic or even to make much of a fuss.

'No. I'll phone them, that's a good idea,' I said. 'He's bound to be there.' I began to dial, already imagining telling Deborah Wimbourne that I was sorry to bother her.

'Hello?' Deborah always answered the telephone without saying her number, which I thought was very peculiar of her.

'Is Eddie still with you?' I said, as brightly as I could. 'I'll walk down and get him, shall I? It's getting a bit dark, isn't it?'

'Eddie?' said Deborah. 'Oh, no, he left a while ago. David! Day-vid!' She yelled away from the receiver, but the force still made me hold it from my ear. 'When did Eddie leave? Because his mother wants to know, that's why!' I heard a background kerfuffle and more shouting. 'About an hour ago, he thinks. Shall we send out a search party?' She suggested this with a little laugh, as though it were a ridiculous idea.

'No.' I could barely speak. 'I expect he'll walk in any minute. Thank you.' I hung up, trembling. What was I thanking the woman for? I wanted to speak to Michael, but he would be on his way home by now, so I couldn't ask him what to do. He wouldn't comfort me this time, anyway. He wouldn't tell me it would be all right. Instead, he'd berate me for being so distracted that I hadn't noticed the time. 'What on earth were you doing,' he'd say, 'when you were supposed to be getting his tea ready?' I was choosing clothes to be unfaithful in, I thought. The envelope was propped against the telephone directories. I picked it up. It came open easily, the glue barely held. *Sweet Marion*, I read, *I'll pick you up at two next Wednesday, to whisk you to our adventure. Seaside town, nothing fancy.* He named a guest house and gave a telephone number. *Counting the days! A*, it finished. He'd written the note on a page torn roughly from an exercise book, edged with a line of incomplete paper circles.

It was like watching something precious disappear down a drain. You knew where it was, you could still see it twinkling, but it was completely out of reach. I can't possibly go, I thought. I shouldn't have even imagined it was possible. And now I'm being punished. I'm going to be punished for ever. The darkness outside seemed swamping now. I was certain that Eddie was lying injured somewhere, far beyond the reach of his cries for help. Or that he'd been taken. At this very moment he was probably pinned under a blanket in the back of a van. Wherever he was, he'd be afraid and calling for me. And all the time I'd been selecting my treacherous underwear. I sank on to the stairs, rubbing my forehead with both hands. Adrian's flimsy missive lay in my lap. It was a moment before I made sense of the sounds I could hear: the fridge door opening and closing, a chair pulled out from the table.

Eddie sat drinking milk straight from the bottle. He started when he saw me, because I was hurling myself at him and screaming his name. 'I was going to get a glass, I really was,' he said.

'It's not that, you stupid, stupid boy!' I wanted to strike him in relief, to hurt him physically to exorcise my pain. 'Where have you *been*?'

Eddie hesitated. 'Getting rosehips,' he said. He looked despondent, as if he knew any answer he gave would be the wrong one. He pointed at his satchel. 'They're in there,' he said. 'Got loads. You tip the seeds down people's necks. S'itching powder. There were loads of blackberries, too,' he added helpfully. He was encouraged to see that, so far, his explanation hadn't made me any crosser.

I knelt in front of him. I examined him as carefully as if I were seeing him for the first time. His lips and teeth were faintly stained with purple. His hair stuck up at the front of his head like a crest. He stared back, his eyes wide, pulling his mouth down at the corners in preparation for his punishment. I felt a great rush of happiness, which cascaded through me like the fall of pushed pennies in the arcade game. Of course! His safe return didn't mean I *shouldn't* go away, it actually meant that I *should*. That was how fate worked: it made you suffer, then rewarded you.

'Eddie,' I said, 'come straight home next time. Please.'

The simplicity of my request melted him. He began to cry. 'I'm sorry,' he said, 'I didn't know I was late.' His weeping got steadily more exaggerated and operatic. 'I'm really sorry,' he sobbed, enjoying his misery.

'It's all right.' I put my arms round him. The paper in my hand crackled behind his back.

'What's that?' he said, twisting to see. 'Is it a hankie? Can I have a hankie?'

'I'll get you one. It's not a hankie, Eddie.' It's a passport, I thought. I got up and left the room hastily, because I wanted to howl with joy.

'Someone's happy,' said Michael, watching me singing as I stirred dried parsley into white sauce.

'She fucking wasn't earlier,' Sarah said.

Eddie hiccupped in surprise.

I laid the wooden spoon aside on a little rest with *Let's spoon together* painted round the edge. 'Come here,' I said. She didn't move.

'Say sorry, Sarah,' said Michael.

'Sorry's not enough,' I said. 'Come here.'

She got up and stood in front of me. Her eyes were half closed in contempt.

'What did you say?' I said.

She paused. Tendrils of her hair trembled against the light. 'I said: She. Fucking. Wasn't. Earlier.' She sliced each word with precision.

I leaned across the sink and picked up the washing-up liquid and poured a small quantity into my hand.

'She's sorry, Marion,' Michael said, his voice low. 'Say it, Sarah, in case Mummy—'

'She's not,' I said. 'Open your mouth.' I spoke directly to Sarah, as if it were only the two of us in the room.

Eddie was silent. Michael looked appalled. My hand dripped.

'Mummy!' Eddie said, loud with excitement.

I ignored him. Grabbing the back of Sarah's head, I pushed my soapy fingers inside her mouth.

'A filthy mouth has to be cleaned out.' I ran my hands under the tap, brisk as a nurse after a procedure. I picked up the spoon and went back to my task, hoping that none of them could see that I was shaking.

'I hate you,' said Sarah conversationally. 'And I'll get you back. I promise I'll get you back.' She spat into the sink.

'Um,' said Eddie, delighted. 'You shouldn't spit. You shouldn't spit, should you, Mummy?'

'There's lots of things you shouldn't do,' I said. 'You shouldn't threaten people, either.'

'What's fretten?' he said.

Nobody answered him. Sarah filled a glass with water and swilled her mouth out several times, her head low, holding back her swinging hair with one hand. She grabbed the nearest tea towel, wiped her mouth on several of the oast houses at once and left the room.

Chapter 71

13 October

I think hating someone is like having an animal you have to feed even when it's not hungry. It growls all the time, too.

Bobbie came over to me at break, but she was with her crowd so we couldn't speak to each other properly. Actually, I don't think she wanted to. She told me I couldn't come over to hers after school; she said something about an uncle, but I couldn't really hear her because my ears filled up with a sadness as solid as sand. She said can you give your mum this and gave me a letter. All the girls around her went OOOH on a rising note, like a siren going off. I asked what it was. She pressed the envelope to her eyes and said, no, she didn't have X-ray vision.

Every time I opened my satchel, I saw the letter. *Marion*, written in big handwriting, as loud as shouting. *Marion*, he'd written, but not with *Michael* beside it or *Mrs* in front of it. Just *Marion*, because she would know who it was from. She was waiting for it. I wished I was brave enough to flush it down the toilet or dump it in a bin. On the way home, it stuck to my bus pass when I got it out, because it wasn't completely glued down at one end. It made me feel weird to think of someone's tongue, his tongue, on the flap. I inspected it carefully, which is to say I wiggled it, to see if it might give a bit more. I don't know if I intended to open it completely but it wasn't difficult.

I thought if I wasn't meant to see what was inside then God would have given the person who sealed the envelope more spit.

Sweet Marion. Reading those words made my eyes hurt, as if the letters themselves bruised me. *Sweet Marion*. Adrian Mr Cavanagh shouldn't ever use that word about her. I thought I could actually feel cracks and fissures forming in my heart, like when the glaciers created fjords. *Counting the days*! *A*. He'd torn a page from Bobbie's rough book leaving little strands attached.

Eddie came into my room without asking. I was taking *Adrian Mr Cavanagh* out of the box, separating him from the others, screwing him up. Eddie said what's that and could he see it. I went to close the box and put it out of his reach, but I was too slow. He knocked it out of my hands sending Jesus and his beams flying. All the bits of paper spiralled to the floor like sycamore seeds. I picked up *Greg* and *Kev* straight away, but he held *Adrian Mr Cavanagh* very tightly and it tore in half when I tried to pull it from his hands. He asked me what it said, although he only had '*ian*'. We fought for the rest of them. I chased him round my room and when he tried to crawl under the bed I held on to him and walloped him, hard. He opened one of the little slips of paper and read '*John*' aloud. He was starting to cry and rubbing his arm.

He asked me if I could still taste washing-up liquid. I said what was he doing, coming into my private bedroom without asking. He said he didn't like me and Mummy fighting. He was still holding some of my names, balled up in his fists. He said if he gave them back to me, would I take him to the stables. He said please please please.

I said okay but he mustn't tell anyone, or I wouldn't. He looked as dizzy with excitement as if I'd spun him round. He crossed his heart as he promised, flinging his arms across his body, his little hands tightly clenched over his trophies. He handed them all back to me solemnly. I said we could play Sorry. I knew that by the time we'd each thrown the dice he'd have forgotten I'd hit him.

I have a plan now. Just like when you're trying to open something that seems closed and you get in first your fingers, then your whole hands, until it gives and widens, I could feel it all becoming possible.

Chapter 72

From time to time, Michael refreshed the details of my trip, asking, 'When do you leave? Wednesday afternoon?' or 'It's North Yorkshire, isn't it?' as though he really did have trouble remembering. I answered as cordially as I could. I was treating him like an irascible teacher who might refuse me permission to leave if I behaved badly in any way.

I woke each morning dazzled by my secret. A girl at my school had claimed she could see auras. She'd insisted that a cloak of colour hung over everyone, more revealing of their true selves than their clothes or their skin. She'd said my aura was mauve, because I was sad, which I thought was very unimaginative of her. Anna Paterson had cried for two weeks after being told that she emanated only yellow. 'It can change,' the girl said, 'when you're happy or something.' How could Michael look at me now without shielding his eyes?

I had a small, cream suitcase with my initials on it, a wedding present from my father. Typically, he had used my maiden name and not Michael's surname, so I would always be Marion Rose Edwards when I was in transit. It was quite small, little bigger than a vanity case, so I wouldn't be able to take much. 'I suppose,' Michael had said, as he checked my arrangements for the umpteenth time, 'you'll be able to share Bridget's things, won't you? Her toothpaste and flannel and so on? No point in taking them, just for one night.' He'd thought it through a lot more carefully than I had.

I laid the case open on the floor. I put a stout pair of lace-up shoes in first. We might go for a walk, perhaps, I thought, imagining clinging to Adrian as we crossed rutted fields or wet shingle. He holding me to him. The shoes took up so much space that there wasn't much room for anything else, but I added a cardigan. I didn't know where we were going to be and in what weather.

'Is Bridget in the country or the town?' Michael asked, stepping over the case on his way to bed.

Of course, I didn't know precisely and made a mental note to telephone her and find out. He'd been so assiduous in his attention to detail up to this point that I suspected he'd require sketches afterwards, like a detective investigating a crime.

I'd rung Bridget as soon as everyone had left the house that morning. She'd hardly spoken, beyond noting down the address and number of my hideaway. 'Can you tell me about where you live, just in case I need to know?' I said.

Bridget had sighed and given me only the briefest of details. I had found it hard to concentrate anyway, I was already in Adrian's car and his arms. 'Are you *sure* you know what you're doing?' Bridget had said. Offstage, I could hear the assorted whines and snuffles of small dogs demanding her company.

I tucked a felt beret in beside the shoes and added a scarf with 'J'adore Paris' written on it. The looping letters weaved in and out of the Eiffel Tower and the Arc de Triomphe. I'd only ever worn the beret standing alone in the hall, snatching it from my head at the last moment before I left the house. I sat at the dressing table and coaxed my hair into shape. I caught sight of myself in the three mirrors. I smiled.

I was ready too early, but I persuaded myself that my case would slow me down and I ought to set off. As I opened the front door, a slew of leaves on the mat outside hurled across the threshold on the draught and arranged themselves haphazardly in the hall. I had to resist the temptation to fetch a dustpan and brush and sweep them up. I knew that they'd still be there on my return.

The case was heavy, despite holding so little. It must be the shoes, I thought. They moved from side to side as I walked, making me feel lopsided and awkward. I had only my handbag in my other hand to balance my stride. I wished I'd gone back upstairs to spray perfume on my pulse points. I hadn't even packed my cologne. I didn't hear Sheila's advancing tread behind me until she tapped me on the shoulder. I spun round.

'Where are you off to?' she said, taking in the case and my expression at a glance.

'Visiting a friend,' I said. 'I think I told you. I'd better keep going, hadn't I?' I gestured ahead in the direction of the bus stop and the open road. Sheila fell into step with me. For a few moments she didn't say anything. We walked on side by side, as if we had just finished the day's labour together.

'She died,' said Sheila eventually.

'Who?' I said, but as soon as I'd spoken I knew who she'd meant. 'Your mother?' I said.

Sheila nodded.

'I'm so sorry,' I added, because Sheila couldn't speak for crying. I didn't know what to do. It seemed heartless to continue on my way, but I didn't want to stop. I didn't want Sheila to accompany me much further, either, though I suspected her tears would dry up soon enough if she spotted Adrian's car on the horizon.

Sheila cried silently for a while then stopped abruptly, as if someone had set a time limit on her weeping. She sniffed and produced a minute handkerchief from her pocket. The lace edging was larger than the usable area. 'Life goes on,' she said at last, folding and refolding the hankie and holding the increasingly small piece of cloth to her nose each time. I heard her draw in her breath through her open mouth. 'You remind me of a friend of mine, Marion,' she said. I glanced sideways at her. She was resolutely facing forward. 'Except you're more your own woman.' She cleared her throat. 'And she, my friend that is, the one who's like you, she had an affair. That's where you're – different.' Her voice broke on the last word.

She's rehearsed saying this, I thought. 'I beg your pardon?' I said. I stopped walking, forcing her to do the same. 'Well, she left her family, you see. To be with him. I said to her you probably think they'll welcome you back as if nothing's happened. But they may not. You might change things too much.'

I was aware that one of my shoulders was lower than the other with the weight of my case and I tried to adjust my position, little by little, so that I could face Sheila square on. She was close enough for me to be able to see tiny lines on her face, like the weathering on a statue.

'I didn't think she'd fall for him,' Sheila said. 'I told her about where he likes to go, but I thought: she'll leave him dangling. I tested her because I thought she'd resist. I knew the man, you see.'

She sounded nervous now. I thought I could hear anger in her tone, too.

'He thought he could just have anyone he wanted, you see. He's – he was – that type. I really believed she was too strong for him.'

Beneath my coat, my buttoned suit jacket made me feel hot and confined.

'I know she was bored and of course he was attractive, but I thought she'd be better than that. Better than him.'

I could think of no way to stop her talking like this. I couldn't think of anything to say in reply, either. The road stretched ahead of us. If anything, it seemed to be getting longer, reaching out endlessly as if it were bewitched.

'He liked the chase,' she said. 'He said to me, *Go on, Sheila. Tell her where I'm going to be. She's very sweet. But she's not incorruptible.* She didn't reject him. She really thought she meant something to him. He left her high and dry, of course. He came and told me all about it afterwards, as usual. And he expected me to say he hadn't done anything wrong. It's all just a habit with him. I'm sure I don't have to tell you she wasn't the first.'

I was rooted to the spot.

'He'd never have walked out on his marriage, of course, his bed was far too comfy there. It was his wife's money that kept him afloat, you see. You can be very sure of that.'

She hates Adrian, I thought. I remembered the image of Sheila smiling and bright beside him in her wedding photo.

'I really thought she'd send him packing,' she said. She reached for my arm. I was too startled to shake her free. 'You don't have to go,' she said. 'It's not too late.'

For a moment, I imagined walking back home with her, laughing over near-misses and scoundrels. 'I don't know what you're talking about,' I said. 'I'm going to stay with my old school friend; I can't imagine what *you* think I'm up to. Excuse me, but I've got to get a move on or I'll be late.'

Sheila stared at me. I saw a flash of tenderness in her expression. 'Of course,' she said. 'I apologise. Take no notice. It's losing Mother, I expect.' She corrected herself as though she'd simply turned over two pages of a book by mistake and misunderstood the plot.

'You've had a shock,' I said. 'It makes the world feel out of kilter when you lose someone. You'll feel better soon.'

'I have, I suppose,' she said. 'You think they'll go on for ever, don't you? I'll be lost without her. Serves me right, doesn't it, after all my moaning.' We fell in step again.

'It's utterly awful, losing your mother,' I said. 'Did she suffer much?'

'I don't think so. She was pretty cross, though,' she said. 'It's all the same if you suffer or you don't, in the end. I don't suppose dying is at all comfortable, however you do it. The funeral is the week after next. I do hope you'll be back by then and you'll be able to come.' We were just neighbours again.

'Yes, of course I'll come. I'm only away for one night,' I said. 'Goodbye, Sheila. Look after yourself.' I raised my eyebrows at her. 'Are you off home now?' She's fighting the urge to come with me as far as she can, I thought.

She leaned forward slightly, propelled by inner turmoil, then accepted defeat. 'Well, yes,' she said. 'That's me, then. Shall I keep an eye on everything for you, while you're gone?'

'If it's no trouble,' I said. 'Thank you.' Something close to a true friendship between us had seemed possible, for a moment. It had been like seeing what appeared to be some bird's unusual, bright plumage high up in a tree, only to realise, on closer examination, that it was a carrier bag caught on a twig. 'What happened to your friend?' I said. 'The one who had the affair.'

Sheila looked momentarily nonplussed. 'Oh,' she said, recovering swiftly. 'She took up dressmaking. It's always good to have something to do with your hands, isn't it?'

On the other side of the road, Tom Spencer walked past with his head down, ignoring us. He wouldn't find the book if he went to look for it. I doubted that he'd even try.

There was a slight dip in the road beyond the bus stop. I usually wished buses into existence, hoping their curved roofs would soon crest the slope like triumphant green beetles, but now I stood there hoping that none would come. I'd had to signal an apology to three bus drivers – each one stopping courteously for me, although it was a request stop and I hadn't – before Adrian drove up. I didn't recognise the car but the lights flashed as it slowed down. He didn't get out, he only indicated putting my case in the boot with a wave of his hand. I looked at the time as I pushed the catch on the lid. He was forty-five minutes late. When I got in beside him, he ruffled the hair on the back of my neck like a man petting a dog. 'Okay?' he said, spinning the car rapidly away from the kerb.

I didn't think we were in the same sort of car as before. I wasn't sure as I'd hardly been concentrating the last time, but I didn't recognise the dashboard and when I put my hand over the door release, I was sure it was different.

'Thinking of escaping?' said Adrian, seeing my fingers on the handle.

'Is this your car?' I said.

He paused. 'It's not. It's Aggie's.' He glanced sideways at me. 'Domestic stuff. Very dull. Full tank of petrol, though. Hey!' He gestured angrily at the driver of the car alongside. 'Move over. Wanker!' Unlike Michael, who drove with the exaggerated courtesy of a much older man, Adrian yelled and gesticulated at other drivers constantly. He argued with traffic lights and harangued road signs. For him, the road was peopled with idiots and beset with confrontation. I smiled at him. He caught my eye. 'You all right?' he said. We were on a long, uncontroversial stretch of dual carriageway, with nothing around for him to confront. He hummed a tune and tapped the rhythm against the steering wheel as if he were alone.

'I can't really believe we're doing this,' I said. 'I think it's rather clever of us to have managed it.'

He flipped the indicator stick down with a flourish. 'You bet,' he said, swinging the car into a lay-by. We came to a halt with a lurch. 'I need a couple of things,' he said. 'One of them is a wazz.' I watched him pick his way over to a tree. I looked away as he prepared himself. He got back into the car and leaned over and kissed me.

'The other thing I want is you,' he said. 'Let's not wait till tonight.'

'Here?' I looked around nervously. I had no idea where we were. The road was empty, but surely someone could appear.

'Yeah. Good idea, isn't it?' he said, and kissed me into agreeing, which didn't take long.

He undid his trousers while I levered myself forward till I was almost off the seat. I managed to pull everything I was wearing below my waist to half mast. Every so often, one of us collided with the hard surfaces or unexpected protrusions inside the car. There were a lot of them. I was just wondering how much more pain I could bear from the point where my thigh met the handbrake when he stopped.

'Are you on the Pill?' he said.

I shook my head.

'Christ, why not?' he said, shifting round and opening the glove compartment. He retrieved a packet from beside the little figure of a toy soldier. One plastic arm was raised in salute. 'We should have got in the back seat,' he said when it was far too late to move much at all.

'All right?' he said afterwards.

It was like the view from a not-very-high hill: there was not much effort involved but no real reward, either. Despite that, I felt curiously comfortable. I thought I'd like to stay there for a while, with his weight on me and my arms on his back. I liked the heavy, dense smell of him and the sway of his regular breaths. I dozed for a while, tangled with some dreams.

Adrian looked up from where his head lay against my shoulder. 'Oh Christ,' he said in a low whisper. 'Don't look now.'

And of course I looked, wriggling from underneath him with some difficulty so that I could follow his gaze. An enormous lorry was parked behind us. It was some distance away, the cab a long way from the ground, but I could see the driver. His face was impassive. 'Are we safe?' I said, horrified.

Adrian started to laugh. 'Safe?' he repeated as though it was an incongruous question. 'Yeah, we're safe.' He pulled on as much of his clothing as he could in the confined space of the car, then tidied himself up standing beside it. When he was finished, he waved in the lorry's direction as he walked round to his side of the car.

'What did he do?' I said, as we drove away.

'Gave me a thumbs up,' Adrian said. He squeezed my leg. 'Great performance, eh?' He was still laughing.

'Are we nearly there?' I said, not sure if I wanted him to say yes or no. An indeterminate background of fields and low barns slipped past the car window. As the buildings began to gather first into the separate sprawl then the busy assembly of a little town, I was almost disappointed. It began to rain.

Chapter 73

When the car drew up by the kerb, Adrian turned off the windscreen wipers. Almost at once, heavy drops of rain burst and fused on the glass. He leaned over me and pushed the handle down. 'Out you get,' he said. 'It's one of those.' He nodded towards the squat houses beside the road. 'I can't park here, by the look of it, so you go on ahead.'

I wished it wasn't raining. I wanted to say: 'Let's arrive together,' or: 'Don't make me go in alone.' But the water washed away my resolve. 'Shall I take my case?' I said.

He nodded and I hurried round to the boot, keeping my head down. He drove away as soon as the boot was closed.

Most of the houses had names as well as numbers: Dunroamin, Wavecrest, Two Trees, Sea View. Not entirely accurate that one, I thought, looking around. The street dipped away to where the owners had unanimously decided that the sea must be, but it was out of sight behind other grey buildings. The houses clustered steeply on the hills behind me, as if they were standing on each other's shoulders to get a better look at the view. Number 43, Ocean Cottage, had a tiny, patched lawn at the front with a cluster of gnomes as garnish. Two panels of frosted glass above the letterbox were covered on the inside with a thick screen of nylon curtain. I couldn't see a bell anywhere. I lifted a miniature knocker in the shape of a windmill and let it fall, with a tinny *ping*, back on its rest. I could see a grey shape behind the curtain, like something large and dense moving under water. The door opened. The woman standing there made me think of an illustration in *Woman's Realm*. She wore a blue twinset and a skirt of nondescript tartan. Her face powder was so newly-applied it almost sat proud of her face. There were two tumbles of powder at either side of her nose, like tiny peach avalanches. On her head was a suspiciously even thatch of auburn hair. Spectacles hung on a beaded chain round her neck.

She squinted at me through blue and glassy eyes. 'Yes?' she said, as if it were slightly odd that anyone called round at this time of day.

I took a step towards her. I could feel the rain on my shoulders and spraying the backs of my legs as it bounced off the ground. 'Mrs Marshall? I have a booking,' I said. The woman stepped back too, as though I had brought the weather with me and she didn't want it inside.

'Welcome,' she said carefully.

'Mrs Thomas,' I said.

The woman raised her eyebrows. Perhaps I wasn't saying my pretend name with enough casual familiarity. When you've been called something for a long time – the length of a marriage, for instance – you don't have to think about announcing yourself, you're already in the conversation beyond that point.

'We're staying one night,' I said, to fill the silence.

'That's right,' said the woman. She didn't seem interested. We were just another reason to change the sheets.

'Ade– Mr Thomas is parking the car.' I indicated vaguely in the direction that Adrian had driven away. Supposing he'd just kept driving? Perhaps he wasn't going to appear at all.

'Do you want to wait here?' The woman indicated a velveteen-covered stool in the hallway. The area itself was minute and the furniture was Wendy-house-sized, too. If the intention was to make the space look bigger by putting small objects in it, it failed.

'May I go up? I've got my things.' I pulled my suitcase closer. Fat drops of rain still sat on top of it, threatening to spill at any second.

The woman regarded it doubtfully. 'Oh dear. I'll get a cloth,' she said, hurrying away.

For goodness' sake, I thought, everyone must bring in a case and they'd hardly all be pristine, would they? The woman reappeared with a fistful of J-cloths and set about dabbing the surface. She used all of them. She was wearing carpet slippers so worn down at the back that the heel had concertina-ed into a thin line.

'You're first floor,' she said at last. 'Follow me.' She left me to carry my case. The handle was still damp.

I walked behind her up the stairs. The woman wore dark stockings and her bulbous calves stretched the fabric to a shining circle with each step. Every available surface was covered in an array of little china bowls and glass animals, or vases too small to hold anything more than a daisy. I wished Adrian was with me so that we could catch each other's eye and smile at the display.

The woman shuffled along the landing past three flowery-name-plated doors and stopped in front of Pansy. 'In here,' she said.

The door opened stiffly. The unmistakable smell of new carpet was almost cancelled out by an aggressive room freshener. It smelled floral but not of any particular flower. I couldn't remember if pansies had a scent. The bed looked very small. It was covered with a candlewick spread and a quilted counterpane. The pillowcases had a deep frill, which hung over the edge of the bed on either side, threatening to dislodge yet more ornaments if they were moved.

'Breakfast is seven until nine thirty,' the woman said. 'Full English, I expect?'

I don't know, I thought, I should have asked him. I began to feel slightly hysterical, as if each seemingly innocent question was in fact a trick designed to reveal our unmarried state. The woman was probably going to ask me which flowers I'd had in my wedding bouquet or where we went on honeymoon. There was a television programme like that, but you were supposed to find it funny if the husband and wife didn't know much about each other.

'Yes, please,' I said.

'Right, I'll wait downstairs for when your husband comes.' The woman sighed, as though couples not arriving together added a huge workload.

'Thank you,' I said. 'I'll unpack.' I wondered if the woman had spotted the fact I had the wrong initials on my case. They were embossed evidence of my guilt.

'Wardrobe. Chest of drawers.' The woman pointed to each. 'Facilities are next door. Would you explain to your *husband* about breakfast?'

She likes saying 'husband' to me, I thought, and she is looking to see if my pupils contract when I hear it, or if I do something else that gives the game away.

The woman wrestled the door shut over the carpet as she left. Little lozenges of wool sat on the surface like lava spewed up from the underlay. There was not a single smooth surface anywhere. The runnels of the candlewick, the deep clefts of quilting and the flounces of fabric that sprouted from the bed swelled everything to well beyond their actual sizes. The anaglypta on the walls stood proud, despite the blurring of several layers of magnolia paint. There were fat lace mats underneath all the pot plants and at intervals on the dressing table, raising the little china trays and dishes high above the Formica. I had imagined both of us on a wide, untidy bed, with disordered covers and large, soft pillows. It was a vision of the bedroom I'd glimpsed through the open door on the landing at the party. That was the bed I wanted him on.

I laid my case flat on the floor and opened the catches. My nightdress sat on top. I'd packed it last, because the thought of Adrian seeing me in it had made me feel nervous. I went to put it beneath the pillow and hesitated. I slept on the right-hand side of the bed with Michael. Adrian might be a right-side person, too. I put it back in the case. There was a small basin in the corner of the room. I ought to put my toothbrush there. The bowl didn't look as if it had been used recently; there was a thick, white caking of limescale round the plughole.

I was standing in the middle of the room when Adrian knocked at the door. 'Hello, is that Mrs Thomas in Pansy?' he said in a high falsetto, then shoved it open. He carried a small, battered holdall. It was almost ostentatiously shabby. He began to take his coat off.

'Careful,' I said. 'You'll make everything wet.'

He looked surprised. 'Why?' he said. 'It isn't raining any more.'

Of course, it isn't, I thought. 'Lucky you,' I said. 'I got soaked.'

'Old Wiggy down there said you'd be in Pansy,' he said, rather too loudly. He closed the door with exaggerated effort. 'Ooh, that's stiff,' he said, going to sit on the bed. 'This is a little one, isn't it?' he said, bouncing gently. 'Christ, Marion, it's like being in a *Carry On* film, everything's a double entendre.' He surveyed the room. 'What a pad,' he said. 'Our Mrs Thingy doesn't seem to have heard of modern design, does she?'

'Why did you choose it?' I said. I hoped it hadn't just been with a pin in a directory. I feared that was exactly what had happened. I sat beside him.

'It's so perfectly un-"us", that's why. It's a terrible little town and this decor is enough to give you a headache, but because it's so different it's all so ridiculously jolly, isn't it?'

'Which side do you want?' I said. 'Which side of the bed?'

He looked at me for what seemed like a long time. 'Shall I show you?' he said. He slid his arm round my shoulders and kissed me, tipping me back on to the quilt. His kissing quickly escalated in tempo. He began pulling at my blouse, untucking it from the waistband and sliding his hands underneath. I was aware that I was still wearing shoes. Every item of my clothing seemed to have increased in weight and girth. I wished I was wearing silky things that slipped off, or soft, light wool that offered only the thinnest barrier to his hands. 'You'd better get out of this yourself,' he said eventually, after some attempts to unzip my skirt.

I stood up and instinctively tucked in my blouse before remembering that I was supposed to be taking it off. He was pulling off his clothes on the other side of the bed, dropping them where he stood. It was like getting ready for a games lesson at school, I thought, putting my shoes neatly beside a frantically tapestried chair. When I put my hands behind my back to unhook my bra, Adrian said, 'Not yet, come here.' He was lying on the bed. His small underwear was so tight it might have been painted on to his body. He looked incongruous against the riotously feminine bedclothes, on a bed that seemed to suggest that, while it was just about big enough for two, it was really intended for one chaste, female occupant. Adrian was categorically the opposite.

I wished I could turn off the daylight. It made me feel ungainly, as if I were wearing a suit made of someone else's skin. Adrian extended his arms out wide and they hung easily over each side. 'I'm lying . . . in the middle. That answers your question, doesn't it?' He watched me take the few steps to the bed.

I lay down carefully, as if I were measuring myself against him. I closed my eyes, but it didn't make the room reassuringly dark. Instead, the light pressed red against my eyelids. He unhooked my bra and helped me out of my knickers efficiently, then wriggled out of his own. I was glad he didn't want me to do it, I worried about getting them off over his trembling erection. He took my hand and placed it very deliberately on himself, the way you do when you want someone to help you with tying a knot. This part of him, which I couldn't name even to myself, still felt utterly unfamiliar. The tip of it, bobbing beneath my fingers, was smooth and round, while Michael had a circle of skin there. They are all different, I thought. Like noses. This was such an inappropriate but vivid image that I smiled.

Adrian caught my eye. 'You like it?' he said. 'Me too.' He looked down and regarded himself with affectionate pride, as if my hand was curled around him only to demonstrate his girth. He reached for another small packet from his discarded jacket and covered himself deftly and fast. He began to kiss and then touch me, spending just the right amount of time in each area. Sometimes he groaned or I yelped. I hoped the abundant soft furnishings would muffle the sounds. The mattress itself was as dense as marshmallow and about as supportive. It didn't seem to have any springs at all. I tried to help him, moving my hands or twisting and turning as he instructed, but I felt out of step. It was as if he were hearing music I was deaf to and the rhythm of it was difficult to determine. It didn't seem to matter to him that he was dancing on his own but when he slid inside me I stopped feeling as if I were in the way and joined in. The side tables shook, rattling their cargos of ornaments.

He leaned up on his elbows and smiled down at me. 'Having a nice time?' he said. I was as startled as if someone had shouted out in a library. It was going to be difficult to have a conversation at this point. 'Do you want me to come?' Adrian said.

It was, I thought, a rather peculiar question. 'Yes,' I said. It turned out to be the right answer.

'Sweet,' he said afterwards, tracing my silvery stretch marks.

The room was cold. I wished I could reach for the enormous, ungiving flowery bedcover beneath me but it would have been an awkward manoeuvre. Adrian lay unconcealed and unabashed. There was something celebratory in his unapologetic nakedness. Before I'd slept with anyone, which meant before I'd slept with Michael, I'd thought everything would happen remotely, as if you could step behind a screen while your body got on with it on the other side. Even with Philip, I'd found it extraordinary how very *present* you had to be. People always expected nurses to be matter-of-fact about being naked, that they'd have a kind of practical frankness that transcends any embarrassment. But despite seeing plenty of bare bodies of all shapes and sizes, I was still squeamish about my own.

Adrian slid down and put his face between my legs. I didn't want him to carry on being there if he didn't want to, but it was impossible to tell him so. He wouldn't have been able hear me, my legs were pressed to his head like earmuffs. I rested my hands gently on his head as if to convey to him that, if this was a mistake, I didn't mind. After only a few seconds I discovered the absolute and entire purpose of what he was doing. I laced my fingers into his hair. I had several strands of it caught in my wedding ring afterwards.

He turned away, removing the condom and putting it on the floor. 'Better sort that before old Mrs Wiggy finds it,' he said. 'Shock her to death. I bet these rooms don't see much action.'

He had a mole in the centre of his back. Two strands of hair grew upwards from it, flicking a V at the world. I could see, as he could not, that they were grey.

Chapter 74

20 October

Sweet Marion. I could taste the words in everything I ate. I could see them everywhere, as though they were solid objects. *Sweet Marion.* I watched her pouring tea, shaking the little strainer until it stopped dripping and I saw them falling into the cup. She looked out of the window when she was getting Eddie's beaker and I could see them hanging from the trees. As she folded the tea cloth and hung it over the rail in front of the cooker, I thought they would fall out of it on to the floor. Eddie hadn't come down for breakfast. She told me to go and get him, which was the first thing she'd said to me for ages. I thought she ought to say *'please'* too, but I kept quiet.

Eddie's curtains were still pulled. He was lying on his bed, flicking the switch to change the pictures on his toy projector. The room was dark enough for the slides to show up on the ceiling; the little nightlight's beam didn't reach very far. I asked him what he was doing and called him a cretin as it was nearly time to leave for school. He looked up as Donald Duck gave way to Pluto. He said he didn't want Mummy to go. I said it was only for a night, but I supposed he wasn't very good at measuring time – a night must feel like a month to him. I told him we'd go to the stables after school but I made him promise absolutely one hundred per cent he wouldn't tell Mummy or Daddy.

I tore a page from the owl pad in the kitchen. I wrote a message with my left hand. The words crawled across the page as if they didn't want to be there. I went up to her room and I put it in her case, tucked inside her silly shoes. Eddie hugged her as if she was going away for ever. She touched his head without concentrating as if she'd already left him.

By the time we walked through the chalk pit after school, Eddie had forgotten how much he'd minded her leaving. He stood under the trees as the leaves fell, trying to catch one and make a wish. He kept jumping up and falling down until he was decorated with little twigs and bracken. His legs stuck out from his corduroy shorts like bleached chicken bones. He'd kept his school shoes on. I'd have to get the mud off them later or I'd be in trouble. Mum had asked a woman from the village to make our tea. She doesn't really know us, or what we're allowed to do, so when I said we were going out she hardly reacted. I told her we'd be back later, without saying when. As we walked into the stable yard, Eddie slipped his hand in mine. It was the first time anyone in my family had held my hand for a very long time.

Horse's heads hung over all the half doors and for a moment I saw them as Eddie did. They swung and shook and whinnied in constant motion. Eddie stood very close to me. I told him to wait out of sight while I went into the little office. Bo looked up, surprised to see me. He was always doing paperwork, I've no idea what sort. He said well I never, it's Sarah. Long time no see. I had to chat to him for a while before I asked if I could saddle up, just for half an hour. He looked doubtful and said it'd be getting dark soon and winter draws on. Then he saw me pleading – I literally put my hands together as if I was praying – and he said I could, just for a while, as he was sure I knew what I was doing.

I didn't tell him I was planning to put Eddie on the pony. I wouldn't have told him that I was heading to Rebel's stall, either. I had to avoid her quick teeth and unpredictable hooves as I eased the halter over her ears and guided the bit into her mouth. Eddie watched from the doorway; he seemed to be shrinking every time she stomped and snorted. I swung the saddle on her back and adjusted the leathers for his small legs. I think if I'd asked him then if he still wanted to ride, he'd have said no. Even when I lifted him up and he struggled to find the stirrups with his kicking feet, even when I put the reins in his hands and took hold of the halter to set off, we could have stopped what we were doing. We might have done one or two circuits of the yard, perhaps, the pony's hooves chinking loudly on the cobbles like a sound effect, then turned round. He'd have pretended to be disappointed. He'd have protested a bit. And I'd have cursed about the waste of my time and gone home smelling of the stables and put Eddie to bed unbroken. But a plan was a plan and I thought it was all happening as it should.

Just outside the gate into the yard, the ponies always tremble and shiver as they remember the wide fields further on. I felt the pony twitch as she saw the lane extend. It was narrow, and I could only just fit alongside as I led her. I glanced up at Eddie. He said he was a cowboy, and held his legs out wide, then he dashed them as hard as he could against the pony's side. I yelled at him to stop. The animal tried to move sideways, away from my restraining grip, jerking my arm hard as she tried to pull away. The sudden pain in my shoulder made me angry and fierce. I said do you want to ride her on your own, then? I shouted across the pony's flailing head at him. Eddie looked down at me, scared but defiant. He said he really was a cowboy. I said I'd had enough and let go, thinking the lane itself would restrain her. Almost at once, she broke into a trot. Eddie half turned back to me, then he was jolted forward again as she picked up speed. He had no time to pull on the reins, even if he'd known what to do. I saw him trying to grab handfuls of her mane as he bounced on her back, leaving his seat as she trotted, rising higher each time. The gate to the field at the end of the lane is permanently ajar, it's too rusty and twisted to open or close. The pony rounded the corner as if she had no one on her back at all. Eddie began to slip sideways. He fell as if in slow motion in contrast to the pony's frantic gallop. Then he stopped sliding altogether and lay on the ground without moving.

I couldn't get to him fast enough. My shoes stuck to the ground as if they were magnetised and all the while I kept thinking that Eddie would get up and shake himself and laugh. Although I knew he wouldn't, because the closer I got, the more still he seemed. The pony stood a little way off, her head down as she tugged at the grass. Eddie's colours were all wrong. His face was white and his hair was red. There was too much blood outside his head. His little chest rose and fell, making his thin shirt tremble. His legs were bent at the knees and both his shoes had come off. I could only see one of them. There was a noise, too: a really high, loud screaming. It was only when I could see someone running from the end of the lane that I realised it came from me.

Chapter 75

Eddie felt scared of Sarah when she was in this mood. She was cheeky to the village lady and kept making signs at him behind her back. He wasn't really sure what they meant but he knew they weren't polite. He'd forgotten his mother wouldn't be there until he got home and the village lady stood in the kitchen instead. He'd felt tearful, but then Sarah reminded him about the riding, so he'd decided not to cry. It was getting late by the time they left the house. The way Sarah lied to the village lady about being allowed out made him feel as if she was cutting them adrift from safe moorings.

He feared she might change her mind just to upset him, so he kept his distance from her on the way to the stables, in case he provoked her by mistake. She was momentarily cross about him still wearing his school shoes but it only seemed to sharpen her purpose. In the yard, the horses threw their heads over the stable doors and looked straight at him, as if they were choosing him, not the other way round. It was only when she let go of him that Eddie realised he'd been holding Sarah's hand.

The hooves bothered him. They seemed at odds with the expression in the pony's eyes, and out of their owner's control. They stamped heavily, taking the pony two steps back and three steps forward, as Sarah buckled the halter and coaxed it out of the stall. He wished he could just be lifted straight on to the pony's back, as easily as he placed the wide-legged man on his little plastic mount. The fact of the animal was much larger and wilder than the horse in his head. Sarah grunted as she hoisted him up. With a huge effort she pushed too hard and for a moment he lay face forward against the pony's neck. When he righted himself and slid his muddy shoes into the stirrups, he felt as if all the pieces of him were properly joined up at last. His height on the pony was exactly the size he wanted to be. He could see the top of Sarah's head and the beginning of the lane beyond the gate. When he gave the pony's sides a tentative kick it picked up its speed in answer. This instant response was as gratifying as it was exciting. Sarah frowned up at him and tightened her grip on the reins. She'd have to let go when they got to the field.

He held out both legs and brought his heels in hard. The pony's squirmy, slow gait gave way to a hard, muscular acceleration. Sarah said she'd let go and he felt a surge of triumph. He turned round as the pony moved forward to make sure she wasn't chasing him and then he lifted his arms because suddenly he wasn't holding on to anything any more. He wanted to shout, but the air jumped in his lungs, making him pant instead. The warm, coarse hair under his hands and against his legs scratched him as he slid first forward then sideways. He heard the hooves, the fearsome hooves of all his nightmares, very loud and very close. He surrendered to his fall.

Chapter 76

'Fish and chips,' Adrian said, rummaging in his holdall. 'There's got to be good fish and chips round here.' He pulled a thick jumper over his head. It had leather patches at the elbows and a great deal of lumpy darning everywhere else.

I laughed. 'Don't you want a new jumper?' I said. For the first time, I saw a flicker of annoyance.

'It's what I wear,' he said.

I put the clothes I'd travelled in back on.

It was chilly outside and we walked briskly towards the seafront. After a while, he put his arm round me. The street was deserted. The solitary boy behind the counter in the chippie only asked, 'Sollenvingar?' and didn't respond to Adrian's bonhomie or his comments about mushy peas. We went outside and found a bench. The wood was still slippery from the rainfall. There was an iodine smell and a distant rhythmic swish but I could only make out an indistinct blur where the land probably ended and the sea began. Pinned papers flapped from a notice-board beside us. I got up to inspect it. They were the usual messages for a community, announcing church fairs and children's outings.

'Vernon House Open Day,' I read aloud. 'Oh, it's tomorrow. Shall we go?'

Adrian tipped the crisp ends of his chips into his mouth from the newspaper. 'Why do *all* you women want to *do* things?' he said. In the beat that followed, we both understood exactly and completely what he had said. 'I just want to stay in Pansy with you,' Adrian said. He stood up, wiping his hands on his jumper.

He's doing what he always does, I thought, about both the wiping and the women.

'We're like those little wooden ducks in the fairground, aren't we?' I said. 'You fish us out and if you find the right number on us, you claim your prize.'

Adrian looked at me as if he was struggling with something. He was trying not to laugh. He didn't fight very hard. 'Ducks,' he said. 'Have you got a number on your bum, then?' he said. 'Are you a good duck, Marion? I like a good duck.'

'Oh God,' I said, 'I wanted to try to tell you something important. Please don't make me laugh.'

He put his hands to my cheeks and lifted my face. 'I hope I always do make you laugh,' he said, in mock seriousness and with a terrible American accent. He kissed my forehead. 'We're not here in a "for ever together" kind of way. You know that, don't you? That's just not me, is it? Ask Aggie. Don't flinch when I say her name,' he said. 'Aggie's a fact. Michael's a fact. But so's this. And it's fun, isn't it?' He spun me round and ran his hands over my skirt. 'Let's see, what number are you, then?' he said. 'Thought so. Your number's come up.'

I looked at the grey wasteland, fuzzy in the low light. The air was wet, as if the sea were evaporating, and my fringe stuck to my forehead. My fingers were still greasy. I wiped them on my skirt. I thought I probably wouldn't wear that outfit again, anyway.

Chapter 77

20 October

I wished it was just me and Eddie. I wished I could hold up my hands to time as if I was a lollipop lady stopping traffic, to let us go and leave everything behind. The running woman was getting closer and I could hear people coming up the lane behind us. I wanted to pick him up and take him away. I wished I could nurse him all by myself until he mended. Then we could live somewhere high up above the trees for the rest of our lives, looking down on everyone.

Molly Spencer stood over Eddie at last; she was out of breath and nearly as pale as him. When she saw it was me, she looked as if she might change her mind. She told me to stop screaming. She said that noise didn't help. She crouched down and felt his pulse; her fingers looked huge against his wrist. She wore a headscarf tied under her chin, like the Queen. She knelt beside him and her mackintosh fanned out around her like a train. She bossed people into calling an ambulance. She woke them up as if they'd been in suspended animation until she arrived. While we waited, the crowd around Eddie grew denser until I could hardly see him in the middle of it. Someone clopped the pony away and everyone formed a line to let her past, like a guard of honour. I could see Eddie's other shoe lying near where she'd been cropping the grass and tried to retrieve it, but they wouldn't let me through. A man told me to stand back, because a little boy was badly hurt.

Molly Spencer caught my eye. She called me to come to her and I ducked under the man's arm to reach her. She hugged me, so quickly that it hardly happened. She told someone to go back to the stables and telephone Daddy and tell him to go straight to the General. I didn't know his number, only the name of where he worked. They kept saying what? speak up, but my voice didn't work properly after the screaming. Molly Spencer said I could come on the bus with her. She said she'd got time, she wasn't going anywhere else in a hurry.

Eddie looked monstrously tiny on the hospital bed, his head bandaged in hundreds of layers like a broken toy. The room smelled of disinfectant and there was another thin, sickly-sweet smell laced through it, like when you can smell the toffee apples on the pier through the scent of the sea. People spoke about me in loud whispers that I think I was meant to hear. Things like *She's his sister. Waiting for her parents. She was with him. Let's leave her there for a minute. She came in alone. We'll send her to the visitors' room when her mum and dad get here.* His eyes hadn't opened. It was the opposite of that staring game where you dare each other to look away first. He was definitely winning at keeping still.

I didn't get up and run to Daddy when he arrived, because my sobbing seemed to stick me to the chair and also because he only glanced at me. He stroked Eddie's hand, which looked plump and pink against the bobbly blue hospital blanket. There was a fat, white lump of dressing stuck on top. Daddy was still carrying his briefcase. He squeezed my shoulder. I said would Eddie be all right. He said he didn't know. He said he hoped so. He sounded very formal. There was a nurse sitting beside Eddie; her little paper hat was stiff but her face was soft. I felt jealous of her because she knew what she was doing. She had an upside-down watch pinned to her apron. When the doctor came in, she jumped up at once and said good evening sir and stood against the wall. The doctor only spoke to Daddy. After that he said we should go and have some tea and they'd fetch us. He didn't meet my eye.

I don't like tea, but I let Daddy pour me some. The urn in the visitors' room was enormous and there were hundreds of chairs, but we were alone. The urn hissed and gurgled as if it had made a lot more effort than provide hot water for two tiny cups. Daddy leaned forward on his chair, rubbing his fists in his eyes. I was waiting for him to ask me what had happened. Why I hadn't even bothered to find Eddie a hat. He might end up stupid like Tom Spencer and it would be my fault. Molly Spencer had left me at the desk downstairs; she seemed to shrink away from me as we got nearer the hospital. She hardly spoke on the bus, either. The last thing she said was that she hated hospitals, but she didn't really say it to me.

Neither of us touched our tea. And all the time I kept thinking about where Mum was and who she was with. At last, Daddy said he'd better telephone Bridget. I said I thought he'd have already done that. He swung his arms behind his head, leaning back into the cradle of his linked hands and said no, he hadn't. He was looking up at the ceiling. There was a poster on the wall opposite us. It was a picture of a crying child, screwing up its face and clutching its jaw. It looked about twelve. It was probably a boy, but I wasn't sure. The words *Is this what we want for our children?* ran along the top and then, along the bottom, it read *Support Water Fluoridation.* I was going to see how many words I could make out of *Fluoridation* when I caught sight of Daddy. Tears streaked from each eye, running backwards towards his ears as if someone had drawn glasses on him with water.

I felt as though I was playing that game on *Crackerjack*, where they load people up with puzzles and prizes till their arms are full, then hand them a cabbage. If they drop anything they're holding, they can't keep it. I was already weighed down with my secrets. Daddy's tears were the cabbage that was going to topple everything.

I said she wasn't at Bridget's, was she? He said no, she wasn't, he knew that. I didn't say anything about Adrian Mr Cavanagh because I didn't know the right words and I didn't want even the idea of him in the room. I couldn't believe I was the same person sitting there while my father cried as the one who leaned against a wall smoking a cigarette. I wanted to be a little girl again. I wanted my mother. Why hadn't she found the note and come home?

I found *Lift. Rid. Din. Nil. Loaf.* I asked him how he could have let her go, if he knew. He said she'd needed to know where home is. He said you can see things more clearly if you stand a little way away. I thought you never really grow up, you just get better at disguising all the bad or wrong things in yourself. In my mind's eye, I tried to imagine her when she was a child. She had my face.

I started to cry. Another nurse, a different one, came into the room. She seemed awkward and didn't look at us properly. It was like when Joy Findlay came on stage two scenes early in the school play. The nurse whispered for Daddy to go with her. He stood up and wiped his face briskly. He told me to wait.

I saw *Daft*. Then *Rat. Float. Dirt*. Eddie had blood, dried brown, in his ears. In the scapha, between the helix and the antihelix. The one on the poster in the biology classroom had each different part labelled and brightly coloured. The picture didn't look anything like Eddie's actual little ear. There was a black stain on my left hand from the ink on the owl pad. I'd have to wait ages until it was completely gone.

I found *Ration*. Somewhere, in this same slice of time, Bobbie Cavanagh definitely wasn't thinking about me. They'd put a wire across one of the fields last year, with a big sign next to it, saying ELECTRIFIED. We'd all dared each other to touch it. One of the boys had flung himself several feet away after he'd put just one finger on it, writhing on the ground in convulsions. I'd known he was pretending, they couldn't risk cows twitching about like that. I'd placed my hand carefully on the wire and waited. Nothing happened. I'd curled my fingers around it, holding it tightly in my fist, but I couldn't feel anything. I concentrated hard now, summoning Bobbie's face and her quick smile, but there was no current. I couldn't even feel my own heartbeat.

Chapter 78

Michael had expected to feel shocked by Eddie's appearance, but the sight of him was bewildering in its awfulness. They'd moved him into a ward with three other boys by the time Michael arrived. The place smelled like a canteen, cloaked in the dense, heavy aroma of food prepared long ago. The other boys watched him from their beds as he crossed the ward to sit by Eddie. It was long past visiting hours and they must have wondered at his presence, especially as the patient only slumbered and did not respond. Eddie was both shrivelled and swollen under the bandages. His narrow arms were bound in wooden splints and his face was puffy and pale. Michael tried to concentrate as the doctors described his injuries in their determinedly unemotional way. He wouldn't have been able to recognise any of them again, even moments after they'd spoken to him. Anguish blurred his vision and silted up his ears. He wanted to hurt Marion. He wanted to punish her. He wanted to see her struggle to explain herself and he wanted to tear up her lies, one by one, until there was nothing left to say. Despite that, even though he was almost immobilised by her selfishness and her betrayal, he was amazed to discover that he craved her presence. He dreaded it, too. He knew how easily she'd be able to trace the scars of his sadness with her cruel, sharp fingers and open them up again.

He'd wanted to be a train driver. It was an ambition based on only one train journey, because otherwise they went everywhere by car. His father was inordinately proud of their enormous Humber. He was fond of saying that there was room for the entire carry-cot on its cavernous back seat when they'd brought Michael home from the hospital. He washed it every Saturday morning and manoeuvred it with great care into the garage on Sunday evenings. It was, he said, the car of kings. Sometimes he'd let Michael stand on the running board as he drove it slowly, for just a few feet, down the road. He'd catch his father's eye as they embarked on this risky venture and they'd smile in collusion.

Just once, though, they'd visited a relative by train. Michael couldn't remember why, or anything much about the visit, but as they stood on the station platform his mother had said, 'Wave to the driver,' and he saw an actual person framed in the window of the cab. Behind the man, the carriages lined up at his command. He slowed the train to stop at exactly the right point. He did this without a change of expression. He'd waved back, but several other children had joined them by that point and Michael didn't think the gesture was just for him. He'd watched the man climb out of the cab and stand on the platform for a moment, exchanging pleasantries with the station guard. He'd seemed a giant, his uniform sharp beside his father's soft suit and trilby. Michael knew he'd dwarf them all, even if he wasn't wearing his hat.

Everything about that train had struck Michael as beguilingly loud and rough: the doors shut with a mighty thunk, the engine and the brakes screeched. The steam thundered recklessly and even the smell was impolite and clung to his clothes for days afterwards. It was all the exact opposite of his solitary play and their tidy household. It was a chaos he hadn't known he desired. And riding along the uncurling tracks at the front of that unpredictable machine, the driver was in god-like control. To be him, Michael decided, was to reach unimpeachable adulthood. Even now, when his daily commute had gone beyond being routine to some hypnotic state, after which he would seldom remember the journey at all, Michael would sometimes feel a jolt of joy at the sound of the guard's whistle or a sudden stop.

There was nothing remotely exciting about this journey, of course. They also seemed to be travelling too slowly. Michael wanted to wrench open the driver's door, haul him from his seat and take his place. He wanted to hurl the train along at top speed, ignoring stations and disregarding signals and level crossings. Ever since the telephone call, the slow speed of the world was at odds with his need to travel quickly. Rosalind had put the call through to him with her usual politeness. She kept everything as ordered as possible for him and this untidy intervention must have caused her almost physical discomfort. 'Excuse me, I have a call for you, Mr Deacon,' she said, as she always did.

When the woman from the hospital had spoken to him, in his alarm Michael didn't recognise the Edward Deacon who'd had an accident as his small, robust son. 'Eddie,' he'd said to her, 'we call him Eddie.' If he only heard them saying his full name, he'd think he was in trouble.

As he sat in the taxi on his way to the station, he admitted to himself that he'd gathered his belongings and tidied his desk and left the building without contacting Marion. He acknowledged this fact without apology. What he had to do to find her, the tortuous web of untruths and difficulty he'd have to cut through, wouldn't change for the sake of a few hours. Time in which he could come to some accommodation of the situation, prepare himself for seeing her. There was even a grace in letting her hear the news on her own. She wouldn't need to share her discovery with him, he was already on the way to dealing with information, rather than reacting to it.

When Rosalind had handed him his coat she didn't say, 'I'll see you tomorrow,' because she'd probably imagined that something involving hospitals might take him away for more than a day. She didn't ask what it was. He had contributed to a congratulatory present when she'd got married, but he'd never enquired about the wedding or her home life. He remembered that she'd once been late to work. She'd spent the rest of day tense and irritable, a state he'd never seen her in before or since.

The evening he'd kissed her had been unusual from the start. Employees had travelled from the St Neots office to mark yet another decade in business but, after only a couple of hours and a few drinks, they'd made it clear they weren't going to spend an entire evening in London with colleagues. He'd suggested to Rosalind that they take the table he'd booked. In the taxi to the station afterwards, he'd kissed her and then slid his hands under her coat to touch her breasts when she kissed him back. It wasn't that he found her any more attractive or suddenly saw her in a different light. It was, somehow, a physical expression of how fond they were of each other. It was an acknowledgement of their comfort in each other's company every day. He was grateful to see no new appetite in her eyes the next morning. Neither was there embarrassment. He relegated her to her previous role without any effort and had chosen to think that, underneath her clothes, she was as smooth and solid as his cousin's dolls. But the memory of her round and satisfying breasts sometimes caught him unawares. Her lavender scent haunted him, too.

The thought of telephoning Bridget and going through the charade of asking her to tell Marion what had happened was exhausting. He felt like that chap in *The Pilgrim's Progress*, wading through the Slough of Despond, every step an effort. He leaned back against the leather seat. He hardly ever travelled in a cab. He and Marion had taken one on the night they'd got engaged, allowing themselves that thrilling extravagance to celebrate. He hadn't planned on proposing to her quite so soon. He was happy with the way things were. He knew he liked her a great deal. She was good company, they laughed at the same sort of things and she didn't seem to mind that he hadn't leapt on her whenever they were alone together. Their relationship seemed a lot more pleasant than the volatile tantrums and complicated sex lives of his peers. He had no particular timetable in mind and might well have kept going in that state, making easy plans and sticking to them. He hadn't been with many women. The first time had been a disaster. He'd torn a tiny flap of skin on his most sensitive part and bled profusely. The girl had said she'd seen it happen before (there was, she'd said, laughing, no question that the blood was hers) and was annoyed rather than horrified, but he was mortified. It made him understandably nervous about subsequent encounters. He became adept at translating this anxiety into an approach that could be interpreted as respect. If he went further, he was as quick as a teenage boy.

The train seemed to pause for longer than usual at the station stops. There was an endless shutting of doors and a babble of goodbyes at each one. His fears for Eddie crystallised into a single, terrible image of him, lying inert on a gurney, looking more dead than unconscious. Where was Sarah? He couldn't remember much of his conversation with the hospital; once he'd noted where Eddie was, the rest of what the woman said crackled like radio interference. He thought she'd said Sarah was there with him, but he couldn't be sure.

Even if she hadn't unintentionally laid a trail of clues (an insistence on being out of the house and suspiciously detailed excuses for being late), he'd have guessed Marion was being unfaithful to him again. She had a pertness to her, as if she'd suddenly been singled out for an award. She looked down on him and the rest of the world, sure of her winner's status. In bed, she was unresponsive and didn't meet his eye. It had happened before, when Sarah was small. They were still living in the cottage then. He'd wondered if perhaps she was pregnant, but he couldn't ask her. She'd guarded herself against him after she'd lost the baby. He hadn't known what to say.

Their lovemaking was sweet when they were first together and he'd loved their habits and endearments. Their inexperience only enhanced their trust in each other. She'd conceived Sarah easily and they'd joked about the storybook perfection of their family. But since her miscarriage, she'd sometimes seemed distant and almost angry with him. It made him feel as if she were only allowing him to make love to her. Logically, they'd both lost the baby, of course, but he knew that his initial hesitation, and his reluctance to celebrate her announcement when the pregnancy began, made her shut him out of her grief when it was over. She never discussed it with him or referred to it in any way. But when she'd told him Eddie was on the way, she put her arms round him and closed the distance between them, undoing any hurt as easily if she were untangling a knot.

Michael had always imagined they'd carry on side by side. When she fell in love with someone else, he was suddenly in her way. Her glaring irritation with him made her snap at his least transgression. If he hadn't done anything wrong, that annoyed her, too. When he tried to touch her, she bristled. She couldn't sit still, she leapt up from furniture as if everything was a bed of thistles and she hardly touched her food. She glowed with purpose. She was as shiny as a fish. Catching sight of her as she left the house, smiling to herself and walking quickly, he wondered if she might not come home at all and that he'd never know who it was that made her quiver so.

If anybody had asked him, although he couldn't imagine who might have done so, he would have said he was fond of Marion when they married. He'd felt protective of her, too. The way she took his arm the first time they'd crossed the road made him feel properly masculine and when she praised him for anything, he felt heroic. She was sweetly cheerful in bed. When he'd first heard her singing, he was astonished at how lovely her voice was. He remembered standing next to his mother in church. He could hear her voice clearly above everyone else's, mainly because the rest of the congregation were hardly making any sound at all. They slurred the words of the hymns and missed out notes. His mother's deep, rich alto floated easily above the sludge of sound. He'd felt proud to be alongside her and caught her eye and smiled. She'd blushed and stopped singing at once. She'd only mouthed the rest of the verses. He'd felt as guilty as if he'd inadvertently revealed her underwear to the world.

Marion wasn't ashamed of singing. She sang along to the radio or the record player. One afternoon he'd been at home, recuperating from flu. He was at the stage of convalescence when feeling better irritated him. He'd paced about downstairs while Marion ran a bath and cajoled the children to get into it. Their protestations gave way to indistinct chatter and some splashing. Then he'd heard them all singing. He'd crept halfway up the stairs to listen. He was still there when they came out of the bathroom, the children trailing towels and Marion red-faced from the heat. He'd fallen in love with her in that moment. It was a great, specific, unmistakable sensation, both as sharp as a knife and as soft as a blanket. Love had stolen up on him and surprised him, wrestling him to the ground. He had no desire to struggle free.

With bloody irony, the very things he'd encouraged – her singing, the stupid choir – were responsible for his first unhappiness. He'd thought he'd lost her for ever. Over the weeks, he'd watched, helpless, as she slipped away. The ending, when it came, was abrupt, but it was months before he understood why. Their neighbour had stared hard at Marion's obvious distress. He saw Marion recoil and then recover; he'd watched her lie and dissemble. And all the time, the fierce, insistent pain of his grief seeped like poison through his veins and into all the chambers of his heart.

He knew it was happening again now. He'd watched her crystallise into a sharper, brighter version of herself. He'd seen the way she'd looked across the room at the party at the man whose name she'd uttered too often. He watched her twist herself free of them all as she planned her night away. He'd heard with weary acquiescence the brittle, silly lies she'd told him, about where she'd be and who she was going to be with. When she was hurt again, as he knew she would be, she would come back to him. Perhaps, this time, she'd understand that he chose to stay, too. If there was then an unspoken contract, binding them together less lovingly than he'd imagined at the beginning, she would have to undertake not to mistake his tolerance for complacency.

He almost felt sorry for Bridget. She was about to be thrown, unprepared, into a terrible improvisation. And once she'd extricated herself from their conversation, she'd have to tell Marion the news. She'd have to hear Marion's panic, and cope with her fear, all by herself. He thought of Sarah and how young she seemed now, unable to make sense of what she'd done. She was very confused by his reaction to Marion's absence. He wasn't surprised, it puzzled him, too. The other thing that unnerved him was how very much he wanted someone else with him now. He was even more disconcerted when he realised who it was.

Chapter 79

'I'd say "race you", but it's all bloody uphill,' I said, walking away. I could feel where Adrian had touched me as if his hands were still there. Didn't your skin renew itself constantly? In time, then, there'd be no trace of him on my body. I wondered how long it would be before I had sloughed him completely. We passed a pub, its door open to release the thumping jukebox music into the night. Adrian joined in. *'If you want it, here it is, come and get it,'* he sang. *'Make your mind up fast.'* The young man's words in his mouth as he sang along made him look older and more solid. He sang flat, too. From quite a distance away down the street, I could see a bright spill of light in Ocean Cottage's porch. As I got closer, I could make out the woman standing there, shielding her eyes as if she looked into a bright light, not into darkness. I saw her hold her glasses up to her face and then drop them as she confirmed what she suspected. They glinted as they dangled from the chain.

'Mrs Thomas?' she said, clasping her hands together. 'There was a telephone call for you. A Mrs Furlow.'

It was a moment before I registered Bridget's surname. I felt as if I were falling very fast down a bottomless hole, with nothing to hold on to.

'What did she say?' Adrian said, mercifully steady.

'She said it was urgent.' The woman looked earnestly at him, as if he were better qualified to receive any information than his so-called wife.

I gasped and shook my head, trying to concentrate.

'She wants you to call her.' The woman sounded less confident now, faced with the consequences of her words. 'As soon as possible,' she said, with a wobble in her voice. 'I said did she want to speak to Mr Thomas, if he came back first. She said she didn't think so.'

'Where's your telephone?' said Adrian.

The woman pointed to where one was mounted on the wall, above a little podium. I wondered why anyone would think it was better to have to take a step up to make a call.

'No, no. Where's *your* telephone?' Adrian said. 'We're not fishing about for loose change.'

We followed her into a cramped kitchen. It was very recently vacated. A cigarette stubbed out in the ashtray was only half smoked and there was a full mug of tea beside it. A newspaper lay folded open at the puzzle page. The three of us had to stand very close together.

'Here you are,' said the woman, meek now. She patted the hard back of a wooden chair as though she offered a comfy armchair.

I fixed my gaze on the blue, rectangular telephone, anticipating its cruelty.

Adrian's chair squealed on the hard lino as he pulled it up to the table. 'And some privacy?' he said to the woman, smiling at her without any warmth.

She sniffed and picked up the newspaper from the table. 'I'll be next door,' she said.

I lifted the receiver. It smelled faintly of TCP. I replaced it at once. 'I don't know . . .' I said, but it was more to myself than to Adrian. I opened my handbag and found the slip of paper with Bridget's number on it.

Adrian took it from my trembling hands and dialled. When he handed the telephone back to me, I turned away from him as the call connected.

'8788?' said Bridget, from the other end of the map of the country in my head.

For a moment, I couldn't speak. 'It's me,' I said eventually, and tears ran down my cheeks.

'Oh, Marion.' Bridget sighed my name on a downward fall. *Just tell me*, I wanted to shout. 'It's Eddie,' she said. 'Eddie's—'

The Trimphone receiver was too insubstantial to hold it tightly. I caught sight of Adrian and for a split second I couldn't remember who he was.

'He went riding,' Bridget said. 'Michael said he'd wanted to go and—'

'Why was he riding?' I said.

'Stop shouting, Marion,' said Bridget calmly. 'I'm trying to tell you. He'd wanted to go to the stables, apparently, and Sally put him on a horse that was a bit big for him and it bolted and he fell. Concussion. He might have a fractured skull. He's still unconscious. They're keeping him under observation, but—'

'Who's Sally?' I was trembling with anger. Which woman had put my son anywhere near a horse, let alone a wild one?

'Your *daughter*,' said Bridget, with the reasonable tone of one who understands how distress might take a person.

'Her name's Sarah.' This miserable wrongness connected me to my daughter as immediately and strongly as if there were still a cord between us. Bridget's voice squeaked again from the receiver but I put the phone to my chest to muffle her.

Adrian took it from me and continued the conversation, repeating numbers and the name of a hospital and thanking Bridget. He reached for a pen and paper as he spoke, writing everything down in handwriting that would never become familiar. The nearby stove was spattered with grey grease spots and hardened dribbles of something brown. I'd have to telephone Michael. He'd have to walk down miles of hospital corridors to speak to me on a public telephone. The nurses would gossip, I'd have done so myself. *Yes, he's all alone. The wife had to be summoned. She was staying with a friend, or so she said.*

Ignoring Adrian, who was leaning back in his chair, tipping it so that the front legs rose a few inches from the floor, I dialled the number. It rang for several minutes. I could hardly speak to the nurse who answered, she sounded distracted and distant. When I heard Michael's voice, I breathed out with such a rush of relief that the little note on the table in front of me lifted in the air.

'How long will it take you to get home?' Michael said at once.

I winced. I could hardly wait here for as long as it was supposed to take me to travel back from Yorkshire. 'About two hours,' I said, wondering if my voice changed when I told the truth.

When Eddie was three, we'd all gone to the seaside. We were miles from anywhere, or at least a long way from the car, when Eddie had declared he couldn't walk any more. I had tried to carry him but staggered under his weight. Michael had taken him from me and held him as easily as if he were a lightweight jacket he'd draped over one arm. I wanted to be carried now, lifted up like the Baby Jesus on St Christopher's shoulders.

'Where did it happen?' I said.

'Castle Field,' Michael said.

In my mind's eye, I saw the galloping horse, Eddie's inert body and Sarah kneeling by his side. 'Has he come round?' I said.

There was a pause, I heard Michael catch his breath. 'Not yet,' he said. 'Oh, Marion. He looks so small.'

'And Sarah?' I folded and unfolded the piece of paper as he spoke.

'Sobbing,' Michael said. 'Saying it's all her fault. She wants you.'

I remembered Sarah lying in the crook of my arm, the bottle of milk emptying with noisy regularity as she fed, her baby toes twisting and circling. I wanted to fill my arms with her again. I wanted to smooth her hair from the face that was almost my own. My heart had swollen inside me and was forcing its way out through my throat.

'Come home,' said Michael and hung up.

'Well?' Adrian said, righting his chair and leaning forward. He was like an actor who hadn't been in the scene until this point, but now turned over the pages of his script to see, with delight, his own name. 'You need to go home, right? It won't take long to pack, will it? I'll grab my bag and get the car.' A wireless began playing nearby; the woman had obviously tired of respectful silence.

'I'll get a taxi to the station,' I said. 'I don't suppose I've missed the last train.'

He began to protest, but I shook my head. 'Okay,' he said, holding up his hands in acquiescence.

I wondered, briefly, if I should kiss him, but it was too much of an effort to stand up. He'd had all of me now that he would ever get. I heard him run up the stairs. Only moments later he bounced back down. I sensed him pausing outside the door, but his script didn't include a proper goodbye. The front door slammed.

I went up to the bedroom. Someone, presumably the landlady, had smoothed the bedcovers and made little triangles of the corners. The idea of waking up beside Adrian seemed ridiculous. Our time together was tiny, like a scene depicted inside a matchbox. I closed the clasps of my suitcase. The only thing I'd taken out of it was my nightdress. I bumped the case down the narrow stairs and knocked on the kitchen door. The woman squeezed her way out into the hallway. She wore a brown and orange pinafore over her clothing.

'Excuse me, Mrs Thomas.' The woman smoothed her apron as she spoke. The nylon crackled and clung to her. 'I do hope it wasn't bad news?' She couldn't disguise how very much she wanted to know.

I was tempted to lie, but I'd used up my lying for now. 'I need to go home,' I said. 'I expect Ade – I expect Mr Thomas told you we'd have to leave?'

'Yes. No, he didn't. Has he already gone, then?' In Latin you can preface a question with a word that lets everyone know what you expect in answer. *Non* for 'no' or *nonne* for 'yes'. This was a *nonne* question, all right.

'Yes,' I said. 'Do you have a train timetable, please?' I should have let him drop me at the station at least. But I hadn't wanted the shared space of his car, of his *wife's* car, for even that brief journey. The woman produced a tiny book from among the directories. There were still two more trains I could get, thank God. 'Is it far to the station?' I said.

'No, it's not. The thing is' – the woman moved her lips as if she was chewing something – 'the thing is, Mrs Thomas, the room's not been paid for.'

I laughed. I wished I could thank Adrian for this last, perfect gift. The woman bent over a notebook and wrote a bill. She handed it to me with solemnity. I took it with similar care, read it and scrunched it into a little ball. I threw it into the air and swatted it with my palm. We watched it roll down the hall and come to rest beside the skirting. I handed over the money and the woman slid it into the front pocket of her apron.

She pulled out a slip of paper. 'I think this might be yours,' she said uncertainly. 'I found it on the floor in your room, when I was turning down.'

I recognised the size and shape of the pad we kept in the kitchen. There was a capital 'M' on the front of the folded sheet. It must have been tucked into my suitcase and fallen out during my unsuccessful attempt to put my nightdress under a pillow. 'PLEASE COME HOME MUMMY' I read. The writing was unfamiliar and the letters were oddly shaped. 'Thank you,' I said, keeping my head down, so that the woman couldn't see my face and the threat of tears.

'Do you like jigsaw puzzles?' I said.

'Oh, I don't mind them,' she answered cautiously. 'I've a nephew who sends me one sometimes. Country scenes mostly.'

'I'm a missing piece.' I picked up my case. 'I'm going home to slot back in. There's a space where I should be.'

The woman frowned. 'It's annoying when you lose a piece,' she said. 'Do you want a little tip? My nephew told me not to start at the corners. He says that's what everyone does, but it leaves you with so much to do. He says you should begin with the difficult areas first, like the sky, so you feel you've really made progress when you come to the rest.'

'That's very good advice,' I said. 'Thank you. Which way is the station?' The woman took my arm and led me to the door. 'It's not far. Turn right and then follow the road. Mind how you go,' she said, her tone surprisingly kind.

'Yes,' I said, 'I will.'

Not a single car came past me. No headlights illuminated the road and the streetlights were sparse. I stumbled on uneven paving and swapped my bags from hand to hand, to lighten the load. A longing for my children, so fierce it was almost palpable, weighed me down. They seemed like the survivors of a blast, lying untended in the open air. 'I'm sorry,'

I said aloud. 'I'm sorry, I'm sorry, I'm sorry.' I couldn't undo what I'd done. There were no bargains I could make to change things or alter the course of the future. The past was set in stone, a great monolith visible from wherever I stood, eternally recording my stupidity and recklessness. My eyes filled with tears and for a moment I couldn't see anything at all. I followed the road to the station without looking back.

Chapter 80

Eddie couldn't understand what had happened to his arms. They were pinned to his sides and too heavy to lift. He couldn't move them, even though he needed them to take the pain away from his head. He wanted to scoop it out, like getting the last bit of yolk from the egg. People appeared in front of him and disappeared again as if he was watching the slides he projected on to his ceiling. Sarah looked scared in a way that made him feel terrified too. His father's face loomed close enough to touch, if he'd been able to move. Nurses' voices were low and firm as they encouraged him to open his mouth to admit a thermometer. Nobody asked him to do anything else. His real life, and most of the people in it, seemed to have vanished to make way for this new state.

When he'd had his eyes tested, the glasses man had held a huge magnifying glass in front of him and twirled it like a conjuror's wand. He'd demanded to know which side was better for seeing the chart he pointed at. Weighed down by the owl-eyes spectacles that the glasses man made him wear, and not very sure of his letters anyway, Eddie couldn't tell what he was supposed to say, but he was sure there was only one right answer. He'd felt so put on the spot, so afraid of speaking at all in case he was wrong, that he'd cried. The opposite of that experience was happening as he lay on this bed. If he even so much as groaned when they spoke to him, they were happy. His father wept so hard that Eddie wanted to ask him if he was dead. He thought he probably wasn't, but he knew he'd had a very bad accident. He was glad he was still a bit alive, because he didn't want any of them to be able to look at his dead body if he couldn't see what it looked like, too. He wanted to sleep. Very much. He'd try to wait until his mother came, before he slept. He'd really, really try.

Chapter 81

When I arrived at the house, Michael didn't move to embrace me. I put my suitcase down.

He stared at it. 'Just so you know,' he said, 'Eddie's awake. Only just, and very groggy.'

'Thank God,' I said. I could allow myself only the smallest sliver of relief. I didn't ask Michael any questions, I felt I had no right to know more.

'We'll go in the morning,' he said. 'It's outside visiting hours, of course, but I've asked if I can bring you.' He looked at me for the first time. 'I'm glad you're here,' he said. 'It's been very frightening.' He didn't mention where I might have been, he hadn't pretended to enquire after Bridget. He was as polite to me as if I were a visiting relative. His courtesy alone would have broken my heart, if it wasn't in pieces already.

I crept into Sarah's room. The covers were pulled up almost over her head and only a dark spill of hair was visible. Propped on the pillow was a little plastic horse, the sort that she'd once spent hours playing with.

When she opened her eyes and saw me, she gasped. 'I didn't know when you were coming,' she said. 'I only wanted to frighten Eddie. But I didn't mean to hurt him.' Her voice was light with fear.

'I know. You wanted to hurt me. I know,' I said. I started to cry.

Sarah looked alarmed. She leaned forward and put one hand on my arm. 'Don't cry,' she said. 'Please.' Her hand rested lightly, as if she daren't let me feel it. 'Is he going to be all right?' she said.

'I don't know,' I said, and felt her tense.

'He looked so little,' she said. 'When the ambulance men put him on the stretcher there was so much of it empty around him.'

'Why did you want to frighten him?' I said.

She mumbled something and looked away.

'What did you say?' I said.

'I wanted to stop you,' she said. Her face was red with effort. 'Both of you. It's because of you and him.'

'Adrian Mr Cavanagh?' I said.

She frowned. 'How do you know I call him that?' she said. It was too late to pretend.

'I know about the painting,' I said. 'How you met him after school. I know about Bobbie and—'

She began to get out of bed, pushing me away as she untangled herself from the bedclothes. 'Did he tell you?' she said. She was louder now, her face contorted with anger and grief.

'Sarah.' I tried to hold on to her, but she flinched away then lashed out. 'He didn't tell me,' I said. 'I read your diary.' She gasped. 'I'm sorry, I shouldn't have but I thought you and he—'

'I wanted to save you from him,' she said. '*I* didn't want him, why would I? I wanted to get him away from you. I wanted you to see what he was like, how he just wants everyone and we don't matter to him. I wanted you to choose us instead. I didn't want you to go. I thought if you saw the note, you'd think it was from Eddie and you'd come home before—'

I felt as if I were under water, sinking. I couldn't breathe. I could hardly hear her.

'Shall I tell you what he said to me? No, I can't. It's too awful. I hate him. I hate you.' She turned away. I watched her shoulders rise and fall as she sobbed. 'Go away,' she said, her voice flooded with tears. 'You have to go away.'

I couldn't stand upright without swaying. I was unbalanced by grief. I said, 'Please, Sarah, talk to me,' but I knew she wouldn't. I'd thrown away everything I ever was to her. In my mind's eye, I saw her small, plump toddler self stumble towards me, arms outstretched. I heard her calling for me to watch her as she climbed high or danced or swam. I'd soothed her, sung to her, calmed her fears, nursed her wounds. All this was lost now, as scattered as pages torn from a book. I would never get back to where I was. I hadn't even marked my place.

The war had flattened most of the old hospital and a replacement had been thrown up hastily. It was a collection of structures never intended for permanence. The single surviving building, which housed the maternity unit, sat haughtily in the centre, like a dowager surveying youthful folly. As Michael drove, I dug my nails into my palms with embarrassment, remembering Adrian's more hectic style.

The last time Michael and I were here, was when we were leaving with our infant son. Michael has always known who I am, I thought. He's been waiting all this time for me to recognise him. And now it might be too late. I felt as if I'd been shedding layers of myself to reveal this last, and lasting, skin.

When we went into Eddie's ward I couldn't distinguish him from the other patients. In my panic, the identical beds and bedding and the uniformity of illness made them all look the same. I waited for Michael to lead the way, afraid I might go to the wrong boy. Several nurses hovered nearby. I hung back. Eddie's eyes were glassy and deeply set. The splints on his arms kept them rigidly at his sides. I stroked one hand. He was trying to open his eyes but it seemed to be too difficult for him to move anything at all.

I wanted to sit on the bed but it felt out of bounds. I perched instead on the only chair. 'Does it hurt very much?' I said. His white face was splodged at uneven intervals, like an artist's palette. There was a livid, mauve half-moon beneath one eye and a darker, purple circle around the other. He still had dots of brown blood on his cheeks.

He said something I couldn't hear and I put my ear to his mouth, tucking my hair out of the way. 'Not too much,' he said again and him being quieter than he'd ever been before made me want to cry.

'You have been in the wars, haven't you,' I said, trying to keep my voice steady. I didn't want to frighten him with my fear. I stayed where I was for a moment, hearing his breath and inhaling the new, terrible, hospital smell of him. No wonder animals reject their young if the scent of them is wrong. I looked up at Michael. He was watching me.

'Let's go and have a cup of tea,' he said. I kissed the air above Eddie's forehead, afraid of his swollen skin.

The cafeteria was empty. A League of Friends banner drooped on one wall. I sat down at a table still damp with disinfectant. 'You're too early,' the woman behind the counter said to Michael, 'we're not meant to be open yet.' She glanced over at me. 'Oh dear,' she said. 'Have you come from the children's ward? All right, then. But you'll have to wait for the urn.'

'I think this is tea,' Michael said, putting a green cup and saucer, the colour of milk glass, in front of me. 'It behaves like tea does and it's roughly the same colour.' We sat in silence.

I braced myself. I knew what he was going to say and I prepared my defence. Not a defence, exactly, but an explanation: Yes, I'd say, I've been an idiot, it didn't mean anything, I was just feeling lonely. Well, not lonely, but not right in myself. Lost, really. I didn't mean to hurt anyone. Adrian, I was going to tell Michael, was vain and silly.

I waited. Michael said nothing.

A nurse – she looked scarcely older than Sarah – ran up to the counter. Curly hair escaped from underneath her cap. I reached instinctively to my own head, as if Matron were going to admonish us both for being untidy. 'Jean! You open?' the girl said. 'I'm gasping.'

'Not really,' the woman said.

The nurse looked over to where we sat and raised her eyebrows.

'Oh, go on, then,' the woman said and busied herself with cups and plates.

The girl took her cup and went and sat down at the furthest table, turning her back to us and opening a magazine. I felt unaccountably bereft, as if a lifebelt had floated past me just out of reach as I drowned.

Michael half raised his cup to his mouth then replaced it without drinking. I studied the metal tin in front of me, stuffed with serviettes. I felt as if my body were filled with wet cement. I wasn't in shock, I was in shame.

'Sarah hates me,' I said. 'She blames me, too. She's right. She tried to stop me going, but I didn't hear her.' I looked at Michael. His face seemed as familiar and as far away as the full moon. 'What are we going to do?' I said.

'I don't know.' Michael looked down at his hands. 'Do you want to leave me?' he said.

'*Leave* you?' I said, too loudly.

The young nurse didn't turn round but her cap quivered.

'I'm not going to ask you to stay, if you don't want to,' Michael said. He looked as if he might disintegrate with sadness, as if it were taking a huge effort of will to keep himself together, atom by atom.

'Why on earth would you still want to be with me now?' I said. 'I've behaved horribly. I was so selfish. I can never make things right after this, can I? I can't undo what I've done.' Misery threaded itself through me, vein by vein, like a vine.

Michael pulled the sugar bowl on the table towards him and filled and emptied the spoon. The grains were damp. Little grey lumps tumbled and clumped together as he spilled them. 'No,' he said. 'You can't undo anything that's happened. But we can come to an acceptance, an accommodation, after a while. We'll have to, Marion. It's what people do. I'll stay with you. But I don't think I can forgive you. That will have to be enough.'

The nurse carried her cup to the counter. 'Ta, Jean,' she called out as she put it down. She left without looking back.

I looked out of the window. Beyond the rows of irregularly grey Nissen huts, I could just make out the roofs and chimney stacks of the town, stretching away into the distance. I felt as if I were back on land after a long voyage. I could still feel the rocking and swaying of large waves, although there was no longer water beneath me. 'It's enough,' I said.

Chapter 82

I am holding a picture of Eddie. He is looking straight into the camera. You can see he's been persuaded to pose and he is desperate to fizz into movement again. It seemed impossible then that he could ever be still for long.

The end had no beginning. I was holding one small, black plimsoll, the elastic loose and Eddie's name inked inside, smudged with wear. I was feeling annoyed, looking round his bedroom for the other one and cursing his carelessness, out of habit, when the telephone rang. I felt no unease. Michael had gone to the hospital to bring Eddie home. I was preparing to care for him. There were no other calls on my time.

I can see myself, still clutching the shoe, the receiver in my other hand. Even the way Michael drew breath before he spoke was enough to tell me what he was going to say. 'Did he ask for me?' I said.

Michael didn't answer.

'Did he ask for me? Did he ask for Mummy?'

'He asked for Sarah,' said Michael.

I leaned against the wall as the room spun. The house was offensive in its irrelevance. How would I ever go on living here now? Suddenly, I felt something as undeniable and unstoppable as the light of dawn. It was a great, swelling surge of relief. I was giddy with it. I almost laughed. I had nothing to fear now. I was unassailable. The worst had, irrefutably, happened.

When Michael and I stood side by side in the hospital, I was glad I couldn't see his face. I made an enormous effort to control my features as I didn't want to make her job any harder for the young doctor. She was pleasant. She would have been popular at school, I thought. She had the sort of open face that suggested easy friendship.

'There was nothing more we could have done, Mrs Deacon,' she said. 'We couldn't have predicted it. It was very sudden. Haemorrhagic shock.'

I knew what it was. It was page 56 of the textbook. It was a possible question in the exam. It was theory. It wasn't meant to be this *fact*. It wasn't meant to take Eddie. Beside me, I heard Michael sob. Beyond the necessary conversations with, first, doctors, then undertakers, we never discussed that moment again. If ever I began to talk about Eddie, Michael would silence me. He would leave the room to avoid the subject. Afterwards, I would listen while he cried, alone. We moved house twice after that and packed fewer possessions each time. Sarah slid beside us, a ghost of herself, as if she were half dissolved into her surroundings. Our conversations were minimal and prosaic, like the phrases in a guidebook. We were marooned in the present tense. Michael didn't put any pictures of Eddie on display and he relegated his small things to boxes and cupboards. Unless I searched for them, there was no chance I might see anything that would make my heart stop. When we parted, there was no discussion. We were civil to each other, even affectionate, but we travelled onwards as if we shared no hinterland.

It is human nature to turn towards light and warmth. You feel it, unexpectedly, in the smile of a stranger or catch it in a snatch of a familiar song. Despite yourself, you respond. I walked past a high-walled garden on a hot day, a year or so after I had left. I could smell a barbecue, of course, it was that sort of summer, and hear low music. There was the rise and fall of conversation, sporadic laughter and sounds suggesting a game, perhaps, or a child's sudden burst of speed. I didn't envy them their gathering, those people beyond the wall. I felt instead a nostalgic ache for things that had never happened. Eddie coming towards me with a baby in his arms. Sarah placing an array of salad bowls on to a flowered tablecloth. 'Whatever happened to that funny boy, Tom something, I think his name was?' she'd say, not really waiting for an answer. Michael struggling with a reluctant cork, the bottle between his legs, making a great show of the battle, smiling at us all.

This is how it was. Sarah was standing in the middle of her room. The cluttered shelves, the pictures of ponies and nursery scenes on the walls and the rosettes and the certificates pinned over the mirror all marked the liminal space between her charted childhood and the unmapped future. It was as if I couldn't reach her, although she was only a few feet away from me. She rocked backwards and forwards, her arms wrapped around her body and her head lowered. She was moaning: a single, repeated sound; she was almost saying: *'no, no, no,'* but it was closer to keening than words. Her hair swayed, keeping time. A van drew up outside, the driver shouted to someone and opened and slammed shut the doors. The sound of a world continuing so vigorously was vulgar and unwelcome. This is how it will be, I thought. Sarah will pack away the china animals and her books. I will wear clothes that Eddie will never see. We will eat and drink and sleep because we must, but everything will be: *'before'* and *'after'*. We won't speak about the *'before'*.

I hadn't been able to go into Eddie's room at all. Michael said he'd deal with it, he'd clear everything away, but I wondered what he'd do when he found Eddie's energy. Surely it was still vibrating there, the essence of him, like a wasp trapped under a glass.

Sarah turned to me at last, rubbing tears from her cheeks with sleeves already sodden. 'It isn't your fault,' I said.

She stared at me through swollen lids. 'I know,' she said. 'It's yours.'

I wanted to move, to sit down or even just fold my arms, but any movement seemed impossible. Standing still required all my concentration.

'It's funny,' she said, 'at first I was so impressed with them. With Bobbie. With him. They were so unlike us. They were all so hippy and fun and free.'

I thought of Adrian and his callous, casual belittling of anything that might pin him down. I saw him leaving us without a backward glance.

'Then I realised what he was like,' she said. 'I saw the truth before you did. How he made us feel beautiful and special and sexy, when all the time it was really just because he thought he could do whatever he wanted to anyone. It didn't matter who or what it was.'

'I should have protected you,' I said.

'You couldn't have,' she said. 'You were too busy hurting yourself. I thought I could stand in between the two of you, turn his head, make him look at me instead and let you get away and see how stupid he was. But you kept running towards him. I just wanted all of this to go on. To stay exactly how it was. For ever. All of it, you, me, Daddy, Eddie—' She stopped, choking on her tears.

Some time passed, I don't know how long, while we watched each other cry. 'Sarah,' I said, but that was all.

'Do you know what he said to me?' she said. 'He said he wasn't into little girls but if he was, he'd definitely have me. Give it a few years, he said. Then he said—' She stopped, looking distraught.

'He said: if it's any consolation, honey, when I fuck your mother, I'll be thinking about you.'

I couldn't hold on to my frozen heart. I turned to people I didn't know and offered it to them. They thawed it enough for me to survive. The residents at Hillview never question my past, even my present doesn't concern them. They aren't much older than I am, but we choose to believe I am considerably their junior. I sing with them, I wheel their chairs and I slice too-big portions of cake on to tiny plates. They know me as practical, friendly, willing, even kind.

I dispatched most of the contents of the carrier bag to the waste-paper bin. Only two letters survived the cull. This one is written on good paper, not too stiff, and with a nice hand. There's a faint suggestion of lavender as I open it.

Dear Marion,

I completely understand your not coming the other day. Thank you for letting me know in good time. You'll be glad to hear that Sarah was on very good form, both boys are bouncing (even Grandpa Michael looked a little weary by the end of the day!) and she and Matthew seem very happy. The boys have pronounced American accents now. I have to confess it took us rather aback to hear little Ted calling Michael 'Pops'. And another one on the way! That'll certainly keep them busy.

Michael continues to have chest problems and continues *to refuse to see the doctor. Jock was just as stubborn, but I don't say that to Michael. He'd only say that my being widowed before doesn't set any sort of pattern!*

This gives me a chance to say, again, how very fond he is of you. As you know, I regard our life together now as a blessing. When we met again after Jock's death, Michael was very much on his own but you were – and you are – very important to him. My decision not to marry him was greatly influenced by my not wanting to replace you as his wife. That means, of course, that you remain his next of kin. I am more than content with that and I am sure it will present no difficulty in the future.

I do have a favour to ask, though: I plan a trip to Vancouver next month. My cousin's daughter's wedding first and then some sightseeing in the back of beyond. Quite an adventure! Then I can travel on to be with Sarah when the baby arrives. Michael doesn't want to come, he's happy to wait for our next stay in the house in France. Might I put your number down as the first point of contact, if needs be? I can't think you'll be called on, but just in case.

Thank you in advance, dear Marion. I really enjoyed our visit to the Academy the other day. Modigliani is so very calming, don't you find? I thought you looked very well and very chic. Yellow suits you!

Rosalind

I keep the diary. I never read it. I'm wary of hearing that particular voice. I take Sarah's last letter from my bag. It's unsealed, the envelope flap merely tucked in on itself. To make it easier for me to open it.

I can't measure the distance between us or map my path to writing this. I'm not sure how, or when, I knew I should. This seems as inevitable as everything else. Let's meet in April, on the tenth. I've kept a picture of you all this time, which might surprise you. It was taken one Christmas, there's a paper crown on your head. You're holding Eddie. He's little, about two, and he's wearing a knitted romper suit. I won't pretend I have that photograph by chance. I wanted you both with me. I thought I was running away but I have been walking towards you all this time. I understand now why you have stayed so still.

I am, always, your daughter. Ted is the same age as Eddie was. He looks so like him, but he has your eyes. I am not asking for your explanation. You don't need my forgiveness. You are my mother. I want to hear you say my name.

I start and smile, the way you do when someone taps you on the shoulder to return the hat you did not realise had fallen from your head. Sarah was in that photograph, too, of course. I place the letter in the drawer, beside all her others. The entreaties and pleas of years and years balance, one on the other, as fragile as a house of cards. I exhale. They do not fall. For the most part, I have tried to regard everything that happened with a kind of dispassionate curiosity, the way you read the labels in a museum. You note the details as you stand in front of some object or other, but you'll forget them soon enough.

There's a stanza I keep turning over in my head: *The human frame is well designed to hide the secrets of the mind.* I really don't know where it came from. I suppose I must have learned it, parrot-fashion, many years ago. I think I'll make myself something nice for supper. Over the years I have become, to my surprise, a rather good cook.

Acknowledgements

Thanking the following people on this page is the right thing to do, but I owe them much more than words. I am indebted to them all for their support and invaluable input. When I stumbled myopically in the foothills of early drafts and woolly thinking, they threw me ropes and shared their visions. There were innumerable fruitful conversations along the way and their encouragement never waned as the book took shape. Colleagues, friends and family all listened as I wrestled aloud with details and descriptions. I should add that their patience was extraordinary and no one lost their sense of humour in the face of my rambling, self-absorbed, often self-pitying petitions to their friendship, love and expertise.

Fanny Blake, Erin Kelly and Cari Rosen read early and kindly. Their reactions and reports were generous and perceptive. Melanie Cantor and I shared experiences and a lot of good wine. My agent Gordon Wise is a terrific and clever cheerleader and Lisa Highton is the best editor anyone could wish for. Her ability to see a book through the tangle of early drafts and fruitless tangents is quite extraordinary and her gentle insistence on keeping on keeping on is fabulous.

My huge thanks to the terrific team at Two Roads – Rosie Gailer, Emma Petfield, Kat Burdon, and Jo Myler for her wonderful cover design.

My husband John and my children Sophie, Jackson and Martha hugged and chivvyed me in equal measure. I needed lots of both. This is the book I always meant it to be. It just took everyone mentioned above to help me do it.

About the Author

Actress, presenter and author Janet Ellis trained at the Royal Central School of Speech and Drama. Best known for presenting *Blue Peter*, she stars in numerous radio and TV programmes and in 2018 appeared at the Edinburgh Festival in a successful month long run of *Makes, Bakes and Outtakes*, a play celebrating sixty years of *Blue Peter*. In 2016 Janet was awarded an MBE for services to charities and theatre.

A graduate of the Curtis Brown creative writing course, her debut novel, *The Butcher's Hook*, was longlisted for the Desmond Elliot Prize.

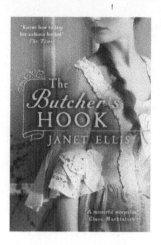

MEET ALL THESE FRIENDS IN BUZZ BOOKS:

Thomas the Tank Engine
The Animals of Farthing Wood
Biker Mice From Mars
James Bond Junior
Fireman Sam
Joshua Jones
Rupert
Babar

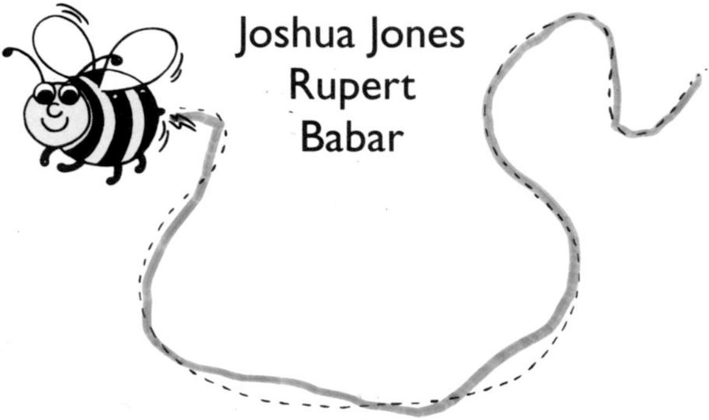

First published in Great Britain 1993 by Buzz Books,
an imprint of Reed Children's Books
Michelin House, 81 Fulham Road, London, SW3 6RB
and Auckland, Melbourne, Singapore and Toronto
Reprinted 1994

Based on the novels by Colin Dann and the animation series
produced by Telemagination and La Fabrique for the BBC
and the European Broadcasting Union.

ISBN 1 85591 325 9

Printed in Italy by Olivotto

Heroes

Story by Colin Dann
Text by Mary Risk
Illustrations by The County Studio

buzz books

The animals of Farthing Wood had found their lost leader. Fox's new mate, Vixen, was with him.

"Oh Fox, you're safe," sobbed Mole.

"Crying again, Moley!" said Badger. "What a shame your tears are salty. If they weren't, we'd never have to go thirsty!"

"I'm thirsty now!" said Baby Rabbit.

"Me too!" squeaked the mice and voles.

Kestrel, who had flown up high to spy out the land, swooped down again.

"Kee! Follow me!" she cried. "There's an old quarry nearby and it's full of water!"

"I remember it, mateys!" said Toad. "Lovely it is. A treat of a place!"

But a fence surrounded the quarry.

"So near, yet so far," sighed Vixen.

"Most disappointing," said Badger.

"What'sss all the fusss about?" said Adder. She slipped through the fence with ease, hissing at the mice and voles along the way.

Mole slid down off Badger's back.

"I could make a tunnel underneath, couldn't I, Badger?" he said.

"Oh, Moley!" said Badger, smiling at his friend. "What would we do without you?"

Mole started at once.

"You're digging in the wrong direction!" said Weasel, and screamed with laughter.

"Oh, sorry," said Mole.

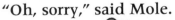

Mole started digging again. Soil flew out of the hole and onto the other animals.

"Oi! Stop it!" shouted Father Rabbit.

"My husband's being buried alive!" cried Mother Rabbit in a panic.

"He's all right," said Fox sternly.

Mole popped out of his new tunnel on the other side of the fence. The hedgehogs dived down after him.

"Wait!" said Mole. "Let Badger look at it first. It is a good tunnel, isn't it, Badger?"

"Very good indeed," said Badger. "Well done, Moley."

Mole glowed with pride.

Soon, everyone was drinking at the water's edge. Vixen looked round at her new friends. Weasel was teasing Adder. Owl was asleep. Mole and Toad were grubbing in the mud for worms.

"Look at greedy Mole!" she laughed.

"Toad's greedy too," said Mole, with his mouth full.

"So I am, mateys! So I am!" said Toad.

Suddenly, there was a strange whistling noise overhead. The animals looked up, startled. A heron was flying over the water, his great wings beating the air. He dived into the water, scooping up a fish.

The little animals scrambled for cover. Even Adder slipped quietly under a rock.

The heron landed.

"Good evening," he said politely.

"I hope you don't mind us being here in your quarry, Heron," said Fox.

"Guests are always welcome," said the heron. "And please, call me Whistler."

"Funny name," said Weasel rudely.

Whistler showed her his wing. "A human shot at me once," he said. "The bullet made a hole in my wing. Now the air whistles through it when I fly."

"The noise must make hunting difficult," said Owl.

"Fish can't hear," said Whistler. "Watch."

He took off, and plunged into the water. A second later he surfaced, carrying a gleaming fish in his beak.

Toad was watching excitedly. "I can fish too! Look at me, mateys!" he shouted, and dived into the water.

Owl looked on disapprovingly. "Pride goes before a fall," she said.

Toad didn't hear. He had seen a fish. He darted through the water after it.

"I'll show 'em," he thought happily.

He caught the fish by the tail, then surfaced. He didn't see the big carp hiding in the reeds, waiting for him.

"Look what I've got!" Toad shouted.

The carp was right underneath him now. She opened her gaping mouth, and pulled Toad back under the water.

The carp was hungry, but Toad was fat. Try as she might, she couldn't swallow him. She thrashed about in the water.

The animals watched anxiously from the bank.

"Where's Toad got to now?" asked Fox. "We mustn't lose him. He's our guide!"

"He's been caught!" said Whistler. "I'll take care of that old carp."

He dived into the water, his sharp beak searching. The carp tried to swim away, but her heavy mouthful slowed her down. She was no match for the heron.

Whistler snapped her up, Toad and all, and dropped them onto the bank. Toad fell out of the carp's mouth.

"Is Toad dead?" squeaked Baby Rabbit.

“Stand aside, please,“ ordered Weasel.

She picked Toad up by the feet and shook him.

“He’s opened his eyes!” said Mole. Tears of joy splashed down his cheeks.

“Thank you, Whistler,” croaked Toad in a shaky voice. “You’re a hero.”

The carp was gasping on the bank, dying slowly. Toad felt a pang of sympathy.

"Throw her back in, matey," he said to Whistler. "Poor thing. She's in agony."

"But she was going to eat you," said Whistler. "Anyway, I've been trying to catch her for years."

"Please," said Toad. "One more favour."

Whistler sighed, picked up the carp, and dropped her back in the water.

"You're a funny lot, you are," he said.

"We're fellow travellers," said Fox. "We've taken an oath to help and protect each other while we're on our journey."

"*Live and let live,* that's our motto," Badger explained to the heron.

"How interesting," Whistler remarked.

"I suppose you want to come with us," cackled Weasel.

"Well, actually..." said Whistler.

"You're welcome to join us," said Fox.

"But first you must take the Oath!" twittered the mice anxiously.

"Very well," said Whistler. "I promise not to eat any of you. Will that do?"

"Yesss! It will!" hissed Adder, relieved.

It was time to leave the quarry and travel on. Toad and Fox led the way.

"Nearly there, mateys!" Toad called out encouragingly. "Not far now!"

"That sssilly whissstling noissse isss getting on my nervesss!" grumbled Adder, looking up at Whistler.

Suddenly, a shot rang out. Toad was so startled, he dropped off Fox's back.

Kestrel dived down from the sky. “Kee! Kee! There are hunters nearby. Take care!”

Fox barked out orders. “Keep together everyone! Get under the hedge. Quick! Rabbits, don’t panic!”

Vixen was trembling at Fox’s side. “Oh Fox,” she whispered. “I hear dogs!”

“We’ll have a better chance if we all keep still,” Fox said grimly.

The rabbits' eyes were wide with fear and their noses twitched in alarm.

"Don't panic! Don't panic!" Mother Rabbit whispered frantically.

The dogs were close now. Everyone froze. Even Baby Rabbit was as quiet as he could be. Finally he could bear the tension no longer. Silly with fear, he darted into the clearing.

A moment later the animals heard a loud explosion. Baby Rabbit fell over.

"Oh, my baby! My baby!" shrieked Mother Rabbit.

She started to run to the clearing, but Hare held her back.

"It's no good," he said gently.

A man with a gun picked up the little rabbit and dropped him into his bag.

Sadly, the animals watched the hunter leave the wood with the bag slung over his shoulder.

"Baby Rabbit saved us," said Badger softly. "That hunter would have found us all if Baby Rabbit hadn't distracted him. He's a hero."

"Yes, he is," Fox agreed. "Unfortunately, the motto *Live and let live* doesn't mean anything to some humans."

He looked round at his little band of travellers. The mice, hares and squirrels had crowded round to comfort the poor rabbits. Overhead, the birds kept watch.

"Glad you joined us, Whistler?" Fox called to the heron.

"Oh yes!" Whistler replied. "I'm proud to have friends like you."

He flapped his wing, and the cool breeze whistled through the hole.